T0274537

A GAME MOST FOUL

ALISON GERVAIS

BLINK

BLINK

A Game Most Foul
Copyright © 2024 by Alison Gervais

Published in Grand Rapids, Michigan, by Blink.

Requests for information should be addressed to customercare@harpercollins.com.

ISBN 978-0-310-15923-0 (hardcover)
ISBN 978-0-310-15919-3 (audio)
ISBN 978-0-310-15923-3 (ebook)

Library of Congress Cataloging-in-Publication Data

Editor: Katherine Jacobs
Cover Illustration and Design: Neil Swaab
Interior Design: Denise Froehlich

Printed in the United States of America

24 25 26 27 28 LBC 5 4 3 2 1

For Maya and Grace,
my reason for everything.

PROLOGUE

The man kept his head down as he walked swiftly across the old cobblestone sidewalk, an icy chill that had nothing to do with the weather settling deep into his bones. The setting sun was beginning to cast eerie shadows along the row of houses lining the street and the man quickened his pace, pulling his coat more tightly around himself.

He was intimately familiar with these streets. At one point in time, he had called them home. In that moment, he longed to be somewhere else—*anywhere* else. He couldn't recall the last time he'd walked these streets without feeling as if someone was breathing down his neck, watching his movements around every corner . . . as if they knew the secrets he carried.

No, it had been quite some time since the man was happy to be in London. So, the offer of part-time employment had been unexpected but flattering. The man had never considered himself a teacher, but perhaps this was fate's way of offering a much-needed change of pace. Perhaps this could be a new chapter for the *both* of them—the man and his well-kept secret.

"*Blast!*" the man muttered to himself as he sidestepped a fallen dustbin in the street.

He would still be awake in their cramped flat above the old pub, waiting for the man's arrival no doubt, in the chintz armchair strategically placed in front of the window. Still in the same dressing gown from a few days ago, hair unkempt with a glass of brandy in hand, reeking of pipe tobacco.

The man found himself wondering yet again how it had all come to *this*, and he stopped suddenly, pressing a fist against the sudden ache in his chest.

The fresh wave of guilt brought with it a suffocating feeling, intense enough to nearly rip the air from his lungs. What had the man been thinking, that he could leave him alone for hours at a time? That he would be well enough to look after himself without stumbling into trouble or some kind of danger?

But he's perfectly capable of taking care of himself, the man tried to tell himself. *At least physically. He's been doing it for over a century...*

Still, the man's reasoning didn't completely erase the feelings of guilt or worry. He didn't think he would ever stop worrying.

The man did his best to shake himself from his stupor as he set off down the street again. By the time he'd reached The Bronze Archer pub, he'd almost convinced himself that all he needed was a strong cup of tea and perhaps a good book to sink his teeth into and all would be right again.

The man paused in the doorway of the pub's rear entrance, clutching the key to his flat so tightly his knuckles turned white. The raised hair on the nape of his neck, the icy sliver of fear causing his gut to constrict, were no stranger to him.

He tried to sneak a look over his shoulder as surreptitiously as possible. The street was empty. The only noise came from a few rowdy patrons in The Bronze Archer. The man stood in the doorway for a moment longer, eyes sweeping up and down the street for any sign of life—any sign that someone was watching him.

The man finally gave a disgusted scoff and stepped inside, slamming the door shut behind him. Must he deal with crippling worry *and* paranoia?

"Bloody losing my mind," he grumbled, trying not to stomp his way up the narrow steps to his flat.

All thoughts of the figure shrouded in black that the man had imagined watching his every movement disappeared as he reached his door.

He could hear the sounds of a violin while still outside on the staircase, and the man couldn't help but smile. It had been a good day then.

He felt himself take his first breath of air that day where he did not feel as if he were suffocating. He'd been worrying for nothing.

He unlocked the door to his flat and slipped inside.

"I'm home."

The sweet tune from the violin cut short, and a hoarse voice spoke from the darkened corner of the nearby sitting room.

"You took your time, my dear doctor."

The man scoffed again as he unbuttoned his coat. "I'm not a doctor anymore. I haven't held a medical license since nineteen ten."

There was a laugh from the corner. "Once a medical man, always a medical man. Or I suppose," the voice continued amusedly, "I could call you *professor*."

The new title still didn't feel quite right either, but perhaps it would with time.

They would make do. Against all odds, they always had.

Keep It to Yourself

I
t was an honest reaction to the loud sneeze that came from the man standing ahead of me in the line at customs.

"Oh, bless you."

The man barely managed a backward glance in my direction; from what I could see of his face before he moved forward, he looked like I'd just told him to pound sand.

I quickly fixed my gaze on my shoes. Did people in London not say *bless you* when someone sneezed? My first half hour in England after a less than thrilling international flight and already I was approaching an anxiety-ridden meltdown. Fantastic.

I checked my cell phone again for the thousandth time, rereading the last text message from my great-aunt Adele.

Just outside customs. Can't wait!

It was a godsend that Adele was putting me up for the summer, I knew that. I never would've been able to attend the prestigious summer writing seminar offered by London's

Ashford College otherwise. Scrounging up enough to cover the airfare by working at a local deli for the last year had been hard enough on top of juggling graduation requirements.

This was just going to be awkward, sharing a living space with someone I hadn't seen since I was in kindergarten. Awkward, but not *bad*. This was what I was telling myself at least.

When it was finally my turn to approach the customs desk, the guard gave me a quick once-over. "Passport."

I slid my passport across the desk and he flipped it open, holding it up to examine.

"What brings you to London?" he asked without looking away from my passport.

"Visiting family," I answered quickly. "Summer college program."

"Hn."

I started to break out into a cold sweat the longer I stood there, watching the guard inspect my passport.

There's absolutely nothing wrong with my passport, I kept reminding myself. *It's not like I'm a felon or anything. I've never even gotten a parking ticket.*

The guard finally nodded, stamped the darn thing, then slid my passport back across the counter toward me.

I nearly tripped over my feet as I made a break for it out of line, stuffing my passport back into my shoulder bag. One hurdle down—about a million more to go.

The area just outside customs was surprisingly packed for a Sunday afternoon. Another bolt of panic zipped through me as I leaned up on my tiptoes, trying to peer over the heads of the crowd. How was I supposed to find Adele in this mess?

"Over here, Juliet! *Juliet!*"

I sighed in relief when I finally picked out the elderly woman waving at me through the people milling around, shouting my name. Great-aunt Adele looked a lot older than I remembered, dressed in a pair of khaki capris and a floral button-down, her hair steel gray in color, framing her face in soft waves. She had me in her arms for a hug the moment I reached her.

"Oh, it's *so* good to see you, Juliet!"

I tried not to cough as I inhaled too much of her amber perfume. "Uh, Jules, please, if that's okay. And it's good to see you too, Aunt Adele."

Adele leaned away, lightly gripping my shoulders. "Well, in that case, call me Adele."

"Adele," I repeated. "Right."

She smiled, touching a strand of my hair that had come loose from my sloppy ponytail. "My, you've certainly grown, haven't you?"

I struggled to come up with a smile of my own. "I mean, it's been a while . . ."

"Right, right." Adele nodded. "The family reunion in Sedona years ago, I remember." She gestured to my shoulder bag next. "Surely you have more luggage than that?"

"Just one suitcase."

Adele put an arm around my shoulders, steering me through the crowd toward baggage claim.

Ten seconds later it became obvious Adele wasn't experiencing the same awkwardness at our reintroduction. She was asking questions left and right, about how my flight was, how my mom and stepdad were doing, if I was looking forward to the first day of the writing seminar tomorrow. Adele apparently loved to talk.

"Ah, the flight was okay. Food was nothing to write home about," I told her, quickening my pace to keep up with her surprisingly long strides. "Mom and Roger are doing well. They just bought a new house closer to the university Roger teaches at. And yeah, I'm . . . super excited about the writing seminar."

It might've been more accurate to say I was *scared out of my freaking mind*, but I wasn't about to share that with Adele.

Ashford wasn't a very big college, but its summer writing program was renowned. The fact that I'd somehow managed to secure one of six slots available was nothing short of a miracle.

Adele must've seen something in my face that let on to just how nervous I actually was; she gave me another friendly squeeze. "You're going to love London, Jules. And I may not have read any of your writing, but I do know how special this seminar is. I'm sure it's very well deserved."

Well deserved.

I knew my writing could stand on its own. I'd known from the age of five that writing was what I was *meant to do*. And the never-ending encouragement from my high school creative writing teacher, Mrs. Gutierrez, was the entire reason I'd applied for Ashford's seminar in the first place. The letter of recommendation from my stepdad Roger, an associate professor of literature, probably hadn't hurt either.

"Thanks, Adele," I said. My smile was genuine this time. "I appreciate that."

I was lucky enough to find my suitcase at the baggage claim without trouble, and then Adele was leading me out of the airport toward the taxi line.

"I try to walk when I can or take the Tube, but I thought you might like to see some of the sights," Adele said to me as we stood in line. "Then we can hit the supermarket just down the road from my flat. Your mother mentioned you're a big coffee drinker, but all I've got is tea right now, I'm afraid."

"Sure," I said. "That sounds great. But, uh, just out of curiosity, how much did my mother fill you in on?"

Adele chuckled as a black taxi pulled up to the curb in front of us. "Oh, nothing, really. Mostly about reminding you to keep a packet of hearing aid batteries on you at all times."

I squeezed my eyes shut, trying not to groan. "Of course she mentioned that."

I was still adjusting to the whole hearing aid thing, even if it had been over a year since I got them. I'd never considered my hearing—or lack thereof—a problem until I'd missed the smoke alarms going off at home and nearly burnt the kitchen down trying to make cinnamon rolls.

I wouldn't deny they came in handy but keeping track of the tiny silver batteries they required was an unexpected pain. It was now a major pet peeve of mine, that little jingle going off in my ears when my hearing aids were about to die, and then the mad scramble to replace the batteries that came next.

Adele climbed into the taxi after me and shut the door, leaning forward to give the driver an address.

I peeked out the window as the taxi took off from the curb. The sky was covered in a thick blanket of gray, threatening rain. From what I could see so far, the buildings and houses were tightly packed together, backyards bleeding into one another.

"Jules?" Adele's voice abruptly yanked me back into the present. "We're here."

I had gotten so lost in taking in the sights that I didn't even realize I'd spent the entire ride with my face more or less pressed against the window.

"Oh, right."

I got unbuckled while Adele paid the fare. The taxi rumbled off after I snagged my suitcase from the back, leaving us on the sidewalk outside a cute little shop painted a faded sky blue. The welcoming sign above the door, written in an elegant cursive, read Dreams of Antiquity.

A display of furniture took up most of the space in the shop window—chintz armchairs, a gleaming writing desk, an intricately upholstered sofa.

Antiquing had never been my thing, but this shop made me want to dive headfirst into it.

"It's not much, but this little shop has been a lifelong dream of mine," Adele was saying as she fumbled with a set of keys. "My own mother left behind a comfortable inheritance, and I was able to purchase the space. My flat is just upstairs, and I've got a—"

"Adele, this is *amazing*."

Adele stopped in the process of opening the shop door and turned to look at me, now pleasantly surprised. "Oh."

"Honestly," I insisted. "This is . . . something else. Can we have a look around first before we go upstairs?"

Adele was still smiling as she finished unlocking the door and stepped aside to let me pass through first. "Be my guest, dear."

I hefted my suitcase across the threshold as quickly as I could, eager to see what treasures lay hidden around the shop. The place wasn't that big, and it was definitely old, the smell of books, furniture polish, and a smidge of dust permeating the air.

Adele instructed me to leave my suitcase by the small table against the far wall where a dated cash register, stacks of receipts, and other papers sat.

I eagerly set off through the shop. Just from the first look I could tell this little antique business had charm. The floral wallpaper, the array of furniture, knickknacks, several bookcases stuffed with old books of varying size.

I loved it all.

The small corner toward the back where an overstuffed armchair sat, a spindly table beside it with a gleaming typewriter perched on top, was what caught me most off guard. The hanging lamp positioned just to the side of the armchair bathed the area in a soft glow, making the space that much more inviting.

I realized this was it. This was *the* writing spot.

Every bit of writing I would do in London—when I wasn't in class, at least—was going to happen right here.

"It doesn't work, I'm afraid."

I jumped at the sound of Adele's voice behind me.

"Sorry, what?" I said once my breathing had returned to normal.

Adele motioned toward the typewriter, looking sheepish. "That Underwood typewriter. It doesn't work. I've spent some time tinkering with it, but I'm no expert. Pretty to look at though, isn't it?"

"I'll say."

Adele was smiling again. She had a nice smile. "What say we get your things upstairs and go pick up some groceries? It'll be time for tea before too long and you've got a big day ahead of you tomorrow."

"Sorry, what's tea? I don't—wait, hold on."

I pulled my phone out of my pocket to check the time; half past four. It took me one long moment to figure out the time difference between London and Monterey, a whole eight hours. It was still early morning in California.

"Oh," I said, taken aback. "I'd be eating breakfast right about now at home."

"You'll adjust," Adele said confidently. "Best to get on a new schedule right away, otherwise you'll never get over the jet lag."

"Good to know."

Time difference notwithstanding, I knew I wouldn't be getting one ounce of sleep tonight anyway.

CHAPTER

MIND THE GAP

I was right.

Not even a grocery store run and the walk back to the antique shop carting several bags, or helping Adele throw together dinner, unpacking, the half-hour video chat with my mother reassuring her that everything was *fine* and that Adele was already taking good care of me, was enough to make me crash.

I rolled out of bed feeling like a zombie and fumbled around putting my hearing aids in before going through the motions of getting ready.

I joined Adele downstairs in the shop after I'd thrown my things into my bag and grabbed the piece of toast and coffee in a to-go cup she'd set out on the kitchen counter for me.

She was strolling through a portion of the shop lined with porcelain dolls, ticking things off here and there on the clipboard she carried.

I was going to have to avoid this part of the shop as much as possible. Even in England, porcelain dolls still gave me the creeps.

"Ready?" Adele asked, checking off something on her clipboard with a little flourish.

"As I'll ever be," I said, rocking back on my heels. "Um. Where did you say the Tube was from here?"

Adele had set me up with an Oyster card for the Tube—the London Underground—last night. With my luck, I was going to need every spare second to navigate it.

"Oh, not too far from here. One of my assistants, Mindy, should be here soon, so I'll show you."

Adele had us out of the shop and down the sidewalk before I could even try to protest. It wasn't a long walk, she was right. Truthfully, I was thankful for the company.

I was turning nineteen in September, an adult at this point depending on who you asked, but still, I was in a foreign country. Who wouldn't be a little freaked out by heading out on their own for the first time in a *foreign country*?

"See? Not so far," Adele said when we came to a stop at a set of stairs leading down into a concrete tunnel. "Just tap your card at the turnstile and you'll be fine. When in doubt, I'm just a phone call away, dear."

"Right. Thanks, Adele."

I gave her a quick parting hug and set off down the steps to the Tube.

I kept up the mantra *You can do this, Jules,* on my way through the turnstile and onto the train. I got settled in for the ride, gripping tight to one of the handrails. A few moments into the journey and I actually felt myself begin to relax. This was another hurdle down—at least partially. I'd made it onto the Tube; the next step was Ashford.

You can do this, Jules.

I kept an eye on the lighted map above the double doors, watching the little light on it moving closer and closer to my stop. The second the doors slid open at said stop, I was off like a rocket, pulling up the directions to Ashford I'd kept loaded on my phone.

There were about forty-five minutes left before the seminar was set to begin, but the closest stop on the Tube was blocks away from Chatham Hall, one of Ashford's smaller buildings where the seminar was taking place.

I tried to focus on putting one foot in front of the other as I walked, but the hubbub on the street was a major distraction. Several different languages were being spoken around me and groups of tourists were clogging up the sidewalk as they stopped to inspect a looming cathedral casting a shadow over half the street.

I was short of breath and wishing I'd brought a bottle of water with me when I reached Chatham Hall with about fifteen minutes to spare. The building looked like one of the oldest on the street, surrounded by a low brick wall covered in moss. There was a simple courtyard out front with an empty fountain smack-dab in the middle, facing a set of double doors that seemed to be the only entrance.

I crossed the courtyard and slipped inside, relieved to find that the stairs leading up to the second floor were just across the entryway. There was definitely a certain charm to it with its wood-paneled walls and plush carpeting. It was nice, but the orderly chaos of Dreams of Antiquity was a bit more my style.

Room 217 wound up being toward the end of the hallway, near a stained-glass window depicting what looked like the garden of Eden (awkwardly out of place in my opinion). I gave myself one last moment to internally panic before I forced myself to open the door.

The sight I was met with standing in the doorway of Room 217 was not what I was expecting.

I thought I would see desks arranged in neat little rows, a chalkboard, maybe a globe and an apple or two somewhere. A nice, tidy place set up for learning. This was absolutely not that.

The only normal thing about the room was the whiteboard on the far wall and, tucked away in the corner, a small desk piled high with dozens of books.

There was a massive Oriental rug that took up most of the floor space, spread out toward the numerous bookshelves crammed with thick volumes in a variety of colors lining the walls. After that came the handful of sofas and armchairs positioned in what was probably meant to be a circle smack-dab in the middle of the room, one long, marble coffee table centered amidst the jumble.

Then there were the thick velvet drapes lining the windows, blocking out almost all of the sunlight, which probably would've looked better in some Victorian house museum.

All that was missing was a crystal ball or a pack of tarot cards and you might have the perfect setup for a fortune teller.

"Er, excuse me?"

"What? Oh, sorry!"

The guy standing behind me had a bemused expression on his face as I struggled to get out a proper sentence.

It might've been the fact that he was dressed in a T-shirt and jeans instead of a pair of loafers and a cardigan like I expected a stereotypical English writer to be wearing that had me so tongue-tied. Or perhaps it was because of his mess of chestnut-colored hair, square-rimmed glasses, the light smattering of freckles across his nose and cheekbones . . .

It also could've been the accent. Probably it was the accent.

"Sorry," I repeated. "Just . . . taking in the sights."

The guy's lips quirked up in a grin as I stepped to the side to let him pass through the doorway.

"Not your average classroom, I suppose," he agreed. "But I've heard Professor Watson isn't your most traditional teacher."

It took a beat for me to realize that the guy was waiting on me with an *after you* motion, gesturing toward the sofas in the middle of the room. We weren't the only ones in the classroom. There were three others already seated, one girl and two guys, apparently ready for class with notebooks and a bunch of pens, pencils, and highlighters strewn about.

I think I managed a smile of my own as I moved toward the sofas. "Have you heard much else about the professor?"

During my many visits to Ashford's website, the only mention of the professor overseeing the program was that he was a former doctor, had a great love of the written word, and that he'd been with the college for several years. No picture had been included with the short bio.

The guy shrugged as he took a seat beside me on the sofa, leaving a comfortable distance between us. "About the same as everyone else, I imagine."

"Oh. Right."

I watched as the guy pulled out a leather-bound journal from his backpack and a very expensive fountain pen. I was pleased to see I wasn't the only one who'd dragged along the welcome packet from the college.

I took out my own supplies for something to do, but the guy

next to me seemed to be paying me no mind as he flipped open his journal, writing the date at the top of the page in a neat little scrawl. Just as I was working up the courage to properly introduce myself there came a loud screech of, "Percy Bysshe Byers, is that *you*?!" from the doorway.

I had to stop myself from clapping my hands over my ears as a whirlwind of color came flying toward the couch, squealing with glee the whole way. I caught a look of mild horror on the poor guy's face before a tiny little thing was throwing their arms around him.

"*Oh*, I should've known you'd get into this program, Percy Bysshe, you little bookworm! Look at you! How long's it been?"

"It's, er, good to see you too, Suruthi," Percy said awkwardly. He looked like he didn't quite know what to do with the sudden arrival. "It *has* been a while."

Once they got settled on the couch, I saw that Suruthi was a girl of about my age, of Indian descent, with glossy black hair piled up into a stylishly messy bun, and a bunch of bracelets on both wrists that were jingling happily as she started unpacking her bag. Her skirt was electric blue, her T-shirt naming some band I didn't recognize, and the look definitely worked for her.

"But you would, of course," Suruthi was saying, twirling a pink gel pen between her fingers, "seeing as you were *always* writing in some notebook or other, even in nursery school, Percy Bysshe. Oh, do you still write with that one green pencil with the little frog on it too? You were *so* adorable carrying that thing around with you!"

"Can't say I do, given that I'm an adult now," Percy said. A flush was starting to work its way up into his cheeks. "And you don't need to call me by my full name. Just Percy is fine."

Suruthi laughed, giving Percy a playful nudge. "Well, *just Percy*, I'm glad to see that your sense of humor is still there. Good, good."

"Happy to oblige," he muttered, looking anything but.

I failed miserably in turning my bark of laughter into a cough and both Percy and Suruthi turned to look at me. Suruthi perked up, as if she'd just realized I was sitting on the couch alongside them.

"Sorry," I said. "Tickle in my throat."

"Making friends already, Percy?" Suruthi said, nudging him again. Percy shot her a look, and she just wiggled her eyebrows at him. "And an American too, I suspect?"

"Correct," I answered. "This American's name is Jules, by the way. Short for Juliet."

I saw Percy's lips twitch again with a barely there smile as he looked down at his journal, and I knew the literary reference hadn't gone unnoticed. Even if I did happen to be named after one of the sappiest romantic characters of all time, I was thankful my name didn't come from a doomed poet.

Suruthi's laugh was a little louder this time. "D'you know what, Jules from America? I've decided I like you."

"Lucky you," Percy said.

I didn't get a chance to say much else besides a very confused, "Thank you?"

Someone else had just entered the classroom, announcing their presence with a quiet *ahem*.

"I've always considered it a good sign when my students arrive before me on the first day of class, I must say."

CHAPTER

WELCOME, WELCOME

Every pair of eyes immediately went to the man now heading toward the front of the classroom.

He was rather tall, almost thin in the extreme, with neatly combed graying hair. He was dressed in a pair of slacks, button-down shirt, and a tan waistcoat. With what I thought was overly formal dress for a college classroom along with the very out of style mustache that had me thinking of a vintage shaving ad I'd seen in Adele's shop yesterday, the man looked strangely out of place.

I might have spent less time inspecting the professor's appearance if I hadn't noticed the scar next. It wasn't a very long scar, but it was considerably wide and noticeable on the side of his neck where it stopped just beneath the edge of his jaw. I had no idea what could've caused something like that—a scar that didn't seem to have completely healed.

The professor didn't seem oblivious to the curious stares that followed him as he went to his desk and began rifling through his leather briefcase. He pulled out a manila folder and a journal bound with a golden clasp that he tucked up under his arm before turning to face us.

He stared at us with an almost unnerving gaze for a few seconds, then cracked a small smile. "No need to look so anxious. I don't bite, I assure you."

There was some awkward laughter at this, but the tension in the room slowly began to ebb as the professor took a seat in the winged armchair at the head of the circle. He crossed one leg over the other, uncapping a ritzy fountain pen he'd retrieved from the pocket of his waistcoat.

"I am Professor J. Watson, your instructor for the next eight weeks," he announced as he undid the clasp on his journal. "And all of you are here, presumably, because you too enjoy writing."

"I think *love* might be the better word for it," I heard Suruthi sing happily under her breath.

Professor Watson gave a half smile at Suruthi's enthusiasm and kept going. "By the end of this seminar, each of you will have completed a one-to-two-hundred-page manuscript over a topic or genre of your choice. The only demand I will make of you is that you truly devote your time and energy to this project. I will be carefully selecting one of your completed manuscripts to send on query to Brookhaven Press here in London."

My hand was unsteady as I took notes. The first line I wrote was *one-to-two-hundred-page manuscript*, followed by *publishing opportunity*. This I underlined three times, digging my pen into the paper so forcefully I almost ripped a hole in it.

This shouldn't have come as such a shock. The whole purpose of this seminar was to write. But a manuscript that was upward of *two hundred pages*? I couldn't even remember the last time I'd written more than two or three pages.

"Not only will you be spending a great deal of time writing over the coming weeks, but we will be exploring various genres of literature as well," Professor Watson continued. "Nothing longer than a short passage or two, but it should still be enough for you to grasp the concepts. As the old saying goes, the greatest writers steal their inspiration from their fellow authors."

He removed a small stack of papers from the folder in his lap and passed it to the girl sitting to his left. She took one sheet and handed the rest to the guy sitting beside her. I was the last to get a copy of the paper, which turned out to be a list of books. From a quick glance I saw that most of the titles were outdated and more than a handful I'd read in high school. With any luck, revisiting them wouldn't be all that bad next to the copious amounts of writing we'd be doing.

But this wasn't a problem. Of course not.

"Well then," Professor Watson said. "Now that our serious housekeeping duties are out of the way, I'd like to take the time for you all to—"

The rest of the professor's words were drowned out by the sound of someone's cell phone ringing—*my* cell phone. I quickly scrambled for it while the LED light flashed, vibrating wildly on the couch beside me.

"Sorry," I said, stumbling over the word as the professor and my new classmates all watched. "Won't happen again."

I was going to have to a serious talk with my mother about making phone calls at two in the morning California time.

Suruthi was the first to break the awkward silence. "Was that Metallica?"

I blew out a sigh, wondering at the probability of the couch cushions swallowing me whole. "Yep."

Metallica was *loud* and that was the kind of music I preferred these days.

Suruthi started to giggle, and a few others soon joined in. I couldn't tell if this was a good thing or not.

"Well then," Professor Watson repeated, his clear blue gaze now centered on me. He thankfully didn't seem too annoyed at the interruption. "Why don't you introduce yourself first, Miss...?"

"Montgomery," I answered.

Professor Watson jotted something down in his notebook, gesturing for me to continue. "Please do go on, Miss Montgomery."

"Um." *Great start*, I thought with an eye roll. "Well. My name is Jules Montgomery. I'm from California. I grew up in a kinda small city not too far from San Francisco. I just graduated high school a couple weeks ago and I'll be attending my first year of college in San Diego—that's near Los Angeles—this fall. For creative writing. Obviously. Because... I like to write. Yeah."

Another round of silence followed my extremely awkward introduction, and I tried not to grimace.

Professor Watson nodded, still jotting down notes in his journal. He might've been smiling, but I couldn't be sure. "And do you have a preferred genre you like to write?"

"Mystery, mostly," I admitted. "It might be a little cliché, but I'm an Agatha Christie fan. Haven't read too many of the Hercule Poirot stories, but *And Then There Were None* is one of my favorite novels. Edgar Allan Poe's not too bad either."

This time Professor Watson did smile. "Classics indeed. Will we perhaps be seeing a bit of the macabre in your forthcoming manuscript?"

"Ah. Maybe?" I tried not to start chewing on my bottom lip. "I think I'm still finding out what else I like to write."

Or just writing, period.

Professor Watson nodded again as he gave a quiet, thoughtful hum. "Hopefully this seminar will bring you one step closer to your goal then, Miss Montgomery."

"Yeah," I agreed. "Me too."

I felt a flood of relief as everyone's attention moved on to Percy next. He'd barely opened his mouth to speak before Suruthi threw a hand in the air, announcing, "I'd like to go next, Professor!"

Professor Watson gave her the same gesture to continue. "Please do."

Suruthi dived right in. "I'm Suruthi Kaur, born and raised in London, the youngest of five kids, blah, blah, blah." She was tapping out a beat on the cover of her notebook with the gel pen, her foot bouncing. "You can definitely expect some of the macabre from me because I happen to be an ardent fan of true crime." She gave me a little finger wave next. "I think you and I will be partnering up on our manuscripts before too long, Jules Montgomery, because crimes are often full of the macabre, aren't they?"

I couldn't be sure what with my hearing aids and all, but it sounded an awful lot like Percy muttered, "*God help us.*"

"Sure," I told Suruthi, mustering up a smile. "Sounds great."

It was way too early to tell if Suruthi was being serious or not, but I was beginning to like her too.

The next hour and a half seemed to fly by as we went around the circle, my new classmates each introducing themselves. No one seemed quite as eager for their turn as Suruthi had been, but it ended up being a fun way to pass the time.

There was only one other student from North America, a girl by the name of Ashley James, who'd grown up living with her grandmother in Ontario.

"I'm going to give us a change of pace and say that my preferred genre would be historical fiction," she told us with a grin. "There's not a lot of historical fiction for young adults out there that focuses on the Viking Age—at least not that I've found—and I *really* want to be the one to change that."

Professor Watson looked intrigued. "Vikings, you say?"

Ashley nodded, her grin a full-blown smile now. "Women during the Viking Age had a lot of autonomy and power despite being of the 'lesser sex.' So I figure there has to be a story there somewhere."

"I imagine there is," Professor Watson agreed. "I look forward to reading your work, Miss James."

Suruthi leaned over to offer Ashley a high five.

I decided that I was going to like Ashley James as well. I could get behind the Vikings.

After Ashley came Willem from Belgium who I think shared with us that he was a fan of science fiction, but I'd admittedly had a hard time understanding his accent at first. Willem seemed shy; as soon as he'd finished speaking, he ducked his head, throwing himself into the folding and unfolding of the paper Professor Watson had passed out.

After Willem came Thierry, who hailed from France, and proudly declared that he'd been writing political thrillers since the age of seven.

"And political thrillers about your own charming country," Thierry added, throwing a smile I didn't particularly care for in my direction. "I went to the United States last summer and found my time touring your capital so very enlightening. I am sure you feel the same."

"I've actually never been to Washington, DC," I told him. "I think there's about three thousand miles between California and the US capital."

Thierry didn't seem too amused by my answer.

The last to give an introduction was Percy.

"I'm from Kent, so not too far," he started, his grip on his pen *very* tight. "Both my parents are in academia, and I've got three elder brothers. I found a flat share in the city for the summer, thankfully, and my genre of choice happens to be fantasy."

"That is *so* you, Percy Bysshe," Suruthi said with a laugh. "Princesses and dragons and whatnot."

Percy shot her a disgruntled look. "More like Tolkien, but I appreciate the support."

From what I'd observed so far, this seemed fitting for Percy. His pen looked even fancier than Professor Watson's and could probably spin some epic fantasy story that could rival *The Lord of the Rings*.

"Thank you for those illuminating introductions," Professor Watson said once Percy had finished. "It is helpful to put a face to the names of the submission pieces included in your applications for this seminar. I am not exaggerating when I tell you that I am very much looking forward to reading each and every one of your manuscripts this summer."

I started chewing on my lip before I could stop.

That *manuscript*.

"Hey, Jules. Jules?"

I gave a start at the sound of Suruthi's singsong voice saying my name. Both she and Percy were eyeing me with curious stares as the rest of our classmates gathered up their things. Professor Watson had already retreated to his desk and looked busy jotting down more notes in his journal.

"Sorry, must've zoned out," I said awkwardly.

Suruthi shrugged. "We've got an hour break now and we're going to nip across the street for a coffee. You wanna come?"

"Sure," I said, grabbing my bag as I got to my feet. "Coffee sounds great."

As I followed Percy and Suruthi out of the classroom, I tried to look on the bright side of things.

I was pretty sure I was making friends. Friends were good. The professor seemed nice too, if not intimidating. I already knew I was going to enjoy staying with Adele for the summer. The only difficult part about all this was going to be figuring out what the heck I was going to write about. I wondered if it would seem a little suspect if I asked Suruthi or Percy how they handled writer's block because it was undeniably a universal experience. Less appealing was asking the professor himself for some kind of guidance. Granted, it *was* his job, but we were barely halfway through the first day of the seminar. My first breakdown (probably one of many) could at least wait until the second day.

I snuck my wallet out of my bag as we left Chatham Hall, checking the wad of pounds I'd shoved in there before my flight yesterday.

I needed to calculate how much coffee I could afford to buy to make it through the rest of the day.

4

Inspiration, Meet Brick Wall

Y ou look upset. Why do you look upset?"

These were the first words my mother spoke as I answered her video call. Somehow she had timed it perfectly and called right as Professor Watson released us for the day.

"Hello to you too, Mother," I said. "My day was great, thank you for asking."

The connection was poor, but I could make out my mother's trademark scowl. "Not funny, Juliet. Tell me what's bothering you."

"Nothing," I insisted. "Nothing's bothering me. I think I still have some jet lag."

My mother did not look convinced at my pathetic excuse, but she let it go with a short nod. "How was your first day?"

"It was fine," I answered. "Great. There are some really nice people in the seminar."

"And what about the writing? The professor?"

"The professor is nice too. The writing will be . . . a lot."

A lot didn't even begin to cover all of what the writing in this seminar was going to involve.

I ended the video chat after promising I would give her a detailed account of exactly how my first day had gone and a general idea of what I wanted to write about later.

And *that* was the problem. I had absolutely no idea what I wanted to write about yet. To make matters worse, Professor Watson wanted an outline by Friday.

I found my way back to the Tube in a daze. Barely one day in and I felt like I was already treading water.

Somehow, I managed to get off at the correct stop and arrived at Dreams of Antiquity before too long. The scent of old books was strangely comforting as I stepped inside, as was Adele's greeting as the door swung closed.

"Oh, Jules, you're back! How was your first day?"

"It was great," I said. I was beginning to sound like a broken record here. "I'm really excited about everything."

Adele cocked her head, a shrewd look passing over her face.

"It's just going to be a lot of writing," I added quickly. "Maybe a little more than I was expecting."

"I see." Adele came forward to grip my shoulder, squeezing lightly. "Well, it's only the first day, so try not to panic *too* much."

"Right," I said. "No panicking here."

Adele grinned, squeezing my shoulder again. "Have a little faith in yourself, Juliet. Obviously, your writing speaks for itself, otherwise you wouldn't have been accepted into the program."

She wasn't necessarily wrong. I'd poured my heart out into the piece I sent in with my application and I was proud of it. Unfortunately, I'd written it over a year ago and hadn't produced anything like it since.

It wasn't for lack of trying. Every time I'd sat down with the

intention to write, a buzzing in my fingers that had me itching
to type, I was left feeling hopelessly frustrated. The words were
there, *somewhere*, but it was like they were stuck behind some
figurative brick wall, and I didn't have a bulldozer handy.

"Now, go upstairs and fix yourself something to eat," Adele
said in a tone that made it clear this was nonnegotiable. "You
look peckish."

"Sure," I said. "An afternoon snack. On it."

Upstairs in the flat, I pulled out some fruit and yogurt from
the fridge and was taking a seat at the table with Professor
Watson's reading list when my phone went off. I was expecting
it to be another call from my mother, but instead it was from a
long, unfamiliar phone number.

> Jules from America!!!!
> It's me, your new fav writing
> mate! (Suruthi, that is)
> Wait
> Please tell me you have international messaging.

I was smiling by the time I'd finished reading the barrage of
messages. I'd given Suruthi my number before Professor Watson
had let us go for the day, but I didn't think she'd start texting me
so soon.

> Hi, Suruthi!! It's me, Jules from America
> Luckily my stepdad set me up with
> an international phone plan, so we
> are good to go. Text away!

Suruthi's response came a minute later—:D:D:D:D:D followed by a Good, good. So, you writing yet?

Snack first. My aunt told me I look "peckish."

Maybe fruit and sugary yogurt would provide some inspiration.

Suruthi's response was a simple: SAME

I was halfway through my snack when I got another text, this time a group chat from Suruthi and another long number I didn't recognize.

So, you're probably wondering why I have called you both here today . . .

A reply came from the unknown number a moment later.

Let me guess. This is Suruthi.

I sat back in amusement as the two chat bubbles kept going off, one after the other.

Correct!! You deserve a prize, Percy Bysshe.

Percy texted back with perfect punctuation: How did you get my number? I don't recall giving it to you.

I'd only just met the guy today, but it wasn't difficult to imagine Percy frowning the whole time he was texting back and forth with Suruthi.

Had my mum ask your mum for it :D Suruthi replied.

Of course you did. Percy wrote back. I really shouldn't be surprised.

Suruthi texted back with another few smiley faces. You know me so well, Percy.

A second text popped up a beat later: You're being awfully quiet, Jules.

Just enjoying the witty banter, I texted after taking the last bite of my yogurt.

My condolences, Jules, was Percy's response. You're probably frightening the poor girl, Suruthi.

Nah, I texted back. We're writing mates now, didn't you know?

Suruthi quickly followed up with, That includes you too, Percy. I am happy to invite you to be a part of this sacred writing circle. You're welcome.

I can barely contain my excitement.

I slipped my laptop out of my bag, snatched the professor's reading list off the table, and headed downstairs into the shop.

I could hear a few different voices chattering away and something that sounded like the beeping of a cash register as I navigated my way through the neat little aisles to the nook I'd designated as my official writing spot.

I got settled in the cozy armchair and booted up my laptop. I had absolutely no idea what I was going to write up to two hundred pages about, but Professor Watson was going to have an outline of it by Friday one way or another.

But my brain apparently had other plans. I frowned as I

stared at the blinking cursor. I felt like it was laughing at me. All I had to work with was a big, fat *nothing*.

Ugh.

I groaned, scrubbing my face with my hands. Was this massive brick wall looming over me at the prospect of this manuscript fate's way of telling me I didn't actually deserve to be here?

Or maybe I'd foolishly pinned all my hopes on my writer's block suddenly disappearing the moment I arrived in London, and now I was going to have to face reality: I was already terrified of screwing up when I hadn't written anything yet.

I spent the next hour or so going through the folder of short stories and assignments I'd saved from my last semester of creative writing class. Mrs. Gutierrez always seemed to have a never-ending supply of writing prompts for her students; surely I could find *something* in all these old files.

This was a good place to start.

I shifted around in the armchair, tucking my legs up underneath me. I was not going to move from this spot until I had at least started my outline.

"Jules? Juliet, dear."

I tore my gaze from my laptop at the sound of my name. "Huh?"

Adele was standing in front of me, clipboard tucked up under her arm, and she had a knowing smile on her face. "Bit lost in thought there, are we?"

"You could say that," I agreed, glancing back at my laptop.

The two pages I'd managed to come up with were, in short, a hot mess—but a hopefully workable hot mess.

"Well, I hate to interrupt, but I've just finished closing up shop and thought I'd head upstairs to get a start on tea. Would you like to join me?"

There was a loud tapping noise that had Adele pausing just as I'd been about to ask if she meant the tea you drink or the one with the meal. "What on earth?"

The tapping noise started growing louder until I figured out that the sound was actually someone knocking rapidly on the shop's front door.

"You're closed for the night, aren't you?" I said to Adele.

"Yes, I am," she said, frowning.

I followed Adele as she made her way to the door. I had no idea what I'd be able to do in the event of a break-in, but my step-dad had informed me that my scream was worthy of shattering glass (I *really* hate spiders).

All I could see at first through the stained glass on the shop's front door was that there was a very *large* figure standing outside. I watched again as their hand raised and the knocking started up again, this time faster.

"Adele, are you really sure you want to open the door?" I asked uncertainly.

Adele was apparently a lot braver than I was; she opened the door without a moment's hesitation.

"*Oh!*"

Adele's exclamation had me rushing forward, but I was apparently worried for no reason. Adele seemed to know the unusually dressed man standing on the doorstep as she said, "William, it's you. What a lovely surprise."

"My apologies, madam," the man she called William said in a weirdly formal voice. "It appears that in my haste to reach your establishment I have frightened you."

"Not at all," Adele said, laughing. "Think nothing of it. Unfortunately though we *are* shut for the day, William."

Just from the one look, it seemed to me that this William was not the type of person you'd want to give bad news to.

The man was tall, for one, but so overwhelmingly lean that it made him seem even taller. His gaunt appearance was a little unsettling to take in at first.

"*But*," Adele continued, and I could hear the smile coming into her voice, "I have no issue making an exception for my favorite customer."

She stepped aside to let the man pass through and shut the door behind him.

Oh no, I thought. *Why are we letting this man through the door, Adele?*

"Thank you indeed, Ms. Duncan," William said, perfectly polite. He seemed to have noticed me standing just a few feet away but he said nothing, his gaze moving around the shop with blatant curiosity. For as out of place as his mannerisms were, his dress, which looked like some kind of silken bathrobe, fit right in with the shop's aesthetic. "I must say, those lab manuals on display in your window caught my eye. I have been meaning to purchase them for some time."

"Of course, of course," Adele laughed. "I wondered if I should've set those aside for you. We also have a microscope that I just picked up through another dealer, circa 1890s I've been told."

William raised an eyebrow, looking momentarily interested,

then shook his head. "Just the manuals today, I'm afraid. But I would take great pleasure in seeing this microscope for myself at a later date."

"Jules, would you mind going to fetch those two red books from the window display?" Adele asked me, like she'd suddenly remembered I was present too.

"Sure," I said slowly, shuffling back a step when William's gaze finally moved to me. Polite he may be, but kind of creepy looking he most definitely was.

"Oh, William, this is my great-niece, Juliet," Adele said, putting an arm around my shoulders as she introduced us. "She came all the way from California to stay here for the summer. Jules, this is William, and he's been stopping by my humble little shop for years now."

It looked like William was amused by this, but quickly smoothed it over with a short statement of, "How very nice."

"Sure," I repeated. "Loving it so far."

I tried to telepathically ask Adele if she was going to be okay being left alone with this man, but she seemed to completely miss my concern, giving me a nudge toward the window display.

I tried to listen to their conversation as best I could as I went rummaging through the display, trying not to disturb anything. The books Adele had been referring to were actually two giant, red, leather-bound books about as thick as my forearm and quite heavy.

"*Are you kidding?*" I whispered, looking down at the books.

They would be put to better use as a doorstop.

Brick-like as they were, I was able to heft the things up into my arms and cart them over to the desk where the shop's cash register sat. Adele was making polite chitchat with William, who hardly glanced over when I dumped them onto the table.

"Thank you, Jules," Adele said, busying herself ringing up the manuals. "William here was just telling me he's going to see about reproducing some of the experiments in these manuals."

"That's . . . cool."

"*Cool* indeed," William said, sounding a little miffed. "I look forward to the results."

He said something else about chemistry, but his voice started to become background noise the more I watched him. It seemed like he was touching everything, picking up little trinkets on a nearby shelf, flipping open one of the chemistry manuals to read off some equation.

The man didn't seem to be able to stop *moving* and it was making it difficult to understand much of what he or my aunt were saying.

"Jules?"

"Sorry, what?" I said, startled. "What did you need?"

Adele was staring at me somewhat in concern. "I asked if you wouldn't mind helping William carry the—"

"Oh, no need for that, Ms. Duncan," William said, and promptly picked up the two books as though they were as light as a feather. "I look forward to seeing that microscope you mentioned earlier. As always, you have my eternal gratitude for allowing me access to your marvelous inventory. Take care."

Somehow he'd gotten the shop door open despite his full hands and that was it.

I was left standing there with my mouth hanging open as Adele went to shut and lock the door again.

That had to be, without a doubt, one of the strangest interactions I'd had to date.

"Are you alright, Jules?" Adele asked when she'd turned to face me.

"Yeah, but—okay, who *was* that?" I said, my words coming out in a rush. "That was—was a little *odd*."

"Oh, really? William?" Adele laughed, flicking the curtains closed over the front window. "Don't be silly, dear. William is harmless. Been coming in here for ages, like I said, and not afraid to spend a pretty penny either."

"Okay, sure, that's great, but it kinda seemed like he was trying to break down the door," I pointed out.

Adele was apparently so used to this William's behavior that she didn't find it odd in the slightest and just laughed again. "He does get a little impatient from time to time, yes, but who doesn't? I promise you, dear, he's a gentle thing. Not to worry."

I opted not to push the matter any further and followed Adele upstairs to her flat as she directed the conversation toward what we were going to eat.

Adele probably did know her regular customers pretty well after running the business for so long, but that wasn't going to stop me from going back downstairs later to double-check the locks.

5

CHAPTER

400 Milligrams is the Recommended Daily Intake of Caffeine

"Hey, Jules."

I half expected to see Suruthi barreling her way into the coffee shop across the street from Chatham Hall, but it was Ashley who had said my name, my fellow aspiring writer from "across the pond."

Ashley was a lot shorter than I'd realized, standing behind me in line, one earbud in. Despite the giant yawn, she still had a smile and a wave for me.

"Hi, Ashley," I said, grinning. "Fancy running into you here."

"Oh, I suspect we'll all be spending a lot of time here during the next eight weeks," she said humorously. "At least those of us who drink multiple cups of coffee a day."

"Guilty as charged," I agreed.

We made polite chitchat as we stood in line waiting to order our drinks. Between the steadily growing noise inside the coffee shop and the soft tone of Ashley's voice, trying to understand a word she was saying was becoming increasingly harder. I snuck a hand up and tried to surreptitiously turn the volume up on my hearing aids, and if Ashley noticed, she kept quiet.

". . . and, okay, I have this one story I've been working on for years now, but when I think about creating an outline for it and all that, I'm a little intimidated," Ashley was saying, pulling a grimace.

"Me too," I said. I almost felt relief hearing her say that. I wasn't the only one terrified of our manuscripts. "We came here to write, yeah, but the whole concept of deadlines kind of freaks me out."

Five minutes of conversation standing in line at a coffee shop had told me that I'd found another kindred spirit. Not bad.

"Yeah, deadlines aren't my thing either." Ashley grinned, tucking a strand of her dark hair behind her ear. "I have it on good authority that I have a problem being told what and when to write."

"Hey, that's a cute bumblebee," I said as Ashley rummaged around in her bag for her wallet to pay for her drink and I saw the little bronze pin nestled into the strap of her bag.

"Thanks!" Ashley said cheerily without looking up. "From my grandma. She's always called me her "little honeybee." Embarrassing, but you know, she's my grandma."

"Sounds like a grandma, yeah."

We left the coffee shop a short while later, drinks in hand, along with a slice of lemon pound cake that looked too good to pass up. There was still a bit of time left before today's session began, but I turned to ask Ashley if she wanted to head up to the classroom anyway. I heard my name being shouted before I'd even opened my mouth.

Suruthi was sprinting her way down the sidewalk toward us in another neon-colored skirt and band T-shirt, waving madly.

"Good *morning*, darlings!" she sang when she reached us, then threw her arms around me and Ashley.

Ashley shot me a startled look when Suruthi let us go and I shrugged in return. Twenty-four hours since we'd met and somewhere during that time, I'd already come to accept the fact that this was simply how Suruthi was.

"I dunno about you two, but I stayed up *way* too late last night trying to work on that outline. I'm going to need three of those," Suruthi said, pointing to my coffee. "And I've already had two cups of tea."

"Then I hope you enjoy standing in that queue," another voice chimed in.

Percy joined us on the sidewalk, two large coffees in hand. Judging by the even messier hair and sleepy look in his eyes, he'd been up late working on Professor Watson's outline too.

"Whatever do you mean?" Suruthi said, batting her eyelashes at him. "I see a coffee for me right there in your hand."

"That's where you're wrong, I'm afraid," Percy said, taking a long slurp of coffee. "These are both mine."

I had to respect a person who could drink two large coffees in one sitting.

I hid a smile behind my hand as Suruthi gasped in mock outrage. She spun on her heel and swept into the coffee shop without another word.

"Suruthi's always been like that," Percy said to Ashley, who had watched the whole exchange with a stunned look. "You get used to it."

Suruthi came breezing out of the shop in what seemed like a

minute with coffee and a scone in hand. "I may or may not have just bribed my way to the head of the queue. Now we may proceed to class," she announced, gesturing grandly with her coffee. "After you."

The four of us zipped across the street, through the courtyard, and went inside Chatham Hall, the last ones to reach the classroom upstairs. Thierry and Willem had taken the same seats as yesterday, so Ashley made herself comfortable in the paisley armchair she'd chosen previously, and the rest of us wound up squished on the couch.

Unlike yesterday, Professor Watson was already seated at his desk, head down, and it looked like he was writing in his journal again. He didn't join us in the circle until the clock hit nine on the dot exactly.

"Judging by the amount of coffee cups and energy drinks I see here, I take it there was quite a bit of writing going on late yesterday?" the professor said, settling into his winged armchair.

There was a smattering of laughter from the rest of the group, but my laughter felt forced.

I watched with some interest as Percy flipped open the journal in his lap and started thumbing through the pages. My jaw dropped when I counted at least a dozen pages packed full of neat, precise handwriting. This, along with the two giant cups of coffee, had me thinking Percy hadn't actually gotten a lick of sleep last night.

"Do you always write by hand?" I asked in awe.

"Usually, unless it's a final manuscript," Percy answered quietly. He gestured with the same fountain pen he'd been using yesterday. "I think it adds something to the creative process this way."

And hand cramps, I thought.

"That is . . . seriously impressive, Percy," I told him.

He looked mildly embarrassed as he mumbled out a thanks. I wondered if it was possible he had a few tips he'd be willing to share.

Professor Watson took the class through a lecture about outlining that ended up lasting most of the morning. It was still a whirlwind of information even if I'd covered similar topics in other creative writing classes; when we took a midday break, I had a few good pages or so in my notebook filled with blocks of notes and plot diagrams.

A few others got up to head to the restroom or dash across the street for another coffee, but I stayed put. I tucked my legs up underneath me on the couch and pulled my bag toward me, digging for some colored pens.

"Yoo-hoo!"

I looked up from my mess of notes at the singsong voice floating somewhere above my head and saw Suruthi perched on the arm of the couch beside me. The classroom was empty, save for the two of us. Apparently spacing out and missing important announcements, like we were going on a break, was becoming a new habit of mine.

"You really get into it when you write, don't you?" Suruthi said, nodding toward the notebook open in my lap.

"I try to," I said, flipping my notebook shut. "Lunch?"

"That it is," Suruthi said, straightening up. "Percy went to get in the queue for a fish and chips stand and I've been craving chips for ages now."

I opened my mouth to tell Suruthi that she was going to have to remind me what chips were, but nothing came out when a cheery little tune suddenly filled my ears, and the world became remarkably quiet.

Well, sort of.

The audiologist I'd become *very* familiar with over the last year had informed me multiple times that I wasn't deaf—my hearing loss was just severe. I was still able to mostly hear people with lower voices when they spoke and loud noises like someone playing the drums or slamming doors . . . or a garbage truck. Sometimes it took me a little longer to figure out what was being said, but I could do it.

Higher frequencies, on the other hand, were now pretty much lost on me—like Suruthi's voice, for example.

She was still talking rather animatedly as she played with the strap of her bag, her lips moving way too fast for me to even attempt to lip-read—something I wasn't that good at to begin with.

Okay, I told myself. *Don't panic. Do* not *panic.*

This was easier said than done, but my mom had reminded Adele to always keep a pack of hearing aid batteries on me for a reason. This was hardly the first time my hearing aids had died in a public place, and it wasn't going to be the last.

I could fib my way out of this, no problem.

"Uh, you go on," I said as Suruthi stood there in the doorway, waiting expectantly. So far she didn't seem like she suspected anything, but feeling my own voice reverberating inside my head when I couldn't hear much of it was just *bizarre*. "I'm pretty sure my mom called earlier, and I need to check my voicemail."

I quickly turned around and busied myself with rummaging through my bag, pretending to be looking for my phone. I snuck a peek over my shoulder as my hand closed around the little plastic case holding my hearing aid batteries just to make sure Suruthi really had gone.

But the coast was clear, so I carefully popped open the plastic case with one hand and reached up to pull out my left hearing aid. The thing was dark brown in color to match my hair, something I'd picked in the hope that they would be unnoticeable. Most of the time I was pretty sure they were.

It was beyond annoying trying to pop open the thing's battery compartment while making sure the miniscule battery didn't go flying, but I somehow managed to successfully change the battery in one hearing aid before moving on to the next.

I popped the battery compartment open on my right hearing aid next, shook out the dead battery, and had just gotten a new battery out of the case before my stupid butterfingers dropped the thing. As I watched the new battery hit the floor and start rolling, I thought about just leaving it there and getting a new one, but hearing aid batteries were expensive. Besides, the battery would still work even if it was a bit dirty.

"Crap."

I made sure the case of batteries was carefully shut before I set my bag on the couch and got to my knees, on the hunt for the rogue battery.

There didn't seem to be anything underneath the coffee table besides a whole lot of dust, and the same went for the couch. I grabbed at the arm of the chair beside me to get to my feet, only to let loose with a squeak of shock at the sight of Professor Watson standing before me, hand outstretched. The tiny hearing aid battery I'd dropped sat perfectly in the middle of his palm.

With the one hearing aid on, Professor Watson's voice

was only a little muffled as I heard him say, "I believe you dropped this."

"Yes," I said, holding in a defeated sigh. "Thanks."

I accepted the battery with another quiet *thanks*. I did my best to ignore Professor Watson as I swapped the batteries out in my right hearing aid and got it safely back on, but without much success.

Professor Watson had an intensity to his gaze that was almost unnerving. I didn't care for the way it made me feel as if I were being examined under a microscope; I was bracing myself for an onslaught of questions given the almost analytical expression that had taken over the professor's face as he watched me work. Hadn't his short bio on Ashford's website said he'd been a medical doctor at one point?

Several beats of awkward silence had passed before the professor spoke again, and it was just a simple: "How's that outline coming along, Miss Montgomery?"

It's an absolute mess.

"It's . . . coming along fine," I answered. I hoped I sounded more confident than I felt. "I think I've got something good going so far."

That part was mostly truthful. I *did* think my outline had potential to turn into a real nail-biting thriller—mostly. It just needed a little fine tuning.

"Excellent," Professor Watson said. "I did rather enjoy your submission piece about the detective working in the paranormal division of the New York City Police Department. I suspect we will have a rousing discussion over your outline at our individual conference next week."

"Uh, right." I cleared my throat, squeezing the strap of my bag tightly between my fingers. "Thanks, Professor."

Professor Watson gave me a polite nod and strolled over to his desk, humming that same tune he'd been yesterday.

It took more effort than it should have to put one foot in front of the other and leave the classroom. I felt somehow trapped in a strange daze.

On the one hand, I'd managed to change the batteries in my hearing aids in public without the world coming to a complete stop just because someone saw me. That was a good thing. On the other hand, Professor Watson just said he'd *rather enjoyed* my submission piece and was *very much looking forward* to reading more of my work.

Because that wasn't an insane amount of pressure or anything.

6

CHAPTER

Hemingway and Faulkner

I think this is it, you lot. I think I've *finally* got it."

Percy sighed, shoving his glasses up into his hair so he could rub at his eyes with the heels of his hands. "Suruthi. You've told us this at least a dozen times already."

"Yes, well, *this* time I mean it." Suruthi slammed her laptop shut and threw a triumphant fist into the air. "It's probably three pages too long and some of it might not be in English, but my outline is done, I tell you."

"Good for you," I muttered around the pen between my teeth, flipping to a fresh page in my notebook.

A few hours' worth of trying to make some headway with our outlines in a study room on the first floor of Chatham Hall that Wednesday night had left us all feeling exhausted and crabby.

I was ready to call it a night before I started getting any weepier at the sight of my half-blank Word document, and Percy and Suruthi seemed to be of the same mind. We started clearing our things off the table, packing up, but the congenial silence was broken when Suruthi spoke suddenly, her voice low and austere.

"Percy Bysshe Byers. Is that a *tattoo* there on your arm?"

Percy's arms fell to his sides from where he'd been leaning back in his chair to stretch. I could see the tips of his ears going red through his mess of hair as Suruthi stared him down from across the table.

"Ah, well . . ." He cleared his throat, his gaze moving to the ceiling. "It might be."

"And what, pray tell, is it of?" Suruthi demanded at once. "It's all black and gray, I can't make much out."

Percy refused to answer, his lips a thin line as he finished packing up. I only ended up with a glimpse of the tattoo that was clearly on his inner bicep as he moved, but it looked strangely rectangular.

"When did you get a tattoo?" Suruthi insisted. "And more importantly, Percy Bysshe, *what* did you get a tattoo of?"

There was really no excuse for it on my part. The perfect opportunity came as Percy scooted back from the table and bent down to grab a fallen pad of sticky notes off the floor. There was one split second where I was able to get a good peek at the black and gray ink on his right arm, and I went for it.

"It's a typewriter," I said in surprise. "You have a tattoo of a typewriter."

I knew nothing about tattoos, but Percy's was intricately done, the detail of each key almost lifelike. A typewriter wasn't the first thing that would come to mind when I thought about getting a tattoo, but that somehow fit Percy.

He exhaled slowly, shoulders slumping in defeat. An embarrassed flush was steadily working its way into his face, but he didn't sound that put out when he said, "That it is."

"A typewriter?" Suruthi repeated. She looked a mixture of confused and amused. "Why a typewriter?"

"Why d'you have to say it like *that*?"

"Sorry, it's just . . . I mean, do you even know how to use one?" Suruthi said, fighting back a laugh. "Seeing as how most people use a computer these days . . ."

"I'm well aware, thank you," Percy said crisply. "But I've always found the simpler, the better. And of *course* I know how to use a typewriter, Suruthi, don't be daft. I've told you about my mum's collection before."

"I like it," I cut in, quickly adding, "Seriously. I think it looks amazing."

Percy only looked mildly skeptical as he now glanced my way. "Well, thanks . . ." He cleared his throat, looking like he was trying to keep from fidgeting. "I appreciate it."

The question was out in a rush before I could bite it back.

"Can you fix one?"

There was a good chance there would be no repairing that typewriter sitting in Adele's shop, but it was worth a shot. It had been sitting there on that table collecting dust for who knew how long. Maybe with a little TLC it would be back in working condition, and if Percy's mother collected typewriters, maybe he knew a thing or two about them.

Percy threw up a hand to cut Suruthi off before she had the chance to answer for him. "Why do you ask?"

"There's this typewriter in my aunt's antique shop that doesn't work," I explained, scooting my chair closer to Percy's. "I think she said it was an Underwood?"

I knew the second his eyes lit up when I said the name that Percy was on board.

"Now *that* is a *classic*," he said, scooting his chair toward me in turn. "A lot of famous authors wrote with Underwoods, like Faulkner and Hemingway."

"You spend a lot of time reading American authors?" I asked curiously.

"Why wouldn't I?" Percy said with a dismissive wave. "Now does this Underwood have a—"

Suruthi groaned loudly. "Oh, for heaven's sake, Percy, just go over to the shop!"

The look that came over Percy's face was pure elation. "Can I?"

"What, right now?" I said.

"No time like the present, is there?" Percy said eagerly. "Besides, I'll be of more use if I can actually look at the type-writer in person."

That was a fair point. And Adele probably wouldn't mind the after-hours company if that typewriter was going to get fixed up and possibly sold—probably.

"True," I agreed. "Uh, sure, we can go now, I guess."

Percy was out of his seat, backpack thrown over his shoulder, halfway out the door by the time I'd finished speaking.

"Oh, don't mind me!" Suruthi hollered after him. "I'll just stay here all on my own, shall I?"

"Oh, no, you can come too if you want!" I said, immediately feeling guilty. "We can just—"

But Suruthi was shaking with silent laughter as she passed a hand over her face. "No, no, you go on, Jules," she said, heaving a sigh. "You two are bloody perfect for each other, I swear."

"Excuse me?" I spluttered. "It's not like *that*. Geez, I've only known you both a few days."

"And yet it strangely feels as if an entire lifetime has already passed us by." Suruthi was out of her seat now, ushering me toward the door after Percy. "Go on then, don't keep Percy waiting."

"But—"

"*Go*, Jules! I'll see you both tomorrow."

I grabbed my bag off the table and left the study room, only for Suruthi to shout after me, "You'll have to let me know how your little date goes later!"

"It's *not like that!*" I yelled back, shoving open the front doors to head outside.

Percy had already made his way across the courtyard and was waiting for me out on the sidewalk.

"I don't actually know where your aunt's shop is," he stated as I approached.

"Right," I said. "I don't know street names very well, but I can get from point A to point B on the Tube well enough."

Percy gestured for me to lead the way. "After you."

I almost ended up in a jog just to keep up with Percy's much longer strides. He was of average height, but I suspected when Percy was on a mission, that was the only thing on his mind.

I was also becoming a little distressed that it was taking more effort than it should have to ignore Suruthi's teasing words still floating around my brain.

Sure, Percy *was* good-looking, and yeah, my face got a little too warm when I witnessed some of his cute, nerdy charm, but this was hardly a date.

My head was mostly back on straight by the time we were off the Tube, making the short trek over to Dreams of Antiquity. At some point Percy had started off on a little spiel about

Underwood typewriters again that I was desperately trying to pay attention to, but a lot of what he was saying flew right over my head.

"It's after hours, so we'll have to go in through the back," I said as the little blue shop came into view. "My aunt might still be downstairs though."

Percy followed me down the narrow alleyway beside the shop while I dug my key ring out of my bag. I unlocked the back door with the patchy red paint and let us inside, calling out to announce our arrival.

"Adele? I'm back and I've brought company!"

I stepped aside to let Percy enter, curious to see his reaction as he took everything in. The shop was even more cramped in the back, mostly full of various pieces of furniture too large to fit up front.

"This is nice," Percy said, breaking into a grin. "It's got character."

"I agree," I said with a smile of my own.

Adele suddenly appeared from behind an armoire painted midnight black with a lot of floral accents, her hair thrown up into a messy ponytail. Judging by the smudges of furniture polish on her left cheek, she'd been a little busy. "Oh, hello, dear!"

"Adele, this is Percy," I said lamely, gesturing in his direction. "We're in the writing seminar together. He's going to take a look at that typewriter."

Adele looked surprised, clearly not the answer she was expecting. "Is that so?"

"I'm a bit of a collector," Percy admitted sheepishly. "I can't promise anything, but I might be able to get it in working order."

"Well, now, you don't come across many typewriter

collectors these days, do you?" Adele was smiling, gesturing toward the rest of the shop. "Feel free to help yourself, Percy. I sent Mindy home for the day not too long ago," she added, more for me. "So it'll be tea soon, Jules."

Adele disappeared back to wherever she'd come from, probably to polish more furniture.

I turned to Percy, trying not to gnaw on my bottom lip. "Um. Shall we then?"

There was a similar excitement to a little kid finding their presents under the tree on Christmas morning on his face as Percy nodded.

I led him through the shop to the little alcove I had taken over since my arrival. Yesterday morning an old afghan smelling strongly of amber perfume had been folded across the arm of the chair, and I'd spent hours with it thrown over my shoulders as I tried to make sense of my outline.

"Well, this is it," I said to Percy, flicking on the nearby lamp.

The Underwood sat there under a bit of dust, but from the look taking over Percy's face as he eyed the typewriter, he didn't mind it one bit. He was staring down at it as if he'd just come across a literal mountain of gold.

As the silence stretched on, I began to feel a little anxious. I hadn't yet decided if it was because I was weirdly desperate for the typewriter to get fixed, or if it was because I was standing too close to Percy.

"I, uh, hate to ruin the moment," I said, "but any chance you'll be able to tell what's wrong with it?"

"Oh, right," Percy said quickly. "Sorry."

He slipped his backpack off and set it on the floor beside the armchair before crouching down in front of the typewriter. He spent one long moment running his fingers over the keys and started fiddling with some piece that looked like a rolling pin.

"Well, this is more than a bit rundown, I won't lie, but overall, it's not in bad shape," Percy said thoughtfully as he worked. "Now I *think* this model is early twentieth century or so, which unfortunately will make finding any replacement parts rather difficult, but not impossible."

"That kinda sucks," I said, frowning.

It would be a shame if Percy couldn't get the thing up and running again. I was curious to know what the keys would sound like click-clacking away as someone used the typewriter to write their next great novel.

"I didn't say it was broken," Percy said. "It certainly needs a new ink ribbon and it's rusted in some places, but it looks as if the carriage is just jammed."

"The what?"

Percy pointed to a small piece of machinery near where I at least knew a piece of paper would be fed through in order to be typed on. "This right here is the carriage. It's the bit that holds the paper in place and moves it while you type." He hit the return key to demonstrate, but there was only a tinny, clicking noise in response. "When the carriage is jammed, there's not a lot of typing to be had."

"I can see that," I said. "So how do you get it unjammed?"

"That depends," Percy said, sitting back on his haunches. "With a model this old, we'll have to take our time."

Good that Percy was apparently willing to help, but also not so good because there was a high chance I'd end up making an idiot out of myself sooner or later around him.

"Makes sense," I answered.

There was another bout of silence as Percy went back to inspecting the typewriter, and then he started mumbling to himself. It was fascinating watching him at work, clearly engrossed in what he was doing, as he started taking pieces of the typewriter apart.

He was in his element here, and I suddenly felt jealous because I had been feeling disconnected from what I had always thought *my* element was—writing.

When Adele came around later to announce that it was getting late, I was surprised. It had been easy to forget just about everything else going on as I listened to Percy explain the finer points of early twentieth-century typewriters. Not my area of expertise, but it felt like I'd been safely hidden from all the stressors I'd been facing—like writer's block—even if only temporarily.

Truth be told, I liked it. I liked it a lot.

I was going to put off deciding whether that was a good thing until much, *much* later.

CHAPTER

The Proper Usage of the Oxford Comma

I was doubtful the few pages of my manuscript I'd managed to type had been worth staying up well past midnight, so I'd followed Percy's line of thinking and bought two cups of coffee this morning. I was currently halfway through my second as I sat on the stone wall surrounding the courtyard outside Chatham Hall.

Suruthi was dozing with her head on my shoulder while Ashley sat on my other side, nursing her own cup of coffee, still looking half asleep. The only one who seemed even remotely awake was Percy.

"...and did you know that the Bodleian Library is actually a system made up of *twenty-eight* smaller libraries?" Percy informed us, skimming a page of facts written down in his journal. "We'll be going into the main portion of the library though, so we won't actually be—"

Suruthi's loud groan drowned out the rest of Percy's

sentence. "*Percy*. Mate. You know I adore you, but would you please put a sock in it?"

"No," Percy said brusquely, flipping to a new page of facts. "I can't remember the last time I went to Oxford, and I'm quite looking forward to it."

"Really?" Suruthi said sarcastically. "We couldn't tell. Not like you didn't have the opportunity to go for a visit any old time the past twenty years or so."

I took another swallow of coffee to keep from laughing.

"Don't get me wrong, I enjoy books just as much as the next person," Suruthi continued, sitting upright now. "But I think I prefer having a lie-in more."

"We've about an hour sojourn this morning to Oxford, Miss Kaur," an amused voice said from behind us. "I'm sure none of your cohorts will mind if you catch up on your sleep on the way there."

Professor Watson had joined our small group on the sidewalk, leather briefcase in hand, and the rest of our group was quickly gathering around, eager to hear about today's adventure.

The trip to Oxford, an hour or so outside of London, had come as a surprise to finish off the second week of the seminar. A contact of Professor Watson's at the university had reached out last minute to offer a private tour for his students, and he'd happily accepted on our behalf.

When I'd told my mom about our field trip destination during one of our regular video calls earlier that week, she'd gone a little misty-eyed as she gave me the rundown on the library system at Oxford. The fact that we were being presented with the opportunity to tour a library hundreds of years old that held books even older than that was out of this world.

It wasn't long before a small bus was pulling up to the curb and Professor Watson went over just as the doors slid open and took a moment to talk to whoever was driving. A moment later he beckoned us over.

"Should be a smooth ride, right?" Ashley said as we gathered up our things.

"Oh, definitely not," Percy said. "London drivers are *mad*."

Ashley blew out a sigh as she hugged her bag to her chest. "Great. Just what I love hearing. I get motion sickness way too easily," she added at our confused looks.

"You should take the window seat, if you think it'll help," Suruthi offered.

"I may just have to do that," Ashley said, mustering up a feeble smile.

Thierry was the first to climb aboard the bus. I was about to say *good morning* to the professor as I waited to board the bus, but Professor Watson was suddenly slipping a hand into his pocket to come up with a cell phone ringing a jaunty little tune, turning away to answer it.

I couldn't see Professor Watson's face as he answered the call, but I still managed to hear his harsh whisper, "There had better not be one pen out of place on my desk, or you're in for it."

Okay, so that was *odd*.

"What's with the funny look on your face?" Suruthi asked when I took a seat beside her. "You're scowling."

"No, I'm not," I said automatically. Oops. "Sorry. I mean, I... haven't been able to stop thinking about that conference with Watson the other day."

Suruthi groaned loudly. "Don't remind me! That was *awful*, wasn't it?"

The individual conferences that had been scheduled with Watson earlier that week had been nothing short of a disaster in my opinion. Not only had my outline been bleeding red, but I'd left with one stark piece of advice from Watson I hadn't been able to forget: *You need to learn to write with more passion and intrigue.* Not really the rousing discussion he must've been expecting.

"You could say that," I said, trying not to grimace.

"Mine wasn't so bad," Percy commented from the seat behind us.

"Sure it wasn't," Suruthi said, a note of suspicion in her voice. "Ashley, what about yours?"

From the seat ahead of us came a muffled little groan, and I peeked around the seat to find Ashley sitting with her head between her knees. "Mine was pretty bad. Watson said I used too many exclamation points."

I settled in for the ride once Professor Watson had joined us on the bus, pulling my notebook out of my bag to hopefully get some writing done. We'd barely rounded the corner onto the next street before I realized that writing a single sentence on this bus was going to be impossible sitting next to Suruthi. She was already slumped against me, fast asleep with her head on my shoulder. Five minutes later, she was snoring.

"You can shove her off, you know," Percy said, peering around the high-backed seat. "Or I can, if you'd like."

I bit my lip, trying and failing to hide my smile. "Nah, I don't mind. She probably needs the sleep anyway."

"Don't we all," Percy said.

I made myself as comfortable as I could with Suruthi still passed out on my shoulder. My eyes were flying open what felt like only a minute later as the bus came to a lurching stop, almost sending me and Suruthi toppling onto the floor.

"Sorry, sorry," the bus driver apologized loudly from up front.

I pulled myself upright, trying to blink the sleep from my eyes. Suruthi looked just as confused, frowning as she peered out the grimy bus window.

"Was I asleep the whole time?" she asked, fighting back a yawn.

"Nearly," Percy answered from behind us. "We'll be there in about ten minutes I suspect."

Percy's estimate was right. The bus was soon coming to a stop on a side street by yet another old church, and we filed off onto a cobblestone sidewalk, huddling together while we waited for Professor Watson to wrap things up with the driver.

I had been in London two weeks now, but I still really hadn't seen much of England beyond the city. Standing on a sidewalk in Oxford, it was like stepping into an almost entirely different world—maybe a little Dickens or Brontë, but I was instantly enthralled.

"You're looking a little misty-eyed there, Jules," Suruthi said, nudging me with an elbow. "You okay?"

"Oh yeah," I said quickly. "I'm just thinking I'll have to come back here some day with my mom. She's a librarian," I added at Percy's questioning look. "She'd really love it."

"Our tour won't begin for another half hour yet, but that gives us time to discuss the city we've just arrived in," Professor Watson said, calling for our attention. "Shall we?"

I fell into step beside Suruthi and Ashley as we set off down the sidewalk, Professor Watson leading the way.

"It's very Harry Potter-esque, isn't it?" Ashley said, grinning. "More than Ashford's dorms, I'll tell you that much."

I laughed. "A bit. I wonder how many bookstores we might be able to visit while we're here."

There was a continuous hum of conversation around us as we made our way to meet our tour guide at one of the smaller entrances to the university. Professor Watson was throwing out facts here and there along the way, but I wasn't sure how much of it I was absorbing. I was taken with Oxford more than I'd been expecting. There was a different atmosphere here than in London, and I wanted to explore it more.

I was pretty sure I had a literal skip in my step by the time we reached a set of gates off the high street Professor Watson ushered us through.

There were only a handful of people milling around the small courtyard we entered, and a short man in a puffy red vest with thinning blond hair came striding over to us, hand outstretched as he greeted Professor Watson.

"It's good to see you, John," he said eagerly, shaking the professor's hand. "It's been too long."

"And you, Joel," Professor Watson said with a polite smile. "We appreciate the invitation to join you for a tour today. You're too kind."

Percy chuckled as the professor and his friend exchanged more pleasantries.

"What's so funny?" I asked.

"Nothing," Percy said. "It's just . . . well, the professor's first name is *John*."

"Okay, so the professor's first name is John," I said. "Why's that funny?"

"That makes his full name John Watson," Percy explained. He actually looked a little affronted now when my confused expression only deepened. "And he used to be a doctor. So, *Doctor John Watson.* You know, like from Sherlock Holmes?"

"*Oh.*"

"It's amusing," Percy insisted. "Isn't it?"

"I guess," I said. "Sorry, but I've never read those stories."

Percy's jaw dropped. "*Really?* But you said you like mysteries! And you haven't read *Sherlock Holmes*? They make up the backbone of the entire mystery genre!"

Okay, so I could see where Percy had a point. After the one time I'd tried to flip through a copy of Sherlock Holmes stories I'd uncovered in Adele's shop, I hadn't really been pulled into it.

"Well," I said. "I guess I never really—"

A loud clearing of someone's throat put a stop to our suddenly heated conversation, and we both looked around to find everyone staring at us.

Professor Watson looked unamused as he said, "Ready to join us, Miss Montgomery? Mister Byers? Or is there something you'd like to share with the rest of the group?"

"Yes, sorry," I said quickly, my face flooding with heat. "We're ready."

"Our apologies," Percy added sheepishly.

"Lover's quarrel?" Suruthi muttered to us slyly.

"Shut up," Percy and I snapped in unison.

Suruthi was still snickering to herself as Professor Watson beckoned us forward, and I very intentionally put a good deal of space between me and Percy, standing on Ashley's other side. From what I could see out of the corner of my eye, Percy was just as hot under the collar as I was.

I almost slapped a hand to my forehead. I was here to focus on my writing and lose myself in a bunch of old books not a . . . whatever it was that Suruthi was imagining going on between me and Percy, which was *nothing*. A mutual enjoyment of type-writers, maybe, but that was it.

"Right then." Our tour guide, Joel, clapped his hands together, calling us to attention. "I'm here to show you around one of the most impressive sights this university here has to offer, if you ask me. Now the Bodleian Library, or the Bod, as we call it . . ."

Joel, as it happened, was quite the enthusiastic tour guide as he began to show us around. His voice, on the other hand, was a little more difficult to understand with the way it was being thrown around against the courtyard's high walls.

I did my best to focus on the facts and dates Joel was shar-ing, but my brain didn't seem to really be comprehending much. I was itching to get inside the library. There *had* to be some spark or stroke of inspiration waiting to be discovered, and I was going to take full advantage of it if I could.

I was at least paying enough attention to get my legs moving and followed the rest of the group as Joel led us to the library's main entrance. We passed through a set of double doors that I wanted to stop and run my fingers over when I saw several of Oxford colleges' coats of arms artfully engraved into the wood.

That ended up putting me at the back of the group, right behind Willem. With the way Joel was quickly moving us along, firing off little tidbits of information left and right, I gave up try-ing to force my way to the front of the group to hear better. I could just as well enjoy the library without all the dates and facts.

And there really was *a lot* to enjoy about this library, with the stone walls and floors, the old furniture, not to mention the *books*...

It wasn't difficult to imagine scholars and professors alike from hundreds of years ago exploring these halls. Odds were some of them had been aspiring writers too. Seeing as writer's block didn't discriminate, I was willing to bet they'd also suffered from it at times.

8

CHAPTER

THROUGH THE WARDROBE

I looked down at the takeout box Percy held out to me. "What is this?"

"Steak and kidney pie," he said, shaking the box for emphasis. "Side of mashed peas."

"What, like baby food?"

"Hardly, Jules. I promise you'll enjoy it. C'mon," Percy insisted. "If you're going to be a tourist here, you're obligated to have steak and kidney pie at least once."

"Am I?" I said, struggling to keep down a laugh. "And here I thought I just flew across the pond to spend the summer writing."

"Oh, live a little, would you?" Suruthi said, lounging beside me on the bench. She was helping herself to some chips she'd gotten from an indoor market after we'd left the Bodleian Library. She'd also been talking with her mouth full the entire time. "Next time Percy's in America you can treat him to some greasy fast food or something. Fair's fair."

"Fine," I said, accepting the box Percy was still holding out. "Should you ever find yourself in California, we're going to In-N-Out."

"Noted," Percy said, offering me a fork.

I popped the top on the takeout box and tried not to examine what I was about to eat too closely. It smelled pretty good at least, so it couldn't be that bad, could it? I stabbed some of the food with my fork and took a bite.

"Well?" Percy asked. "What do you think?"

I finished swallowing my bite of food before answering. "It's . . . okay, it's actually pretty good. I like it."

"*Hah!*" Percy looked incredibly pleased with himself. "And now may I say: *I told you so.*"

Next I took a bite of the mashed peas and was pleased to find it tasted pretty good too.

Percy used his foot to nudge Suruthi over on the bench and he sat down, pulling out a lunch of his own.

It was pleasantly warm sitting outside on the bench, the sun peeking out through a thin layer of gray clouds, and the vibe of Oxford was infectious.

After the tour at the Bodleian had wrapped up, Professor Watson announced that we were being given the latter half of the day to explore what else Oxford had to offer on our own before he disappeared with Joel the tour guide.

It hadn't taken long before Suruthi took charge and dragged us off to buy an early lunch. I was very much on board with this, seeing as my breakfast had consisted primarily of coffee.

Where the rest of our group had wandered off to, I wasn't sure. The professor had been adamant that we be on the bus back to Ashford precisely at two o'clock, so they couldn't have gone far.

"What d'you reckon?" Suruthi said as she polished off the last of her lunch. "Think we ought to get a little shopping in?"

"If by shopping you mean going to that place where I can find replacement ink for my pen, then yes," Percy said.

They turned to me next, waiting for my response, and I struggled to finish chewing the last bite of my food without choking.

"I'm pretty much up for everything," I said. "We could always—"

I stopped when I caught sight of Ashley striding down the sidewalk across the street. She was walking briskly, disposable cup in hand, earbuds in, and even at this distance I could see her face was set in a hard, determined expression.

"Oi! Where are you headed, Ashley?" Suruthi called over to her before I could do the same.

Ashley looked around at Suruthi's voice, gave a wave, and she took a detour to jog across the street when there was a break in the traffic.

"Hi," she said, breathless as she approached. "Sorry, I didn't see you over here."

"You look like you're off somewhere," Suruthi said. "Have you eaten yet?"

"Sort of. Peppermint tea," Ashley said, gesturing toward her cup. "Still too afraid to eat after that bus ride."

"*Boo*," Suruthi said, frowning. "I think I saw a Boots somewhere nearby, if you wanted to pick up some antacids."

"I'm fine, really," Ashley assured her. "Just in case though I'll find a barf bag for the trip back. No, I'm actually just wanting to go see the Narnia door before we leave."

"The what now?" I said, confused.

"Oh, there's this story out there that says C. S. Lewis discovered the inspiration for The Chronicles of Narnia from a set of doors here in Oxford that have carvings of lions on them," Percy jumped in to explain. "There's supposed to be a lamppost nearby too."

Ashley nodded excitedly. "I read all the books with my grandma, growing up, so I wanted to see it in person. Take a picture back to her and all that."

"Well, there's no evidence to suggest that C. S. Lewis was even in Oxford at the time, so we don't really know if—"

I jabbed an elbow into Percy's side before he could finish his sentence, shooting him a dirty look. Why rain on Ashley's parade like that when she was so clearly looking forward to it?

Percy thankfully took the hint and fell silent.

"Do you mind if I come with you?" I asked, looking back at Ashley. "My mom used to read me those books when I was little too."

"Sure," Ashley said, her smile widening. "The company would be nice."

"Off you go then," Suruthi said, giving me an energetic push to my feet. "Percy Bysshe and I are going to be on our way to the shops."

Percy caught my wrist before I could get very far, tugging me back a step. When I gave him a questioning look, he said in a panicked voice, "You're not going to leave me alone with her, are you?"

It took almost too much effort not to laugh. "You'll be fine. You guys are best friends, aren't you?"

"Up you get!" Suruthi said cheerfully and gave Percy a hearty shove off the bench. "We'll see you both in a bit, yeah?"

I could still hear Percy's loud protesting and Suruthi's cackling even after Ashley and I rounded the corner onto the next street.

"The door shouldn't be too far from here," Ashley said as we walked, scrolling around a map on her phone. "Hopefully it won't be too hard to find."

"We'll find it," I assured her. "How hard could it be to find a door with lions carved on it?"

Exceptionally hard, it turned out.

Maybe flying across the Atlantic had made the both of us directionally challenged, but it took us over ten minutes to realize that we'd been walking *away* from the little red dot on the GPS screen Ashley had pulled up on her phone for reference.

"Crap," she muttered, holding her phone up skyward. "I think I've lost reception. How's yours looking?"

I checked back in with my own GPS. "Not good. Looks like we're standing in a bunch of gray right now."

Ashley's scowl was something spectacular. "This shouldn't be that hard! Last time I looked at the GPS, we were only a few streets over, I swear."

"Well, maybe we should try to—"

I watched in awe as Ashley strode over to the first person she happened to lay eyes on, a man in a red shirt and gray exercise shorts, sitting atop a bike with his own phone out.

"Excuse me!"

The man looked up at Ashley, pulling out an earbud. "Yeah?"

She got straight to the point. "We're trying to find the Narnia door. How do we get there?"

A minute later Ashley was headed back my way with an almost thunderous expression.

"We went in the complete opposite direction! We're supposed to have gone *that* way." She pointed at the street directly behind us. "Let's go!"

Whatever directions the guy on the bike had given Ashley were thankfully not terrible. There were a few people gathered around the side of a building, cameras out and taking pictures, so I figured we were probably in the right place.

"*Ah!* There it is!" Ashley squealed happily as we approached what was definitely the door. "I feel like such a lame tourist, but I don't even care. I'm going to enjoy this."

If only I could be that self-confident, I thought wistfully.

"I like your style, Ashley James," I said with a hint of admiration.

Ashley tossed me a wink over her shoulder and pulled her phone out again, waiting her turn for a closer look at the door. I followed suit and snapped a couple pictures of what I could see of the door, followed by some of the lamppost a few feet away.

"Now I can literally envision what C. S. Lewis must've seen out here in the dead of winter in the snow," Ashley gushed, rocking back on her heels. "Can you see the carving of the lion up there?"

There was a very tall woman with long braids standing in front of me, blocking my view, so my answer was an unfortunate no.

When we finally did get close enough to the door to be able to see more of the intricate details carved into the wood, I was feeling a little giddy myself. It had been ages since the last time I'd read any C. S. Lewis, but this was like a trip down memory lane.

"Think it's worth a video call?" I asked Ashley, checking the reception on my phone. "My mom would flip seeing this and just about everything else in Oxford."

"Why not?" Ashley said, peeking at her own phone. "I'll try giving my grandma a call too. Hopefully she's awake."

I pulled up my mom's number and hit the little video call button. It took a minute before the call actually started to go through, and another minute or two before my mom's face popped into view on the screen. Half of the picture was all pixelated, but I could make out enough to tell that my mom was already at work, despite it barely being six in the morning in California.

"Jules? Is everything alright?" Her voice came out warbly through the speakers. "I thought you—in Oxford—?"

"Yeah, I am in Oxford," I said. "But listen, we're at this place called the Narnia door and I wanted to show you." I gave her an abridged version of the background info Percy had shared earlier as I tried to get a little closer to the door. "Apparently this is where C. S. Lewis—Mom? Hello?"

My mom was frozen on the screen, her mouth open as if she'd been caught mid-sentence. Ugh.

"*Hello!*" I sang loudly. "Mom? Mother? *Janine!* Can you hear me?"

"No reception again?" Ashley asked, and I looked around to see her glaring at her phone too. She was tapping her foot, biting into her lip. The unreliable phone service had obviously ruined her good mood.

"Looks like it," I confirmed.

I probably looked like an idiot holding my phone away from me, then up, down, and side to side, but that usually ended up doing the trick, right?

My mom's face remained frozen on the screen, and I groaned in frustration.

"You know what? I think I'll just hang up and try again," I said. "If anything, we can find a café or something that might have internet so we can try to . . ."

My voice trailed off into nothing when I looked up from my phone and Ashley was no longer standing in front of me.

"Hey, Ashley?"

I looked over my shoulder, but she wasn't there either. The sidewalk was now strangely empty, and I seemed to be the only one left standing by the Narnia door—which I was positive hadn't been the case thirty seconds ago.

"Ashley?" I said again, this time louder.

Nothing but silence.

I went to peek around the corner of the building, but only found a group of tourists all wearing matching red T-shirts.

Then I went to the other side of the building to look for any sign of Ashley, peeked down a nearby alleyway, and ended up making a full circle again before I realized I could've saved myself the trouble. I tried to call her instead.

The line rang a few times, but Ashley didn't pick up on the other end. Instead of leaving a voicemail, I shot her a text:

> hey, looks like we got separated.
> Where'd you end up?

I went over to a bench opposite the Narnia door and sat down, looking at my phone, waiting for Ashley's reply. I would think she hadn't gone very far. Granted, we both had been a little directionally challenged, but surely not enough to get completely lost.

When ten minutes had passed with still no response, I sent Ashley another text:

> everything okay?

I was starting to get nervous. The reception around here hadn't been bad enough to where Ashley couldn't respond to a text message. Another five minutes of waiting and I decided to call again instead of texting.

This time the call went straight to voicemail.

Okay, so maybe her cell phone ran out of juice. It wasn't unlikely, but I was starting to get increasingly nervous now. Where could Ashley have ended up?

As if the universe was somehow mirroring my quickly darkening mood, I felt a few raindrops land in my hair. I looked up at the sky and groaned when I saw the gray clouds rolling in, quickly followed by several more raindrops. By the look of it, I'd have maybe another minute at best before a downpour was likely to begin.

It had taken awhile to fine-tune, but at this point, it was instinct to quickly slip my hearing aids off and tuck them safely away in their case. Six-thousand-dollar pieces of assistive technology and rain *so* did not mix. Luckily, I got my bag zipped up before the rain *really* started.

I was drenched in the short amount of time it had taken me to figure out my next move, which was to go find the closest coffee shop to hunker down in and wait out the rain. I ended up only one street over from the Narnia door, which should've been easy enough for Ashley to find if she'd gotten a bit turned around.

Once inside, I pulled out my phone again and sent another text to Ashley, letting her know where I'd gone to take cover from the rain. Judging from the time, we had a little over a half hour before we needed to be back on the bus to return to Ashford. That was still plenty of time for the rain to stop, and maybe Ashley had just found another shop to wait it out in.

I stepped in line to buy a drink and used my debit card this time so I wouldn't have the added worry of trying to make the correct change. Once I had my coffee in hand, I found a seat at the bar along the shop's front window and checked my cell phone again. Still nothing.

I blew out a sigh, drumming my fingers on the bar. We still technically had time before we were due back at the bus, but— something about this felt off. It wasn't as if I thought Ashley couldn't take care of herself (obviously she could) but we were still in a foreign city. A nice, foreign city, but with the rain, it probably wouldn't have been a stretch to say that she took a wrong turn somewhere if she had been in a hurry to stay dry.

I took a few sips of coffee and decided to send a message directly to Percy instead of the group chat Suruthi had made.

> Got caught in the rain and somehow ended up separated from Ashley at the Narnia door. Is she with you?

Percy's response was almost instantaneous: No, she's not. Where are you?

I sent him a pin of my location, and he immediately replied with a short: Stay there. Suruthi and I are coming to you.

As if I have anywhere else to go, I thought.

I tried calling Ashley again, fingers crossed that she would answer this time. The wave of disappointment that came when the call went straight to voicemail again was crushing.

So the battery on her cell phone had definitely died then.

I sent another message to Ashley anyway— are you okay? — and swallowed down more coffee as I waited.

My mom had always been fond of the saying *a watched pot never boils*, but that's all I could do; keep my eyes on my cell phone, waiting for any text or call that might come through from Ashley. We were now about fifteen minutes out from needing to be back at the bus for Ashford. It also didn't seem like the rain had slowed down.

I went for another sip of coffee and nearly jumped out of my skin at the hand on my shoulder. Suruthi stood beside me with her palms up, looking very apologetic. Percy was close behind her, and they both looked about as bedraggled from the rain as I was.

I wasn't sure how I didn't notice it at first, that I wasn't hearing anything that was coming out of Suruthi's mouth, and then belatedly I realized it was because I hadn't put my hearing aids back in after coming in from the rain.

Percy seemed to catch on before Suruthi did that I was missing whole chunks of the conversation—probably by the glazed look of confusion in my eyes. He put a hand on Suruthi's shoulder, and while still looking at me, said very clearly, "Slow down for a minute."

Suruthi stopped talking at once, looking back and forth between Percy and me, and then she frowned in confusion.

"Just give Jules a minute," was Percy's reply to whatever Suruthi had said that I'd missed.

There was nothing else for it. I was going to have to put my hearing aids back in and there would be no way of hiding it.

I held up one finger, signaling that I needed a minute, and unzipped my bag to carefully extract my hearing aids from their case. I kept my attention focused on my cup of coffee as I put my hearing aids in and waited until I heard the cheery little tune that signaled they were turned on to look over at Percy and Suruthi again.

Percy had a small grin in place when our eyes met, and it occurred to me then with the look of understanding on his face that he must've known from the beginning. He'd known all along that I wore hearing aids, and he hadn't said anything about it.

Then I began to wonder why it would've bothered me so much in the first place if Percy—or anyone else, really—knew that I wore hearing aids.

"Jules?" I heard Suruthi this time around when she said my name. She'd noticed the hearing aids too, obviously, and she also hadn't said anything. "You okay?"

"Yes! Sorry," I said quickly. "Sorry. I'm fine. Just spaced out for a second."

"Well, what happened then?" Suruthi asked, taking the seat next to me. "Percy only said that we needed to find you. Where's Ashley?"

"That's exactly it," I said. "I don't know where Ashley is."

I spent the next few minutes giving Percy and Suruthi an exact replay of my and Ashley's trek to the Narnia door.

"And she didn't say anything about where she was going?" Percy asked when I'd finished.

"Ashley didn't say she was going anywhere," I answered. "All she did say was that she wanted to try and video call with her grandma so she could show her the Narnia door."

"Are you sure?"

"*Yes*, I'm sure! I took my hearing aids out just before the rain started. I would've heard her if she'd said she was going somewhere else."

Right?

Our conversation took an abrupt pause when my cell phone started to ring, blaring Metallica with the flashing LED lights and all.

"It's Ashley, thank God," I gasped when I saw her name on the screen, scrambling to answer the call. "Hey, Ashley! Where'd you end up? You okay?"

There was not a single sound to be heard in response.

"Ashley?" I repeated. "Hey, you there?"

More silence.

I checked the reception on my phone and saw three cheery green bars at the top right-hand corner of the screen.

"What's going on?" Suruthi asked, leaning toward me. "Is she okay?"

I quickly tapped the speakerphone button and placed my cell phone on the bar between Suruthi and me, beckoning Percy over.

"Ashley, it's me, Jules," I said, raising my voice a notch. "Can you hear me?"

The silence I continued to be met with was causing an icy feeling of dread to encompass me whole.

"*Ashley!*" My voice cracked when I said her name. "Please, can you just tell me you're okay?"

The line went dead.

"I'm sure the rain is just messing with the reception," Percy announced, sounding far more confident than he looked. "Always happens with my mobile."

"Mine as well," Suruthi agreed quickly. "Must be that."

When they both looked at me, I could only shrug. What else was I supposed to do?

"We'll find Ashley," Suruthi said, patting my hand. "She can't have gone too far, can she?"

A Missing Persons Report Should Be Filed as Soon as You Suspect Something Is Wrong

Two o'clock came and went without any sign of Ashley. We were standing on the sidewalk outside the same church we'd been dropped off near this morning, huddled together against the brisk wind. Professor Watson stood off to the side, phone in hand, and I figured he was trying to call Ashley again.

I had my arms crossed tightly, fingernails digging into my palms, doing everything I could to keep the worry at bay. It was still afternoon, and there was still sunlight. It was a good thing Ashley would not be having to make her way back here in the dark.

"You two still haven't heard from Ashley at all?" Percy suddenly asked me and Suruthi.

He'd been watching Professor Watson talking on his cell

phone a few feet away but had turned back to look at us. The professor didn't seem to be doing a stellar job of keeping the worry off his face either.

I shook my head while Suruthi said, "If we had, you'd be the first to know, Percy."

But I did check my phone just in case I *had* gotten a message from Ashley and had just missed it. I hadn't.

"Just to reiterate," Professor Watson said when he approached our group a moment later. "No one has heard from Miss James except for Miss Montgomery?"

"That's right, sir," Suruthi answered for the group.

I'd already informed the professor of what went down in front of the Narnia door with Ashley, how she'd been there one second and gone the next, followed by that unnerving phone call where no one had actually spoken on the other line. I sincerely hoped he wasn't about to ask me to repeat that story again in front of the rest of the group.

"Ring her again," Professor Watson said to me. His voice was short, far from his normally polite tone. "Now, if you please."

I quickly did as instructed, hitting the redial button. All eyes were on me as I waited, praying Ashley would pick up the phone. She didn't.

"Straight to voicemail," I said, not bothering to hide the tremor in my voice.

For one impossibly long moment, no one spoke.

I couldn't have been the only one that felt like something was *wrong* here. Yes, we'd only met barely two weeks ago, but Ashley didn't seem like the type to suddenly go wandering off on her own without explanation. Willem and Thierry had managed to make their way back to our meeting spot, so there had to be some reason why Ashley hadn't.

"Right then," Professor Watson said, nodding to himself. "I think it would be best if we were to—"

"Phone the police?" Percy cut in before I could ask the same thing.

I didn't know the first thing about how the police operated in the UK, but they'd be able to help. At the very least, they had more means to throw together a search party than we did and could cover more ground, seeing as none of us had a car.

"Let's not act too hastily, Mister Byers," Professor Watson said, looking down at his phone. "I'm going to reach out to Joel, and in the meantime, I highly encourage you all to *stay together* while we get this sorted out. And please do not leave the area."

I was not the only one who watched Professor Watson until he disappeared around the corner. When I finally looked back to the rest of the group, I was certain we were all sporting identical anxious looks.

"So," Suruthi said. "Now what?"

"You heard the professor," Thierry said, and for the first time, he didn't look as if he knew exactly what he was doing. "We stick together."

We ended up back at the same coffee shop as before while we waited for Professor Watson to return, hopefully with an update to share—or better yet, with Ashley herself. Percy and I pooled resources to buy us all tea this time and Thierry purchased the shop's entire stock of chocolate biscotti.

With no idea of when Professor Watson would come back, we settled in for the long haul.

Dusk had fallen, biscotti and drinks long gone, by the time Professor Watson reappeared. I was thinking about finding something more substantial to eat than biscotti with dinner time so close when the professor came striding into the coffee shop, accompanied by two men who were obviously police officers—and no Ashley.

"Jules? *Ow.*"

I jumped at Percy's yelp, oblivious to the fact that at some point I'd gotten his hand in a viselike grip, squeezing hard.

"Oh, sorry," I said, quickly releasing his hand. "I didn't mean to."

The seriousness of the situation couldn't have been more evident, watching Professor Watson join our group with the police in tow. Suruthi wasn't even cracking a joke at the fact that I'd just been holding Percy's hand.

"Did you find Ashley?" I asked at the same time Thierry stood up and demanded, "*Well?*"

I could tell by the expression on the professor's face that he had no good news to share before he even opened his mouth to respond.

"Miss James has yet to be located."

In the few brief seconds it took to process the professor's announcement, I had somehow already decided that nothing about the rest of this trip to London and everything that had come with it was going to be the same.

"Jules?"

Someone was touching my elbow, and I looked over my shoulder to find Suruthi trying to urge me back down onto the small couch we'd been holed up on. When had I even stood up?

"C'mon, sit down," Suruthi whispered, squeezing my arm. "It's okay, Jules."

It wasn't though. Nothing about this was *okay*.

I sat down anyway, wrapping my arms around myself like that was somehow going to keep me from falling to pieces.

Ashley was missing. What part of this was my fault?

The two police officers Professor Watson had brought with him, who introduced themselves as Detective Constables Evans and Thomas, told us that they would need to speak with all of us individually and take down our contact information before we would be able to return to London.

"And we're starting with you," Evans said, fixing his gaze on me. As everyone else followed suit, my face started to burn. "The professor here says you were the last one to see the girl."

Okay then. So, there was a very real chance I might puke right here, but I could handle being questioned by the police.

"Her name is Ashley, and yes, I was," I said all in one breath.

Without another word, Evans gestured for me to follow him out of the coffee shop while his partner, Thomas, announced that he would be staying behind with Professor Watson and the rest of the group to start taking down contact information.

"*Jules!*"

I snuck a look back at Suruthi when she hissed my name as I got to my feet, and she leaned in close to whisper, "Remember, you do have the right to remain silent. The police here have their own version of Miranda rights, but—"

"Thank you for the advice, Suruthi," I whispered back, cutting her off. "But you do know I'm not actually under arrest, right?"

"*Still.* Oh, and the police here aren't allowed to lie to you like they can in America, so make sure you—"

"For heaven's sake, Suruthi!" Percy said exasperatedly, giving Suruthi's arm a gentle tug to get her to sit down again. "You can blather on about the criminal justice system when it's *your* turn to be questioned by the police. Let Jules go."

With those words of encouragement to aid me, I exited the coffee shop after Detective Constable Evans.

CHAPTER

In the Aftermath

Before my parents' divorce and before my dad disappeared to some small town in Vermont to run a bed-and-breakfast with his new wife, we used to watch action movies all the time. They were all a little too intense and graphic for my six-year-old self, but it'd been a steadfast routine of ours. And in every movie I watched with my dad where there was a big explosion during some high-speed chase that had you thinking the hero might not make it out alive, there were always those few seconds in the aftermath when all you could hear was a piercing ringing.

The hero would stumble around, a hand to their head, waiting for the ringing to stop and for their hearing to return to normal before carrying on like nothing had ever happened.

The aftermath of Ashley's disappearance was a lot like that—except I wasn't a hero, and my hearing wasn't going to return to normal. At some point the ringing stopped, but I knew it would only be a matter of time before it returned. I spent most of that Saturday and well into Sunday following our ill-fated trip to Oxford curled up in my favorite armchair down in the shop. I'd tried to work on my manuscript, but my heart wasn't in it.

I'd made it a few sentences in before I slammed my laptop shut and stuffed it under the armchair so I didn't have to look at it anymore.

If my cell phone hadn't been confiscated by the police, I would've been sending message after message to the group chat with Suruthi and Percy, because surely they had to be just as frantic as I was about what happened. Ashley was missing and yet here we were, sitting around over the weekend, twiddling our thumbs and waiting to be contacted by the police. Although this was still probably preferable to dodging all the phone calls and messages from my mom through Adele's cell phone.

I couldn't blame my mom for wanting me on the next plane home, but I had point-blank refused the first time she'd even mentioned it. I hadn't worked tirelessly for the last several months to get into this seminar only to go home two weeks in. Before I could explain all that, Adele had taken the phone into the other room and spent the next half hour in conversation with my mom.

Whatever she'd said had worked and my mom had laid off—somewhat. Adele had finally turned her phone off for a short reprieve from my mom's continued messaging. This was also partially the reason why I was hiding down in the shop after hours.

I slumped down in the armchair with another frustrated groan, scrubbing my face with my hands. I'd spent the last however long staring up at the ceiling, wondering when I'd wake up from what I wasn't convinced was not a nightmare.

I hated feeling useless like this. I wasn't a detective, and I didn't know the first thing about solving a missing persons case, but there had to be *something* I could do, right?

I began gnawing on my lip when that awful feeling of guilt started unfurling in the pit of my stomach again. There was a part of me that felt responsible for what happened because I'd been the last person seen with Ashley. According to Suruthi, this at the very least made me a person of interest to the police.

But I'd had my hearing aids in, and I still genuinely hadn't heard a thing. One second I'd been on a video call with my mom and then—nothing. Ashley was gone.

Just as I was debating whether I should smother my face in a throw pillow so I could get out some frustrated screaming, I shot upright when I heard loud knocking coming from what I thought was the back of the shop. There was a pause for one moment that had me thinking I must've been imagining things before the knocking started up again, this time louder and more insistent.

I saw myself with two options here. I could run upstairs and tell Adele and we could call the police (although I had to admit I wasn't too fond of this option at the moment). Or I could investigate myself.

I was on my feet, snatching the first heavy object I could get my hands on as I made for the back of the shop. The knocking hadn't let up, and as I drew nearer, I couldn't figure out if I was also hearing muffled conversation behind the door. Standing around thinking about it wasn't going to get me anywhere though.

Here goes nothing, I thought.

I unlocked the back door and flung it open, ready to attack with my makeshift weapon if I had to.

"*Cripe*s, Jules, it's us!"

It was Percy and Suruthi standing in the narrow alleyway behind the shop, both with mildly terrified looks on their faces.

I leaned against the doorjamb, pressing my free hand against my chest where I could feel my heart pounding frantically. "What are you two doing here? You scared the daylights outta me."

"*We* scared *you*?" Suruthi said with a disbelieving laugh. "Jules, you were about to attack us!"

Percy pointed at the object in my grasp when all I could get out was a very confused, "*Huh*?"

"Were you really about to beat us with a candlestick?" he asked carefully. I wasn't sure if he was struggling not to laugh or just had a tickle in his throat.

I stared down at the golden candlestick I was still clutching. "Oh. I just grabbed the first thing I could find."

"Have we suddenly found ourselves in a game of Cluedo?" Suruthi said, sounding way too excited. "*The culprit was Jules in the antique shop with the candlestick.*"

"Haha," I said, deadpan. "Could we please get to the part where someone explains what you two are doing here? It's after hours if you hadn't noticed."

Also, in case you forgot, one of our classmates went missing less than forty-eight hours ago, the police have no leads, and somehow I still can't help but feel that this is all massively my fault.

Who was to say that one of us wasn't going to be next?

"Funnily enough, we have noticed," Suruthi said. "Now would you please let us in? And please put down the candlestick, Jules."

I stepped aside to let Suruthi and Percy into the shop and shut the door, double-checking the locks. I put the candlestick safely out of reach on top of a small armoire and followed the other two deeper into the maze of antiques.

Despite having only been here once, Percy seemed to recall

where *the spot* was at the other end of the shop. Suruthi made herself at home on the couch crammed in next to one of the many bookcases, stretching out with a pleased little sigh. I returned to my favorite armchair and Percy wound up on the floor rather than try to squeeze onto the couch with Suruthi.

"Cute little place, isn't it?" Suruthi said, picking up a decorative pillow.

"Yes, it's adorable," I said. "But again, I have to ask, what are—?"

"Yes, yes, what are we doing here," Suruthi said, waving a hand. "Isn't it obvious?"

She did not have to say much more than that for me to understand what she was implying. It left me trying and failing to keep from shifting uncomfortably in my chair. Naturally the reason behind their visit would be about the one thing I was about one hundred percent positive I did *not* want to talk about.

"What she means to say is," Percy began slowly, "that we wanted to . . . make sure you were alright. You know, with everything and . . . stuff."

"*And stuff* covers a lot of ground," I said.

"Well, it's not like we could've sent you a message with our mobile phones being confiscated and all," Suruthi pointed out. "Otherwise we absolutely would have and saved ourselves the trouble."

"Then how *did* you two decide you were just going to show up here unannounced on a Sunday night?"

"Telepathy," Suruthi said.

"Email," Percy corrected, rolling his eyes. "Wasn't such a difficult task when our mums still get on even though it's been years since we last went to school together."

"Be that as it may," Suruthi said, shooting Percy a snooty look. "We're here now at this late hour to ask you what on earth happened the other day in Oxford."

I had no way of telling how much time had passed until I was able to formulate a proper response to Suruthi, but it was long enough for her to start bouncing impatiently where she sat.

Even if it had only been a few weeks since we'd met, I'd already come to really like these two. Spending several hours a day together like we had at the seminar, discussing all things writing, all the little things we loved about it, what we hated, what we hoped to accomplish one day, seemed to be a pretty good way to learn a lot about someone.

I felt comfortable enough telling the truth—especially since I now knew that the only one who'd made a big deal about my hearing loss was me.

"I had nothing to do with it, if that's what you're asking."

The atmosphere turned tense the second those words were out. It hadn't exactly been what I'd planned to say, but maybe there was a part of myself that had wanted to make that perfectly clear.

I felt my face flood with heat as Suruthi's eyebrows shot up her forehead. She blinked a few times while she seemed to struggle to come up with something to say. I was now debating whether I could get away with smothering myself with one of those decorative pillows to avoid any further embarrassment.

"Er. Well, the thing is, Jules," Suruthi said. "No one . . . thought that you did? Had anything to do with it, that is."

"I know," I said. "Of course not. Because I didn't . . . I—"

The tension was increasing by the second, swiftly turning awkward just for good measure. Percy repositioned himself where he sat on the floor a couple times and cleared his throat like a professor about to launch into some stuffy lecture.

"We wouldn't presume to think that you did." He was enunciating each word carefully, which had me feeling like I was some sort of child he was getting ready to reprimand.

"Because I didn't!" I exclaimed.

"We *know*!" Percy and Suruthi fired back in unison.

"But you *were* the last one who was with Ashley, Jules," Percy added quickly. "Surely you must've seen something."

"And I'm telling you I *didn't*," I insisted.

I spent the next however many minutes giving Percy and Suruthi a play-by-play account of exactly what had transpired during our trek to the Narnia door.

"And that is *exactly* what happened," I said when I was done, pulling in an unsteady breath.

More silence—the perfect opportunity for some crickets to do a bit of chirping.

"Okay," Percy finally said.

Now I felt my own eyebrows go up. "Okay? That's it?"

Percy simply shrugged. "What else is there to say? You say that's the whole story and I believe you."

I sat back in my armchair, suddenly feeling winded. Just like that, Percy supposedly believed me now. It seemed like a far cry from the skepticism that had accompanied these two inside earlier; they could deny it if they wanted, but the aura of disbelief had definitely been there to start with.

"I believe you too," Suruthi said quickly when Percy nudged her leg with his elbow.

"*But*?" I pressed.

"There's no—"

"There's always a but."

Suruthi mumbled something under breath, squeezing her eyes shut as she pinched the bridge of her nose. "It's just ... well, are you sure you didn't maybe ... you know, just not *hear* something?"

Ah, there it was.

I threw up my hands with an exasperated huff. "Well, *maybe*. But, if you'll recall, I said I had my hearing aids in, and Ashley was standing about a foot away from me the entire time."

All of this had sounded reasonable and perfectly factual in my head, but coming out of my mouth, it felt a little sour. What evidence did I have that proved I hadn't accidentally missed something? I wasn't so sure how reliable a gut feeling was going to come across.

"That's a fair point, Suruthi," Percy said, looking over at her. "And I trust Jules's word."

"I do too!" Suruthi said, shooting upright. "I do, really."

And maybe Suruthi really did believe the words she was saying, but that same *gut feeling* told me there was still doubt there—maybe a lot of it.

"Ashley was wearing a blue-and-white-striped blouse on Friday with a pair of dark jeans and that gray jacket she got from one of those kitschy tourist shops that says *London* on it. She had one earbud in her right ear and she was trying to do a video chat with her grandma while also channeling her inner C. S. Lewis. So, there," I finished, crossing my arms and legs. "I think I noticed plenty even if I *didn't hear* everything going on."

There was more of that awkward silence from before in the wake of my little rant. My imagination must've had me thinking I was hearing the loud *ticktock* of the large grandfather clock across the shop by the front door.

"I take it all back then," Suruthi finally said, sounding awed. "You do notice things."

"So there," Percy said, failing at hiding his smirk.

He squawked next when Suruthi leaned over to ruffle his hair and he slapped at her hand, making her laugh.

Just like that, the tense atmosphere disappeared. I felt like I was about to get whiplash from all this, but I was relieved we had gotten all of *that* out of the way.

"So then." Suruthi tucked her legs up underneath her on the couch, arranging her skirt neatly around her. "Now what?"

"Um." I looked to Percy for backup. "I'm not really sure."

He frowned, his eyebrows pinched together as he fell deep into thought. It seemed a little anticlimactic when all he came up with was a lackluster, "I have no idea."

"Well, it's not like waiting around for the police to phone with any updates will do us any good," Suruthi pointed out after another beat of silence. "I suppose we could always—"

The rest of her words were drowned out by the sudden loud *crash* that echoed through the shop. I was on my feet before I could consider the fact that I wasn't thinking straight here—like *I* would be equipped to handle some sort of intruder attempting to rob the antique shop.

"Jules, wait!" There was a mad scramble behind me as Percy leapt to his feet. "Something probably just fell over, you should—"

I was off through the maze of antiques anyway. I was trying to locate the source of the crash—the sound of breaking glass, maybe?—but I didn't think I could trust my sense of direction to figure out where the noise had come from.

I'd gone down two separate aisles, on the hunt with Suruthi and Percy hot on my heels, when there was another *crash*! It was quieter this time, followed by what sounded like a very creative stream of curse words. I was pretty sure Adele might spontaneously combust if she ever cursed, so we were almost certainly dealing with an intruder here. Crap.

Where was that stupid candlestick when you needed it?

"Jules!" Suruthi hissed behind me. "Would you just slow down? We should phone the police to—"

"*Hey*! What do you think you're doing?"

The figure bent over in front of a curio cabinet against the wall, obviously fiddling with its lock, froze. On the ground by their feet was a silver serving tray and a large ewer—the objects that had been atop the cabinet. There was a beat of silence where the person must've been debating whether to make a break for it through the front door a couple feet away, then thought better of it. They drew themselves up to their full height before turning to face us, cool as you please.

There was enough light left in the shop from the few lamps I'd turned on for me to get a good look at the figure's face, and I gasped.

"Hang on, I know you!" I might've been shouting by the way the man winced, but who cared? "You were here the other day! You were here after hours because you wanted to buy those old chemistry manuals. What was your name again?"

The man standing before me deflated a bit, losing some of their impressive height as their shoulders slumped. Whatever fear there might've been unfurling at the base of my spine was gone.

The man had seemed pretty harmless when I'd encountered him just a few days ago, if not entirely too fixated on the items he'd happily made off with. The intensity he carried himself with, his purposeful stride, might've been a little off-putting, but that was gone now too.

Now he looked like a toddler who'd gotten caught with their hand in the cookie jar.

"I'm not really sure how they do things in the UK, but in the US, breaking and entering is pretty frowned upon," I said, crossing my arms.

"And rightfully so," the man agreed. "But, as luck would have it, I realized the other day that I'd forgotten to purchase the microscope in this cabinet here that your aunt so kindly informed me of. Naturally, I had to rectify the situation as soon as possible."

"And you couldn't have waited until normal business hours to do it?" I asked.

"The door was unlocked," the man said huffily. "Forgive me for assuming that meant this establishment was currently conducting business."

No, it wasn't, I thought, panicked. *The door absolutely was not unlocked.*

I knew, because I'd locked the darn thing myself, had watched Adele yank tightly on the handle to double-check that the door was indeed locked.

"If that were the case," I said, choosing my words carefully, "then surely the fact the lights are all turned off in here would've clued you in to the fact that we're *closed*."

There was a short laugh from behind me and I suddenly remembered that I'd started off the hunt for the source of all this racket with some backup.

"She got you there," Suruthi crowed happily, pushing forward to stand beside me. "So it's probably time for you to, you know, jog on."

"*Before* we phone the authorities," Percy added.

The man kept staring at me with a slight frown, like he wasn't quite sure what to make of what he was looking at. That made two of us.

Percy cleared his throat loudly and the man's gaze moved to Percy.

"Perhaps that would be best," the man finally agreed, his voice curt. "But I will—"

"Be back for the stupid microscope, yeah," I said hurriedly. "Whatever. Just get out. *Now*, please."

There were no further complaints from the man as I made a sweeping gesture toward the front door. He marched on past, a strong stench of pipe tobacco wafting after him. He wrenched open the door and was whirling out into the night a second later, and that was it.

I quickly went to the door, shut it, triple-checking all the locks, then made Percy and Suruthi check too while I went back to inspect the cabinet. The thing was surprisingly still locked, the dusty vintage microscope set neatly on the top shelf, undisturbed. Laying abandoned on the floor by the tray and ewer was a small leather case, something you might put a pair of glasses in. I bent down and carefully picked it up, bringing it over to the table where Adele kept her cash register to examine it more closely by the light from the small lamp there.

"What've you got there, Jules?" Suruthi asked as she approached. "You drop something?"

"No," I said. "I'm pretty sure that man did." I held the case out for Suruthi and Percy to see for themselves. "It's a lock picking kit."

An uncomfortable silence fell as we all stood there considering what that meant.

"Should we actually phone the police?" Percy asked at large. "Just to be sure."

"No," I said at the same time Suruthi said, "For what?"

I was circling back to those gut feelings again, but this one I could at least be somewhat certain of.

"I told you, I've seen that man before," I said to Suruthi and Percy. "My aunt calls him one of her favorite customers. Always likes to look at old books and whatever science-y stuff he happens to find. Polite, I guess, but obviously a bit of a jerk too."

"So he's harmless then," Percy said, taking the leather case in hand.

"Save for the whole breaking and entering thing," Suruthi added. "Mustn't forget the attempted larceny as well."

"I'm not sure about that," I admitted. "I can't tell if he's entirely harmless, but I . . . don't think he means to do any harm."

Suruthi went over to peek out the window. "Well, whoever he was, he's long gone now."

I'm not sure about that, I thought.

The man had seemed pretty interested in the microscope. Besides, he'd dropped his lock picking kit. He'd be back.

11

CHAPTER

Things Aren't Any Better the Next Day

"And you're quite sure about this, dear?"

Adele was hovering as I stuffed my notebook and a few extra pens into my bag.

Monday morning, going on seventy-two hours since Ashley had disappeared, and again Adele was asking if I *really* wanted to go to class today.

As if there were any other option at this point.

"Honestly, Adele, I'm fine," I said, swinging my bag up onto my shoulder. "Wouldn't the best thing be to keep a normal schedule?"

"Yes, but are you *sure*?" Adele insisted, wringing her hands again—something she seemed to have taken up recently.

"*Yes*," I said, reaching over to take her hands in mine. "I promise. I'll message you during breaks and come home right after class lets out."

Adele freed one of her hands from my grasp to pat my cheek, sighing heavily. "You must think I'm a silly old woman. You're an adult, Jules, and you can obviously look after yourself, but this whole thing has me unnerved, I won't lie."

Well, the adult part was debatable—I still couldn't legally drink in the US and you could forget about renting a car. We were on the same page about being unnerved though.

"You're not silly," I said to Adele. "It's still scary. I was with Ashley when she disappeared and now she's . . ."

I couldn't—maybe didn't even *want to*—find the words to finish that sentence. Every time I'd said it aloud it seemed to chip away at the calm, collected demeanor I'd been trying to maintain.

The truth of the matter was that *Ashley was missing* and I *was* the last person she'd been with. And all I could muster up to tell the police was: *I don't know what happened.*

"Oh, darling girl." Adele suddenly had her arms around me in a fierce hug. "You mustn't think this is your fault."

"I don't think it's—"

"Because it *isn't*. You did nothing wrong, Jules."

I hugged Adele back just as tightly, resting my chin on her shoulder. I didn't bother trying to come up with a response; I didn't have one anyway.

Adele obviously already knew I very much felt like this was my fault.

She gave me one last squeeze before letting me go, taking a step back. "Best be off then. Don't want to be late."

"Right," I said, clearing my throat. "I'll let you know when I get to class."

Adele saw me to the front door of the shop with another line about keeping my chin up. She was still standing in the doorway when I looked back over my shoulder before I turned the corner down the street. I tried to smile as I gave a small wave; it must've worked, since Adele waved back.

It felt like I was wandering in a daze as I made the now familiar trek to the Underground. I was following the same routine this morning as I had every other morning since arriving in London, but everything felt *off*. It didn't take a genius to figure out why: Ashley was gone.

As much as I might've desperately wished otherwise, Ashley was gone, and she was not going to be the first in Room 217 this morning. As quiet and softspoken as she could be, we'd all had the chance to witness her wicked sense of humor and quirky remarks; her absence was going to be painfully noticeable.

I managed to make it to Chatham Hall in one piece with only one minor mishap of tripping over my shoelaces. I stood outside in the middle of the courtyard for a moment, wondering if I might be able to locate the window in Room 217.

I wondered too whether if I looked closely enough I might see Ashley sitting on the windowsill, book in hand, or pencil scribbling away in her notebook.

"Are you too chicken to go inside or what?"

"Probably," I said as Suruthi came to stand beside me.

Also like me, Suruthi looked as if she hadn't gotten a lick of sleep last night. Her clothes matched her mood today too; there wasn't a single scrap of neon on her shorts or T-shirt anywhere.

I was pretty sure we stood there for another few minutes, both lost in our respective thoughts, staring up at Chatham Hall like it somehow had all the answers to our burning questions.

"Good morning. I trust you two had a pleasant weekend."

It was a mixture of angst and unease that I felt at the sound of that voice somewhere behind us.

Suruthi met my eye and gave a firm nod before we both worked up the courage to turn and face Detective Constable Evans. I may have also imagined the way she mumbled, "He's come back with a warrant," but it still seemed to fit the moment.

Behind Evans, toward the courtyard entrance, I could see his partner, Detective Constable Thomas, deep in conversation with a man and woman who I immediately pegged as likely candidates for Willem's parents.

Willem was standing about a foot away with his arms crossed, gaze fixed firmly on a crack in the cobblestone, and I could clearly see his grimace.

The woman was speaking animatedly with a lot of hand gestures, clearly taking charge of the conversation. DC Thomas kept shaking his head, trying to interject, but the woman wasn't letting him get a word in edgewise. All in all, it was probably a good thing I couldn't understand Dutch.

"My weekend was great, thanks," I said to Evans, forcing some pep into my voice. "What about yours?"

Evans fixed me with his blank, gray stare and I tried and failed not to shiver. Yikes.

"My weekend was perfectly adequate, Miss Montgomery."

"And my weekend was crap, thank you for asking," Suruthi said casually, like we were all having a chat about the weather. "So have you found Ashley yet?"

"Regrettably, no," Evans said shortly. "Hence our visit this morning. We have some follow-up questions we'd like to ask."

There was a deeper, more rational part of my brain that knew if Ashley had been found, we'd know by now. With Evans and Thomas back for more questioning, that obviously meant Ashley was still missing.

Seeing the tight set of Evans's mouth and the way he wouldn't quite meet Suruthi's gaze as he responded to her question made it difficult to stay positive. It wasn't a very good look. And yet the hope I still clung to that Ashley would be found, unharmed and reunited with her grandmother, wasn't keen on being silenced.

Evans gave a polite nod and stepped around us to finish the trek across the courtyard.

"What do you reckon then?"

I jumped when Suruthi gave me a hard nudge with her elbow. "Huh?"

"I said, *what do you reckon*?" she repeated, now frowning.

"Oh, yeah, I . . ."

Looking back to Evans and then again to Suruthi, I realized I must've missed the last minute or two of conversation, too caught up in cataloguing all of Evans's aloof little mannerisms. The way he was leaning to one side, how his gaze was roaming around the courtyard, almost like he was looking for the best escape route . . . Or maybe it was just my overactive imagination filling in the gaps.

"It kinda seems like Evans would rather be just about anywhere else but here, doesn't it?" I said, watching as the man in question disappeared into Chatham Hall.

"Bloke really does seem to hate his job," Suruthi agreed.

"That's one way to put it," I said. "Either that, or he thinks this is a major waste of his time."

It was disconcerting to see the genuine look of apprehension that flitted across Suruthi's face before she managed to school her expression. "But you do think they're trying to, you know, *find* Ashley, right?"

"Yeah," I said. "Of course they're trying to find her. That's their job."

Suruthi nodded, her eyes now downcast. "Of course."

She linked her arm through mine and gave me a gentle tug to get walking, pulling me inside. I couldn't shake the feeling that it was just *wrong* to be going about our day like this, up to Room 217 where we would all sit around on the couches and chairs and talk about writing and how our manuscripts were going, without Ashley there.

Ashley was an aspiring writer just like the rest of us, one of the group. There was a member of our group now missing, and that was becoming more and more difficult to stomach.

Suruthi still hadn't let go of my arm as we walked side-by-side up the stairs, and I was holding on to her just as tightly by the time we'd reached the second floor.

Percy and Thierry were both standing outside the classroom door, but Percy was the only one who acknowledged that we were approaching. Thierry was leaned casually against the wall, face buried in a book, and seemed determined not to look up.

"Well, you look about as great as I feel," Suruthi said to Percy. "Rough night too?"

"Massive understatement." Percy rubbed a hand across his face, and I could practically feel the exhaustion radiating off him. His hair was even messier than usual, the dark circles under his eyes suggesting a serious lack of sleep. "I found it . . . a bit hard to relax last night."

You don't say, I thought.

I tried to stop myself, but the words were out before I had the chance to bite them back. It was pointless to ask because Percy would've let us know if Ashley had contacted him in the twelve hours since we'd last seen each other, but I was asking anyway.

"But you didn't—? I mean, Ashley didn't—?"

Percy gave a small, apologetic smile. "No. Afraid not."

"Right." I pursed my lips, willing myself to ignore the sudden feeling that I was about to cry. "Never mind then."

It looked like Percy was about to fiddle with his glasses again, then thought better of it, and crossed his arms. "The, er, professor's just gone to have a word with Detective Constable Evans, I believe, and then we'll be starting today's lesson."

It was to be business as usual in the meantime then. The writing seminar would go on with or without Ashley. It made sense and yet the whole thing seemed impossible when I wasn't sure I'd even be able to get into the right mindset to try and write (not that I'd made much progress on my manuscript to begin with).

The door to Room 217 swung open and Detective Constable Evans stuck his head out, beckoning us inside with a crook of his finger. He pointed us toward the couches and chairs as Professor Watson stood up at his desk and came forward to greet us.

I did a double take at the professor. Suruthi let out a low whistle.

"Oh dear," Percy muttered.

Professor Watson, to put it delicately, looked terrible. He'd obviously forgotten to shave over the weekend and his hair was the farthest thing from neatly combed. His shirt was wrinkled, sleeves rolled up to his elbows, and his waistcoat was missing. It was almost like looking at a different person, and it definitely wasn't leaving me with any hope that things weren't actually as bad as they were feeling.

I did my best to shake myself out of my stupor and greeted

the professor before quickly taking my seat on the couch between Suruthi and Percy.

We all ended up staring at Ashley's empty seat—even Thierry who had finally looked up from his book. We were still staring when there was a flurry of noise in the hallway, and then the door swung open with a loud *bang*.

The man and woman we'd just seen outside arguing with the other detective constable came storming inside, a very embarrassed Willem shuffling along behind them. The woman had barely crossed the threshold before Professor Watson was stepping right into the line of fire, preventing them from getting any farther into the classroom.

"Mr. and Mrs. Maes, I presume?" Despite the rumpled appearance, Professor Watson sounded cool and collected. "What a pleasure it is to meet you. Willem, if you'd like to join your classmates, I daresay your parents and I will be a touch more comfortable in a private study room downstairs to continue this conversation further."

"Sure," Willem said, skirting around his parents to join us in the circle of furniture.

Professor Watson managed to usher Mr. and Mrs. Maes out into the hallway, closely followed by both detective constables. The door had only just shut with a quiet little *click* when Suruthi pounced.

"So what time do you expect to be on a flight back to Brussels?"

"By breakfast tomorrow, if I'm lucky," Willem griped, dropping into an armchair across from Thierry.

There was a collective grumble from the rest of the group, except—

"Can you really blame them though?" Thierry interjected, snapping his book shut. "We all know Ashley isn't coming back. Oh, don't look at me like that," he added, rolling his eyes in Suruthi's direction. "You are the true crime expert, right? They say the first forty-eight hours are the most crucial in a missing persons case, and we are well past that now."

Thierry's words, spoken so casually, cut like a knife. The resounding silence felt painful.

"Why would you say that?" Percy demanded at the same time Suruthi said, "What is *wrong* with you?"

I was too stunned to have any intelligible kind of response.

None of that seemed to bother Thierry though. He made himself more comfortable in his chair, flipping his book open again. "Fret all you want, but you know I'm right. And that being the case, I think our time would better be focused on our manuscripts."

"Oh, yeah, like that'll be so easy," Suruthi said sarcastically. "Let's all just keep writing away while one of our mates is missing. You mean to tell me that you really think something— something happened to Ashley?"

Thierry gave Suruthi a look that very obviously said *don't be stupid*. "You don't? And she is not one of my *mates*. I barely know the girl."

I had the immediate thought that that wasn't quite true. We'd learned quite a bit about each other since the start of the seminar. Ashley adored the historical fiction genre and wrote her first story at the age of fourteen. She talked about her grandmother a lot, her prized possession was the little bronze bumblebee pin her grandmother had given her, she would only drink coffee if it had a bunch of caramel sauce in it, and I'd never seen her do any kind of writing without earbuds in. I'd never gotten the chance to ask her what she was listening to.

"Is that really fair?" Willem said, straightening up in his armchair. "We *have* spent the last two weeks together."

"And?" Thierry said, arching a brow. "That still doesn't change the fact that we are *not* friends, simply … acquaintances."

None of us were given the chance to respond to Thierry's rather cold sentiments. Detective Constable Evans reappeared in the classroom then, and that same knife from before cut a little deeper when he took the paisley armchair Ashley had diligently occupied the last two weeks.

Evans crossed his legs, leaning casually into the armrest, and my heart gave a painful lurch.

"Now that we're all here," he began, diving right into it, "I'd like to speak with you all individually this morning to ask a few additional questions about Miss James. Your mobile phones will be returned to you as well. Now, one by one, we would like to—"

A shrill voice suddenly drowned out Evans's, floating into the room from somewhere down the hallway. Willem went scarlet in the face as we all glanced his way because it was pretty darn obvious his mother was currently tearing into Professor Watson loud enough for half of London to hear.

"Forget tomorrow morning," Percy said quietly, resting his chin in his hand as he leaned into the arm of the couch. "Willem's going to be out of the country by afternoon tea at this rate."

Percy's guesstimate was an overly generous one. It was a mere half hour later, Detective Constable Evans just having excused himself to question Thierry first, when Mr. and Mrs. Maes returned to the classroom. Professor Watson was just a few steps behind, and if it were possible, he seemed to have a few more strands of gray hair.

It only took one look for Willem to figure out this was all a lost cause.

Mr. Maes stood to the side with his arms crossed while Mrs. Maes snatched Willem's backpack for him and started ushering him toward the door. Whatever she was saying in a string of rapid Dutch had Willem scowling, looking more and more perturbed by the second.

"Will you at least let me say goodbye?" Willem suddenly burst out.

He'd planted his feet firmly in the middle of the classroom and was refusing to budge. Mrs. Maes made a face like she'd sucked on some sour candy and turned back to Mr. Maes. They seemed to have some sort of short, nonverbal conversation before Mrs. Maes said, "Fine, Willem. Be quick about it."

"Yeah, yeah," Willem grumbled. "Whatever."

He turned his back on his mother's indignant scowl to face the rest of us and I felt myself start to get a little choked up.

Thierry had a point; two weeks really wasn't a great amount of time to get to know someone. Strangely though, I felt like I had already gotten to know the people in this room pretty well—save for Thierry, maybe. I was going to miss Willem and his quick wit, and his action-packed sci-fi short stories.

Suruthi, Percy, and I got to our feet, and then we were all just sort of standing there awkwardly, unsure of what to say, until Suruthi finally made the first move.

"We're going to miss you, Willem," she said with a mournful sigh, pulling him in for a tight squeeze.

Willem patted Suruthi on the back, looking very unsure of what to do with the sudden hug. "Uh. Yes. You as well."

Next came a firm handshake and a nod from Percy. When it was my turn, I just decided to throw caution to the wind and give Willem a quick hug too.

"Good luck with everything, Willem," I said when I stepped back. "Be sure to tell us when you have your first book signing."

Willem mustered up a small smile. "You'll be the first to know."

Mrs. Maes cleared her throat loudly and Willem blew out a defeated sigh, shoulders slumping. "Guess this is it then."

We all waved as Willem grudgingly followed his parents to the door. Professor Watson put out a hand to stop him before they could get too far, speaking directly to Willem when he said, "You have incredible talent, young man. Please do not let your early departure keep you from pursuing your passion for writing."

Willem shook the professor's hand, mumbling something that I couldn't really make out with the way his back was turned. Mrs. Maes got a grip on her son's shoulder and gave him a hearty shove out the door before Professor Watson had the chance to say anything else.

Just like that, Willem was gone. I spent a moment fixated on the doorway, wondering if the universe was maybe playing a twisted joke, and both Willem *and* Ashley would suddenly show up in the doorway, pretending like the last few days had been some kind of prank.

That didn't happen.

"And then there were three," Suruthi said as Professor Watson quietly shut the classroom door.

"Four," Percy corrected. "Thierry's only downstairs. Oh, hang on, Willem didn't get the chance to—"

"What, wish Thierry well?" Suruthi scoffed, tossing herself down on the couch. "Don't be daft, Perce. There's no love lost there."

"I'm sure Mr. Maes will have the opportunity to bid Thierry farewell if he wishes," Professor Watson interjected quietly. "He won't be going far."

Professor Watson hadn't moved from where he stood by the classroom door, also watching the thing intently, like he too was waiting for some sort of miracle.

"What do you mean, Professor?" Suruthi asked curiously.

Professor Watson waited until he had taken his regular seat at the head of our unusual circle of furniture to answer Suruthi.

"Regrettably, Miss Kaur, the police have not yet located Miss James, and as you heard Detective Constable Evans say earlier, he and his partner will be needing to ask you all some additional questions. This includes your classmate, Mr. Maes."

"Because we've all got something to hide, don't we?" Suruthi said with a sarcastic laugh. Then she sat upright, a panicked look crossing her face. "Wait. We're not suspects, are we?"

"I believe the correct term would be *persons of interest*," Percy said casually.

Suruthi managed to chuck a small throw pillow at Percy while somehow maintaining direct eye contact with Professor Watson the entire time.

Professor Watson did not look amused. "None of you are a suspect to my knowledge, nor are you a person of interest. This is merely standard operating procedure, Miss Kaur. The police need to know what exactly occurred in the hours leading up to Miss James's..."

An interesting expression crossed the professor's face as he lapsed into silence. He seemed to have forgotten the rest of what he was going to say and didn't seem entirely *present* anymore. Maybe I was just projecting, but Professor Watson was currently seeing something that wasn't visible to the rest of us.

It took both Suruthi and me saying his name a few times before Professor Watson returned to the present.

"I beg your pardon," he mumbled. It was odd seeing him fidgeting with the cuff links of his shirt. "I'm afraid I did not... that is to say, my weekend was perhaps not the most restful."

"I think we're all in the same boat, Professor," I said reassuringly.

"But Professor?" Suruthi leaned closer toward Professor Watson, almost hanging off the couch now. "You *do* think the police will find Ashley, right?"

It didn't take him quite as long to answer Suruthi's question. As he spoke, I didn't believe a single word he said. I didn't think the professor did either.

"Of course, Miss Kaur. I have every confidence that the police will find Miss James."

12

CHAPTER

Anything You Do Say May Be Given In Evidence

As it happened, being questioned by the police for the second time was not really what the movies made it seem. This left Suruthi massively annoyed.

For one, Detective Constable Evans greatly miscalculated how long "a few simple follow-up questions" was actually going to take. It took *hours*—long enough to have to take a break for lunch.

While the rest of us sat around waiting to be questioned, Professor Watson made a valiant attempt at doing another writing exercise, but it was about the same as an act of Congress to get any of us to focus. None of the words that I actually managed to get down on paper were making any sense and every so often there would be an annoying burst of ringing in my ears that had me wincing.

"You okay, Jules?" Suruthi leaned over to ask the third time I stuffed a finger in my left ear to fiddle with my hearing aid.

"Yeah, I—I'm fine," I said quickly, grabbing my pen for something to distract myself with. "My ears itch a lot."

When it was my turn to be questioned, I followed Evans out of the classroom, downstairs, and into a private study room. Detective Constable Thomas was seated at the table with a notepad opened before him and a pen in hand that he kept rapidly clicking and unclicking. If I had to pick a word to describe his face, he looked *bored*.

"Have a seat, if you please, Miss Montgomery," Evans instructed. "This won't take long."

I tried not to roll my eyes as I sat down. "Sure. And call me Jules, please."

I got enough *Miss Montgomery* throughout the day courtesy of the professor; I didn't need to hear it anymore from the police.

"Jules then." Evans nodded, flipping his notebook open to a fresh page once he'd sat down across the table from me. "We'll start from the beginning, shall we?"

"Beginning of what?" I asked carefully.

"Last Friday," Thomas clarified. "Your trip to Oxford with your classmates. We need to know exactly what happened in the hours leading up to when you lost sight of the girl."

"Oh, you mean *Ashley*," I said. "Okay, yeah, we can start from the beginning."

And start from the beginning we did. Because they were asking for it, I started to tell them *everything*.

"So we all had to wake up a little earlier than normal that morning, which, you know, none of us were really all that thrilled about, but we got here on time to catch the bus. I sat next to Suruthi—you met her upstairs, she's great. Then we fell asleep on the way there even though I'd had two cups of coffee. I don't usually do that, but that morning specifically I was *really* feeling tired, so I thought I'd—"

"Let's pause for a moment here, Jules," Evans said, raising his voice a smidge to speak over me. "We don't need you to go back *quite* that far."

"But you said—"

"Just skip to the part where you go off with the girl," Thomas cut in, raising his voice to speak over me. "You wanted to see the Narnia door."

"Yeah, *Ashley* was dead set on seeing it," I said, leaning back in my chair, crossing my arms. "So was I, since we'd both grown up reading all the C. S. Lewis books. So, anyway, we left Suruthi and Percy sitting on a bench near a bunch of shops, I guess. Suruthi had been eating chips for lunch and Percy made me try steak and kidney pie with, like, mashed peas or something. A little gross, but still kinda good, I guess. Ashley had just gotten some tea because she said the bus ride to Oxford left her feeling sick, and I wanted another one too even though I *really* knew I didn't need one, since three cups in a day is *a* lot of caffeine and all, but I still wanted to—"

"Jules."

"Okay, anyway. Ashley and I went off to find the Narnia door, but we had trouble with the GPS on our phones," I went on. "We ended up stopping to ask someone for directions, but they didn't—"

"You spoke with someone?" Now Thomas looked interested, clicking his pen again. "Who?"

"Dunno," I said, shrugging. "Some dude who had been riding his bike, I guess. He told us we were going the wrong way and sent us in the opposite direction."

"Some dude," Thomas repeated. I couldn't tell if he was irritated or amused. "Did this *dude* happen to tell you his name?"

"Nope," I answered. "After he told us where to go, he got on his bike and pedaled away down the street."

Evans must've seen the way Thomas had rolled his eyes at my response and intervened before Thomas could say anything else. "And what did this gentleman look like?"

I took a moment to mull it over. The man who'd pointed us in the right direction of the Narnia door had been pretty nondescript, but I was mostly certain I could come up with a mental image.

"Stocky," I settled on saying. "Balding, with some facial hair. He was wearing gray shorts and a red T-shirt with some sports logo on it. Red bike, with one of those little cup holder things on it where you can put your water bottle."

Thomas quickly wrote my description down in tiny, chicken-scratch writing.

"Did anything else stand out to you about this man?" Evans asked. "His demeanor? The way he spoke, perhaps?"

I took even longer to think about the follow-up questions.

"No," I finally said. "He was nice enough to help us out and that was pretty much it. The whole exchange lasted maybe like two minutes and then we went our separate ways."

"I see." Evans took his turn writing a few lines down in his own notebook before speaking again. "And when you did reach your destination with Miss James, what then?"

"We took a bunch of pictures on our phones," I told him. "Geeked out a bit over how cool the door was. Then I tried to do a video call with my mom in California and Ashley said she was going to try and call her grandma so she could get a look too."

The closer I got to the part in my retelling where Ashley was there one second and gone the next had my heart stuttering through a few anxious beats.

"And did Miss James speak with her grandmother?" Evans asked, back to scribbling down more notes. "Did you happen to overhear their conversation?"

I shook my head. "No. I ended up walking around a bit to try and get reception. The connection was crappy."

"I see."

Evans continued to write in his little notebook for the next minute, and when Thomas went back to scribbling in his own notebook, it was a struggle to keep still and not start bouncing my knee. Why was this taking so long?

I thought about trying to read their writing upside down, but another quick peek at Thomas's chicken scratch and Evans's tightly packed cursive made me a little nauseated. When Thomas tossed his pen aside and cut a look to Evans, some sort of silent exchange passing between them, I couldn't bite it back anymore.

"She didn't run away. Ashley, I mean," I said. "This isn't some case of a teenager running away while on vacation."

Evans arched an eyebrow. "What makes you so sure of that, Jules?"

I started counting off on my fingers. "Because I was with her? Because I've spent every day of the last two weeks getting to know her? Because she *wanted* to be here. She'd saved up for ages to be able to afford the airfare. And she told me as much," I added at the skeptical look that had taken over Thomas's face. "Why would she lie about that? What reason would she have for throwing that all away?"

Evans was far quicker with his response than I was expecting, catching me off guard.

"Because you only met the young lady a fortnight ago," he

said, surprisingly calm. "Not a considerable amount of time in the grand scheme of things, no matter how good a judge of character you claim to be."

I bit down on the inside of my cheek to keep from shrieking in frustration and scrubbed my hands over my face.

This was *infuriating*. Yes, I could understand that the police were just doing their due diligence, but it seemed like a massive waste of time to just be sitting here, answering questions I'd already been asked.

"How about a search party then?" I threw out, almost desperately. "We've already got a couple people here, why can't we just—"

Evans held up a hand to cut me off. "I appreciate your concern for your friend, Jules, but we don't need you wandering off either."

"Excuse me?"

"This is your first time in London," Thomas elaborated. "You're a tourist. You don't know the area. You'd wind up God only knows where, no matter how much you mean well."

"What about her family then?" I said. I wasn't ready to let this go; there had to be *something* we could do besides just sitting around waiting for the police to tell us something. "I bet her grandmother would come if you just—"

"The only emergency contact Miss James provided when enrolling in your writing seminar was her grandmother," Evans said, his voice hardening. "When we contacted Miss Edith Longmont of Ontario to inform her of the situation, she stated that she is Ashley's only living relative and her physician will not allow her to fly to London because she is in poor health."

That information came as a slap to the face. My expression

must've given that away with how Evans briefly looked mildly pleased with himself.

"I take it Miss James didn't share that information with you, did she?" he asked.

"No," I answered quietly. "She mentioned she lived with her grandmother and that they were close, but that was it."

"Then I believe I rest my case."

As if to purposely change the subject, Thomas reached into a bag on the empty chair beside him and slid what I quickly recognized as my cell phone across the table to me. Suruthi would be disappointed that it was in a simple sandwich bag instead of one marked in bold letters declaring it as evidence. "Your mobile, Jules. Thank you for your time."

"We'll be in touch," Evans added as I picked up my phone.

He immediately went back to scribbling in his notebook and Thomas leaned over to mutter something to him in an undertone.

My dismissal was obvious, but I stayed seated. This couldn't be over yet.

"Do you have any business cards?" I asked.

Evans didn't even look up from his notebook. "Pardon?"

"Your business cards," I said again. "Do you have any? I'd like to—"

"None on us at the moment, I'm afraid," Thomas cut in. "Don't worry though; we'll be in touch if we need you."

What was obviously left unsaid here was: *we won't need you.*

13

CHAPTER

Now It's Getting Really Bad

That's the right time, yeah?" Suruthi said, peering up at the clock on the wall above the whiteboard.

Percy checked the time on his watch. "Half past nine."

"Huh."

I looked around at the wide-open classroom door behind me, half expecting Professor Watson to come rushing in with some apology about running late this morning. I'd been hoping that by being released early yesterday after being questioned by Evans and Thomas, we would come back today having had a reset. That didn't seem to be the case.

Last night I'd managed to get a few sentences down in my manuscript before I'd fallen asleep early. It hadn't been a restful sleep though; I kept having weird dreams about Ashley's empty chair in Room 217 and a bunch of random letters floating around. If I had to guess, my subconscious was now squeezing Ashley and my lack of writing into the same box.

So for someone who'd arrived promptly at nine o'clock for the past two and a half weeks, it was *odd* Professor Watson had apparently picked today to not show up.

"Maybe the professor just overslept," Percy suggested.

I appreciated the effort he was putting in to sound positive, but the expression on his face was telling a different story.

Thierry heaved an exasperated sigh from where he sat across the classroom, a new leather-bound journal open in his lap, pen scribbling across the paper. Suruthi and I exchanged annoyed looks.

Since he'd shared his rather morbid stance on Ashley's disappearance, he'd been pretty tight-lipped. Other than to be a major suck-up to the professor or blab about how brilliant he thought the first few chapters of his political thriller manuscript were, Thierry kept to himself.

"Something you'd like to share?" Suruthi asked him sweetly.

"Not with you," he answered without looking up.

Suruthi stuck her tongue out at Thierry and then threw herself backward into the couch, tossing an arm over her face. "Oh, what a *shame*. How will I ever go on knowing that *Monsieur Thierry Garnier* won't bless us with his—"

"Suruthi."

Percy's sharp tone managed to silence Suruthi before she got any further into her rant and then she stuck her tongue out at him too.

"My apologies, class. It would appear I was rather ... delayed this morning."

We all looked around at the sound of Professor Watson's voice and simultaneously tried not to gasp. If he'd looked haggard the other day, he looked *awful* now. He'd apparently decided to keep working on growing the beard, and he didn't have his briefcase. As he crossed the classroom to his desk, I saw the deep circles under his eyes and the aura of pure exhaustion that followed him.

Professor Watson spent a moment at his desk rummaging around in the drawers, growing more and more frantic when he couldn't find whatever he was looking for.

"Uh, Professor?" Percy said tentatively. "Are you alright?"

The professor kept at it, obviously not having heard Percy's question. I couldn't tell for sure, but it sounded a lot like Professor Watson was mumbling to himself. He swore loudly when he knocked over a pen cup with his elbow as he wrenched open another drawer.

Percy looked over at me with raised eyebrows and I shrugged helplessly. Obviously the professor was having . . . issues this morning, but what were *we* supposed to do about it?

"Professor?" Suruthi called loudly. "Watson? Sir? You alright?"

"*What?*"

I flinched at the professor's loud bark of a response and the way it echoed uncomfortably in my ears. The others, even Thierry, were openly gaping at Professor Watson, and then I was doing the same too once I recovered.

I would've thought it impossible for Professor Watson to raise his voice like that. Just as quickly as the enraged look had darkened his face as he glared at us, it was gone.

He collapsed into the chair at his desk and sighed, passing a hand over his face. "I beg your pardon, Miss Kaur. It's no excuse, but things have been rather . . . tense of late. My apologies."

Suruthi opened and closed her mouth a couple times before she managed to come up with a response, mumbling something about how we all got a little tense now and then.

A little tense might've been an understatement though. Professor Watson looked way beyond "on edge" as he grabbed a fresh notepad from a desk drawer and came to join us, taking a seat in the armchair reserved specifically for him.

"Well then." Professor Watson cleared his throat as he uncapped his fountain pen. "Where were we?"

"We ended yesterday's discussion with character development," Thierry supplied.

Thierry seemed to have already gotten over the shock of Professor Watson's outburst and was now behaving as if this was just another day in class. I didn't think the rest of us were faring so well.

"Yes, of course," Professor Watson said, nodding along. "Let's begin, shall we?"

Suruthi was on us the second we were outside in the empty courtyard that afternoon.

"What was *that* about? Professor Watson was looking a little deranged there, wouldn't you say?"

Percy frowned. "He did seem rather . . . a fright."

For once, Suruthi didn't tease him about his choice of words. "Yes, exactly!"

"That's one way to put it," I agreed. It didn't quite seem like that touched all the bases though. "I think we can all agree that there's something bothering the professor."

"Obviously," Suruthi said with a snort. "But what I want to know is—"

"It's none of our business," Thierry said in a singsong voice, passing us on his way through the courtyard.

"Oh, *go on*, why don't you?" Suruthi called after him. "We all know how you feel!"

Thierry simply waved farewell.

As much as I hated to admit it, maybe Thierry had a point.

Yes, Professor Watson obviously had something going on that was clearly *way* beyond the pressures that came with leading an esteemed writing seminar, but we were still faced with the same question as before: What could we do about it?

"Perhaps he's right," Percy said, blowing out a sigh. "Perhaps we should focus on—"

"Let me stop you right there, Percy Bysshe," Suruthi said, throwing up a hand. "Thierry can sod off for all I care. Something's up with the professor and I want to know what."

"This isn't one of your true crime stories, Suruthi!" Percy shot back. For the first time since we'd met, he looked genuinely upset. "And you're not a detective either. Professor Watson simply is under a lot of pressure with Ashley's disappearance and probably feels somewhat responsible, so what we can do now is let the police do their job and find Ashley while we make the most of our five and a half weeks left in this seminar and *finish our manuscripts.*"

Suruthi's eyes narrowed as she crossed her arms, glaring up at Percy. This was the first time I'd ever seen her look *annoyed.* Her glare wasn't something I wanted directed at me.

"You can keep telling yourself that if it'll make you feel better," she said, her chin jutting out. "But I know something *is* wrong, I'm going to figure it out, and Jules is going to back me up on this."

"Excuse me, but when did I say that?" I said in alarm. "I don't remember agreeing to anything, Suruthi." The next words out of my mouth felt a lot like a lie, but I said them anyway, maybe to convince myself just as much as Suruthi. "Professor Watson probably *is* under a lot of stress like Percy said, and we did come here to write. Maybe that's where our focus should be."

My focus was far from my manuscript though. I'd managed to write one measly page last night before I'd given up and rolled over in bed, stuffing my head under a pillow. I must've spent more than one fitful hour trying to force myself to sleep, replaying those last few moments standing at the Narnia door with Ashley repeatedly, before I finally drifted off.

It was thankfully a dreamless sleep, but one that still left me feeling like I'd been hit over the head with a baseball bat in the morning. I barely managed to throw on some clothes before stumbling my way out of the flat. When I was finally passing through the little stone entryway into the courtyard outside Chatham Hall, I figured I was probably about as functional as I was going to get.

I didn't notice at first how quiet it was inside. It was summer, but there were still classes being held in the hall, with a gaggle of students always on their way in or out of the building at any given time.

I heard no snippets of conversation as I reached the second floor or laughter or some ongoing lecture. Suruthi was usually responsible for a lot of the noise, but she hadn't arrived yet—same with Percy.

Equally as strange was finding Thierry seated on the floor outside the classroom.

"What are you—?"

"Door's locked."

"Excuse me?"

"Door's locked," Thierry repeated without looking up from his journal.

I tried the doorknob, gripping tightly, and pushed. Nothing.

"Believe me now?"

"Just—double-checking."

I'd probably been yanking and tugging on the doorknob for a solid minute or two before I had to admit defeat. I leaned against the wall, pulling my phone from my pocket to check the time; it was past nine by this time and the classroom door was locked. It seemed an awful lot like the universe was sending me a message here.

"Lost cause, is it?"

"How long have you been standing there?" I asked Percy as he came to stand beside me.

"Long enough. Let me have a go."

"By all means," I said, gesturing grandly toward the door.

Percy stepped around me to try the door for himself, giving the handle a tremendous yank. I had to give him credit; he kept at it longer than I had, yanking and tugging, before he finally gave up too.

"Well, I don't know about you, but it seems to me that class has been cancelled for the day," Percy grumbled, pulling out his phone. He spent a moment scrolling around on it before he gave an annoyed huff. "Didn't even send an email. It's not like Professor Watson to just not show up for the day."

Percy was not wrong. From day one Professor Watson seemed to have carried himself like a man who knew everything; he'd carefully crafted a perfect agenda for these eight weeks, and he was going to stick to it. Professor Watson not showing up to class *was* incredibly strange.

"Okay then," I said. "I think it's probably worth coming up with plan B now."

"Er." Percy frowned in confusion. "Do we need a plan B? I reckon we ought to just—"

"Ought to talk more about how Suruthi is right, and we've got a mystery to investigate!"

I broke into a smile as Suruthi's loud voice carried up the stairs. She was skipping up the last step by the time we reached the end of the hallway, a little out of breath but looking ridiculously pleased with herself.

"I'm calling it *The Case of the Bedraggled Professor*," she announced. "I'm starting to suspect the police must've kept him overnight in a holding cell after hours of questioning and *that's* why he was late for class yesterday morning."

"I seem to recall having this conversation yesterday," Percy said. "I thought we all agreed that we weren't going to—"

"Oh, no, Percy Bysshe," Suruthi said, wagging a finger at him. "*You* decided that all on your own. So now we are going to—"

"Have this conversation somewhere else," I said in an undertone, grabbing Percy and Suruthi's forearms to tug them a little closer.

"Good idea," Thierry called from his seat on the floor. "You're all starting to sound like a bunch of conspiracists. Best not let anyone else catch on."

"Lucky us!" Suruthi called back. "And lucky for us," she continued, lowering her voice, "I know exactly what to do first."

"Oh no," Percy said as Suruthi quite literally started to drag us back down the hallway in the opposite direction. "Oh no. Oh *no*."

"You wanna fill us in on where we're going?" I asked Suruthi, nearly stumbling over my feet trying to keep up with her.

She shot a devious smile over her shoulder. "You'll see."

Percy figured it out first as we rounded the corner at the end of the hallway and immediately stopped, pulling free from

Suruthi's grasp. "We are *not* going to go ransack the professor's office."

"It's not ransacking," Suruthi disagreed. "I call it *having a look around.*"

"If the classroom is locked, won't the professor's office be locked as well?" I said. "What if he's in there now and just lost track of time?"

"Well, let's find out then!" Suruthi insisted. "Come on, I can't be the only one who noticed how *awful* the professor looked yesterday. What if he's passed out in his office and he needs emergency medical attention? If *we* don't help him, who will?"

Suruthi turned on her heel with a twirl of her hot pink skirt and marched down the short hallway, heading for the third door on the left.

"*Suruthi!*" Percy hissed after her. "Now you really are going to get arrested for breaking and entering!"

"Live a little!"

Percy looked to me for backup, but I could only shrug, just as lost as he was. It really didn't seem all that possible to stop Suruthi when she was dead set on doing something.

"Might as well keep an eye on her," I reasoned, "seeing as she'll just drag us into whatever she's got planned anyway."

Percy sighed, shoving up his glasses so he could rub at his eyes with the heels of his hands. "I hate that you're making far too much sense right now, Jules."

Once his glasses were back on, we quickly followed Suruthi and came up short by Professor Watson's office door just as she began to knock.

"Professor?" she called politely. "Professor Watson, it's Suruthi. Are you in? It's nearly half past nine and we were wondering if we were going to start class. We also wanted to make sure you were conscious."

We waited for one long moment, straining to listen for any kind of movement or sound from behind the door. I was almost certain the office was empty. There was no light peeking out from beneath the door, no sound of anyone on the phone, or typing away at their computer.

"Hang on, do you hear that?" Suruthi said, moving closer to the door.

"Hear what?" Percy and I asked in unison.

As far as I could tell, there wasn't a single noise to be heard beyond that door. Then again, I probably wasn't the best one to ask for confirmation.

Suruthi leaned against the office door; her eyes closed as she had her ear flat up against the surface. She was frowning in concentration, and very carefully said, "I think... I think there's someone watching the telly in there."

"You're serious?" Percy said, eyebrows raised. "The professor doesn't strike me as someone who watches a lot of television."

"Listen for yourselves then."

Suruthi beckoned us over, and the three of us found ourselves packed in against the office door like a few sardines in a tin can. I wound up squished in between Percy and Suruthi, positioned at a somewhat awkward angle so I could get an ear to the door too. This left me pressed mostly into Percy's side once I finally managed a decent position.

Under normal circumstances, I would've just ignored the awkwardness and got over it. It didn't help the situation in any way feeling firsthand how *warm* Percy was. It definitely didn't help when I snuck a glance up at him and saw that he'd gone scarlet in the face, determinedly looking anywhere but at me.

So I decided to do the same and pretend like my heart wasn't skipping into a frantic, pounding beat against my chest. Thankfully Suruthi didn't seem to have caught on to any of this, still listening diligently with her ear pressed against the door.

I was straining to listen, but it was a struggle to hear anything beyond heavy breathing from the three of us as well as my rapid pulse. A handful of moments in and I was pretty sure I actually could make out a low mumble of voices. Then came a bit of canned laughter and a second, somewhat louder laugh.

"Hang on," Percy said, trying to inch closer to the door. "That sounds like . . ."

"*Fortune and Glory,*" Suruthi said, snapping her fingers. "I think it was a sitcom."

"That's the one!"

"You can hear all that?" I said, pressing harder against the door.

I closed my eyes this time, focusing as much as possible with how closely I was standing next to Percy. I had a hard time telling if I really was hearing some TV show, or if it was all just my imagination. It was a stroke of luck there was another, much louder laugh next.

Suruthi started knocking again. "Excuse us, Professor. Professor Watson? Hello in there."

The laughter stopped at once, silence following.

"Professor Watson?" Suruthi tried the doorknob, and it held fast. "Excuse us, sir, but we were hoping we could talk to you."

Our only response was more silence.

"How long are we going to stand here?" Percy muttered. "He's clearly not going to answer the door."

"If it even is Professor Watson in there," I said without thinking.

Suruthi and Percy turned questioning looks my way.

"You said yourself the professor doesn't seem like the type to watch television," I pointed out.

"Well, then, who else would be in there?" Percy asked. "I don't think Professor Watson's teaching any other classes this summer, and I don't think he has a teaching assistant or some other kind of aide."

"Perhaps it's his sister's cousin's aunt's nephew, twice removed," Suruthi said sarcastically, taking a step back from the door. "*But* it's probably not the best idea to waste the day away standing outside the professor's office."

Percy looked relieved to hear Suruthi suggest this. "That's a fair point. We really should be focusing on our manuscripts. What say we—Jules, are you coming?"

Percy and Suruthi had already started off down the hallway again and I was still standing there, pressed against the professor's office door.

"Oh yeah," I said lamely. "Sorry."

I stepped away from the door, giving it one last questioning look. The answer to the question of *Who's been watching sitcoms in Professor Watson's office?* was probably going to plague me a lot longer than I wanted.

"Jules," Suruthi prompted. "Shall we?"

"Sorry," I repeated. "I'm coming."

I only managed a few steps toward Suruthi and Percy before it hit.

CHAPTER

For Whom the Bells Toll

I had to clap my hands over my ears with a pained groan, squeezing my eyes shut, the piercing ringing only I could hear growing louder and louder with each second. It felt quite literally like my head was vibrating from the force of it and my hands weren't doing anything to stop it.

I kept increasing the pressure of my hands covering my ears to give myself the illusion that I was keeping my head still, but the feeling of having intense shockwaves radiating through my skull did not recede.

I was vaguely aware of the hand on my elbow, another on my shoulder that carefully guided me down to the floor where I could sit. If anything, sitting down made me feel even worse, and I was convinced I was seconds away from throwing up.

I slipped off my hearing aids, not caring in the moment about keeping up the pretense that I didn't wear the things, and stuck a finger in my right ear, desperately trying to get the agonizing ringing to just *stop*.

My hearing aids were closed tightly in my fists when I gave up and bent over, sticking my head between my knees. I kept forcing myself to take deep, even breaths, in through my nose and out through my mouth.

I wasn't sure how long I stayed in that position, but I did not sit up until the ringing had subsided into something like dull background noise. It was still there, but it was manageable, and thankfully not near the level of making me feel as if my skull were about to split open.

"...Jules? You okay?"

I was wary to open my eyes again when I made out the sound of Percy's voice floating somewhere beside me, and then came a hand on my shoulder. For the most part, the sickening feeling of being thrown around on a roller coaster had subsided now, and I was going to have to face the world again sooner or later.

I didn't open my eyes until after I'd slipped my hearing aids back on. It took a moment for everything to settle again, and Percy's voice asking, "Are you alright?" was the first thing I could really hear clearly.

Percy and Suruthi were seated on the floor on either side of me, both looking like anxious mother hens.

"'M okay," I said. My voice sounded weirdly muffled to my ears. "Sorry."

"Quit apologizing!" Suruthi said, whacking me playfully on the shoulder. "You gave us a real fright there, Jules. I swear I thought you were about to keel over."

"I'm sorry," I said again anyway. "It's—it's just the ringing in my ears, that's all, not anything serious. And I've never fainted because of it. Sometimes the ringing just gets really, *really* bad."

"I have heard that about tinnitus," Percy said grimly.

"Bless you," Suruthi said.

He rolled his eyes, shooting Suruthi an annoyed look.

"Thank you, but the condition of having ringing in your ears is called tinnitus."

"What he said," I agreed, when Suruthi looked at me for confirmation. "Most of the time it's manageable and I can ignore it. Sometimes it's so bad though I feel like my head is about to split open."

Suruthi winced. "Ouch."

It is what it is was automatically on the tip of my tongue because that was my normal response to this sort of thing—the subject of my hearing loss and all that had come with it.

It *was* technically the truth. There wasn't a single thing I could do about the fact I had permanent hearing loss or awful ringing in my ears or that I had to wear hearing aids if I wanted to actively participate in a conversation where I could understand what was being said.

This had become my new reality, but a year and some change into it, and I still wasn't sure if I'd ever really adjust.

So when the next words out of my mouth were, "Yeah, it *sucks*," I was surprised.

I would have to take some time to think it over, but I didn't think I'd ever said as much before, that this really did suck, but it felt . . . freeing in a way. It felt good to say it.

"I'll bet," Suruthi said. "I like your hearing aids, though. They're a nice color."

That got a burst of laughter out of me. "Thanks. It's called *mahogany*. I thought the color would blend in with my hair."

"I think it does," Suruthi agreed. "What d'you think, Perce?"

Percy looked like a deer caught in the headlights, and he was still a little flushed by the time he managed to school his expression. "I think you look . . . very nice, Jules."

Suruthi did a poor job of choking back a laugh. "I was asking about the color of the hearing aids, Percy, not whether Jules looks nice. Which you do, by the way," she added, nudging me with her elbow. "A real looker, isn't she, Percy?"

He didn't answer this time around.

"Thanks, I guess," I said. It came out more like a question.

It would probably be a waste of time trying to figure out what that whole exchange was supposed to have meant—*I looked very nice*—so I left it there.

We lapsed into silence then, sitting on the floor in the hallway, and without a single clue as to what we were supposed to do now that Professor Watson was just suddenly not showing up to class.

Beyond that, Ashley had been gone several days now and the jury was still out on whether we were going to be hearing much from the police after being questioned. Even if Suruthi was letting her love of true crime and mysteries cloud her vision, Percy was going to have to admit it sooner or later— Something odd was going on here. And I *really* wanted to figure out what it was.

"You know, when I imagined what this seminar was going to be like, this wasn't what I had in mind," I said, ending the silence.

"Likewise," Suruthi said while Percy hummed in agreement.

"What a memorable first trip overseas this is turning out to be for you," Percy added ruefully.

"I was hoping to get past this *awful* rut I've been in, but now I think it's worse than ever, funnily enough," I said.

"What do you mean?" Suruthi asked curiously. "Seems to me like you've been doing pretty well so far. How many pages have you got in your manuscript now?"

I had to think about that.

"If we're not counting all the pointless outlines or notes that make absolutely *no* sense, then maybe . . . five?"

Percy looked startled. "But—you submitted an outline to the professor, didn't you?"

The unintentional laugh that escaped was a disparaging one. "Yeah, and it was a load of crap," I said. "Professor Watson had a field day marking that thing up with his red pen. I should show you sometime."

"If it's any consolation," Suruthi said after a moment, "mine wasn't any better. Professor Watson told me that I should spend less time blathering on about the unimportant and stick to the facts. Apparently, I let my own opinion cloud my writing too much."

"Well, the professor told me that I need more passion and intrigue in *my* writing," I said, pulling a smile.

We looked over at Percy next.

"What?" he said defensively. "The professor was perfectly pleasant with his review of my outline, thank you."

Suruthi arched one eyebrow, and that was all it took to make Percy crack.

"Alright, so he did say that I was a little too . . . long-winded," he admitted, refusing to make eye contact. "That I shouldn't spend so much time on world building and that I need to focus on character development as well."

"Ah, there it is." Suruthi sighed, closing her eyes as she placed a hand over her chest.

"What?" Percy demanded crossly. "There what is?"

"Proof that Percy Bysshe Byers really is human like the rest of us. I'm going to savor this moment forever."

Percy turned an offended look on me when I cracked up laughing, unable to keep it back.

"Sorry, sorry, I don't mean it," I got out through the unintentional laughing fit. "I have this really bad habit of laughing at inappropriate times."

This had Suruthi busting up laughing too.

"Yes, alright, thank you. I realize the humor in it," Percy allowed with a small smile of his own. "I never said I was an otherworldly writer though. None of us are."

"Except for maybe Thierry," Suruthi said, smirking. "Per his own account, of course."

"At least one of us is," I said, leaning my head back against the wall, blowing out a sigh. Now that my laughing fit was over, I was left feeling exhausted. "It's an honest miracle I got into this seminar and now I'm not even sure I can hack it."

"Don't you think you're being a little too hard on yourself?" Suruthi said, nudging me again. "Percy's not wrong; we're all amateurs. We came here to get better at writing. Of course we're not going to be perfect at it."

"Yeah, sure, but I used to be able to sit down and write at least a dozen pages in one go, and now I can barely get out one." I was starting to sound a lot like I was complaining, but I suddenly couldn't stop. "Writing was the *one* thing I was able to do without even having to think about it and now it's like pulling teeth, I swear. It has been for the last year. I told you, Percy, my submission piece for the seminar was something I wrote ages ago, not recently. Writing was the one thing I felt like I had any sort of control over in my life, but now I don't even have that anymore, just like my stupid hearing."

I wasn't sure what kind of reaction I was supposed to expect from Percy and Suruthi after that confession. It would've been hard to swallow if there had been pity in their gazes, and it probably wouldn't have helped either if they'd tried to tell me I was wrong in some way.

"Oh, Jules." Suruthi sighed, slumping over to rest her head on my shoulder. "You really should give yourself some grace."

"I'm only saying I—"

"I think Suruthi's right," Percy said suddenly, catching us off guard. "You *are* being too hard on yourself. You haven't really given yourself time to grieve."

"Excuse me?" I said, completely stunned. "What do I have to grieve for?"

Percy debated his answer as he picked at a thread on his pant leg. "What you used to have. In this case, the way you used to write. Your hearing."

I began to realize at once just how much sense Percy was making.

It had been a gradual thing, but quick; in a matter of months I'd developed such a severe hearing loss that my doctor and the audiologist I'd been seeing still weren't sure why it had happened. Something sensorineural was a likely cause, but I'd put a lot of effort into blocking it all out.

A part of myself hadn't wanted to understand it, because in the end, what did it matter? It still wouldn't have changed the outcome. I would still have hearing loss, regardless of the cause.

"That makes a lot of sense," I said. "I guess I've always just swept it under the rug. Not really because I'm embarrassed about it or whatever, more because I just get ... *angry* with myself. That I haven't adjusted the way I think I should have by now."

"Adjusted how?" Percy asked. "Like with sign language?"

"No, not sign language," I answered. "Although I have learned a bit. I mean more like how I should be used to my hearing aids by now. I've had them about a year now, but sometimes it's just... just..."

"Go on," Suruthi encouraged. "Let it out, mate."

That was all the permission I needed.

"Sometimes it really just *sucks,* and it can be really, really difficult to wear them. Hearing aids don't actually help me understand what someone is telling me, they just make everything louder. They don't clarify the noise for me, they just amplify it. I have to work a lot harder most of the time to understand what's being said to me and I just get, I don't know, *tired.* I get tired of having to put in all that extra effort. I get tired of the look people give me when I'm having a hard time keeping up with the conversation. It's so much easier for me to just... have it be kind of silent for a while, I guess."

And the tense silence from before returned, although not nearly as depressing. I felt like I might have moved into the *oversharing* category, but it didn't seem to have bothered Percy or Suruthi much.

Suruthi was grinning at me actually and reached up to pat me affectionately on the head. "Do you feel better now, Jules?"

"A bit," I said. "It was kind of nice getting all that off my chest, to be honest."

"Been a while, has it?"

"Actually, no." I was starting to feel embarrassed about it, but since I was already on a roll here... "I've never shared that with anyone before."

Suruthi put a hand over her heart again like when she'd been teasing Percy, but her smile was genuine. "I'm honored. You might think about sharing more often then."

"As long as it stays between us," I said, wagging a finger at her.

Suruthi gasped in mock outrage. "Whatever are you implying, Jules? I can keep a secret, thank you."

"Maybe you should try writing about this," Percy blurted.

"Excuse me?" I said, looking over at him again.

"If it's not too forward of me to say," Percy continued in a rush. "But why don't you try writing about this? Your struggles with writing. Even your hearing, maybe. Turn it into something usable. Seems to me like you've got a lot of experience to draw on. That ought to give you something to work off, right?"

I was left staring open-mouthed at Percy's little speech. It was something I'd never considered before, but *maybe* . . .

"Are you a shrink in your spare time, Percy?" Suruthi asked, not unkindly.

Percy gave a short laugh, sneaking an arm behind me to ruffle Suruthi's hair. "Maybe I should consider that as a secondary career option."

"You know, maybe you have a point, Percy," I said later when we were walking outside into the courtyard. "Maybe I'll give my manuscript another try from a different angle this time."

Percy looked pleasantly flushed as he grinned down at me. "I think that's a grand idea, Jules."

I found myself grinning back in response and would have kept the conversation going if I hadn't seen a flash of color behind Percy, just above his shoulder. It took a second to realize what I was looking at, and when I did, I felt a chill slip down my spine.

We were being watched by a figure peering out a second story window. I couldn't see well enough to make out any distinct characteristics of the figure, but I knew that whoever the figure was, their gaze was fixed directly on me.

15

CHAPTER

The Opportune Moment

Juliet, you look *horrible*."

I dropped my head back against the wall in my bedroom with a long sigh. "Mom, it's six in the morning." I'd also gotten maybe two hours of sleep last night, tops. "Of course I look horrible."

"Well, indulge your mother in a conversation, would you?" my mom said briskly. I could hear shuffling papers in the background even though it was ten o'clock in the evening—burning the midnight oil in her home office then. "You didn't answer any of my texts yesterday."

Telling my mother the real reason why wouldn't have gone over well, so I settled instead for, "Yeah, I'm sorry, Mom. I got caught up editing the first bit of my manuscript."

Well, *rewriting* would've been the more appropriate word, but the specifics didn't matter so much.

"It's been a little hectic and . . . stuff," I continued lamely. "But I'm doing well. *Really* well, I promise. Adele's having me help in the shop more and I've gotten to hang out with Suruthi and Percy—the two from my class I was telling you about earlier?"

These half-truths were sort of keeping the feeling of guilt at bay. Maybe they weren't outright lies, but it still felt an awful lot like I was being dishonest, and I couldn't really see any other way around it. God only knew what had transpired between Adele and my mom during the private half hour conversation they'd had over the weekend, where Adele had somehow managed to convince my mom to let me stay, so I wasn't about to push my luck any further.

"Stuff, huh?" My mom had one eyebrow raised as she started flipping through a green legal pad full of notes. "Elaborate, please."

"Oh, you know," I said, clearing my throat. "If I'm not in class, I'm writing or spending time with Adele and a bunch of antiques."

I spent the next few moments spinning a few tales about the adventures in writing I'd had with Percy and Suruthi lately. I wasn't sure if I'd managed to convince her of anything by the time I ended the call, but we'd at least avoided the topic of Ashley's disappearance—for now.

I dragged myself out of bed and padded my way down the hallway into the kitchen where Adele was seated at the table in the small nook, a book and a cup of tea before her, like every other morning since I'd first arrived in London.

"There's a fresh coffee on the counter for you," she said, looking up with a smile. "I heard you on the phone with your mother," she added at my confused look.

"Oh. Thanks, Adele."

I joined her at the table with my coffee and we sat in silence for a bit while she read, and I sipped at my drink.

"So," Adele said when I returned to the table with a refill of coffee. She'd set aside her book and was drinking from her tea-cup. "How's class been this week so far?"

"Weird," I said immediately.

It was the only adjective that made sense: *weird*. Bizarre might've also worked in this context too.

"Weird," Adele repeated. "Weird in what way?"

"Weird in the way that one of my classmates is still missing and we have no idea what happened?" I said helplessly. "I don't know, Adele. The professor doesn't seem to be handling the whole thing very well."

Adele frowned, and took her next sip of tea through pursed lips. "You know, Jules, I'm sure we could still arrange for you to go back to—"

"I'm okay to finish the seminar, honestly," I said quickly, trying to stop her before she could finish her sentence. "Everything being weird, it's not *bad*. It's just weird, that's all. Nothing I can't handle, I promise. I'm not about to waste this trip to London."

Adele's expression turned thoughtful as she sipped more tea. "I think you've far from wasted this trip, Jules. Based on what you've told me, I imagine you'll still be in touch with Percy and Suruthi long after the seminar's over."

"You might be right," I agreed. If the heart-to-heart we'd had yesterday sitting on the floor in the hallway of Chatham Hall was anything to go by, I'd already found myself with two *very* good friends. "At any rate, I'll be excited to see what happens next... I think."

I finished my second cup of coffee while Adele drank the rest of her tea, then dragged myself off to the bathroom to get ready for the day. I'd checked the email app on my phone about a dozen times once I'd showered, dressed, and attempted to do something presentable with my hair and a bit of makeup.

I spent most of the journey to Chatham Hall wondering what surprise might be waiting for us in the classroom this morning—if Professor Watson even showed up. Maybe yesterday had just been a fluke. For all we knew, the professor could've had some twenty-four-hour bug and hadn't been able to send out a mass email cancelling class.

I'd almost had myself convinced we'd all but imagined yesterday's unusual events by the time I was inside Chatham Hall and walking up the stairs to the classroom. When I didn't see Thierry camping in the hallway outside the door, I figured it was a good sign.

Some of the tension I felt in my body started to ebb when I heard quiet conversation as I neared Room 217. Peeking inside just to be sure, I breathed a sigh of relief when I saw Percy and Thierry in their normal spots in the circle of armchairs and couch along with Professor Watson.

I nearly tripped over my feet on my way inside when I got a better look at the professor. It was almost like looking at another person occupying the same armchair. Compared to the other day, Professor Watson was an entirely new person; he was clean-shaven, hair neatly combed, dressed smartly, just like every other day since the start of the seminar.

This was a good thing then. Right? Professor Watson was obviously doing better now.

"Ah, good morning, Miss Montgomery," Professor Watson said, nodding politely when I entered the classroom. "I trust you're well."

"Yep," I answered quickly. "I'm peachy." I'd taken my seat

next to Percy on the couch before I decided to just ask the burning question we were all probably dying to know. "And yourself, Professor? Are you . . . well?"

"I'm faring much better this morning, fortunately," Professor Watson answered breezily. "I'm afraid I was under the weather yesterday and I apologize I was not able to contact you and your peers to cancel class. Thank you for asking, Miss Montgomery."

Professor Watson's tone of voice had been perfectly pleasant, but it was the way he had averted his gaze to the journal in his lap as he spoke that was a little odd.

I snuck a curious glance toward Percy to see if he'd noticed the same thing, but he was caught up jotting something down in his own notebook.

It was mostly quiet until Suruthi came barreling into the room, firing off a rapid stream of apologies. She managed to conceal her shock at seeing Professor Watson looking so put together this morning and took her seat beside me, shooting me a look with raised eyebrows.

"Quite alright, Miss Kaur," Professor Watson said breezily. "Still two minutes to spare. Shall we begin?"

We got straight down to business like we were pulling overtime for having missed yesterday's class.

Professor Watson pulled out a packet of papers from a folder he'd gotten up to retrieve from his desk. "I've prepared passages for each of you from well-known pieces of literature loosely based on the topics of your manuscripts. I would like you to take the time to rewrite these in your own voice, using the characters you have developed thus far. I suspect this will take you some time, so no need to watch the clock."

Okay, this exercise I could handle. I'd done something

similar in my last creative writing class, so I could do this no problem. At least I thought so until I saw what neatly printed passage wound up in my lap.

"Uh, Professor?" I said, raising my hand. "I haven't read *Hamlet* since the tenth grade in high school."

I was struggling to find any similarity between my developing manuscript and this passage. Here Hamlet was being confronted by the ghost of his dead father for the first time, so obviously the topic had to be a murder. I was pretty sure that was the route I was headed down in my manuscript—a mystery needing to be solved around an unexpected murder—but I was still remarkably undecided.

"Indeed," Professor Watson remarked. "And this worries you?"

"Well, no," I said carefully. "I'm just not sure that I'm familiar enough with the passage."

"Yeah, I agree with Jules, Professor," Suruthi chimed in. She looked a little nervous as she held up her own passage. "I can't remember the last time I read *Murders in the Rue Morgue*."

Thierry interjected then with a short monologue on the fine choice Professor Watson had made in choosing *The Scarlet Pimpernel* for him that left all of us rolling our eyes.

"And, er, *The Princess Bride*, sir?" Percy added last, looking mildly embarrassed.

"Indeed," Professor Watson repeated. "A fine piece of literature, don't you think?"

"Of course," Percy said quickly. "It's a wonderful story, but I don't know if I . . ." He shrugged in defeat when he couldn't seem to find the words to finish his sentence. "Alright then. *The Princess Bride*."

Professor Watson spent the next few minutes explaining the finer points of the exercise. "If you'll recall, I mentioned at the beginning of this seminar that the finest authors of our age are said to have stolen from other authors. This is what I'm asking you to do here. I want you to consider what you can draw on from these passages that you might implement in your own writing. What are the themes? The motivation behind the characters' actions?"

I looked down at the printed sheet in my lap, skimming over the passage again.

I supposed I liked Shakespeare well enough, but the ye olde English language that was his style sometimes left me more confused than anything else. The passage was short, so I could probably pick it apart easily enough, but the prospect was still intimidating.

Professor Watson had shared with us such specific expectations that I wasn't sure I wouldn't completely mess up by missing some minute detail he wanted us to focus on.

"Take all the time you need," Professor Watson said. "And do not hesitate to ask me for assistance if you should find that you need it."

Right, I thought. *Because that's something I'm comfortable doing.*

After our one-on-one conference about my manuscript outline, I wasn't going to be asking Professor Watson for any kind of help unless absolutely necessary.

Once he'd decided we were ready to tackle the exercise, Professor Watson retreated to his desk in the corner and left us to get to work.

Suruthi snatched a pillow off the couch and promptly

stretched out across the floor, highlighter in hand. Thierry went to some desk on the opposite side of the room while Percy stayed put, biting his lip as he got to reading his passage from *The Princess Bride*.

I made myself comfortable on the other end of the couch after I pulled a pen and my notebook out of my bag.

"Alright, Hamlet," I whispered to myself. "Let's do this."

I'd gone through the passage about three times before I felt like I was somewhat understanding what I was reading. There was one bit of lines that stood out to me in particular:

Ghost: *Revenge his foul and most unnatural murder.*
Hamlet: *Murder?*
Ghost: *Murder most foul, as in the best it is.*
But this most foul, strange and unnatural.

Strange and unnatural. The words kept floating around my mind as I began to write my opening scene. My main character had just been questioned by the police and was left pondering what happened to her friend . . . a lot like what I had recently experienced.

The whole experience was strange and unnatural. But those types of things happened all the time. *Strange and unnatural.*

Strange, like Ashley's disappearance. Unnatural, because it went against what I had learned of her character so far.

"Jules?"

I looked up, startled at the sound of my name, and found Percy leaning toward me.

"You alright?" he said quietly. "You've been mumbling to yourself."

"Oh, sorry," I said automatically. "Just . . . thinking."

Percy grinned. "I gathered as much. A murder most foul, I imagine."

"Murder, murder, murder!" Suruthi sang from on the floor. "For once, I think I'd rather *not* talk about murder." She sat up, fixing Percy with a devilish little smile. "Let's talk about *the most passionate and purest kiss in all of history.*"

"That is *not* the passage I was given," Percy said firmly. "So put a sock in it, Suruthi."

She burst into laughter. "As you wish. Lucky you weren't given *Romeo and Juliet*, eh?" She threw me a playful wink before she lay back down on her pillow, picking up her highlighter and the passage Professor Watson had given her.

"Please tell me you've taken to ignoring her just as much as I have," Percy said to me in an undertone.

"Yeah, a bit," I said, trying not to grin.

For the sake of staying focused, it was probably best *not* to think about the words *kiss* and *Percy* in the same sentence. I needed to get back to the subject at hand: murder.

I'd made decent progress—at least I thought I had—in my rewriting of the scene when the silence of the classroom was disturbed by a jaunty little ringtone that sounded like a bunch of bells.

Professor Watson stood up at his desk, cell phone in hand, grimacing at whatever caller ID must've been showing him. "My apologies, class. I'll be back momentarily."

He walked swiftly from the classroom, answering the call with a quiet, "Hello?"

Professor Watson had only just disappeared through the doorway before Suruthi leapt to her feet and quickly crossed the room. I thought she'd been off to the bathroom, but it became obvious what she was doing a second later: she was making herself comfortable at the door to eavesdrop on Professor Watson's conversation.

"Suruthi Kaur!" Percy hissed after her. "What do you think you're doing?"

"Oh, don't get your knickers in a twist, Perce," Suruthi said, flapping a hand. "He's gone down to the end of the hallway, so I can't hear much. I only want to watch."

"That's beside the point!"

"*Will you two be quiet*?" Thierry demanded crossly from his corner. "I am trying to concentrate here."

I stayed put, even though I was itching to get up and do a little snooping with Suruthi. The only other time I'd seen Professor Watson take a phone call, he'd seemed to have ended up in a pretty bad mood. If he was stepping out to answer another call, I wondered if it was because he wasn't going to enjoy speaking to whomever was on the other line.

Suruthi spent a minute peeking out into the hallway before she reported, "He looks angry now, to be honest. A bit of hand waving going on."

I gripped my pen tightly. Here was another thing that was strange—maybe not unnatural, but still a little strange, because we didn't often see Professor Watson angry, did we?

"*Suruthi*." Percy gave an unhappy moan. "Would you just stop it?"

"Nah," Suruthi said happily. "Gathering evidence. He's been chatting with those detective constables for days and he's been pretty tight-lipped about it. I want to know what they're up to."

"Don't you think the police would've contacted us if they actually needed something?" Percy asked.

Suruthi didn't answer, just let out a squeak and came zipping back across the classroom. "He's headed this way!"

A moment later, Professor Watson was walking back inside, and his expression had gone from unpleasant to downright grim.

"Everything alright, Professor?" Suruthi asked casually from her spot on the floor.

"I ... apologize, class, but I'm afraid that I must end our lesson early today," Professor Watson said briskly as he went to his desk, gathering up his things and tucking them into his briefcase. "Detective Constables Evans and Thomas have returned and are requesting access to Miss James's dormitory. I am to provide immediate assistance. You may remain here if you'd like to continue your writing exercises, or you may leave, but please have your finished piece ready to share tomorrow morning."

I'd always thought the saying *quiet enough to hear a pin drop* was a weird one, but it was an accurate description of the silence that suddenly fell over the room. By the time my brain caught up with my mouth, Professor Watson was halfway out the door, and I was left scrambling after him.

"Wait, sir, did Evans or Thomas say if they needed to speak to us too?"

"No, they did not, Miss Montgomery," the professor answered stiffly, and with that, he was gone.

I could feel myself opening and closing my mouth, like I was trying to speak, and no words were coming out. I looked over at Suruthi for some sort of backup, but she looked just as confused as I felt.

Thierry, on the other hand, had no issue sharing his thoughts on the matter.

"Well, what did you expect?" he said, coming over to the circle of armchairs to grab the rest of his things. "Obviously they were going to look through her things sooner or later."

"Yeah, but . . ." I forced out, my voice sounding hoarse. "Don't you think they would've gone through her things the first time they came to Ashford?"

"Agreed," Percy said unevenly.

Suruthi was gnawing on her lip, occasionally glancing back toward the door. "Well, the police *are* incredibly short-staffed most of the time. Perhaps they hadn't the time."

"Well, it's good they are looking now, yes?" Thierry said, heading over to the classroom door once his possessions were in hand.

"I thought you didn't care that Ashley is missing, Thierry," Suruthi reminded him helpfully.

She'd used Professor Watson's preferred armchair to push herself up off the floor and had taken a seat, watching Thierry curiously.

"That's correct. I feel nothing at all," Thierry said. *"Au revoir."*

The moment Thierry left the classroom, Suruthi was on her feet and went to stick her head out into the hallway again.

Percy groaned. *"Oh no."*

"What?" I muttered. "What's wrong?"

"I *really* don't like that look she's got on her face."

"What look?"

Percy was right to have been wary. When Suruthi turned to face us, still standing in the doorway, she was twirling a small gold key ring around her index finger with a devious little grin.

"Oh no," I said.

"Oh *yes!*" Suruthi said excitedly. "*Obviously* we are going to need to return the professor's key ring and *obviously* the safest place for them would be in his office."

Percy was on his feet in a flash. "Absolutely not, Suruthi. I seem to recall us having a conversation the other day about breaking and entering being frowned upon in this country. How'd you get those anyway?"

"Ah, don't be a spoilsport, Percy!" Suruthi said, now bouncing on the balls of her feet. "Besides, it's not breaking and entering if I've got a key, is it? Maybe the professor left them behind for us to find."

"More like they fell out of his pocket," I said dryly.

"We are *not* about to break into the professor's office," Percy said, moving around the couch to confront Suruthi. "Forget it."

Suruthi's face turned exasperated. "I'm not suggesting we steal anything, just return his keys!"

I took a step back when Suruthi looked to me for backup, palms up. "Don't drag me into this."

"Oh, come on, Jules!" Suruthi whined. "You're American, aren't you?"

"What's that got to do with anything?" I said, now thoroughly confused.

"You're from the home of the brave!" Suruthi said, like this should've been obvious to me.

"You're talking about committing a *crime*, Suruthi!" Percy exclaimed before I had the chance to answer.

I couldn't help it at this point; I slapped a hand to my forehead, unsure if I wanted to start laughing or cry out of frustration. First, a writing exercise that made me want to bang my head against a wall. Second, the police were now requesting Professor Watson let them do a search of Ashley's dorm. And now Suruthi wanted to sprinkle in a little B&E on top of it all.

What on earth had this day turned into?

"*Listen*, you lot," Suruthi said, her tone abruptly serious. "We all want to know what's going on with Ashley's disappearance. If the professor isn't going to tell us and the police aren't going to give us the time of day, then we're going to need to push back a little, aren't we? *Maybe* Professor Watson's taken those detective constables back to his office for a chat first and *maybe* we just so happen to overhear their conversation on our way to return the professor's keys to him."

"That's still a bit of a stretch, don't you think?" Percy said nervously. "We can't just—"

"Fine then," Suruthi said loudly, speaking over Percy. "I'll just go return the professor's keys myself."

And then she turned on her heel and went from the room in a flash.

"Do we just . . . let her go then?" I said, glancing at Percy.

Percy's answering sigh sounded a lot like someone who was carrying the weight of the world on his shoulders. "Of course we've got to stop her."

I was surprised at how quickly I was on board with this. Going after Suruthi seemed like the more exciting option compared to working on my pitiful attempt at a rewrite of a scene from an old play.

We snatched up our things and dashed out of the classroom after Suruthi in enough time to see her disappearing around the corner at the end of the hallway with a swish of her skirt. I was suddenly thankful I'd decided to wear slip-on shoes today instead of my sneakers, otherwise I would've tripped on my laces and fallen flat on my face as Percy and I took off running.

It wasn't even that long of a distance from Room 217 to the end of the hallway, but I was just about gasping for air by the time we rounded the corner. Suruthi was already skidding to a stop in front of Professor Watson's office door, fiddling with the key ring.

It was impressive the way Percy zipped past me with his much longer strides and managed to reach Suruthi just as she was beginning to try the first key in the lock.

"You are going to get us in *trouble*!" Percy huffed, trying to snatch the keys from Suruthi. "Give me the keys, Suruthi."

Suruthi easily slipped out of Percy's grip and jabbed him in the stomach with her elbow when he turned around to reach for her again.

I was wheezing by the time I reached the two squabbling right outside Professor Watson's office. "Seriously, you guys," I struggled to say between gasps for breath. "We're going to get caught!"

Suruthi must not have heard me. She somehow located the correct key without even trying and had the office door unlocked a second later.

I watched Suruthi's face fall as she stood in the doorway to the office. She'd gone from excited to confused in a heartbeat, and Percy looked the same as he peered over Suruthi's shoulder.

When a raspy, deep voice suddenly joined in the foray, causing us all to freeze right where we stood.

"Well, I say. I was beginning to wonder whether you would ever cease the inane chatter and unlock the blasted door."

CHAPTER

YOUR SCHEDULED PROGRAMMING WILL RETURN AFTER THESE BRIEF MESSAGES

Sometime in the future—decades from now, probably—I was going to be impressed with how quickly I managed to pull myself together once I saw what, or rather *who*, had been holed up in Professor Watson's office.

The man was sprawled in an old, winged armchair that sat opposite a small black-and-white television perched on a folding table, slippered feet propped up on the narrow windowsill. The armchair was surrounded by empty teacups, a bunch of candy wrappers, and cigarette butts. There was barely any space left for the one bookcase and desk stuffed in the corner of the office. The overall effect was alarmingly claustrophobic.

Possibly strangest of all were the stacks of coins *everywhere*—lined up neatly on the windowsill next to the man's feet, in a circle along the edges of the bookcase, some copper or silver, some smaller than a dime, and others that looked the size of my palm. If there was some kind of treasure chest hidden away in here too, the professor would have himself a decent replica of the Pirates of the Caribbean ride at Disneyland.

"Do come in," the man said, gesturing at us with a spoon. He was halfway through a carton of ice cream and his gaze hadn't once left the television. "And shut the door if you would, please. I've found you students make far too much noise always stomping up and down the hallway like a herd of elephants."

Suruthi opened and closed her mouth several times like she was trying to say something, but nothing was coming out. I wasn't fairing much better.

"Sorry, what?" Percy blurted out, his voice several octaves higher than normal. "You want us to—*hah*?"

The man sighed heavily, finally dragging his attention away from the TV to look at us. "I said, *do come in*. And I might recommend you close your mouth before you attract every insect in the country."

That was when my brain seemed to catch up with the rest of my body and I was suddenly shouting, "*You!*"

Just a few nights ago we had discovered someone snooping around after hours in the antique shop, intent on stealing an old microscope, and now that someone—the man Adele had called William—was frowning at me with a rising sense of contempt. "Have we met, young lady?"

Had we—?

"Yes, we've met!" I exclaimed. "You're William, right? You're the one who's been breaking into my aunt's antique shop trying to steal old science stuff! By the way, would you like your lock picking kit back? Thought you would've come back for that once you realized it was gone."

William's frown deepened as he tapped his spoon on the rim of the ice cream carton. "Old science stuff, you say?"

"*Yes!*"

He shrugged after a very long, uncomfortable pause. "I'm afraid I don't recall."

"*Excuse me*? You were just—"

"Let's not argue with the man, Jules," Percy cut in, grabbing my wrist.

I'd started marching into the office without realizing it, pointing threateningly at William. "But just the other day you were—"

"Yes, Jules, perhaps he simply has an identical twin brother," Suruthi added unhelpfully.

"Oh, *c'mon!*" I said. "I'm not about to just let this guy—"

"So sorry to interrupt, sir." Percy raised his voice to drown out mine. "We'll just be on our way now."

"Please stay, by all means," William said, stabbing at the carton of ice cream with his spoon. "It has been some time since I have last entertained guests, but I believe I remember how."

"No, no, that's alright," Percy said with an anxious laugh. "We'll just be—"

"May I ask what you three think you're doing?"

I imagine jumping headfirst into an icy lake would feel a lot like the sensation that hit at the sound of Professor Watson's curt tone. I figured it wasn't necessary to turn around to face the professor, because I could hear perfectly well by his voice that the professor was *not* happy.

"John!" William gave a happy wave with the spoon, mouth full of ice cream. "How kind of you to join us. Please, have a seat."

"I think not, Holmes." The professor's voice had become frosty. "Did we not agree that you would stay put and *not* open the door?"

"But I did not open the door," William said, now sounding bored. "Your students had that honor. I have been here, in your office, like the obedient little schoolboy you desire. I will require more ice cream, however."

"*Oh?*"

Suruthi, Percy, and I exchanged looks and we all seemed to be of the same mind: we were going to have to fess up to breaking and entering. We turned around as one to face Professor Watson. He had not moved from the doorway, and I saw I had been right, of course; he was obviously upset.

"Yeah, about that, sir," Suruthi said, forcing a chuckle. "Well, you forgot your keys, you see, and we wanted to . . . return them."

"Indeed," Professor Watson said, not buying the lame excuse. "How very kind of you, Miss Kaur."

"Oh, no need to thank me, Professor," Suruthi told him. "I'm always looking for ways to help."

There was a loud bark of laughter from William. "What amusing students you have, Watson. I'm curious to know how their writing abilities compare to their intellect."

"Please, Sherlock, save your commentary for another time," Professor Watson said, exasperated. "Preferably when I am not deciding on the best way to address my students' breaking and entering. Perhaps with expulsion from my seminar?"

I gaped, Suruthi immediately looked nauseated, but it was Percy who said, far too loudly, "You must be joking, right, Professor?"

"I beg your pardon?" Professor Watson said, taken aback. "I sincerely hope you are not questioning my reasoning, Mister Byers."

"That—that man—" Percy jabbed a finger at William, now

back to watching the TV. "You—his name is—it's not *seriously* Sherlock, is it?"

"What's that got to do with anything?" Suruthi hissed at Percy. "I think we have more pressing matters at hand!"

Percy looked like he'd become hot under the collar as he rounded on Suruthi. "Do you—that is—are you really not seeing what I am here?"

"That depends," Suruthi said. "Let me borrow your glasses."

"*No*, that's not what I—surely you—" Percy gave an aggravated huff as he shoved his glasses up to rub at his eyes. "That is—*their names*. The professor called that man Holmes, not William, and he's John Watson? All the—the stories? *Surely* you at least know that the stories—"

Hearing those two names aloud, one after the other, had the pieces falling into place as I finally understood what Percy was getting at. His joke from the other day in Oxford came flitting across my brain.

So that makes his full name Doctor John Watson. You know, like from the Sherlock Holmes stories?

The next words out of my mouth were, "This is some sort of joke, right?"

"Please tell me you understand now," Percy said to me, sounding desperate.

"Understand *what*?" Suruthi demanded impatiently.

"Oh dear," William—Holmes?—commented, followed by a little *tsk*. "It would appear your little game has been found out, Watson."

Professor Watson had become very still as he witnessed our back-and-forth. I thought I'd gotten pretty good at reading facial expressions, but the professor was a blank slate, and I had no idea what to think. Instead of answering, he stepped inside his office and shut the door. Before he turned to face us again, I heard him give one *very* world-weary sigh.

"Would you care to join us then?" Professor Watson said to Holmes.

"No, indeed," Holmes said, casting aside the now empty ice cream carton. "I'm rather anxious to finish this series. But, please, don't let that stop you from sharing our sordid history with your students."

Professor Watson quickly crossed the room, jostling Percy to the side, and snatched the TV remote off the small table to shut the thing off. "This is really *not* the time, Holmes."

Holmes tilted his head back, exhaling slowly, his eyes closing briefly.

"Well?"

Holmes took his time responding to the professor's prompt, digging around in the pockets of his tartan bathrobe. He came up with a bag of nuts and popped a few in his mouth, chewing as he said, "How may I be of assistance, Watson?"

"Holmes." Professor Watson pinched the bridge of his nose, eyes squeezed shut. "Do not speak with your mouth full, I beg of you."

"Might I point out that *you* prompted *me*," Holmes said when he was done chewing.

There was a red flush beginning to creep up the professor's neck; give it another minute and there would probably be steam coming out of his ears too. "Do not attempt to change the subject. Clearly, we have more pressing matters at hand."

"Indeed." Holmes nodded toward Suruthi, Percy, and me squished in the corner. "The presence of your students when you have kept me prisoner in your office does seem out of character for you, Watson."

He was almost sneering the word *prisoner*, and by the look of the place, maybe that wasn't an inaccurate term.

"I did not imprison you," Professor Watson snapped. He seemed to have forgotten we were even in the office as he spoke to Holmes. "I have insisted you stay here for your own *safety*, Holmes. You know you cannot continue to simply go gallivanting across London all on your own. Times have changed. It's not the same as it was in our day."

As in our day. What was that supposed to mean?

"Oh no?" A dark look crossed Holmes' face. "If you are not keeping me prisoner, then why do you lock the door?"

"For your safety!" Professor Watson exclaimed. "You cannot deny that you have become even more reckless, Holmes. I am concerned you are not . . . taking your own well-being into account!"

"Psh." Holmes waved a dismissive hand and tossed back some more nuts. "I have been traversing London on my own for well over a century now. One might argue it was far more dangerous *in our day*."

"Was it not just last week you threw yourself off a bridge into the Thames?"

In the time it took me to blink once, Holmes was upright in his chair, brandishing what looked like some kind of rusted coin at the professor. "For *this*, John. I have told you countless times."

"Adding to your ridiculous collection of currency is *not* worth throwing oneself off a bridge," Professor Watson said sharply. "Do not compare the two."

Everything that had rapidly unfolded since Professor

Watson's sudden arrival had been strange enough. Now it was downright bizarre.

I tried to do the mental math as Holmes and Professor Watson devolved into more squabbling. In the end it didn't matter once the realization hit me like a lead brick.

Holmes. Watson. *Well over a century.*

Now I knew this had to be some massive joke.

"Hang on," I interrupted loudly. "Could we, like, back up here for a second?"

Professor Watson looked almost surprised to see the three of us in his office when he turned at the sound of my voice. "Yes, Miss Montgomery?"

"Clearly you two have some deep-rooted issues to work out amongst yourselves, probably with the help of a good therapist," I said. "But before you do that, could you *please* explain what exactly is going on here?"

There was a long, uncomfortable silence.

Then Holmes gave an unpleasant laugh as he wadded up his empty snack bag and chucked it on the floor. "Oh, Watson, what a truly spirited pupil you have. Magnificently outspoken, I daresay."

"This isn't the nineteenth century, Holmes," Professor Watson told him. "Most women in this day and age have no sense of the meaning of the word *demure*."

A snort of laughter escaped from me before I could choke it back.

Demure was hardly a word I'd ever use to describe myself, and apparently Suruthi found the humor in it too, seeing as she was now giggling along with me.

Percy still hadn't stopped staring at Holmes and Professor

Watson as though they might suddenly disappear if he so much as blinked.

"Well, I would invite you to have a seat, but . . ." Professor Watson gestured at his office at large like it needed no further explanation.

There was still an unnaturally tense atmosphere in the room, but Holmes and Watson no longer seemed like they were about to start throwing punches, so that probably had to count for something.

"No matter," Holmes said, distracted with his pockets again.

Professor Watson shot Holmes a dirty look. Holmes simply smiled in return when he looked up. It was not a very nice smile.

"I believe this is the part where you begin to *tell our story*, although I must ask that you stick to the facts, Watson, and save us all your overly romanticized opinion."

"Yes, *thank you*, Holmes." Professor Watson perched himself on the edge of his desk, crossing his arms. "I intend to."

Holmes shrugged. "Simply offering my assistance, old boy."

Professor Watson looked ready to snap at Holmes again about talking with his mouth full, but Suruthi spoke up before he could.

"Oh, *please* don't start squabbling again. Could you just tell us whatever story you've made up to explain how bloody weird this thing you have going on is, and then we can be on our merry way?"

For some reason Professor Watson smiled at Suruthi's comment. "You wouldn't be the first to make that request. I am sure you're aware by now that I've made at least a partial living off making up stories. And I must ask that what you are about to hear does not leave this room."

The professor may have used the word *ask*, but one look at the expression that crossed his face made it clear that he wasn't asking—he was telling us. I wasn't keen on finding out what would happen if we chose not to listen.

I heard a gross slurping noise that I quickly realized was Holmes sucking up a few gummy worms he must've found in his pocket. "A loose interpretation of the word *living*, I would say, but please continue, Watson."

Now that's interesting, I thought, taking note of the look of disdain Holmes was doing nothing to hide.

Professor Watson ignored Holmes, giving us his undivided attention as he spoke again. "As Mister Byers so helpfully pointed out, Holmes and I do in fact share the same names as the world's first consulting detective and his assistant whose adventures were first published over a century ago."

"So you must *really* be into cosplay," Suruthi said. "Good on you."

"Beg pardon?" Holmes and the professor said in unison.

"Cosplay," Suruthi repeated. "You like to dress up and parade about pretending to be a fictional character."

Professor Watson looked somewhat stunned at Suruthi's explanation before he looked over at Holmes, and they both sported wry smiles.

"Yes, fictional characters," Holmes said, popping another gummy worm in his mouth. "Perhaps that's it."

The urge to laugh was beginning to build up again because what *was* this? We were currently standing in a room with two grown men who I could tell were about to tell us what had to be the most ridiculous story of all time.

On the first day of the seminar, I had picked up on the fact that Professor Watson was a little odd, quirky maybe, with his out of style clothing and old-fashioned way of speaking, but the man was also a writer. Usually, a strong imagination and a creative streak went together with being a writer, so I hadn't thought much of it. The professor was simply good at his job.

Now though? I could hardly be sure I hadn't walked into some freakish nightmare.

"Cosplay aside," Professor Watson said. "The facts are these: we are the very same Holmes and Watson from those stories, or rather summaries, of cases we actually did solve. *I* wrote them, you see."

17
CHAPTER

Is This Considered Copyright Infringement?

There was nothing but silence in the wake of Professor Watson's bold statement.

I stuck my index fingers in both ears to make sure my hearing aids were working properly; everything checked out there.

The first to break the silence was Percy. It wasn't a gush of awe like I might've expected, seeing as he was our resident Sherlock Holmes fan. It was rather a blunt, "Now I know you really are taking the mickey."

Gaining momentum, Percy's voice got a lot louder as he went on. "Your biography on Ashford's website said you used to be a doctor, didn't it? So obviously you would know that *human beings are not immortal.* You—you'd have to be, what? Over one hundred and fifty years old?"

"Give or take a decade, yes," Holmes said thoughtfully. He'd plowed through the gummy worms and seemed to be on the hunt for another snack. "What say you, Watson?"

"I believe so," the professor agreed slowly. "Although the years do start to blur together after the first century or so. I do appreciate your skepticism though, Mister Byers; however, I assure you, I am not taking the mickey."

Percy went to me and Suruthi for backup, but I was beyond lost. None of what Professor Watson or Holmes had said so far made an ounce of sense. How could it have made any sense?

"So let's say we humor you for the sake of this little . . . exercise," Suruthi said, clearing her throat. "What about the author, Conan Doyle? I thought he was supposed to have written all the Sherlock Holmes stories."

Professor Watson answered her question far too easily. "In name only. You know I was once a doctor, and so was Sir Arthur Conan Doyle. We were in the same year together in our schooling. After I was sent back to London to convalesce from the war and I'd taken up a flat share with Holmes, Arthur and I crossed paths when Holmes and I were working one of our very first cases together."

This had Holmes chortling. "*A Study in Scarlet*, I remember. You've always had a flair for the dramatic, haven't you, Watson?"

Professor Watson pointedly ignored Holmes's comment and kept going. "One of the things we were taught in our studies was to document *everything*. A written record of each patient we saw would be invaluable should we need to refer to them later, and for future record, of course. This I did from the moment Holmes and I first began working together.

"When I'd shared with Arthur what I had compiled after the completion of our first case, he encouraged me to share with the public. I had little desire to, but Doyle was . . . persuasive. I agreed to share my chronicles on the condition that they were published under Arthur's own name. From then on, the profits were split between the two of us accordingly."

I raised my hand without thinking and then felt heat rush to my face as everyone stared at me.

"Yes, Miss Montgomery?" Professor Watson said. "You needn't raise your hand to speak. We're not in class."

I quickly dropped my hand. "Right. Sorry. But—well, okay, my question is, supposing all that you're telling us is true, how are you and Holmes still alive? You don't look that old. Maybe fifty, tops?"

"Not entirely incorrect," Holmes reasoned. Their smiles were growing a lot bigger.

"Ah . . . okay," Suruthi said slowly. "I suppose that makes sense."

"No, no, no." Percy shook his head, somehow managing to pace in the small office. "No, I am sorry, but none of this makes one ounce of sense! Those Watson and Holmes stories are fiction, and you can't tell me that you honestly expect us to believe you were both born in the eighteen hundreds. It *isn't* possible. I'd like to see you produce one shred of evidence that you are who you say you are."

"You cannot fault the boy there, Watson," Holmes said. He'd somehow managed to produce a giant Toblerone bar from somewhere and was pointing it at Watson. "Perhaps you should go procure some proof. You could always find a way to *accidentally* injure yourself to demonstrate you no longer bleed."

"The only one who will be sustaining any injuries is *you*, Holmes," Professor Watson said darkly.

Holmes gave a humorless laugh. "Are we to come to fisticuffs here in your office, John, or shall we perhaps step into the ring this time? You might insist my *mind isn't what it used to be*, but I assure you, I still remember how to fight."

"Now you've done it," Suruthi said in an undertone, nudging Percy. "They're going to have a scrap right here in this office and it'll be all your fault."

Professor Watson drew himself to his full height as he took a step closer to Holmes, who quickly abandoned his chair to stand as well. Holmes was only a few inches taller than the professor, but his overly lean figure and the way he stared Professor Watson down made him seem *much* taller.

"I would not even entertain the idea, Sherlock," Professor Watson said in a frighteningly calm voice. "Now sit down."

"I think not. I'd rather we address the issue here and now."

And with that, Holmes gave Professor Watson a good wallop over the head with the giant Toblerone bar.

"Oh, dear," Percy said. "Er. Perhaps we should—"

"See ourselves out," I finished, and Suruthi quickly nodded in agreement.

"Yes, let's."

Trying to politely excuse ourselves wound up being pointless, as the two gentlemen were now otherwise occupied; Professor Watson had somehow managed to get Holmes in a headlock, and Holmes was attempting to beat the professor again with the candy bar.

"Yeah, I don't think we're going to be missed," I said once I'd shut the office door behind us.

Percy winced when a loud crash came from inside the office, followed by a colorful array of curse words.

"They remind me of my brothers," Suruthi said. "We should go before the professor changes his mind and decides to expel us."

We quickly made our exit, down the stairs, onto the first floor, and out into the courtyard. We hadn't been running, but I'd broken out into a nervous sweat anyway, and my heart wouldn't stop beating painfully against my chest.

"Can we—sorry, can we just stop for a second?" I said breathlessly, stumbling over to a stone bench to sit down. "Let's take a breather."

"I feel as if we should keep going," Percy said, glancing over his shoulder at the building. "Before we get beaten with a giant Toblerone bar too."

"Did you see the way they were going at it?" Suruthi said. "I'm thinking it'll be a while before they wrap things up in there."

"Yeah, okay, but still," I said. "Were you listening to a word the professor and that man were saying back there?"

Suruthi pondered this for a moment. "A bit. Honestly, I was a little distracted by all the eating Holmes was doing. I'm not sure if I'm impressed or horrified at everything he put away."

"I think more concerning would be the fact that Professor Watson got into a physical altercation like that," Percy pointed out.

"So," Suruthi said to Percy. "Do you believe me now?"

"About what?"

Suruthi threw up her hands with a disgusted scoff. "That the professor is a nut, obviously!"

"No, he isn't." Percy's answer was surprisingly calm. "The professor isn't a nut. Holmes, on the other hand . . ."

The jury was definitely still out on Holmes.

Suruthi gave an unhappy moan, literally stomping her foot. "No, no, no, *no*. Don't do this to me, Percy Bysshe."

"Do *what*?" Percy demanded. "I haven't done anything."

"Oh, yes, you have!" Suruthi said. "Please don't tell me you're actually starting to *believe* all this, Percy. *Please*. I know you've always been obsessed with Sherlock Holmes, and you love the stories and whatever, but any of what Holmes and Watson said back there? It's all nonsense! There is no way on earth any of it could be true!"

Percy hesitated just a moment too long to deny Suruthi's accusation, so she rounded on me next.

"Back me up on this one, Jules. Please tell me you think this is a load of rubbish too."

"It's all a load of rubbish," I said quickly, stumbling over my words.

"I *never* said I believed any of it," Percy cut in, sounding exhausted. "But—"

"What do you mean, *but*?" Suruthi said shrilly. "There shouldn't be any *buts* about it. The professor's having us on and Holmes is obviously a very good actor. *None of this is real!*"

Logically, I knew Suruthi was right. She *had* to be. Things like *eternal life* or *immortality* were concepts that didn't have much base in reality. Those fantasy-like themes were better suited for a Tolkien novel or a low-budget vampire movie.

I was unnerved though at Professor Watson's intensity as he'd shared his backstory with Holmes. He'd spoken as if he genuinely believed every little thing that had come out of his mouth—which was fair, I supposed. That was their truth.

The things they had said about wandering around London for over a century, being over a hundred-fifty years old, and especially the part where Professor Watson supposedly couldn't bleed . . . all that had the lovely side effect of leaving me thoroughly confused and unsure of what I had witnessed back in the professor's closet-sized office.

Percy took off his glasses to rub his eyes again and looked significantly more tired when he put them back on. "When you have eliminated the impossible, whatever remains, however improbable, must be the truth."

"That is ... okay, I guess. That's true," I said to Percy. "That's a weird way to phrase it though."

Suruthi let out a shriek between clenched teeth. "*Ugh*! He's quoting Sherlock Holmes at you, Jules!" She turned and started stomping her way down the sidewalk. "I'm going to go home now so I can pretend this day never happened!"

"Wait, Suruthi—"

"Let her go," Percy said, catching my arm before I could follow. "She'll be fine."

"I'll be fine!" Suruthi shouted back. She was already across the street, her skirt swishing angrily around her knees. "I'm not cross with either of you, I'm just lashing out because I don't know how else to handle the situation right now!"

She disappeared around the corner without another word, leaving Percy and me behind in a mess of confusion.

"That was . . . insightful of her," I said uncomfortably. "Now what?"

Percy looked pained for a moment as he tried to come up with an answer, and he shrugged. "Now maybe we follow suit, go home, and we also pretend like this day never happened."

I almost busted up laughing. I knew Percy had a giant anthology of Sherlock Holmes stories and we also had Google in our arsenal.

There was no way any of us were going to sleep a wink tonight.

Lying in bed that night, I almost wished my phone had been confiscated by the police again. It was well past midnight and apparently Suruthi was still awake too, sending links to articles or blogs to our group chat, every single one of them about Sherlock Holmes. She'd been doing this for some time, and every few minutes without fail I'd get a new message alert, LED light on my phone flashing with the notification, briefly illuminating the room before it inevitably happened again.

After the first few times this happened, I put my phone on *do not disturb* mode.

There had been nothing but radio silence from Percy. He was probably too busy reading every copy of Sherlock Holmes stories he could get his hands on. There was also the chance he'd given up and turned off his phone after Suruthi started up with the messaging.

When it became very obvious that sleep was probably going to evade me for the rest of the night, I caved and started scrolling through the links Suruthi had sent, because what else was there to do? She'd provided us with plenty of reading material.

Sherlock Holmes: Genius or Menace?
Debunking the Science of Deduction—Do Sherlock Holmes'
    Methods Actually Work?
Why We Can't Let the Great Detective Go: Holmesian
    Obsession in the 21st Century

The two that stood out to me the most were:

*The Overidealized, Codependent Relationship of Our
Favorite Consulting Detective and His Boswell
The Effects of Prolonged Cocaine Usage on the Brain*

Without the background knowledge of having read any Sherlock Holmes stories (that apparently our professor had written) not a lot of this made much sense to me. I kept reading anyway.

I'd spent two hours reading, maybe three, by the time I finally shut my phone off—not so much because I was tired, but more because I felt like my eyes were permanently crossed from having stared at my phone screen for so long. I chucked my phone on the floor and rolled over, covering my head with my pillow. I wasn't sure what I was trying to block out, but the virtual silence that came with it was strangely comforting.

I forced myself to close my eyes and my breathing eventually began to even out, but I still didn't feel anywhere near falling asleep. The events from this afternoon kept replaying behind my closed lids, one after the other in quick succession. There was Holmes towering in the doorway to the professor's office; Professor Watson's thunderous expression when he found us in conversation with Holmes. The way he had so casually announced that *he* was responsible for all of the Sherlock Holmes stories, that they weren't fictional characters, but actually two very real, very much *alive* men who were supposed to have been born sometime in the Victorian era.

But there were significantly more important things at hand that were more grounded in reality—like the fact that *Ashley was still missing.* Suruthi had made a pretty good point earlier; if the police were so eager to keep to themselves, we needed to come up with a way to stay in the loop. But apparently that way was not going to involve Professor Watson.

It's not true, I kept telling myself over and over again. *It's not true. This* can't *be true.*

I'd been a pretty average student when it came to subjects like science, but as far as I was aware, nobody had yet cracked the code behind halting the aging process. Assuming that people could realistically live well beyond one hundred fifty years, wouldn't Holmes and Watson have looked *very* shriveled and wrinkly by now? Percy had been pretty spot-on when he'd made the comment that they didn't even look middle-aged.

My brain was unhelpfully offering the suggestion that maybe Holmes and the professor were actually vampires. The only problem with that theory was again that whole point of immortality not being a thing. There was also the fact that Holmes hadn't stopped eating once during that incredibly awkward interlude today and I'd seen Professor Watson drink dozens of cups of tea at this point. If they *were* vampires, surely they would've had a few bags of O positive tucked away somewhere. And there was the whole thing about not being able to go out in the sunlight, but maybe Professor Watson or Holmes had perfected some sort of vampire sunscreen that would protect them during daylight hours—Holmes *was* supposed to be a genius after all.

I groaned, wondering how difficult it would be to smother myself with a pillow. I was currently lying in bed and wondering whether my professor was a blood-sucking mythical creature. Maybe my mom had been right, and I needed to book myself a ticket on the first flight back to California.

18

CHAPTER

Earl Grey, No Sugar

Another first I got to experience while in England was screaming the moment I first opened my eyes the next morning.

I'd mostly gotten used to the vibrating alarm clock that a lot of people with hearing loss used, so that wasn't responsible for my suddenly racing pulse and the scream in my throat—it was Adele hovering over me. That, or the bizarre dream I'd been having about Ashley's vacant seat in Room 217.

Adele leapt away with a wince, so I must've been screaming *loudly*.

"*Ack*! What the—*Adele*! What are you doing?!"

Adele's lips were moving frantically, but whatever she was saying was completely lost on me, and then I realized it was because I didn't have my hearing aids in.

"Hang on," I forced out, holding up a finger. "Just let me—" I snatched my hearing aid case off the bedside table, got the things in my ears, and turned on. "Okay, now go for it."

"I'm *so* sorry, darling," Adele burst out at once. "I didn't mean to frighten you, only it's half past eight, and your seminar—"

"*What?*"

I leapt for the alarm clock on my bedside table and felt my gut constrict when I saw Adele was right. It *was* half past eight in the morning and Chatham Hall was not close by; I'd be lucky if I could make it down to the Tube before nine o'clock, which was exactly when the seminar was supposed to begin.

"I meant to wake you earlier," Adele was going on remorsefully, "only I lost track of time when Mindy showed up early, and I—"

"It's fine! It's fine," I said, tossing my alarm clock aside and scrambling out of bed. "I'll just get going, it'll be fine."

It was not *fine.*

My suspicions were proven correct when I was squeezing my way through the crowd of Londoners trying to start their morning by catching the Underground too and it was already pushing nine-fifteen. I'd thrown on the first shirt and pair of pants I could get my hands on, chucked all my things into my bag, and literally run out of the shop, but I still hadn't been fast enough.

I spent most of the ride mentally berating myself for sleeping through my numerous alarms—something I hadn't done often since the vibrating alarm clock. Then came the barrage of text messages, mostly from Suruthi but also one from Percy, and all variations of: WHERE ARE YOU?!

I broke into a run as soon as I was off the Underground. My lungs were burning, there was an awful stitch in my side, and I was grossly sweaty when I went zipping through the courtyard outside Chatham Hall and inside the building.

My knees nearly buckled more than once on the stairs and I clutched at the handrail for support, desperate to reach Room 217 before the clock struck ten.

In the end it didn't matter because for the second time this week, the classroom door was shut and locked when I tried the handle.

This time I was *sure* I could hear voices behind the door—something that sounded like one dramatic soliloquy with a French accent. So class was still in session then; I was just *very* late.

I rapped my knuckles on the door, still breathless when I called out a hesitant, "Hello?"

Silence fell beyond the door, and it swung open a beat later, Professor Watson standing before me. He'd been wearing a lot of different expressions on his face throughout yesterday, but today he was sporting a new one: disappointment. That was somehow the most unnerving.

It was enough—at least for the time being—to make me forget all the outlandish claims he'd been making yesterday because I *hated* having someone disappointed in me.

"How kind of you to join us an hour late, Miss Montgomery."

"Professor, I'm *so*—"

Professor Watson held up his hand, cutting me off mid-sentence. "No apologies necessary. However, this seminar begins promptly at nine o'clock."

"But—"

"I do not condone tardiness, and as such, I'm afraid you'll be unable to join your peers today. You are free to join us again tomorrow morning, provided you arrive *on time*."

And with that, Professor Watson shut the door in my face.

There were a lot of thoughts that crossed my mind in the wake of being so sternly dismissed. The one that I said aloud to the closed door was, "That's awfully hypocritical of you, sir."

Hadn't the professor been seriously tardy just the other day? *Ugh*.

What was I supposed to do now?

I really wasn't feeling up for the interrogation Adele would hit me with if I went back to Dreams of Antiquity so soon. I supposed holing up in one of the study rooms downstairs and trying to slug my way through my manuscript was an option.

Instead, what I found myself wondering was, what episode of *Fortune and Glory* was Holmes watching now? And given the rate he'd been plowing through all that candy, he'd probably be due for a restock right about now.

My feet took me down the hallway toward Professor Watson's office seemingly all on their own, and I decided to go with it. Confirming for myself that I hadn't imagined all that had occurred yesterday seemed like a pretty good use of my now open schedule.

I was taking all the articles and blog posts and the one YouTube video Suruthi sent to the group chat last night with a grain of salt. It would've been a different story if any of those articles had come from, say, Arthur Conon Doyle—alleged close friend of Professor Watson and the public face of the original Sherlock Holmes stories—but I thought I had a pretty good understanding of the "great detective" based on what I'd read.

Most of what I understood was the following:

- The man was a genius (obviously)
- He seemed to have a strong sense of *right* and *wrong* while also occasionally operating in morally gray areas
- His methods were unorthodox, to say the least
- He seemed like a horrible person to share living quarters with

- Doctor John H. Watson was probably the closest thing he had to a friend in this world

Helpful as this information was, it still didn't do much to confirm whether Professor Watson and Holmes were telling the truth. The scuffle with the Toblerone bar yesterday hadn't done them any favors either.

I hesitated in front of the professor's office door, fiddling with the lock picking kit I'd been keeping in my bag. What if Professor Watson had decided it was too much of a risk to continue keeping Holmes in his office?

Or there was also the chance I'd imagined the entire exchange yesterday. But the fact we'd caught Holmes (apparently *not* William) trying to pull a heist in the antique shop a few days ago left me with a smidge of doubt concerning whether he and the professor were actually telling the truth.

It took several attempts with the lock picks to get the office door unlocked thanks to my fumbling fingers.

"I must congratulate you, young lady, on *finally* opening the door."

I exhaled shakily, trying not to scream when I came face-to-chest with Holmes standing right in the doorway. The tartan bathrobe was gone today, replaced with a loose-fitting pair of slacks and button-down, and instead of a chocolate bar, he was currently chewing on what looked like black licorice.

"*Thanks,*" I said, my voice coming out in a squeak. "I mean, thank you."

So, apparently, I hadn't imagined the entire thing yesterday. I still pinched my forearm as discreetly as I could manage, just to be sure.

"And how may I be of assistance?" Holmes asked, leaning against the doorjamb. "Shouldn't you be occupied with your studies?"

"No," I said, tucking the lock picking kit away in my bag. "The professor banned me from class today because I was tardy."

Holmes chuckled around a bite of licorice. "Oh dear. I trust you've learned your lesson on the merits of punctuality, young lady."

"Actually, I've come to spring you," I said.

Holmes raised a brow. "*Spring* me?"

"Yesterday you said you were being imprisoned here," I reminded him. "And I *did* just open the door."

"Indeed," Holmes agreed. "What, may I ask, are you proposing?"

I placed a cup of steaming tea in front of Holmes, per his request. "*Voilà*. Earl Grey, no sugar. Enjoy."

Holmes pursed his lips as he inspected the cup of tea, then leaned over to sniff at it. I supposed for cajoling a suddenly-not-fictional-after-all character to join me for a cup of coffee—or in this case, tea—he could've made a bigger fuss. A giant carton of ice cream might have also worked in this case too.

He was still eyeing the cup of tea like it might grow a pair of legs and scuttle off the table when I sat down and started picking at my maple scone.

"Something wrong with the tea?" I finally asked when there seemed to be no end to his brooding.

Pouting might also have been a good word.

"This is a tea bag," Holmes stated.

"That it is," I said. "It's all they had at the counter."

Holmes exhaled harshly, nostrils flaring. "I see."

"Okay," I said. "I'm probably going to regret asking, but is there something wrong with tea bags?"

Holmes must have taken this as permission to do a deep dive into the science behind brewing tea. "These *sachets*, as they are called, do not allow the tea leaves to properly steep due to the constriction of—"

"You know, I could take that back for you instead," I said. "Get a refund. Watching me drink my coffee and eat my scone will be much more enjoyable, I'm sure."

Holmes's lips twitched like he was considering smiling and shook his head, grudgingly taking a sip of tea.

I began to take some mental notes as I munched on my scone. There I was, sitting at a table in a café with someone who insisted they were *Sherlock Holmes,* of all fictional characters, and it was quickly becoming one of the most awkward experiences I'd had to date.

"Out with it then, young lady. I am growing tired of your gawking."

"Excuse me?" I set my coffee down on the table a little too forcefully. "I am not *gawking.*"

"You are incessantly *staring,*" Holmes said impatiently. "You obviously have several burning questions you desire to ask me, and if this is to be repayment for *springing* me from that office as you so put it, then I suppose I must answer them. So, if you would be quick about it, I would be much obliged."

Well, he wasn't wrong. And if Holmes were giving me permission . . .

"Okay," I said. "Sure. So, is it true?" My voice kept dropping as I leaned across the table toward Holmes. "Everything that the professor said yesterday. That you guys are ... whatever it is that you are. Immortal?"

"Dull." Holmes made a face as he took a sip of tea and shuddered. "But yes. I regret to inform you that it *is* true; however, I am not sure immortal is the most appropriate term to describe our current living status."

What was the comment Holmes had made yesterday in the professor's office?

A loose interpretation of the word living, *I would say ...*

"Then what other word would you use besides immortal?" I said. "Eternal? Everlasting? Did you both drink from the fountain of youth maybe?"

Holmes snorted into his cup of tea. "Certainly not."

"Then *what*?"

Holmes set his cup of tea down, resting his now clasped hands on the table before him. "Next question."

I gaped at him. "What? Why? That's an easy one!"

"*Next*," Holmes repeated firmly.

"Yeah, okay, fine." I swallowed down some more coffee before I scooted my chair closer to the table. The place was decently busy, and I didn't really want to take the chance someone might overhear us and suggest we contact a mental health hotline. "Did you really solve all those cases the professor wrote about?"

"Your professor tended to produce sensationalized versions of the cases we worked on together," Holmes said, sounding just the slightest bit fond. "But again, my answer is yes."

"So, in that case, you're a genius," I said. "Highly intelligent and a brainiac and all that."

"Indeed," Holmes agreed.

"Modest too, I see."

"My dear girl, I never claimed to be modest," Holmes said, back to chuckling again. "I only wish to state the truth. Do go on."

I copied Holmes and put my hands on the table before me, lacing my own fingers together. I was trying to sift through the mental catalogue of interesting tidbits about Holmes that I'd filed away from all my late-night reading. Truthfully, I had *a lot* of questions, but some I wasn't sure I could get away with asking outright.

Like, *If you're such good friends, why did you look like you wanted to murder Professor Watson yesterday?*

I pulled a random question from my mental list and went with it. "So why do you eat so much candy?"

"I beg your pardon?"

"The *candy*," I said again. "You were just eating licorice not a half hour ago and yesterday, with the sour gummy worms and chocolate bars and—"

"Yes, I understand, thank you." I couldn't figure out a name for the look that crossed Holmes's face as he leaned back in his chair. *Amused* was a possibility, maybe with some exasperation. "But please, continue. I would very much like to hear more of your *observation* of me."

"Well, you're a slob," I said, diving right into it. "Okay, maybe slob isn't the right word, but you're not the neatest person. Your bathrobe yesterday had a bunch of stains on it, and you clearly don't care about keeping the professor's office clean, which makes sense, because you said he was *imprisoning* you there. Obviously, you're somewhat resentful of him, although I'm willing to bet there's a whole lot more going on than all of what we heard yesterday."

"Obviously," Holmes agreed. "Go on."

I faltered here a bit. "Um."

"*Go on*," Holmes pressed.

"There were a bunch of empty cigarette packs and ashtrays on the floor yesterday too, so you're obviously a smoker."

"Not Watson?"

"Maybe," I said. "But I don't think so. He's never smelled *too much* like smoke before and you're the one who was sitting surrounded by every ashtray under the sun yesterday."

"I see," Holmes said.

There was more awkward silence as I tried to think of what else to say. The whole interaction in Professor Watson's office yesterday couldn't have been more than fifteen minutes.

But then again, hadn't Holmes also been snooping around the antique shop lately?

"You might also be a kleptomaniac," I blurted. "Seeing as you tried to steal from my aunt's antique shop."

Holmes choked a bit on his tea and puffed up indignantly. "I beg your pardon. I am *not* a thief. I intended to *pay* for that microscope." He set the cup of tea down, his scowl deepening. "A kleptomaniac, I ask you . . ."

"Okay, so then you're impatient," I said. "You couldn't have waited until normal business hours to come in and *pay* for that microscope like anyone else would've done?"

Holmes did that lip twitching thing again. "Is there no end to your impudence, young lady?"

"Probably not," I said. "Are my observational skills not up to your standards, sir?"

"I should think it obvious that they are not."

"Glad we've got that settled then, I guess." I finished off the last of my scone before I asked my next question, but when I opened my mouth, nothing sensible seemed to come out. "So . . ."

"So," Holmes repeated, his expression flat. "If that is all you intend to ask me, I must say I'm rather disappointed."

"Why *disappointed*?" I demanded, trying not to feel offended.

"But no matter," Holmes continued dismissively. "Although I am loathe to admit it, I *have* been mistaken once or twice, although I hardly think I—"

"Are you really addicted to cocaine?" I blurted without thinking, then winced.

Smooth, Jules, I thought.

The glare Holmes fixed me with made me wish I could teleport. "And may I ask where you happened upon that information?" he asked frostily. "Is *that* my lasting contribution in this world? Not the results of my numerous academic findings, or the criminals I brought to justice and the cases I solved, or—or—*anything but cocaine*."

I held up my thumb and index fingers to Holmes with a small sliver of space between them. "A bit. Everyone thinks you're a fictional character though, so that's got to count for something, right?"

There was one moment where our eyes met again, and Holmes looked as if he might've been over a hundred years old. It seemed like the look of a person who was very, *very* tired—in more ways than one. The look was gone by the time he had shifted in his chair and choked down some more tea.

"I am not an addict," he began tersely. "I never *was* an addict." Holmes pressed the heel of his hand to his forehead, his eyes shut tight. He didn't speak for a few tense moments. "I do not think my mind has ever been . . . I have never been able to . . .

to sit idly by and not do *something* of value, something produc-tive. I *need* stimulation. I simply cannot be without..."

I waited patiently, sipping at my coffee, until Holmes had stopped clutching a hand to his head like he was experiencing a migraine.

"I don't imagine you get much stimulation from watching television all day, do you?" I said.

Holmes's short laugh was a bitter one. "You would be cor-rect; however, I haven't found any better alternative presently."

Or, my brain supplied, *you don't have permission to.*

"So ..." I took in a breath, holding on to my coffee cup with both hands, looking anywhere but at Holmes.

There was no getting around it: this was awkward. Whether or not Holmes was a literal man out of time, how was I supposed to lead a conversation?

My gaze landed on a lone figure on the sidewalk outside the coffee shop. The man was dressed in a police uniform and seemed to be on patrol, carefully observing his surroundings. Or rather, he was probably *supposed* to be on patrol, but the man looked bored out of his skull.

And that was when, seemingly out of nowhere, the idea fell into my brain.

"So," I said again. "You're probably looking for some stimu-lation then, I imagine."

Holmes's eyes narrowed as he stared at me over the rim of his cup of tea. "I do not like the expression that has come over your face just now, young lady."

I brushed that comment aside, leaning closer toward Holmes across the table. "Well, I have a ... let's call it a mystery that I think you might be able to solve."

Now that the figurative dam had been broken, there was no stopping the rest of the words that came tumbling out of my mouth in a rush.

"One of the professor's students went missing last Friday and the police seem to think that it's a simple teenage runaway situation, but I'm not entirely convinced they're giving this case the attention it deserves."

The fact that Detective Constables Evans and Thomas hadn't even bothered to give me their business cards had stuck with me like an itch I couldn't scratch, and I hadn't been able to let go of it yet.

I couldn't tell at first if Holmes looked eager to hear more or if he was just annoyed. "Watson has alluded to this, I am aware. Unfortunate, to be sure, but what do you propose *I* do about it?"

"Just . . . *something*, I guess," I spluttered out. "You're supposed to be a genius, right? You're looking for stimulation and I want to know what happened to my classmate."

Holmes drank some more tea through pursed lips. By the time he put his cup down, I was practically squirming for an answer.

"What is your personal involvement in this matter?"

"Excuse me?"

"You are choosing to ignore the police when they have, presumably, informed you that they are *handling it*," Holmes said, making quotation marks in the air. "You have a personal investment in the disappearance of your classmate. I want to know what it is."

My mouth opened and closed several times as I struggled to come up with a response, but no sound came out. Then I started to wonder, what did I really have to lose by telling Holmes the truth?

"I . . . I was there, or, um, *close by*, when she disappeared," I said weakly. "But I have hearing loss, so ... I mean, *I know* there's something I probably missed, but ..."

I shrugged helplessly, unable to finish my sentence. I doubted I'd be able to come up with an adequate explanation for how personally responsible I felt for Ashley's disappearance—however misguided that thought was.

Holmes looked far from satisfied with my answer. "I am afraid I am going to need more information than that. Your own sentiments on the matter will hardly be of any assistance."

"But—"

My voice died in my throat when my phone chirped loudly where it rested on the table beside my plate, and I quickly snatched it up.

Please tell me you didn't go far, the message from Suruthi read. We have GOT TO TALK.

"We've got to go," I said quickly, shoving back from the table to stand when I saw the time. "They're going to break for lunch soon and the professor will—"

Holmes was on his feet and halfway out of the coffee shop by the time I could blink, leaving me behind to scramble after him. I tossed out another, "Sorry!" to the annoyed-looking barista behind the counter and flew out the door after Holmes.

Somehow Holmes had already made it down the sidewalk and was about to cross the street toward Chatham Hall. This wasn't normally a crowded street, but it was today, and I'd nearly lost sight of Holmes in a gaggle of tourists shuffling by. Holmes had only gone about two steps into the street before he collided head-on with a bicyclist.

I came up short and could only watch in horror as Holmes hit the ground and was quite literally *run over.*

19

CHAPTER

The Game Is—Maybe?—Afoot

Utter chaos descended upon the street. There was a lot of shouting in surprise and a few onlookers running over to help, some yells of pain from the bicyclist after he'd gone flying over the bike's handlebars. This left me in a panic trying to find Holmes in all the hubbub, struggling not to elbow people out of the way for a better look.

When I did manage to locate him a moment later, he was simply picking himself up like he hadn't just been run over, fixing his shirtsleeves and dusting off his hands. The bicyclist was still on the ground, bleeding from what looked like a serious gash on his arm.

I may have had difficulty making much sense of the things I heard for a while now, even with the help of hearing aids, but at some point, I had decided that I could usually trust the things I saw.

And what I'd just seen was Holmes get plowed over by a bicycle without sustaining any kind of injury—none that was obvious, at least. He was simply standing there, rubbing a hand across the back of his neck as he looked upward at the sky like he was merely contemplating the weather.

I skirted around the group of people attending to the bicyclist and went to Holmes, asking at once, "Holmes, are you alright? That looked like a nasty fall."

He looked down at me in surprise. "You're late."

"I'm—what?"

"You are *late*," Holmes repeated. "I sent word requesting you meet me promptly at ten o'clock in the morning. It is nearly midday."

He was waiting expectantly, obviously wanting an answer, and I was completely lost. What was he talking about?

"I think you might be a little confused," I said carefully. "You've never sent me any note and you've been stuck in the professor's office this whole time."

Holmes made an impatient noise as he glanced over his shoulder. "I would hardly call my rooms at Baker Street an office and we will hardly accomplish anything by discussing your tardiness. Now, did you bring what I asked?"

I tried not to groan as I rubbed my forehead with the heel of my hand.

I hadn't spent enough time around the man to have a good idea of his typical behavior, but this was just weird. *What was going on here?*

"You didn't tell me to bring anything!" I suddenly burst out. "You're not making any sense, Holmes!"

"*Psh.* No matter then." He glanced over his shoulder in the opposite direction, like he was checking to see if he were being followed. "But we must make haste."

A second later I found myself being whisked down the sidewalk, tucked up under Holmes's arm. He had me pinned to his side with a surprising strength and it wasn't easy to keep up with his much longer strides. He was awfully energetic for someone who had just been run over by a bicycle, but maybe Holmes was made of stronger stuff than he looked. At any rate, with all the concern being paid to the man who flipped off his bike, there was no one there to question us as Holmes all but started to frogmarch me down the sidewalk.

"Hang on a minute, will you please just—"

"You read the case notes at least, I presume," Holmes said. "I know Lestrade is only *marginally* competent on the best of days, but the basic facts are there."

"Who?" I groaned when I tripped over my feet for the third time. "I don't know who that is!"

"Come now," Holmes said impatiently. "I am aware you are a novice, but I know you too have had to endure Lestrade's insufferable countenance on more than one occasion."

A novice? Of *what?*

"Listen to me, Holmes!" I managed to break free from his viselike grip and stumbled back a step. "I have no idea who—who Lestrade is and I'm not a novice *whatever* and I really think we need to take you to a hospital now because I think you got a concussion getting run over by that bike back there."

Holmes stared at me. He simply stared long enough to make me even more concerned when I noticed he wasn't blinking. Then the mumbling started. I noticed his lips moving a mile a minute but there was no way I was going to understand a word of what he was saying.

"*Yoo-hoo*! Holmes!" I waved a hand, trying to get his attention. It didn't work. "I wear hearing aids, so whatever you're saying, I don't understand, so can you—HEY!"

I shrieked at the sudden finger in my left ear and slapped Holmes's hand away. He looked mortally offended at this. "*What the—*?"

"I assume the device in your ears are what you called *hearing aids*, and I wish to see them more closely for myself," Holmes said, like I should've known. "I have never seen such a thing before. You cannot blame me for being intrigued."

"*Dude*! You don't just go around sticking fingers in people's ears!" I said shrilly. "I *know* people in the Victorian era didn't do that either, Holmes, so don't try to tell me they did."

Holmes frowned and looked for a moment as if there was more he wanted to say, then thought better of it. "No matter," he said again. "If you are going to insist upon it, we can discuss matters of etiquette later. We really must be on our way. Stamford has left the door to the morgue at Saint Bartholomew's unlocked, but only temporarily. We must—"

"*Whoa*, buddy. Hold up there for a second." I threw up a hand to stop Holmes when he attempted to grab me by the arm again. "I am *not* going to a morgue with you."

"Oh, no?" Holmes raised an eyebrow. "Surely you wish to see the remains of poor Miss Ramsey after all those sensationalist articles about her death that have been circulating."

Funny, I thought. I couldn't think of a time when I'd ever wanted to see a dead body, but hey—stranger things were *currently happening*.

"Uh-huh," I said. "Sure. And, uh, who was Miss Ramsey again? She—what did she like to do?"

Holmes rolled his eyes skyward. "*This* is why I insist you read my case notes ahead of time. Miss Ramsey was the most recent, unfortunate socialite to meet her end after perhaps spending too much of her time dabbling in the occult. She died just this last week in a most unusual manner after attending a séance. Not a drop of blood was left in her veins—allegedly."

Holmes's description had me fairly nauseated before he'd even finished speaking.

I didn't know much about séances or the *occult*. My only visit to the Winchester Mystery House in San Jose for my ninth birthday, supposedly one of the most haunted houses in the United States, had ended up a spectacular blowout between my parents. I hadn't absorbed much beyond the fact that Sarah Winchester, who apparently believed she was being haunted on the regular, liked to hold séances in one of her mansion's many rooms.

Even then, it did sound incredibly strange that a séance would end with someone dropping dead, and without any blood left in their body.

"I thought you just did some table tipping at a séance," I said to Holmes, still a little nauseated. "Maybe a little crystal ball gazing. How'd someone wind up dead?"

"That, my dear," Holmes said, tapping me on the nose with his index finger, "is merely *one* of many questions we must ask ourselves."

"And we need to go see the dead body, why?" I questioned carefully.

"Because although Watson and I have already examined the body, I wish to do so again before the young lady is buried tomorrow," Holmes said in an undertone. I had to lean closer as he continued, "I am convinced that there is *something* missing from the equation here. An otherwise perfectly healthy young woman does not simply *drop dead* without cause. I want to know why."

Don't we all? I thought.

"Hey, Holmes," I said as he began to forcefully lead me down the sidewalk again. "What's the date again?"

Holmes stopped long enough to toss a shrewd look my way. "August the seventh, eighteen hundred and ninety-nine."

"Oh."

"It would seem you are even more in need of further practice to better manage your time," Holmes said.

"Probably," I said.

I'd been over an hour late to Professor Watson's seminar this morning in the twenty-first century, and according to Holmes, I was just as tardy in the nineteenth century too.

And all this was leaving me stuck between a rock and a hard place. Five minutes of conversation with Holmes and it was obvious he was not even remotely in the present. I'd never read any of the Sherlock Holmes stories, so I had no way of knowing if the unusual death of Violet Ramsey was a case he actually solved, or if this was all made up and Holmes was putting on one Oscar-worthy performance.

We were getting farther and farther away from Chatham Hall and I was growing more and more nervous with each step.

What was I supposed to do here? Despite his lean stature, Holmes was deceptively strong, his grip on my shoulder like a vise, and I wasn't sure I could make a break for it so easily without him catching up to me right away. On the other hand, I also didn't want to just abandon Holmes on the street either. He may have kept insisting yesterday that he was fully capable of looking after himself, but I was sincerely doubting it now.

"Hey, Holmes," I said as casually as I could manage.

"*Yes*?"

"Isn't Watson supposed to be meeting us at the morgue too?"

The question made Holmes come up short. He'd already begun frowning in thought. ". . . is he?"

"Yeah! I mean, yes," I said quickly. "I didn't get your note, but I got the one Watson sent along, and it said he wanted us to get him from, um, Baker Street first so we could all go to the morgue together."

Holmes remained silent, and the expression on his face was becoming pained. He started massaging his forehead with the tips of his fingers as he sucked in air through his teeth. "Well, perhaps Watson . . . but no, I'm not sure if I . . ."

I knew I was going to spend a lot of time feeling guilty about this outright lying to Holmes, but I couldn't see any other way to get him back to Watson. I had to strike while the iron was hot.

"Why don't we go and find Watson, just to be sure," I said gently. "He's a doctor, right? It makes sense to have him examine the body."

That seemed to be enough to convince Holmes. He gave a jerky nod, turning back in the direction we'd come from. "Yes, perhaps we *should* go fetch Watson. Although I wonder if it would be easier if we hail a . . ."

I had to spend another minute convincing Holmes that it would be much better to walk instead of trying to find, say, a horse-drawn carriage, and then we were thankfully on our way back to Chatham Hall.

When Holmes suddenly stopped outside some high-end

boutique to pick up a few pieces of change off the ground, I quickly pulled out my phone and shot off a text to Suruthi and Percy:

Send Watson outside ASAP. I've got Holmes.

I received no reply, but one of them must've gotten the message, because Watson was already waiting outside in the courtyard by the time we reached Chatham Hall. Holmes, who had previously been playing with the few coins he'd found, perked up at the sight of Watson and quickly strode over to him once we'd dashed across the street.

I was dismayed not to see Percy and Suruthi in tow, but knowing the professor, he'd probably made them stay put.

"Ah, there you are, Watson!" Holmes cried, slipping the coins into his pocket. "Please tell me *you* are prepared to visit the morgue at Saint Bartholomew's, unlike our companion here."

I could tell for one moment that Watson, while obviously *very* angry, was confused at Holmes's remark, but caught on very quickly.

"I am afraid not, Holmes," Watson said, clapping Holmes on the shoulder. "I was hoping to discuss Lestrade's case notes with you before we went to examine Miss Ramsey."

"It does one well to be thorough," Holmes agreed, "but I insist we be quick about it. I do not know how long we will have access to the morgue before Stamford returns to lock the doors."

"Indeed," Watson said. "I believe we are in luck, as Mrs. Hudson has just prepared afternoon tea, and then we shall be on our way, I assure you. Come now, Holmes."

Given Watson's behavior and how he seemed to know exactly

what case Holmes was referring to, this couldn't have been the first time something like this had occurred.

Holmes was back to massaging his forehead and stumbled over his feet as Watson coaxed him toward the double-door entrance to Chatham Hall.

"I think it best you leave, Miss Montgomery," Watson said without sparing me a second glance.

"Professor, I'm *so* sorry," I said, trying to catch up with them. "I didn't—"

"Regardless of what you did or did not intend, this was very foolish of you," Watson said. He was radiating disapproval and it was awful knowing it was directed at me. "I trust it is evident now why I have been keeping Holmes in my office, where I can ensure his safety."

I most certainly understood that *now*. I was grateful we hadn't ended up lost in London or caught breaking into a hospital morgue. Also, I didn't have to see any dead bodies.

Watson disappeared inside with Holmes, and I opted not to follow.

I sat down on one of the stone benches instead and pulled my phone out again, sending another message to the group chat with Percy and Suruthi: Meet me after class gets out. We've got a lot to talk about.

20
CHAPTER

CALL IN THE TROOPS

W hat, no candlestick?" Suruthi said, grinning as she swept inside the antique shop.

"That one was sold a few days ago," I told her. "But I'll find an even bigger candlestick for you the next time you come over."

It was already decently late, but I had planned another meeting in Dreams of Antiquity with a specific purpose in mind this time around. After having spent the last several hours dissecting my unexpected "adventure" with Holmes that morning, I was in desperate need of consulting my friends.

Percy stepped inside after Suruthi and shut and locked the back door. I was surprised to find him looking so anxious as he stepped closer.

"Jules, are you alright?" he asked in an undertone.

"Yeah, why wouldn't I be?" I said. "I'm totally fine."

"Well, we could've done with a *bit* more of an explanation after your messages," Suruthi said to me. "Percy's been a right mess since this afternoon."

"*No*, I have not," Percy disagreed at once. "I was concerned, Suruthi, there's a difference."

Whatever reasoning they decided on, I still felt a rush of immense guilt.

"I'm sorry," I said. "Both of you. I didn't mean to freak you guys out."

"Ah, we know," Suruthi said, giving me a playful nudge. "Percy will get over it."

"I *wasn't*—"

"Now, are you going to tell us what happened on your little outing with Holmes this morning?" Suruthi asked.

I jumped right into a detailed account of what went down with Holmes earlier as soon as we'd taken our seats in my corner of the shop. I tried to give as much detail as I remembered—what Holmes said, how he seemed convinced I was some kind of apprentice detective, and the "mysterious death" of Violet Ramsey.

By the time I'd gotten through all of it, Percy and Suruthi were looking at me with such dumbfounded expressions that I couldn't decide whether they were frustrated or amused.

"Alright then," Suruthi finally said. "So, either Holmes and Watson are telling the truth and they really have been floating around London since Victorian times, or they both are exceptionally good actors. Which is it?"

"Percy, you're our resident Sherlock Holmes expert," I said to him. He hadn't said a word since he'd taken his seat on the floor by the armchair, and he might've looked a little green. "Was there any case about someone named Violet Ramsey that Holmes and Watson helped solve?"

Percy spent one long moment staring at his hands as if they might have the answer he was looking for. And his answer was, "No. Not that I can recall reading."

"Nothing about a séance or some sort of bloodsucking creature that went around killing people?" I pressed.

There had to be *something* we could work from here.

"I really don't think so," Percy said. "Granted, it has been some time since I last read anything from my Sherlock Holmes anthology, so I suppose it's worth another look."

It was a minor offer and maybe it wouldn't amount to much, but it still made me feel one small surge of hope.

"Well, there you go then," I said, clapping my hands together. "That's one hurdle down."

"One?" Suruthi repeated, raising an eyebrow. "You mean there's more?"

"Obviously," I said. "Ashley's still missing, and the police just searched her dorm yesterday, right?"

"Yes, but if they'd found anything, I would think Watson would tell us," Percy said. "Wouldn't he?"

"I wouldn't be so sure of that," Suruthi said. "According to Jules, he was caught up in going along with whatever memory Holmes was reliving. Also, are we just going to call him Watson instead of *Professor* Watson now? Because that's honestly much easier."

"Sure, let's go with that," I said. "Look, either way, I think we can agree that the police are kind of dragging their feet about Ashley. It took them how long to come back and search her dorm? Why couldn't they have just done that the first time they came down to question us?"

Percy seemed to seriously debate my question before he spoke, sounding like he was trying to convince himself of what he was saying too. "Jules, they're probably just understaffed. They're doing what they can to—"

"*Are they really?*" I wasn't sure when I'd gotten to my feet, but I was pacing now, trying to make sense of the million thoughts bouncing around my brain like a pinball. I knew Detective Constable Evans had made a fair point and I really hadn't known Ashley that long, but *still*. My gut instinct was telling me more was going on. One second Ashley had been there, the next she was gone, and somehow despite being only a few feet away, I'd managed to miss *everything*. "Look, you can choose not to believe me, but I was with Ashley right before she went missing. She was happy to have found the Narnia door, trying to call her grandmother, and she didn't even have a bag packed or any of her belongings with her. *Why* would she have run away? I'm telling you; this doesn't make any sense!"

"Okay," Percy said quickly. "Okay, that's a fair point, but you might want to lower your voice, Jules. You're shouting."

"Oh, sorry," I said automatically. "Sometimes I don't realize how loud I'm being."

There was a brief pause that left us all staring at each other expectantly, waiting for someone to say something. I didn't last too long before I gave in, almost stomping my foot in frustration.

"But *still*! Guys, something about this isn't adding up, and if the police are just going to treat Ashley as some teenage run-away on vacation, then I think it's time we do *a little sleuthing* on our own."

Percy caught on to it first, sitting up straight in alarm. "Oh, no. Please tell me you're not serious, Jules."

"It's not a bad idea, Percy," I said.

"No, I think it's a *very* bad idea!" Percy said heatedly. "You've literally just told us a story about Holmes thinking he was solving some case from over a hundred years ago."

Well, that one I couldn't wiggle out of. "Yes, but—"

"Can someone please fill me in here?" Suruthi cut in, raising her hand. "Preferably *before* you have your little romantic row."

Completely ignoring the teasing remark, Percy turned to Suruthi and said, *"A little sleuthing*, Suruthi."

That seemed to do the trick. Her eyes lit up and then she gave a disbelieving laugh. "You're not talking about asking Holmes to help us do our own investigation, are you?"

"That's exactly what I'm suggesting," I said firmly.

Backtracking somewhat, I went into more detail about my conversation with Holmes over tea this morning once the topic of his "recreational" drug usage came up.

"He said himself he needs the stimulation," I told Percy and Suruthi. "I don't think staying locked up in Watson's office is doing him any favors. He's obviously going stir-crazy, and I think he might actually enjoy the challenge. I mean, the man *is* supposed to be a genius, right? And between the three of us, I think we ought to be able to keep a hold on him."

"He's a grown man, Jules, not a dog," Percy said exasperatedly.

"And a grown man with memory issues who likes to wander," Suruthi added helpfully.

"I'm not suggesting we kidnap him or anything, *geez*!" I exclaimed. "All I'm saying is that I think it might be worth a shot having Holmes help us look around Ashley's dorm."

Suruthi seemed in on it after only a short moment to think it over. I'd sort of been expecting it, but I didn't think Percy would be so difficult to convince, as fond of the Sherlock Holmes stories as he was.

"What makes you so sure Watson hasn't whisked him off to

some safe house by now?" Percy asked me. "After your outing today, do you really think Holmes will be so easy to find?"

The question had me frowning.

"Maybe not," I agreed grudgingly. "But he's been getting out and about somehow. He's a frequent visitor here, remember?"

"That's fair," Percy said.

"Shall we put a note in the front window then to catch his attention and wait to see what happens?" Suruthi said sarcastically.

There was another bout of silence as we all tried to think this one through.

Percy didn't sound very confident when he finally spoke. "Well . . . I realize this might be a long shot, but there *is* the Sherlock Holmes Museum."

"There's the what?" Suruthi said, eyebrows raised.

"The Sherlock Holmes Museum," Percy repeated. "There's an actual 221B Baker Street here in London that was turned into a museum. It was created using descriptions of Holmes's and Watson's flat in the stories. Or that's what I've read, at least."

"Uh-huh." Suruthi rested her chin in her hand as she fixed Percy with a knowing look. "How much did your membership to this museum cost you?"

"I don't have a membership, *thank you*," Percy said frostily, but the tips of his ears had gone pink. "I'm just saying that it *might* be possible Holmes spends time around there, given that the museum literally looks like a Victorian residence, based on where he actually lived."

"I'm not so sure about that," I said, recalling one specific moment from my earlier conversation with Holmes. "I got the impression he only tolerates at best the stories Watson apparently wrote, and he *really* doesn't like it when you mention his, um, fondness for cocaine."

"That's fair," Suruthi said.

Percy threw up his hands with a huff of exasperation. "Then what do you suggest, Jules?"

"It's a bit of a long shot," I said warningly, "but I *do* have an idea."

It took about twenty-four hours after putting the silver coin roughly the size of a plum in the front window of Dreams of Antiquity before Holmes showed up. The coin was nestled in a plush red velvet case and glinted when the shop lights happened to hit it just right. I remembered having added it to the shop inventory the other day, after Adele's assistant had a laughing fit over how garish it looked. It was exactly the kind of thing I thought would attract Holmes's attention, and it sure enough did.

There had been some discouragement when I'd walked into Room 217 the next morning a full twenty minutes before class was supposed to begin and Watson, already seated at his desk, told me point-blank, "Sherlock is at home, *resting*. And I trust you understand now why I prefer to keep a close eye on him."

To say that Watson was disappointed about yesterday's events was putting it mildly, and in some ways, that was worse than him being angry. I couldn't stand it when someone was disappointed in me.

I wanted to think that I understood. If Holmes had just been plowed over by a bicycle and recently jumped off a bridge into the Thames, he didn't seem to be paying much attention to his own personal safety. Given that he had seemingly walked away uninjured on both occasions, maybe that was valid. But combined with the fact that Holmes wandered and occasionally happened to believe he was living in a completely different time period, we couldn't entirely rule out the potential for disaster lurking on the horizon.

Keeping Holmes locked away all day with an endless supply of junk food, cigarettes, and television didn't seem like a better alternative—even if it did ensure Watson could keep an eye on him.

Theirs was undoubtedly a complicated relationship—incredibly codependent, if I were to go by what that one article from Suruthi said—and there had to be a lot more behind the scenes that we weren't seeing. I also didn't see why that should stop me from providing Holmes with some mental stimulation.

"I suppose this was your doing and not your aunt's?" Holmes said as he removed a small magnifying lens from his pocket to inspect the coin.

After he'd shown up, I sent a quick *SOS* message to Percy and Suruthi, which was code for *get down to the shop ASAP*. Adele had seemed pleased when I'd offered to take *William* on a personal tour of the shop after my less-than-polite behavior the first time we'd met. It made the most sense to bring Holmes over to my favorite corner and let him *ooh* and *ahh* over the coin until Percy and Suruthi showed up.

"It might have been," I said. "It worked though, didn't it?"

"So it did."

It was fascinating watching Holmes inspect every inch of the coin under the magnifying lens. I had no idea what he was looking for, but he seemed a little disappointed when he tucked the magnifying lens away and returned the coin to its case.

"Of course you would happen to know the going price for such an antique," Holmes said, tapping a finger on the velvet case.

"There's no charge," I said quickly. "I'll give it to you for free."

Holmes didn't seem surprised by the offer. "In exchange for what?"

"My friends need to get here before I can explain fully," I said.

"Ah." Holmes nodded, as if this were acceptable. "The young man with the spectacles and the young woman who owns a wardrobe comprised of hideous shades of neon, I presume."

"Yep," I said awkwardly. "They would be the ones. But this is about our missing classmate who I told you about the other day."

Holmes didn't answer, just sat himself on the floor directly in front of the typewriter on the table, and the magnifying lens soon made another appearance. I forgot to keep track of the time as Holmes proceeded to inspect every inch of the typewriter like he'd done with the coin. He didn't seem as disappointed with the typewriter and kept studying it like it was one very fascinating specimen.

"I take it you collect typewriters as well as coins," I said as Holmes began pressing down on the first row of keys.

"Well, what else is one to do when one cannot eat or sleep?" Holmes said with a click of his tongue. "I have spent several decades finding ways to occupy my time, and the refurbishment of typewriters is merely one of them."

Percy and Holmes really were kindred spirits after all then.

"Hang on," I said quickly. "If you can't eat, what's with the candy all the time?"

"Insanity, perhaps," Holmes said thoughtfully, on cue pulling a piece of hard caramel candy from his pocket. He unwrapped it and popped the candy in his mouth. "I cannot taste anything, and I have not yet found any food that provides me with nourishment. I have run my own experiments, of course, but the only conclusion I have been able to reach is that I simply . . . exist. I can, and have, gone several weeks without food or drink of any kind, and it did not make one ounce of difference."

"So the candy . . . ?"

"Habit," Holmes said simply, pulling out another caramel. "But I suppose I don't break the habit because I still hope that one day I will be able to enjoy eating a simple meal again."

I considered telling Holmes that he was spot-on about the insanity bit; trying the same thing over and over again and expecting a different result was a pretty well-known definition of insanity. I'd also never thought I'd get upset over a few pieces of caramel candy.

"Maybe one day then," I said, feeling lame.

"Of course," Holmes went on, and I wondered if he was starting to speak more to himself than me. "Not *all* of us have similar struggles."

The bitterness in Holmes's voice was almost palpable, and it didn't take much guesswork to figure out who he was hinting at.

"I guess Watson must spend more time writing instead of looking at coins or typewriters with you then," I joked awkwardly.

Holmes was not amused. He looked ready to tell me as much when we heard a familiar voice coming around the corner.

"Sorry we're late!" Suruthi said cheerily, joining us in the corner. "I had to drag Percy out of bed."

"You did not," Percy corrected, rolling his eyes. "I was only a few minutes behind schedule, Suruthi."

"Either way, thank you for being here," I said, getting to my feet. "Holmes and I were just—wait, what are you doing?"

Holmes was resting his head against the typewriter, tapping the return key again and again as he listened to the sound of the thing jamming.

I shrugged helplessly when Suruthi looked at me questioningly. I didn't have a better explanation as to Holmes's strange behavior any more than she did.

"Er, Holmes, sir?" Percy said tentatively, inching forward. "That's really not a good idea. You might—"

"I might *nothing*," Holmes said, standing so abruptly we all leapt backward. "I know how a typewriter works. Now, if you would be so kind as to explain why my presence here is necessary, I would be much obliged."

"Go on then," Suruthi said, flapping her hands at me. "This was *your* idea, Juliet."

"Yes, I know, thank you," I said, bristling at the use of my full name. "I'm getting to it."

I let myself have about five seconds to be nervous and fret about Holmes's reaction before I made our request.

"Like I told you the other day, Holmes, one of our classmates is missing." It took some effort to ignore the burning urge to cry that was automatically creeping into my eyes. "It's been almost two weeks now and the police don't seem to have any leads. They think she maybe ran away, but I'm not buying it."

Holmes mulled this over for a solid minute. He didn't look disinterested, but he also didn't look eager to hear more. "And

I believe I have already asked this, but why should this matter concern me?"

Percy swooped in to answer before I could. "Because, sir, you're the world's only consulting detective and Jules thinks—okay, *we* think—that there's more going on that we're not seeing."

"Undoubtedly there is," Holmes remarked. "But again, I must ask why I—"

"Isn't it obvious?" Suruthi said with an exasperated huff. "We need your help."

Holmes arched a brow. "Oh? How so?"

"Now that you ask . . ." I reached behind the armchair to grab my bag and unzipped it, pulling out the lock picking kit still neatly tucked away in its case. "Given your track record, we figured you wouldn't be opposed to doing some breaking and entering."

CHAPTER

THE POLICE ALREADY DUSTED FOR FINGERPRINTS . . . RIGHT?

Balcombe Residence Hall was only a few streets over from Chatham Hall in the miniscule section of London that made up Ashford College, but it felt like we were stepping into an entirely different world. For one, Balcombe had clearly been renovated in the last decade, whereas Chatham looked as if it had been virtually untouched since the Second World War.

If it had not been for the fact that I'd been here once before to do a manuscript brainstorming session with Ashley and Suruthi just before our first conferences with Watson, I would've had no idea where to go.

It didn't feel right walking inside without Ashley leading the way up to her dorm, and that burning urge to cry was returning.

I'd been wondering if we would find yellow crime scene tape covering Ashley's door, but everything looked exactly the same as it had the last time I'd been here. The bronze emblem on the door announcing the dorm room as 3F was still there, along with the chips in the wood around the doorknob. I was tempted to put my ear to the door to listen, wondering if I'd be able to hear the sound of Ashley humming along with whatever she was listening to in her headphones.

"You okay, Jules?" Percy had been the one to nudge me instead of Suruthi, but they both looked concerned.

"Yeah," I said, swallowing hard against the unexpected lump in my throat. "Yeah, I'm fine. Let's do this."

"I'll take *that*, thank you," Holmes said, plucking the lock picking kit out of my hands the second I'd retrieved it from my bag.

He bent over by the door for a mere moment, and then the doorknob turned smoothly as he pushed open the door.

No one made any move to step inside.

There was still plenty of daylight, but the room seemed unnaturally dark, and there was some sort of draft emanating from inside that made it about ten degrees colder.

Percy cleared his throat a couple times before he said, somewhat shakily, "Well, ladies first."

"Oh, come on then!"

Suruthi grabbed my hand and pulled me into the room alongside her.

"Do not touch anything," Holmes stated, using his foot to swing the door shut. "If I am to be of any assistance, I must see things exactly as they are."

"Can we turn on a light at least?" I asked. "It's a bit dark in here."

Right on cue, the lamp set on the small desk flickered on, casting a dim glow around the room.

"Don't worry, I used the edges of my shirt to turn the light on," Percy said when Holmes turned a scowl his way.

"As I said, do *not* touch anything," Holmes repeated. "I also require complete silence in order to work."

Suruthi snapped a salute. "Yessir."

Percy, Suruthi, and I ended up standing shoulder to shoulder on the small rug in the middle of the room as Holmes got to work.

The room was rather nondescript; a small twin-sized bed against the wall, a desk, and an old wardrobe were the only pieces of furniture that had been provided by Ashford. There was a faint scent of mothballs and clean linen; otherwise, the place was empty.

Holmes went to the desk first, where we discovered each drawer was empty. The wardrobe was next, and I felt a jolt of excitement when I saw Ashley's duffel bag on the bottom shelf, surrounded by what looked like a pile of dirty clothes.

"See?" I whispered, nudging Percy. "Wouldn't someone who was planning on running away take their clothes with them?"

"Well, not necessarily," Suruthi reasoned in hushed tones. "If someone had to leave in a hurry, they—"

"*Silence.*"

Holmes somehow managed to search through the wardrobe without disturbing any of its contents, then moved on to the bed, quickly searching underneath it on his hands and knees. With a surprising amount of strength I didn't think him capable of, Holmes then lifted the mattress up with one hand to search beneath it.

"Alright, Holmes," Suruthi said when he'd carefully put the mattress back in place. "Let's hear it."

"*It?*" Holmes said, rising to his feet.

"*It,* as in your deductions," Suruthi explained. "What has that great big melon of yours come up with about Ashley?"

Holmes looked somewhat offended at Suruthi's tone but answered anyway. "Nothing that would be of use, I fear. The occupant of this room is neat, but not overly so, and clearly is not intending on staying here a great deal of time, given the lack of personal items." He wandered over to the desk again and ran his fingers over the scarred wood.

"Okay . . ." I crossed my arms, stuffing my balled-up fists in my armpits. "So, can you tell us if Ashley did run away? Or if she's planning on coming back?"

"I wonder if you might be exaggerating my capabilities, young lady. I am not a clairvoyant," Holmes said tersely. "If you intended for me to tell you where your classmate has gone, I am afraid that I cannot. Why she left I also do not know."

There was an interesting feeling taking hold over me listening to Holmes speak. Obviously I knew Holmes couldn't tell the future, but he was all about the past, wasn't he? There had to be something here he could use to tell us about Ashley or give us some clue about what she'd been planning—like maybe packing a smaller bag to run away.

"However."

My gaze snapped to Holmes at his sudden change of tone. "What? What is it?"

He was leaning across the desk now, peering down into the sliver of space between the wall. "If you were to ask me if I thought the young lady had planned to return, my answer would be yes."

"Wait, Holmes, what are you—"

It didn't seem to take much effort on Holmes's part to move the desk away from the wall. He stepped around it and bent down to grab what looked a small book with a dirty purple cover. Holmes flipped open the cover and I saw that rather than a book, Holmes was holding an iPad.

"Aged I may be, but I am not unaware today's youth live their lives bound to these cursed devices," Holmes said, thrusting the iPad at Percy. "If this young lady is similar to the rest of your peers, then I would hazard to say she would have taken this device with her, would she not?"

I inspected the iPad when Percy passed it to me after he had the chance to look at it himself.

"What d'you reckon, Jules?" Percy asked me.

"I think . . . Holmes might not be entirely wrong," I said, carefully considering my response. "This tablet is small enough Ashley could've put it in her purse. If she was going to run off, I bet she would have taken this with her. I know it's how she writes sometimes."

"Then how did the police happen to completely miss it?" Suruthi pointed out. She took the iPad next, trying to turn it on but with no luck.

"If they had been *looking properly*, they would've seen that cord," Holmes answered, motioning to what looked like a charging cable on the floor. "It appeared to have been threaded up the back of the desk in order to utilize the outlet behind it."

"So, for clarification," Suruthi said, crouching down to plug the charging cord into the iPad. "You're saying the police just weren't trying hard enough."

"Or apparently looking in the right places," I added.

Holmes shook his head with a short *tsk*. "That is certainly a possibility. The police are often out of their depth. That much has not changed a great deal over the last century or so, in my experience. It would not surprise me if that were also the case in regard to your classmate."

Suruthi set the tablet on the desk, and we had to wait a few minutes for it to turn back on with the battery having been completely drained. When the screen flickered to life, we were met with the picture of a dog with wiry brown fur wearing a red checkered tie on the lock screen.

"Cute," Suruthi said. "Any idea what the passcode is for this thing?"

"Oh," I said. "I hadn't thought of that."

"Well, we're going to have to proceed carefully," Percy said seriously. "Too many attempts using the wrong passcode and the device will lock itself."

"Yes, I know that, thank you!" Suruthi snapped impatiently. "If we could just—"

Suruthi's voice broke off when the iPad started ringing with an incoming video call. No one moved an inch as we all stared in horror at the name "Grams <3" flashing across the screen.

Suruthi shoved the iPad at me in a panic and I answered the video call without taking the time to consider how this would affect the other person on the line when they realized Ashley wouldn't be the one picking up the call.

"Ashley, *oh,* thank goodness you—" The elderly woman stopped speaking at once, and it was heartbreaking to see the way her face fell. "You aren't my granddaughter."

"No," I said quickly. "No, I'm so sorry, I—um. I'm—my name is Jules. I'm one of Ashley's classmates from the seminar."

"I see." The old woman nodded, her lips pressed together in

a tight line, and she was blinking rapidly. I was doing the same thing too, trying not to cry. "And you have her iPad, why?"

"Oh, I—that is *we*—" I gestured to Suruthi and Percy off screen even though she couldn't see them. "We just wanted to, um, hang out in Ashley's dorm for a while, maybe do a little bit of writing together."

The old woman did not look convinced. I couldn't blame her—it was a lame excuse. But it sounded a lot better than the truth: that we'd asked an apparently *not* fictional detective to do some sleuthing to see if there was something we were missing about Ashley's disappearance, and if that went well, could he possibly help us find her?

"I see," was all the old woman said.

"You must be her grandma," I said, feeling stupid, but I wanted to keep the conversation going. "Ashley, she—she talks about you a lot, but I don't think she ever mentioned your name."

The elderly woman gave a barely-there smile and I realized just how unwell she looked when she used one hand to fix the cannula in her nose used to administer oxygen. She was very thin, with dark circles under her eyes and thinning gray hair.

"My name is Edith." Edith spent another moment fiddling with the cannula before continuing. "Not that it isn't nice to meet you, Jules, but . . . well, foolish as it is, I've been calling Ashley religiously, hoping she might pick up."

Edith's voice cracked on the last word, and I felt my heart skip through a few beats.

"I'm so sorry," I said in a rush. "I'm so, *so* sorry. I wish there was a way I could—"

"Oh, you really don't need to apologize, Jules," Edith said, speaking over me. It sounded like this took her a lot of effort. "None of this is your fault."

Wasn't it though? At least somewhat. I'd been the last one to see Ashley. I'd been *there* with her when she'd disappeared.

"Well, is there anything we can do for you?" I asked. "I know we're in London, but maybe if we ..."

Maybe if we *what*? Held hands and put on a candlelight vigil, Ashley might be found?

Edith gave another halfhearted smile. "I appreciate you asking, but I don't think so. Although ..."

Her lips began trembling as she frowned, and I jumped on it. "What is it?"

"Did Ashley ever mention anything about wanting to see a friend?" Edith asked in a rush. "A friend by the name of Valerie."

It took me a full minute to decipher what she'd said, Edith had spoken so quickly.

"A friend," I repeated. "Um, no. Not that I can think of."

I looked at Suruthi and Percy and said, "Do you guys remember Ashley having said anything about wanting to see a friend?"

"No," Percy answered at once. "You both spent more time with her than I did."

"Likewise," Suruthi said. "Never heard a thing about a friend named Valerie."

"Ah." Edith cleared her throat a few times before she spoke again. She either looked very disappointed or very relieved. "Well, it was a long shot, but I did wonder ..."

"Should Ashley have mentioned anything about wanting to see Valerie?" I asked Edith.

I wasn't sure where this line of questioning was going, but

if there was any chance there was a *reason* Ashley would have run away...

"Valerie used to be Ashley's old babysitter when she was younger," Edith explained, her smile more of a grimace. "More like an older sister, really. They spent so much time together while I had to work to support us. She moved to Britain for schooling a few years ago and Ashley was pretty devastated. Can't remember what university she was going to, but last I heard, Valerie was only a few hours outside London. They've exchanged letters and had phone calls every now and then and of course Ashley always has a standing invitation to visit, but I never really considered that a possibility."

"Why not?" I asked.

"International flights aren't cheap, dear," Edith said, and I felt stupid for asking. "It's a blessing Ashley was able to fundraise the money she needed to afford your writing seminar."

At this point, I was willing to investigate any possible avenue that didn't suggest something bad happened to Ashley.

"Do you think Ashley would've run off on her own to go see Valerie?" I asked.

Edith shrugged. "Ashley likes to put on a brave front and act like nothing ever bothers her, but she was really upset when Valerie moved. Said she felt like she was being abandoned. I do know she would be thrilled to see Valerie, no matter how long it's been."

So maybe... maybe Ashley *had* gone to see Valerie. Why she would've needed to up and leave in the middle of a field trip to Oxford, I didn't have an answer though. Had she arranged ahead of time for Valerie to meet her there?

"And you... you told the police this, right?"

"Of course I did." Edith frowned. "They said they would follow up on it and *let me know.*"

Somewhere behind me I heard Holmes make one of those *psh* noises.

"Well, maybe that's where she's gone," I said, trying to muster up some optimism. "And she's just having trouble reaching out to you or something."

"Maybe," Edith said, and her frown deepened. "Although I have to ask. Did Ashley have her inhaler on her?"

Inhaler? I again looked at Suruthi and she was already shaking her head, mouthing, *I didn't know.*

"I didn't know she had asthma," I admitted. "I don't know if she had her inhaler with her or not."

"She's usually very good about keeping her inhaler in her bag," Edith said, a nervous edge creeping into her voice. "She hasn't had too many asthma attacks over the years, but . . . well, a grandmother worries, you know."

"I know she had her bumblebee pin though," I said quickly. "On the strap of her bag."

Edith's worried expression lessened just the slightest bit, and her smile seemed to reach her eyes this time. "Thank you for telling me that, Jules."

"Of course," I said. "We just . . . if there's anything we can . . . I mean, I just want to . . ."

This was strange for me, not being able to come up with the right words to speak. Thankfully Edith seemed to understand. I gave her my cell phone number and promised to reach out to her if I happened to hear anything from the police on this side of the pond.

When the video call ended, I shut the iPad off and set it on the desk, leaning against the edge for support.

"Well." Percy's voice sounded too loud in the empty dorm. "That was . . ."

"*Awful*," Suruthi said. "I think that's the word you're looking for."

"So, now what?" I said to no one in particular. "We take the iPad to the police?"

"With our fingerprints on it?" Suruthi yelped. "Have you lost your marbles, Jules?"

"Probably," I said. "But we've been in here before Ashley went missing, so that's reasonable doubt right there, isn't it?"

"Might I suggest you children stop playing detective," Holmes interjected, "as that is *my* profession, and let us take this to Watson instead. He has been your primary contact with the police, has he not? From there we can determine what to do with this device."

"Again, Holmes, we're not children," Percy said flatly. "But I suppose that's not a bad idea."

"Uh, it could be," I said. "I don't think Watson's made it a secret he wants us to stay out of this so the police can do their job. If we give him the iPad, I'm not so sure he'll keep us in the loop, and I sincerely doubt the police will let us know what's on this thing either."

"Holmes?" Suruthi said, looking to him.

Holmes took a moment to ponder this. "I would not be so quick to judge your professor, young lady. Watson can be a reasonable man, and no one would doubt the sincerity of your intentions." He reached out to pluck the iPad from my hands before I could object. "Allow me to speak with Watson on your behalf."

"That's awfully kind of you," Suruthi said to Holmes. "But before you go and pull a Houdini on us again, maybe you can give us your mobile phone number first. Much more civilized."

Holmes did so and begrudgingly accepted our own cell phone numbers.

"This is all very well," Percy said, sounding strangely formal, "but where does that leave the three of us?"

"Come again?" I said.

"The three of us," Percy repeated, motioning toward himself, Suruthi, and me. "What are we supposed to do now?"

"Return home," Holmes said flatly. "You have my word I shall be in contact should I have any new information to share."

"Yeah, see, that's not going to work for us, mate," Suruthi said before Percy and I had the chance to object. "Ashley is *our* classmate and we invited you in on this. So, here's what the three of us will do."

Suruthi turned her back to Holmes and beckoned Percy and me closer.

"I can't speak for the two of you, but I'm not about to sit around and twiddle my thumbs while we wait for Holmes to get back to us," Suruthi said in an undertone. "And let's be honest. Are we really sure we can trust him to follow up with Watson? He hasn't seemed too fond of the professor from the start. I'm willing to give Holmes the benefit of the doubt, but there's some kind of bad blood between them. I'd rather not take the risk of Holmes doing something petty to get back at Watson, like holding on to the iPad. We need to have a contingency plan."

"You do realize I am still present," Holmes interjected. "I can hear every word you're saying."

"Yep," Suruthi told him. "So, I propose we focus our energy

on finding out who Valerie is. If Edith was right and there's a chance Ashley *did* go visit Valerie, maybe we can use the power of the Google to find out where she lives."

I tried to keep my anxiety from skyrocketing as I exchanged a glance with Percy. I couldn't be sure what his line of thought was, but I was thinking Suruthi's plan maybe had some merit. At any rate, it was more of a plan than what I'd come up with on my own. Beyond searching Ashley's dorm room, I had no idea what to do next.

"Okay," I said. "I say we give it a shot."

Percy didn't seem so easily sold on the idea, given the fierce scowl he was wearing. But then he nodded and Suruthi clapped her hands together with a little squeal.

"*Excellent!*"

"So," I said awkwardly. "Should we ask Holmes when he plans to talk to Watson, or—"

"We *could*," Percy said. "But he's gone."

"Huh?"

Percy made a sweeping gesture to the door that was now swung wide open, with Holmes nowhere in sight. "Saw himself out, I reckon."

"Clearly," Suruthi grumbled.

I groaned, scrubbing my face with my hands.

It probably wasn't a good thing we were all apparently *way* more oblivious than I'd originally thought.

CHAPTER

Have You Ever Played Armchair Detective?

lright," I said to the blinking cursor on my laptop screen. "This is how it's going to go."

It was a good thing Dreams of Antiquity was empty, otherwise someone might overhear me having a conversation with an inanimate object. I didn't see any other way around it though; I had to lay down the law somehow.

"I'm going to spend the next hour or so writing until Suruthi shows up. There's a story somewhere in my brain, maybe a mystery or a thriller, needing to be written." The thought of having a one-to-two-hundred-page manuscript ready to hand in in just a few weeks, when I only had about a solid twenty or so pages, was nightmare-inducing fuel. "So, I am going to *absolutely* put this time to good use."

I got comfortable in my favorite armchair, tucking my legs up underneath me, and got my hands in the proper position, hovering over the keyboard.

I can do this, I told myself. *You're on a deadline. You can do this, Jules.*

A half hour later, it became evident that I could not do this.

There was one glaring problem staring me right in the face and I felt stupid for not realizing it sooner.

I wasn't sitting down to write because I wanted to. I was doing it because I *had* to. That made trying to write even more like pulling teeth. Not only was I on a deadline, but I'd worked so *hard* to be able to save up to cover the seminar fees, not to mention the airfare. It wasn't as if I had a thriving social life in high school to begin with, but once I'd gotten my acceptance letter from Ashford, any sports games or school dances or weekend get-togethers became an impossibility because I needed to work to save money.

If I couldn't produce a manuscript by the end of all this, then what was the point of my having come to London?

What I wanted to do was find Ashley. Every time I replayed that conversation with her grandmother in my mind, it became easier to tell myself that Ashley really had met Valerie in Oxford. Then maybe they had just lost track of time or decided to head back to where Valerie lived, but Ashley had lost her phone and she didn't have any of our numbers memorized, so she couldn't—

"Jules, why are you sitting upside down like that?"

My eyes flew open in alarm at the sound of that voice, and I was shocked to find Suruthi looming over me, looking equally confused.

"*Geez!*" I struggled to sit upright, not quite sure how I'd ended up sitting upside down in the armchair, my laptop cast aside on the floor. "Sorry, Suruthi, you scared me."

"For a moment there, Jules, I thought the worst had happened," she admitted. "Do you often sleep upside down like a bat?"

"I wasn't sleeping, just—thinking, is all," I said lamely. "Sorry."

I didn't have a good response for this when my honest answer would have been that I was daydreaming about uncovering Ashley's whereabouts instead of trying to make some progress on my manuscript.

"Wait, where's Percy?" I asked, peering around Suruthi. "I thought he was supposed to be coming with you."

"*Supposed to be*, yes," Suruthi said unhappily. "Our charming Mister Byers didn't answer his phone when I called. I even messaged a couple times, and nothing, so I can only assume he's ignoring us for some reason."

I almost did a double take. "Seriously? That doesn't sound like Percy."

Suruthi gestured toward my phone laying nearby. "See for yourself."

I grabbed my phone and quickly pulled up Percy's number. The line rang three times, then went to voicemail.

"He sent me straight to voicemail," I told Suruthi, a little offended.

"I told you."

A new text message popped up on my phone screen before I could start complaining again, and it was from Percy: Sorry, won't be able to make it.

I simply sent back numerous question marks in reply.

Percy wrote back. Doing my own research. Let me know what you two find out.

My response was: ☹

"Right then," Suruthi said after I'd showed her Percy's messages. "Rather than mope, it's probably better we get to work."

An extra pair of eyes would've been more helpful, but . . .

"Right." I grabbed my laptop off the floor and went to the sofa so Suruthi could take a seat beside me. "Let's do this."

And by *this*, we merely opened up a new search engine and got to typing.

"This is . . . well, I'm not going to lie, this is boring," Suruthi said a short while later as I clicked out of the fifteenth profile for *Ashley James* on some social media site.

Turns out there were quite a few Ashley Jameses in Ontario.

"It honestly didn't cross my mind how popular Ashley's name is," I admitted sheepishly. "We could . . . try searching for her grandmother?"

Suruthi narrowed her eyes at me in thought. "Does your gran have social media?"

"No, but that would be because she's dead."

"That would do it."

We started over, typing *Edith Longmont* into the search engine. That narrowed down our results somewhat, but it still left us coming up empty-handed.

"And we're positive Edith never mentioned Valerie's last name?" Suruthi asked for about the tenth time.

"Positive," I said, biting back a sigh. "I suppose we could try texting her?"

"And have her start asking questions about what we're up to? Probably not the best idea, Jules." Suruthi blew a raspberry, slouching back into the sofa. "Well, you know what they say. If you haven't found what you're looking for on the first page of Google results, then it's pointless."

"It's not pointless," I insisted, closing my laptop. "We just need to look at this from a different angle, maybe. Go back to the drawing board or something."

"Meh."

"Look, it's only Saturday," I said. "Holmes said he was going to give Ashley's iPad to Watson, right? Maybe by Monday we'll have more answers."

"One can only hope," Suruthi grumbled.

I didn't consider myself a spiteful person, but I was doing this out of spite: showing up over half an hour early to the seminar on Monday morning. If Professor Watson wanted to instill the virtues of punctuality, then I would show him I'd taken that to heart.

"Why, Miss Montgomery, you're here awfully early."

I looked up from the doodling I'd been doing in my notebook, seated on the floor outside the classroom. Professor Watson was approaching, tucking his briefcase under his arm as he pulled out his key ring to unlock the door.

He seemed considerably less frazzled today, which had me thinking that *maybe* he had managed to find something on Ashley's iPad or the police had had some sort of breakthrough on the case.

"Couldn't sleep," I said, which wasn't entirely a lie. "Thought I'd get a head start on the day and all that."

"Indeed." Watson gave me a curious look as he unlocked the classroom door. "And are you well?"

"No," I said automatically. "I mean, *yes*. Okay, actually, I mean, did you manage to find anything on Ashley's iPad? Holmes said he was going to—"

"I must ask you to refrain from finishing your sentence

until we are inside the classroom, Miss Montgomery, if you don't mind."

I snapped my mouth shut at Watson's abruptly serious expression and scuttled into the room as instructed.

Rather than shut the door, Watson left it slightly ajar, and didn't speak a word until he'd set his things down on his desk.

"I might ask you, Miss Montgomery, if you fully understand just what you're doing."

My artful response to this was a confused, "Huh?"

Watson crossed the room and took the armchair closest to me, leaning toward me with the kind of expression that made me feel I was in for a big scolding.

"Seeking out Holmes as you have been," Watson clarified. "Choosing to involve him in this search for Miss James."

"Okay, yes, I understand that Holmes is—"

"I am not sure you *do* understand, Miss Montgomery," Watson said sharply, speaking over me. "Obviously I am not unaware that Holmes has been . . . ill at ease with the way we have been living the last several decades, and I cannot say I blame him. But undoubtedly as you have seen for yourself, time has taken a toll on him."

It took a lot of effort to sit there quietly as Watson continued speaking.

"I know it appears as if Holmes has kept most of his faculties, but there are times where he . . . isn't entirely in the present, where he's clearly seeing something the rest of us are not. And when these spells come over him, so to say, it is as if he is reliving moments from our previous lives. Eventually—sometimes a few hours, sometimes a few days—he comes back around, but he is . . . that is, Sherlock is not the man he once was."

Isn't he, though? I wanted to say.

Holmes had managed to find Ashley's iPad when even the police hadn't (even if he claimed they were always out of their depth) and he'd been pretty spot-on in his deductions of me and my conflicted feelings around Ashley's disappearance.

But rather than tell Watson this, I said, "The other day, Holmes seemed to think we were trying to solve a case about someone named Violet Ramsey, this woman who apparently died at a séance. He was trying to take us to the morgue at a place called Saint Bartholomew's."

Watson didn't seem surprised by this news.

"Yes, he revisits that moment frequently, being that it is the last case we worked on together before we became ... whatever it is that we are."

"So ..." It took a moment to muster up the right words. "Is that the reason you and Holmes are ... stuck this way? Because that case dealt with the occult or something?"

"That would be a logical assumption," Watson said grimly. "But to be perfectly frank, Miss Montgomery, we do not know with one hundred percent certainty what exactly happened to us that night."

"Did you ever solve the case?" I asked curiously.

"No," Watson answered, his voice flat. "Obviously we did not, given that I am here now in the twenty-first century speaking with you. And I would encourage you, Miss Montgomery, not to dig any further into the case of Violet Ramsey."

"Can I ask why, sir?"

"You only have to look at Holmes to find the answer to that question yourself," Watson said. "Holmes has been gifted with extraordinary skills of deduction and oftentimes has even seemed almost superhuman. But the man is not used to *not knowing*. I can provide you with only two instances where Holmes has been bested, and I can assure you, he's never fully recovered."

I was wishing for the opposite, but Watson was making sense here. When you got down to it, Holmes was a major know-it-all. And apparently he didn't know the exact cause of why he and Watson were stuck the way they had been since 1899.

"He must get pretty . . . upset by all this then," I said carefully. "The not knowing."

"Precisely. And I have discovered that when you have lived as long as we have, memories begin to fade," Watson said, and his tone had become strangely wistful. "I haven't entirely given up hope that one day Holmes might completely forget that last case of ours. I have tried to encourage him toward other pursuits, but I am sure you can imagine I have had little success there."

Other pursuits.

As far as I was aware, Holmes either spent his time binge eating, watching television, or hunting for spare change. Two of those things I could rule out as having to do with their last case.

My stomach did a funny little free fall as I carefully asked, "Sir, does the . . . I mean, is Holmes always looking for coins or whatever because it has something to do with Violet Ramsey?"

"Indeed," Watson said, and he didn't sound that happy about answering. "To what extent, I cannot rightly say."

My fingers started twitching with the urge to immediately send a message to Percy and Suruthi with this information. I wasn't ready to let the conversation end here; Watson had been pretty forthcoming so far, and I wanted to know more.

"I guess you just decided to take up writing after all that

happened," I said, desperate for Watson to keep talking. "As *your* other pursuit."

Watson seemed to lose some of his hardened edge at this. "More or less. I have always enjoyed writing." That wistful tone was back and only growing. "I do not think I would've recovered from the war if I hadn't begun to write of my experiences with Holmes. On occasion, when I decide to revisit my early writing, I feel as if I am greeting an old friend."

This I could relate to. Writing *was* like an old friend. That was what made it all the more difficult when I couldn't even get myself to write a single sentence.

"Do you wish things were different, sir?" I asked Watson after another beat of silence.

Watson exhaled slowly again, leaning back to cross his arms over his chest. "Oh, sometimes. Death plays a crucial part in the balance of the universe, does it not? But it is much easier to endure hardship when one has their closest companion for comfort."

Regardless of the tension that constantly simmered between the two, or that ridiculous fight in Watson's office last week, Holmes and Watson obviously still relied on each other a great deal. The stories hadn't been wrong about that.

"I'm sorry to keep pushing, Professor, but did Holmes at least give you Ashley's iPad?" I asked in a rush, unable to hold it back any longer. "Did you—"

"Of course he did, and *of course* I gave it over to the authorities," Watson said, as if I should've known better. "I had no reason to keep it."

"But even if—"

"I am sorry, but am I interrupting?"

I wanted to shriek out of frustration when Thierry came waltzing into the classroom, clearly not sorry about anything.

"Certainly not, Mister Garnier," Watson said, gesturing for Thierry to join us. "Miss Montgomery and I were merely discussing her manuscript."

Ouch.

23
CHAPTER

You Might Have Mentioned the Literal Conspiracy Board in Your Bedroom

This morning had gotten off to a pretty rocky start. Seeing Percy come dashing into the classroom with about one minute to spare, backpack hanging off his shoulder and his glasses askew, was enough to provide me with some amusement I felt I'd sorely been missing as of late.

Suruthi sat up straight as Percy threw himself onto the couch between us, short of breath like he'd just run a marathon. "What happened to *you*?"

"I may—" Percy sucked in a series of short breaths, struggling to speak. With how hot his face seemed, he must've run all the way here from the Underground. "I may—have overslept."

"Research going well then?" Suruthi asked, leaning in close.

It was like Christmas morning had come early for Percy as his eyes lit up. Despite the exhaustion radiating from him, I'd never seen him look so excited.

A GAME MOST FOUL

"Suruthi, you have *no* idea. I can't wait to—"

"Shall we begin, class?" Watson cut in loudly, taking a seat in his winged armchair. "Mister Garnier has come to me with an interesting idea this morning which I thought we might take advantage of."

I was only able to absorb about half of what Watson was saying about sharing bits of our manuscript, too focused on Percy, who was now scribbling down a note in the top corner of a blank piece of paper in his notebook.

I am almost positive I've found it!!

What was that supposed to mean?

It? I mouthed at Percy.

He immediately started scribbling down his response, a very sloppy *the missing piece for potentially both cases!!!!*

Percy thought he'd solved *both* cases? I definitely knew about one case—that of our missing classmate—but the second? What was he talking about?

Suruthi somehow managed to jot down a note above Percy's as I halfheartedly listened to Watson explain that Thierry had volunteered to share the first chapter of his manuscript today and that it might be a good idea for all of us to consider doing the same.

Did you tell Holmes?

Percy wasn't as sneaky as he answered Suruthi's question with another note.

Already did. He'll meet us at the coffee shop across the street once class lets out and I'll take it from there.

There were about a dozen more questions bouncing around my brain at this point, none of which were making much sense. How was I going to make it through the rest of the day when I knew Percy was apparently sitting on a gold mine of information?

Hopefully he would have told us at once had he found anything related to Ashley's whereabouts, rather than wait an entire weekend.

"Now, if I may have your attention," Thierry began in what I could only refer to as an overly dramatic voice. "I am excited to share with you the first chapter of my manuscript, which I have decided to call *Alias Unknown*."

"Intriguing," Watson said, sounding genuinely interested.

That was all the permission Thierry needed to dive right in. I had to give him credit for an action-packed beginning, kicking his manuscript off with the kidnapping of the US president's son, but I'd never had much of an interest in politics after I'd taken last place in running for student council president in the eighth grade.

I stopped paying attention to Thierry's enigmatic storytelling completely when there was a sudden heavy weight on my shoulder. I looked over to see that Percy had *fallen asleep*. His head was resting on my shoulder, glasses crooked, and the position had to be far from comfortable. But he was definitely asleep.

This made me seriously wonder just how long he had stayed up this weekend doing *his own research*.

The dark circles under Percy's eyes were even more evident up close, which then gave me the opportunity to notice just how seriously long his eyelashes were, and that his nose was just the slightest bit crooked. There was a scar that cut through his left eyebrow too. Where my attention was drawn to the most though were his lips. His bottom lip was slightly fuller than the top, which was curved in a perfect Cupid's bow.

This is so, so *stupid,* I thought. But even that knowledge did nothing to squash the internal panic steadily increasing. I shouldn't have been so fixated on Percy's lips. I should not have been thinking about what it would be like to—

"Could always shove him off," Suruthi suggested quietly, making me jump.

Crap.

"Or would you rather keep mooning over him?"

"*I'm not mooning,* thank you," I whispered back. "Just—surprised."

I blew out a sigh before nudging Percy as gently as I could with my elbow. He came awake with a squeak that left Suruthi giggling.

I could get through this without self-imploding. Percy had only fallen asleep on my shoulder. It was completely innocent.

At any rate, we had bigger fish to fry.

He may have spent the latter half of the day forcing himself to stay awake, but Percy had no problem taking charge once we were on our way to meet up with Holmes that afternoon. Percy looked relieved when we found Holmes waiting for us outside the coffee shop, just like he'd said, immediately calling out, "Over here, sir!"

Holmes regarded us with a mixture of curiosity and probably annoyance as we approached, flicking the remnants of his cigarette on the ground and snubbing it out with his shoe.

"Dare I ask what you want now that you have requested my presence *again*?" was the first thing Holmes asked when we were close enough. "Surely the fact that I did not reply to any one of your incessant messages was clue enough I have no desire to converse. I've other, better ways to occupy my time, I hope you know."

"What exactly did you tell Holmes to get him here?" I asked Percy quietly, who breezily answered, "I told him he could have the pick of my mum's typewriter collection."

"And your mum is on board with this?" Suruthi said, fighting a laugh.

Percy shrugged. "I sent pictures."

"I'm sure there are better things you could be doing," he continued, addressing Holmes. "But you're going to want to humor me on this one, sir."

"Oh?" Holmes arched an unimpressed brow. "Do tell."

"I'm afraid you'll just have to come with us," was Percy's response.

I could definitely stand to see more of this confident side of Percy.

Holmes looked to Suruthi and me as if we might have a better answer for him, and we both shrugged.

"Now, if you don't mind," Percy said. "I reckon we should be on our way."

One very long ride on the underground where Holmes seemed to annoy everyone in a ten-foot radius with his constant fidgeting and playing of the air violin, and we were setting off in a part of London I hadn't been to.

"We're going to your apar—I mean, flat, aren't we?" I said, quickening my pace to catch up to Percy.

"Yes." I caught just the slightest hint of a grin when Percy glanced over at me. "I have a flatshare for the summer, if you'll recall, and *thankfully*, my flatmates have gone on a spontaneous holiday to the Netherlands for the week."

"*Ooooh!*" Suruthi seemed thrilled at this idea. "Are we really going to see Percy Bysshe's inner sanctum?"

"It's a flat, Suruthi," Percy said with an eye roll. "Don't read too much into it."

"Still! You keep to yourself so much in some ways, I can hardly wait to see for myself where you have your morning tea, or how clean you keep the loo. It'll be like some great mystery solved at last."

"I feel it is my duty to inform you, young lady," Holmes said, solemnly addressing Suruthi, "that you are in need of reconsidering your priorities."

Suruthi complained about us *ruining her fun* the rest of the semi-lengthy walk to Percy's flat. There was definitely a more residential feel to the area, and the building Percy led us to was on the shabbier side, but still pleasant, probably made up of a dozen or more apartments.

"Afraid the lift isn't working, so it'll be the stairs," Percy said when we were inside the lobby. "This way."

Up two flights of stairs and down a short hallway had us standing in front of a door marked with a simple 2B. Fitting.

"Any idea what we're about to walk into?" I whispered to Suruthi as Percy fiddled with a key ring he'd pulled from his pocket. "Percy isn't, like, a hoarder or something, is he?"

"With the way he keeps his notebooks organized? No way," Suruthi said, shaking her head. "But your guess is as good as mine, Jules."

Percy stepped aside to let us inside once he had the door open and immediately shut the door behind us, sliding the lock home.

It took a second for Percy to get a few lights switched on and then he was quite smartly ushering Holmes down a short hallway to our left before Holmes had the chance to continue snooping anywhere else.

I was able to see a cluttered living area to our right with a vibrantly orange couch and a plain kitchenette against the far wall before I followed Suruthi into what had to be Percy's bedroom. When the light came on, my jaw dropped when my gaze landed on the display directly in front of me.

Percy looked somewhere between proud and embarrassed as he walked to the oversized corkboard on the wall next to the lone window in the room. It was covered with an array of multicolored tacks that pinned up a series of black-and-white photographs, sketches, newspaper clippings, and pages that looked as if they had been neatly removed from old books.

To top it all off, everything appeared to have been pinned up in chronological order thanks to the long pieces of red yarn connecting each item to the next.

Percy's confidence from before was nowhere to be found when he spoke. "I realize that this is, er, perhaps a bit—"

"Insane?" Suruthi threw out. "Percy, you do realize this looks like something a serial killer might put together, right? How long did this take you? A full twenty-four hours? Or did you—oh." A look of realization suddenly crossed her face. "*This* is the research you've been doing? Why, you little Hermione Granger, you."

Holmes glowered disapprovingly at Suruthi as Percy spluttered out some kind of rebuttal.

"You shouldn't berate the boy, young lady. It is never an inconvenience to have all the facts available when working a case." Holmes gestured to the corkboard. "The evidence here has been arranged well indeed."

"Er. Yes, I thought . . . thank you, sir," Percy managed to say once he'd cleared his throat several times. "I thought it would be helpful to see all the facts laid out in chronological order."

"And so it would," Holmes remarked.

Holmes hadn't once looked away from the corkboard since we'd entered the room, and I was curious to see what he'd observed so far that the rest of us average citizens hadn't.

"Yes, thank you for your service, Perce," Suruthi said seriously, but her devilish grin ruined the whole thing.

"Seconded," I added, nudging Percy with an elbow. "Thank you."

Percy mumbled something that sounded like *you're welcome* and gestured to the corkboard. "Shall we?"

"Indeed," Holmes said. "After you, young man."

"Right then," Percy said. "Er. So."

He went to the far side of the corkboard, pointing first at a copy of what looked like a list, each line item written in a tiny, cramped script.

"Obviously you know that Jules told us everything about your . . . trip down memory lane concerning your last case. So, using that information Jules told me about the case having involved a séance and the death of someone named Violet Ramsey, I started to do some research, beginning in the year 1899." Percy reached for a notebook on his desk, flipping through a few pages before he found the one he was looking for. "Now, I was able to do a search for Violet Ramsey in the university archives where my mum works. I *did* locate a record of birth for someone of the same name in March of 1878, followed by a death certificate issued in 1899. Does that check out so far, sir?"

Holmes's only response was a short nod.

Percy looked like he wanted to jump up and down in excitement, but was able to keep a hold on himself. He uncapped a red marker and circled the date 1899. "Moving on then. I tried to dig a little deeper from there and I *thought* I had something when I came across mention of an autopsy having been performed on Violet Ramsey, but I wasn't able to find any record of it."

"You said her body had been completely drained of blood, right?" I said to Holmes, and again he nodded. "That doesn't sound like an autopsy people would want to get around."

"Could be," Percy agreed. "But without an autopsy to refer to or any other kind of record of her death, I had to approach this from a different angle."

"Which was?" Suruthi said. The fact that she hadn't cracked a joke in several minutes meant she was just as intrigued as the rest of us.

"I started to do some research on spiritualism instead," Percy said. "And blimey, Victorian people sure loved death. Sorry," he added to Holmes, who shrugged. "*Everyone* seemed to be caught up in the throes of spiritualism at some point or another. Going to a séance every Saturday night instead of the opera seemed like *the* thing to do for a while there, which left me with a lot of names to sift through." He tapped his marker on a short list of names next. "Fortunately, I managed to narrow it down to three names that seemed the most promising given the period we're focusing on. First, we have Alexander Johnston. He had a fast rise to stardom, but eventually he excused himself from the public eye after his whole *séance possession act* was picked apart, er, quite viciously in a newspaper."

Percy crossed Alexander Johnston's name off before moving to the second name on the list.

"This brings us to Madame Ophelia Dupont. Now, there's some speculation as to whether she was the real deal or if she was hosting nightly séances because she was actually trying to attract wealthy customers for the high-end brothel she was operating."

"That was very enterprising of her," Suruthi commented.

I caught Percy rolling his eyes at this, but it was Holmes who scoffed loudly.

"I had the misfortune of meeting the madame, and enterprising businesswoman she most certainly was not," Holmes said in clipped tones. "She seemed to enjoy pushing the boundaries of impropriety on a regular basis, but she was, however, a rather gifted gambler. Watson himself lost to her more than once on a few misguided bets."

"So, you remember her then," Percy said eagerly to Holmes. "What else? Can you remember anything specific?"

I could tell at once Percy had said the wrong thing. However innocent the comment may have been, Holmes clearly hadn't taken it that way with the thunderous look now overtaking his face.

"Are you that astonished that I still maintain some semblance of mental acuity?" Holmes demanded, his normally raspy voice taking on a hard edge. "Is it so surprising that I can recall certain events from my previous life?"

"N-No, sir," Percy stammered, immediately backtracking. "It's only that I thought—well, Jules told us that you sometimes seem to—"

"Despite appearances and despite whatever your classmate may have told you, I assure you, I am *not* a madman," Holmes said sharply. "My intellect is as sharp as it ever was."

Holmes was looming now, moving closer to Percy as if he meant to drag him into a boxing ring so he could settle this with his fists. And for the first time, I felt a genuine sliver of fear creep up my spine.

For as little time as I'd known him, it was impossible not to think—at least somewhat—that Holmes was *fragile*, and in more ways than one. I'd seen firsthand that he was still remarkably sharp-minded and good at fighting, but I'd also seen him convinced that he was back in Victorian England, solving a case.

"Sir, no one is saying there's something wrong with your intellect," I said quickly, moving to Percy's side. "We know you're brilliant, not a madman."

"You don't have a deceitful bone in your body, do you, young lady?" Holmes said, head cocked to the side as he stared down at me. "Do you really believe that I cannot see right through that falsely contrite look of yours?"

"Excuse me? I'm not—"

"Rest assured, I am still capable of utilizing the fine art of deduction," Holmes went on, his gaze now moving back to Percy. "Take yourself, for example."

"*Me*?" Percy said, his voice several octaves higher than normal. "Oh, I really don't think we need to—"

"Obviously you're a young man of keen intellect given the timeline of events you've constructed here," Holmes said, gesturing to the corkboards. "Meticulous, organized. Given the amount of information you gathered, this took you a considerable amount of time, but you're a perfectionist, which is why you've waited until now to show it to us. That, combined with the way the items here in your bedroom are organized by height in descending order and by color tells me that you also have, perhaps several, obsessive-compulsive tendencies. You most likely experience great discomfort should items not be arranged to your exact specifications."

Sneaking a peek up at Percy and seeing the look that had come over his face, Holmes's statements checked out so far.

"You're also frequently riddled with anxiety," Holmes said next. He was on a roll here and didn't seem to be showing any signs of slowing down. "You regularly fidget with your glasses, obviously a nervous tick of yours, but also because you're never quite able to rid the lenses of the smudges left behind by your fingers."

"Have noticed that a time or two," I heard Suruthi mumble to herself.

"And then there's the state of your hands."

Holmes caught Percy's right hand between his own, flipping it palm side up. "One can clearly observe that you spend a great deal of time writing. There's the ink stains, of course, but also the callouses *here*, on the ring finger of your right hand, which suggests you hold your pen incorrectly. You wouldn't have developed those callouses were you not regularly writing whilst incorrectly holding your pen."

Percy tried to yank his hand free from Holmes's iron grip, but Holmes held fast, tugging him a step forward.

"Given the way you repeatedly massage that right ring finger of yours, along with your littlest finger as well, means you're most likely experiencing numbness along the outer part of your forearm and that numbness is spreading. Cubital tunnel, I presume?"

Percy finally managed to yank his hand free and step aside, holding his arm close to his chest. "What of it?"

"Perhaps this must mean you're also something of a masochist, seeing as you choose to write through the pain this must be causing you," Holmes said to Percy. Holmes was smiling wryly to himself now, like he was holding on to the punch line of some joke he was enjoying dangling in front of us. "I suppose you'd have to be, given the way you allow yourself to be in close proximity to someone you're clearly attracted to, yet you make no move to see if that attraction is reciprocated."

I had become familiar with the sound of silence as my hearing had worsened over the years. It wasn't as nerve-inducing as it used to be and sometimes, I was almost comfortable with it. But the silence that fell in the wake of Holmes's deduction had me inwardly feeling as if I'd just been thrown out of an airplane for an ill-fated skydiving expedition.

My mouth had fallen open, and Suruthi looked equally stunned. I was too afraid to look at Percy.

"Well, go on!" Suruthi urged, flapping her hands at Holmes. "Keep deducing!"

"Take Miss Montgomery for example," Holmes said, gesturing toward me before I could object. "A bright, clever young lady by all means, somewhat conventionally attractive by today's standards."

"Thanks," I said with a grimace while Suruthi tried and failed to smother a laugh.

"Now, most likely a subconscious reaction on your part, but you gravitate toward the young lady whenever she enters the room," Holmes went on. "To be polite, perhaps, in offering her your full attention, but in all our encounters to date, you tend to maintain a physical distance from her of no more than an arm's length at any given time."

My palms had begun to sweat the more Holmes kept talking. This weird ache now spreading in my chest made me wonder if I was in the first stages of a heart attack.

All I had to do to drown out Holmes would've been to simply reach up to turn my hearing aids off and then maybe start humming loudly. It would've been easy enough to do. But I was frozen to the spot, unmoving, and Holmes's words kept coming.

"And certainly, you are not unaware of the physical responses you must currently be experiencing standing so close to the young lady, Mister Byers." There wasn't a single trace of humor to be heard in Holmes's voice, but it was impossible not to feel like he was saying all this like it was some big joke. "There is an increase in your respiration, of course, but not enough to warrant concern or draw too much notice to yourself. No, the real giveaway, young man, is the constant flush in your face and the way you seem to be unable to observe Miss Montgomery speaking without fixating on her mouth."

There was a sharp intake of air at this last part of Holmes's deduction; I didn't know if it had come from me or Percy. It hadn't been Suruthi because she was full-on laughing now, which I found odd because *nothing* about this was amusing.

"That, my dear boy," Holmes continued, his expression morphing into something incredibly self-satisfied, "makes it quite obvious that you not only find Miss Montgomery attractive, but you also wish to—"

"I think, *sir*," Percy said suddenly, raising his voice to drown out Holmes, "you've said more than enough."

And he turned on his heel and promptly left the room.

Never Did I Claim to be a Good Liar

A moment later, I heard the sound of a door opening, then slamming shut.

My feet remained firmly planted to the ground despite the urge to chase after Percy. If I was left feeling mortified after Holmes's little display, I could only imagine how Percy must've felt, and that was what had me moving forward, jabbing a finger into Holmes's chest, embarrassment quickly being replaced with anger.

"What was *that*, Holmes?! Maybe I don't have a deceitful bone in my body, but you obviously don't have a brain-to-mouth filter!"

Then I turned on my heel and left the room without waiting for a response from Holmes, half-running, half-tripping my way out of the flat. I was out the front door with just enough time to see Percy opening the door to the stairwell down the hallway. I barely remembered to shut the door behind me before I took off running again.

"Percy! Percy, *wait!*"

Percy was well on his way down to the lower floors of the building by the time I came dashing into the stairwell, my lungs already screaming for air.

Man, am I out of shape, I thought, half-hysterical.

Another area I was also out of shape in was this whole romance thing. I had already resigned myself to the fact that whatever feelings I had to admit I'd developed for Percy would have to wait—possibly permanently—at least until we'd gotten to the bottom of Ashley's disappearance. But apparently Holmes felt it appropriate that we address it *now*.

"Percy!" I shouted again, my voice echoing through the stairwell. "Hey, please wait!"

How exactly I lost my footing on the last step before I reached the landing was a mystery to me, but the next second I found myself on my back, staring up at the ceiling. There was a searing pain in my elbow and there were going to be a lot of bruises in some awkward places, but I was pretty sure I was still in one piece.

"Ow."

Once the world had stopped spinning, I couldn't help it. I started laughing. Nothing about recent events had been amusing, and still, I couldn't help it. The laughter just kept coming.

"Jules!"

Somewhere over all the laughter, I could hear Percy's frantic voice echoing up the stairwell. I was still laughing as I struggled my way up into a sitting position, just as Percy reached the landing.

"Are you alright?" He was tutting about me like a mother hen, checking me over for any obvious signs of injury. "Did you hit your head? How many fingers am I holding up?"

The more questions Percy threw at me, the more difficult it became to understand what he was saying.

I ended up shouting just to get him to take a breath. "Percy. *Percy*!"

Percy's incessant babbling stopped immediately and there was that flush creeping back into his face.

"Sorry," he said, his voice hoarse. "Sorry, I only thought you—Jules, are you *alright*? That looked like an awful fall."

"*Yes*," I said, choking down another laugh. "It's the inappropriate laughter thing I have a problem with, remember? I promise I'm fine, so will you stop fretting because I'd really like to tell you how much I find you attractive as well."

Percy's eyes widened, his jaw going slack. The noise that left him sounded like a wheeze before his expression turned shrewd. "How hard did you hit your head exactly?"

His question had me rolling my eyes. "Didn't hit my head, thanks. I told you, I'm *fine*."

"Then why do you—"

"Because Holmes wasn't wrong," I continued, raising my voice to speak over Percy's. "And if we'd stayed up there in your room any longer, he probably would've deduced the same thing about me. I can't help but watch your mouth when you talk, and it's possible you haven't noticed, but my heart also goes into overdrive whenever you stand close to me, and then I start breathing weird too."

I wasn't sure if this was the best way to ... *fess up* to my feelings while using Holmes as a buffer, but it was out in the open now, and I couldn't take it back. There was also the fact that I *didn't want* to take it back. It felt like a strange relief to have finally said it aloud.

And Percy just sat there in the stairwell, his face a blank slate.

"Percy?"

He gave no response.

"Um. So, I'm sorry if I made you uncomfortable or something," I said, biting into my lip. "We can just pretend this never happened and, you know, get back up there to—"

"*No!*" Percy said suddenly, so loudly I jumped. He exhaled slowly as he ran his fingers through his hair, now looking pained. "No, I mean, *yes*, we should go back, but *no*, you didn't make me uncomfortable. Not at all. I'm just trying to . . ."

"To . . . ?" I prompted when he fell silent again.

Percy gave a frustrated laugh as he finally met my gaze. "It's only that I'd like to kiss you, and I'm trying to figure out how to tell you that in a way that doesn't make you think I'm a complete twit, but I don't think I've succeeded."

The only bit that I was able to catch on to was the *I'd like to kiss you* part. Everything else had already floated away into the background. Percy said he'd like to kiss me.

And before I could throw caution to the wind so *I* could kiss *him*, there was a loud *bang!* that ricocheted through the stairwell like gunfire, causing Percy and me to leap apart.

"Are you decent?"

We both looked up and found Holmes leaning over the banister, peering down at us.

"Obviously we are," Percy said flatly. "What would we have gotten up to in all of five minutes?"

"Don't answer that," I said quickly, pointing a finger at Holmes.

Holmes did that lip twitching thing where it looked like he

was thinking about smiling. "I hope you can pardon the intrusion, as I've been sent with orders to apologize."

I exchanged looks with Percy.

"I . . . don't think that'll be necessary, Holmes," I said. He probably wouldn't have meant it anyway. "Turns out you're not a bad wingman."

"So," Suruthi said the moment we'd returned to the flat upstairs. "When's the wedding?"

Percy and I pointedly ignored her.

"Shall we continue?" Holmes said, hands clasped behind his back as he stood in front of the conspiracy board.

Percy jumped into action, grabbing his marker again.

"The last name on our list of potential, er, suspects, is a young woman by the name of Adelaide Shaw." When there was no reaction to the name from Holmes, Percy went on. "From what I've been able to gather, she gained notoriety by putting on impromptu séances right in the middle of ballrooms. She was so good at it, apparently, that *she was invited to Buckingham Palace a time or two.*"

"Okay, so she dined with the royals," Suruthi said, nodding. "What else?"

Percy had a very Holmes-like glint in his eyes as he tapped the name with the marker again. "*So.* Not only did Miss Shaw dine with the royals, but she also happened to be a particular favorite of Queen Victoria after she *may have had contact* with her beloved Prince Albert during a séance."

Percy was really laying it on thick here, working his way up to what had to be his big reveal, and I wasn't sure if I found it amusing or frustrating.

"*But*," he went on, and there was definitely excitement in his voice now. "We know the royal family were major celebrities of their day just like they are now. Which means, provided you look in the right places, you *may* just find—"

"Young man, I must insist you *get on with it*," Holmes said impatiently. "There is little point withholding information simply for the purpose of suspense."

Percy brushed Holmes's words aside and continued speaking with the same trembling excitement in his voice. "You may just find photographic evidence."

I wasn't sure what I was looking at once Percy stepped away from the board, gesturing toward it with a flourish. It took a second look to see that he'd just pinned up an old black-and-white photograph right in the middle of Adelaide Shaw's biography.

There was a sudden, mad dash from the rest of us to get a closer look at the photograph, and thanks to Holmes's bony elbows, he came out on top.

From what I could see standing on my tiptoes, the photo was a blurry shot of a group of people seated around a table in a parlor room. Queen Victoria was the easiest to spot, given that I'd seen her likeness in just about every World History class I'd ever taken. Seated beside her were probably a few other members of the royal family; everything about their clothing and jewelry screamed opulence.

The last figure seated at the table was a young woman in a plain black dress, standing out in stark contrast to the rich attire around her. Her dark hair was styled simply and pinned back from her face. She would've looked like any other Victorian-era woman posing for a photo that took way too long to take—if it hadn't been for the way the corners of her mouth were turned up in a small, knowing little smile.

A smile I'd seen before.

Suruthi noticed it right when I did with a gasp.

"*Holy*—is that Ashley? That's Ashley sitting right there next to Queen Victoria, isn't it?"

"Has to be," Percy said eagerly, rocked back on his heels. "That woman *has* to be Ashley, right? She looks exactly like her twin!"

Percy was practically vibrating on the spot and Suruthi had broken into a grin, but I'd been hit with a sudden uptick of doubt.

"Then what would your explanation be for Edith?" I pointed out. "If Ashley has been alive since the nineteenth century, how do you explain the fact that she has a grandmother?"

"*If* that was her grandmother," Suruthi said after a beat of uncomfortable silence. "Who's to say that Edith isn't actually one of Ashley's descendants or something and they've just been keeping this big family secret all this time. Honestly, Jules, Ashley's grandmother isn't high up on my list of what's strange about this whole case."

Before stumbling across Watson and Holmes and somehow getting caught up in their century's old mystery, I wouldn't even have considered the thought that the woman in the photo was Ashley.

But *now*? Somewhere the line between reality and fiction had become blurred these past several weeks. After all we'd seen thus far, who was to say that *wasn't* Ashley seated next to Queen Victoria?

"Think about it, Jules," Percy said. "Here we've got Holmes and Watson, two men who should've died over a century ago, up and roaming about London, and then we have photographic evidence that this medium who may or may not be responsible for their fate looks *exactly* like our missing classmate? No way can this be a coincidence."

I looked over at Holmes, wondering if he had any statistics floating around his brain about the chances of coincidences being legitimate, but Holmes hadn't once looked away from the photograph of the medium with the royal family. I wasn't even sure he was blinking.

I finally recognized the feeling unfurling in the pit of my stomach as *hope*.

Percy had obviously done his research here and it looked pretty darn convincing at this point. What were the chances of this *not* being a coincidence?

"So, what? We think that Ashley made a run for it once she realized our writing professor was actually Watson?" Suruthi said.

"I don't know about that," I said after a moment of thought. "Wouldn't she have left that first day of the seminar, once she'd seen Watson?"

Suruthi's expression went a little flat. "Well, déjà vu can be *very* creepy. Maybe she just—"

I let out a yelp when Holmes suddenly lunged forward, jostling me aside as he snatched the photograph off the board.

"What, Holmes?" Percy said in alarm. "Do you remember anything about this woman? What is she—"

"It's her."

Holmes's matter-of-fact statement had that sense of burgeoning hope increasing tenfold.

"Are you sure, Holmes?" Suruthi demanded. "You're sure this woman was—"

"I am certain of it," Holmes insisted. "Look at the lady's wrist, here."

We all gathered around Holmes as he pointed to Adelaide Shaw's left wrist in the photograph. It was a little difficult to make out at first, but the silver piece she wore like a bracelet was large enough, round in shape, and etched with an unusual symbol made up of what looked like three rings.

I couldn't be certain of how long it took for me to connect the pieces, but once I did, it was hard to keep the excitement from creeping into my voice.

"That's what you've been looking for this entire time, haven't you? You've been searching for that silver piece she's wearing."

Holmes gave a short nod. "This piece of silver . . . whatever it is. I am loathe to admit that I don't know its exact purpose, but it . . . this has been the *one* thing I remember most clearly about that night. Obviously it had to be of import given the way the woman wore it, but *why*, I . . . I don't know. *I don't know!*"

Holmes's shout had me jumping, and then I felt nothing but a surge of sympathy. I hadn't known it was possible for three words to be filled with such agony.

"Here, why don't you sit down, sir?" Percy said when Holmes began to sway on his feet. "Let's rest for a moment."

Holmes did not protest as Percy and I helped him to the chair at his desk, still clutching the photograph in his hand.

"Do we . . . do something?" Suruthi whispered when several moments had passed, with Holmes sitting in silence, unblinking again as he stared at the photograph.

"I'm not sure," I admitted. "Maybe we should just—"

It was like Holmes had just received some electric shock when he was suddenly thrown into action, shouting, *"Pen!* Someone get me a blasted PEN!"

Percy managed to find a pen in one of the drawers and Suruthi snatched a piece of paper off the corkboard, turning it blank side up.

Holmes's grip on the pen was unsteady as he put it to paper, but it became clear a moment later what he was doing.

"What's he drawing?" I asked, trying to peer over his shoulder. "I can't tell."

"I think it's . . ." Suruthi leaned in a little closer. "It looks like a . . . giant, black blob, actually."

"Well done," Percy said with an eye roll. "Really on to something there, Suruthi."

"Silence!" Holmes's loud bark had all three of us jumping this time. "I must have *silence.*"

Rather than apologize, we shut up.

It was awkward simply standing around, watching Holmes draw, but the awkwardness was quickly becoming replaced by fascination.

Holmes was far from a master artist, but he worked with long, thin strokes of the pen, taking up almost the entire piece of paper. A few minutes in and the object began to take shape.

The page was taken up by what truly did look like a giant black blob at first glance, but then I recognized the shape of a small series of keys.

"It's a typewriter," I said in surprise, forgetting that we were supposed to be keeping silent.

"Certainly looks like a typewriter," Percy agreed.

"Like this one, perhaps?" Suruthi held out the laminated photo of the medium with the royal family. "Look, right there in the corner on that posh little desk. It's a typewriter."

I had to bring the photo almost up to my nose to really make out what Suruthi was pointing to, but it was definitely a typewriter.

"I can't tell if that's the same typewriter Holmes is drawing," I said, passing the photo to Percy next.

"Neither can I," Percy admitted after he took a look. "But—"

"*Aha!*" Holmes was suddenly out of his seat with a triumphant shout. "I knew it. *I knew it!*"

"Now would be a good time to fill us in, please, Holmes," Suruthi said, definitely struggling to sound patient now. "What's going on?"

"The typewriter!" Holmes grabbed Suruthi by the shoulders and gave her a shake. "The *typewriter*, dear girl!"

"Yes, yes, we've seen it," Percy said, reaching over to stop Holmes from shaking Suruthi any further. "What about the typewriter?"

"The typewriter has been the missing piece all along!" Holmes was quickly dissolving into mad rambling territory, and it was a struggle to keep up with the rapid flow of conversation. "Oh, I must have subconsciously known it for some time. Of course I must have. Why else would I have been drawn to that delightfully kitschy shop?"

"You're not talking about my aunt's shop, are you?" I said, wondering if I should be offended on Adele's behalf.

"*Obviously*," Holmes said, not sparing me a second glance.

"At least he called it delightful," Suruthi pointed out.

"Call it a hunch," Percy said cautiously, "but I'm going to

hazard a guess that the silver piece the medium is wearing is somehow connected to the typewriter."

"Precisely!" Holmes said gleefully.

"So what now?" Suruthi said. "We go traipsing across London looking for a typewriter? Do you know how long that will—"

"Perhaps you misunderstood me, dear child," Holmes said, speaking over Suruthi. "Are we not all aware of where we might find a typewriter?"

Once Holmes's statement had sunk in, it was impossible not to laugh.

"Holmes, the chances of the typewriter you're looking for being the same one in my aunt's shop are—"

"Astronomical?" Percy said. "I'm pretty sure we're well past that now, Jules. I think we can all safely agree that everything up to this point has all been connected somehow, and it's not as if we have a better place to start."

An interesting expression crossed Holmes's face as he considered Percy's words. I was worried he was going to start shouting again, but he was rather calm when he finally said, "As a matter of fact, I believe there is another resource we can tap into."

"Such as?" Suruthi hinted.

"Watson was a very meticulous chronicler of the cases we solved together, before he developed a flair for romanticizing everything he wrote from then onward," Holmes said. "And I do recall . . . rather, I am sure I remember *now* how often I used to sit amongst his journals and pour over the pages in the hopes that he had documented *something* about that night we . . ."

"And how did that work out for you?" I asked when Holmes had lapsed back into silence.

"The whole ordeal was terribly frustrating," Holmes answered, and then his expression became somewhat sheepish. "It is my belief Watson finally hid his journals in an attempt to save our rooms any further destruction, and regrettably *before* I had the chance to read them all."

Holmes's confession brought my conversation with Watson from that morning back to mind, where Watson had said that Holmes wasn't used to not knowing, that he didn't handle it well. Apparently Holmes had handled it with violent outbursts.

"If I'm understanding correctly, and I know you'll correct me if I'm wrong, Holmes," I said, "but you're wanting to go dig up Watson's old journals to see if he wrote something about the case you worked on with the medium. If we're lucky, he'll know something about the typewriter too."

"Indeed," Holmes confirmed with a nod.

"If that's the case," Percy said, raising his voice, "then why hasn't Watson mentioned any of this before?"

That I believed I had somewhat of an answer for.

"Watson hasn't made it a secret that he's been trying to protect Holmes and keep him from doing anything dangerous. If Holmes started going on a rampage—sorry, Holmes—any time he couldn't find what he was looking for about this case in Watson's journals, then why would Watson voluntarily bring up the subject with him?"

"Also, you just said Watson hid his journals from you, Holmes," Suruthi added, looking at Holmes. "Do you know where they are now?"

Holmes's previously eager expression turned into something a lot more unhappy. "Frankly, I do not."

After all the excitement and hope that had been building since I'd first got a good look at the photograph Percy had uncovered, that it was looking an awful lot like Ashley was in the same boat as Holmes and Watson, and maybe there was a good reason she'd had to leave, I was beginning to feel the first pangs of discouragement.

This couldn't be where we hit another brick wall, could it?

"*However,*" Holmes said, sanding his hands together. "I am not without ideas."

CHAPTER

Now the Game is Afoot

L et's run through this *one* more time."

Suruthi and I groaned.

"I think we've got it by now, Perce," Suruthi complained. "We know what we're doing, so why can't we just *go*?"

"It never hurts to be overprepared," Percy declared, herding us under the awning of a nearby shop on the street outside his flat.

It felt like we were a bunch of football players huddling together to plan their Hail Mary pass. It seemed like a pretty apt description, seeing as we had absolutely no idea where Watson did in fact hide his journals. Luck was still *somewhat* on our side, though; Holmes had gleefully shared that Watson had been called in for some faculty emergency with the college, so the chances of him catching us in the act of searching his room would be minimal.

"Alright, Jules, Suruthi," Percy said, looking at each of us in turn. "You're both off to the antique shop for that typewriter. Do you think you can get it over to Holmes's without any trouble?"

"Of course," I said. "Probably. I'll just tell Adele that

replacement piece you ordered finally arrived and we're going to do some repairs or something."

"That won't be necessary," Holmes said abruptly, then thrust a rolled-up wad of pounds at me. "I'd prefer you purchase the typewriter instead, as we will not be returning it."

"Uh, okay." I quickly sorted through the pound notes and tried not to gape. "You know, I think my aunt was selling it for seventy-five pounds, not . . . however much this is."

"Consider it a donation," Holmes said, unconcerned. "Watson is a rather smart investor," he added at our dumbfounded looks. "Over a century of perfecting the art of being frugal will, unsurprisingly, leave you with a small fortune."

"That'll do it," Suruthi said as I carefully tucked the money away in my bag.

"Right then," Percy said. "Jules and Suruthi, you'll go *purchase* the typewriter and meet us over at Holmes and Watson's. I'll make sure Holmes messages you the address. Hopefully we'll have found at least one of Watson's journals by then."

"And then what?" Suruthi said.

We all stared at her.

"Elaborate, please," Holmes demanded.

"After we go fetch the typewriter and we *hopefully* scrounge up a journal or two, then what? It's not like we can go to the police and tell them we think our missing classmate is actually a medium from the nineteenth century."

"Why don't we cross that bridge when we come to it?" Percy said after some uncomfortable silence.

I was going to agree with him on this one.

Obviously I knew Suruthi had a point and we needed to address this figurative elephant in the room, but getting our hands on Watson's journals and figuring out the connection between the typewriter and the silver piece Holmes had been fixated on for over a century seemed like bigger hurdles at this point.

All signs seemed to be pointing toward Ashley actually having been a medium by the name of Adelaide Shaw from the nineteenth century, and somehow she'd been involved with the very last case Holmes and Watson had worked before they became . . . whatever they were now.

So I had to believe that Ashley could look after herself after all this time. How else would she have made it this far? Was an extra day going to make that much of a difference in the long run?

"Well, then, what if this doesn't work?" Suruthi said. "Has anyone considered that?"

"It may not," Holmes said, and I was surprised at how calm he appeared. "Failure is oftentimes inevitable. But that doesn't mean one should not make every attempt possible to achieve their goal."

There was an awkward stretch of silence as we considered Holmes's unexpected words of advice. Maybe we *were* about to walk into failure. I had the feeling it was more likely we had no idea what we were about to walk into. That had to be better than not trying, right?

"D'you know," Suruthi finally said to Holmes. "If this *doesn't* pan out well, you might make a good motivational speaker, Sherlock."

"I think not."

"*Listen*, you lot," Percy said, snapping his fingers for our attention. "We don't know how long Watson will be tied up with this faculty emergency of his, and I don't reckon he'll be too pleased if he catches us in the act of going through his things."

"Turnabout is fair play," Holmes said dismissively. "Let us be on our way then."

Looking back on this moment sometime in the future, I'll know it was going to be one of those inevitable things. It would've happened at one point or another, and I decided I wasn't above giving fate a little push.

"Wait, Percy!"

I broke away from Suruthi and had to jog to catch up to Percy and Holmes, already halfway down the street. I could actually hear Holmes's impatient sigh over the hubbub of the street, and I would've laughed if I wasn't suddenly so nervous.

"What is it?" Percy asked, his face drawn in concern as I approached.

"You know how in every epic action movie when the good guys have to go separate ways to help save the day and it's really dangerous and they know they might not make it out alive?" I said all in one breath.

"I suppose," Percy answered slowly, now looking confused. "Why? Are you worried we won't make it out alive? Because I don't think this is going to be *that*—"

"C'mon, catch up!" Suruthi chimed in from behind me. "She's saying she wants to snog you for good luck!"

"What she said," I confirmed at Percy's questioning look. At least, I was pretty sure I knew what *snog* meant by now. "I'm not sure if I believe in luck, but it can't hurt, right?"

I could tell Percy's face had become very hot and he looked just the slightest bit nauseated, but he was sort of smiling and sounded plenty confident when he said, "Best not to risk it."

"Oh, for God's sake!"

Whatever else Holmes started complaining about faded into

the background when Percy slipped an arm around my waist to pull me in close, leaning down to press his lips against mine.

It probably wasn't the most pure and passionate kiss of all time or whatever, but the kiss still made my toes curl in my shoes and my heart skip a funny little beat.

"Thanks," I said breathlessly once we'd had to break apart for air. "You know, for, um, all the luck."

"Anytime," Percy said, just as breathless.

"And *this* is why I find romantic sentiment abhorrent."

"Thanks, Holmes," Suruthi said cheerily. "And on that note, we'd best be off."

Suruthi looped her arm through mine and began leading me away in the opposite direction, giggling the entire way.

"Took you long enough, didn't it?" she said conversationally as we walked.

My heart rate was mostly under control at this point, but I still sounded winded when I said, "What did?"

"Oh, never mind then." Suruthi huffed as she gave me another playful nudge. "But I'm serious, Jules. Make sure you invite me to your wedding, yeah?"

"*Dude*. Shut up!"

Suruthi laughed even louder.

As expected, Adele was very confused but also very pleased with Holmes's payment for the typewriter. It took a lame excuse about him being Percy's uncle and how we were going to deliver it after the typewriter was repaired, but it worked. Soon enough Suruthi and I were lugging the typewriter off toward the Underground, carefully packed in a cardboard box with a bunch of packing peanuts per Adele's instruction.

"Well, we got the thing, didn't we?" Suruthi said, patting the typewriter on the seat between us. "That's one hurdle down."

"Partially, I guess," I said. "Do you think Percy and Holmes will have had the same luck though?"

"Who's to say?" Suruthi shrugged. "If any of Watson's journals aren't in their flat, we know we can at least try his office next."

"Suppose we don't find any journals in their flat *or* Watson's office," I said. "Then what? We keep running around London for however long until we do find something?"

My question had Suruthi pulling a grimace. "No idea. I'd prefer it if we don't have to find out."

We spent the rest the journey in silence, both of us lost in our own thoughts. Once we were above ground again, I pulled out my phone to plug in the address Holmes had given me into the map app.

"Why are you all frowning at your phone like that?"

"Holmes gave me the address of a pub," I told Suruthi, offering her my phone. "Some place called The Bronze Archer."

"Well, good to know in case we need a pint after all this," Suruthi said.

"I'll pass."

It was a long enough walk from the Tube to The Bronze Archer pub that Suruthi and I were both huffing and puffing by the time we reached it, taking turns carrying the stupidly heavy typewriter.

The pub seemed decently packed with a lot of chatter and laughter spilling out the open door, and I felt another wave of nerves.

"How're we supposed to find them here?" I asked Suruthi. "Better yet, what do we say when we get stopped by someone wanting to know what we're up to with this box full of packing peanuts here?"

There was a loud shout of, "UP HERE!" from somewhere above us before Suruthi could answer. We both looked up to find Percy leaning out a window on the second floor, waving down at us.

"There's another entrance around the corner!" he called down to us. "I'll meet you there."

Around the corner we found a narrow door that was almost hidden from view next to the back door of the pub. The door swung open as soon as we approached, and Percy stepped out to immediately take the typewriter from Suruthi.

"Inside and up the stairs," he instructed. "First door to the right."

"How's it going?" I asked, taking the lead.

I couldn't see his face, but I could hear the disappointment in Percy's voice when he answered. "It's only a two-bedroom flat, but they've lived here since they bought it just after the First World War, according to Holmes, and there is an overwhelming amount of rubbish to go through."

"Great," Suruthi said flatly. "Probably a million sweet wrappers everywhere too."

"Maybe seeing the typewriter now that we have that photograph will jog more of Holmes's memory," I suggested, trying to sound positive.

I went to the first door on the right and opened it, moving to the side to let Percy in first, then Suruthi.

I'd barely shut the door behind me before I sneezed—*loudly*.

"Yeah, it's a tad dusty in here," Percy said apologetically.

"You don't say."

The place was so dimly lit that it was difficult to make out what I was looking at until my eyes adjusted.

We were standing in a small, tiled entryway. To our left was a walkway into the kitchen, and directly in front of us was what looked like a sitting room. The furniture was an odd assortment of dated pieces that wouldn't have looked out of place in Adele's shop.

It was unsettling to realize that Holmes must have spent a lot of time shut up in this dusty, poorly lit place, where it probably wasn't the easiest to tell whether he was currently in the nineteenth or the twenty-first century.

"This way," Percy said, nodding toward a hallway directly to our right. "We started in Watson's room."

I'd only taken a few steps when there was a sudden, loud crash, followed by the sound of breaking glass, ending with a very loud curse.

"I see it's been going well then," Suruthi commented.

"Tremendously," Percy grumbled. "All we've managed to do so far is turn the room upside down and break a bunch of stuff. The professor is not going to be happy, I'll tell you that."

The room Percy led us to was the very last at the end of the hallway. The door was thrown open and there were books littering the floor, a pile of clothes, and shoes.

There came another colorful curse when I peeked into the room and narrowly avoided getting hit in the head with a flying book. Holmes was on the floor, digging through a trunk at the base of a four-poster bed, and it was evident he'd been at this for some time.

Percy had been right about the room being turned upside down, and I could only imagine what Watson's fury would be like when he caught sight of this.

How Holmes managed to notice our arrival with the way he was digging through the trunk was impressive. "Put it over there, on the desk."

Percy set the box on the desk pushed up against the wall by the lone window in the room.

"Well, don't just stand there!" Holmes barked. "Start searching!"

"A little hard to tell where you've already looked in this mess, Sherlock," Suruthi said disapprovingly.

Holmes's reply was a short, "Deal with it."

Yikes.

Suruthi went to the closet across from the bed while Percy joined Holmes on the floor.

I knew I needed to join in the search as well, but I was finding it difficult to move. It was *noisy* in this room, Holmes's shouting and the loud thumping of the occasional book or picture frame hitting the wall causing an awful lot of feedback in my hearing aids.

The second time I jumped when Holmes gave up on the trunk and went to the dresser, yanking out the top drawer and letting it fall to the floor, I gave up and just turned my hearing aids off, quickly returning them to their case in my bag.

It was significantly quieter without the hearing aids; I could still hear most of the racket Holmes was making, notice more of the vibration of the objects hitting the floor that Holmes kept throwing around, but it helped me feel more anchored in the moment.

I wasn't thrilled to be ransacking Watson's bedroom, but I could do my part and try to help find his journals.

Even though the desk had clearly been searched, I went over it again, checking in the drawers, underneath it, and came up with nothing. I spent some time searching in the closet with Suruthi, which was surprisingly barren.

It wasn't that big of a room, and the more of a mess Holmes made, the more cramped it became. Soon I was stepping around more articles of clothing, shoes, a few pictures here and there. How much longer were we going to spend in here?

I closed my eyes as I leaned against the edge of the desk and rubbed my forehead with the heel of my hand. I didn't think I was starting to get a migraine, but there was a definite headache blooming.

If I had a stack of private journals, where would I hide them?

I tried to pick through the one-on-one encounters I'd had with Watson so far, but I wasn't coming up with much. Watson was polite and a bit soft-spoken while still maintaining a stern disposition. He obviously enjoyed what he did, and he obviously wanted to see his students succeed in their endeavors.

And then, like the world's biggest cliché, the answer fell into my brain like in one of those silly cartoons where some unfortunate soul gets a piano dropped on their head.

I almost tripped over my feet in my haste to get to the bed and dropped to the floor beside the end table. There wasn't a lot of clearance between the floor and the bed, but there was enough room for me to pull out the flashlight on my phone and start looking around.

It was even dustier under the bed, but mostly free from

debris. Nothing that I was able to see seemed suspicious or stood out to me as strange.

I pulled myself upright with a groan and sat back on my heels, brushing some hair out of my face. At some point Percy had joined me on the floor, close enough for me to hear him without my hearing aids on. "We've already looked under there."

"Well, I'm looking again," I said. "Watson told me that it's like visiting an old friend whenever he reads his earlier stuff. I'm willing to bet he keeps at least one or two journals close by so he can do just that."

"Possibly," Percy said after a moment of thought. "We've already gone through that nightstand too, but maybe . . ."

He motioned for me to move aside and together we went through the contents of the nightstand (a bunch of pens, stopwatch, handkerchief, one very old Bible).

"Here, let's move this," Percy said, gripping the bottom of the nightstand. "Something might be underneath it."

The nightstand was deceptively heavy, and it took the two of us pushing it to the side for the thing to budge. We managed a few inches before the nightstand seemed to hit a snag and refused to move.

It was impossible to squash the zip of excitement that shot up my spine. "There's gotta be something under there."

"A divot in the flooring, most likely," Percy said, ever the realist.

"Maybe," I said.

But maybe not.

I was pretty sure we had both broken out into a sweat by the time we got the nightstand out of the way.

The space where the table had been was empty, save for more dust, and Percy had been right; there was a divot in the flooring, a small hole that couldn't have been any larger than a quarter.

But large enough for someone to slip their finger inside, and that's exactly what I did.

"Wait, Jules, what're you—"

The piece of flooring came up with no trouble at all, and I let out an excited, *"Aha!"* at what lay underneath—several small, leather-bound journals stacked neatly together.

I'd managed to snatch one of the journals before I was quite literally being dragged away so Holmes could see the discovery for himself. His resulting shouts were *definitely* loud enough for me to hear without the hearing aids.

Percy seemed to be attempting to console Holmes as he started piling the journals in his arms, something about it being okay he'd missed this one, everyone was off their game every now and then.

It was easy as breathing to tune everything else out as I sat down at the desk and began to read.

26

CHAPTER

Luckily My Pens Are New

March 18, 1896

*I can scarcely believe it to be true. If it were not for the fact that I have
witnessed it with my own two eyes, Holmes moving about our old rooms as if
he never once left, the blasted chemistry experiments in the drawing room, the
violin at ungodly hours of the morning, I would think him still deceased.*

*But Holmes is alive. Holmes is alive, having suddenly appeared in my
practice not a fortnight ago, and of course in disguise. I confess my response
to his reveal was rather humiliating, losing consciousness the way I did, but
he did not hold it against me. I was then, however, overcome with the urge
to give my old friend a good walloping, regardless of how pleased I was to see
him again.*

*I was filled with a rage unlike ever before at his notion that I would not have
been so affected by his death. I, unaffected? After all that Holmes and I
had gone through together—every case, every perilous situation we happened
across, the injuries, and bloodshed—and I would not have been affected?
What a ludicrous and unequivocally false sentiment.*

Having accused me of wearing my heart on my sleeve more than once, I am sure Holmes was perfectly aware of those thoughts that crossed my mind during our reunion. And yet he did not offer anything beyond a mere, "I must owe you an apology, Watson." Holmes's apology—if one could even describe it as such—was not without merit, but one I was not entirely sure that he sincerely felt. When had the great Sherlock Holmes ever truly cared for a single living soul beyond that of his own intellect?

If I had not been so eager to return to our old rooms in Baker Street, desperate to have even the smallest semblance of adventure in my life again, I would have taken the time to ponder our next move. I will not deny that I am thrilled to be in the same presence as my old friend again, but it would be foolish of me to overlook the fact that Holmes is not the same man he was before his plunge over the falls in Switzerland. What do I know of this man now?

But perhaps I am simply getting ahead of myself. It surely would not be the first time. What with the influx of patients at my practice and Holmes's unceasing desire for the game, I have had little time for much rest these days.

Perhaps all I need is a short holiday. I do not believe I can even recall the last time I went on holiday. Holmes would be welcome to join me, I suppose. He has mentioned more than once a desire to visit the Sussex Downs. Perhaps that is where we will go. Holmes has not divulged much from his time away, but I suspect that wherever he went, there was little time for a holiday.

I have not yet decided whether I will broach the subject with Holmes. That will be determined over time.

John Hamish Watson is no fool. One day I will learn the secrets Holmes still wishes to keep from me. He will not make a fool of me ever again.

April 29, 1896

Today marks the conclusion of our first case solved in over three years. It was not one of the most difficult cases we had ever experienced in our years together, yet nonetheless delicate in nature—a series of children gone missing over the course of several weeks. I am thankful the culprit's reasoning was not any more nefarious than simply desiring more work hands. The children were returned to their families in near perfect condition, if not a little shaken. This will unfortunately be an experience they no doubt will never forget, and I wish them all well.

I had little doubt we would be able to solve it with Holmes at the helm, and rest assured we did, in under seventy-two hours no less. Holmes has proven himself to be the same cold and calculating machine capable of the most extreme deductions, but my suspicions of his changed countenance continue to be proven correct.

Even more short-tempered and reckless beyond a reasonable doubt than before, though he will refuse to acknowledge as much. Something has happened to the man, but he will not say what. I know I must respect Holmes's wishes, but how can I, when that blasted seven percent solution continues to make an almost daily appearance? To prevent his mind from stagnating he has said, I know, but at what cost? It leaves him in the blackest of moods, however stimulating he claims it to be, and increasingly on edge. Mrs. Hudson has begun to complain of the bullet holes riddling the walls of the sitting room, though Holmes continues to insist that he is not responsible (on this he blamed the dog).

Does he truly desire to rid the world of his genius so prematurely yet again—perhaps permanently? The mere notion of losing Holmes to his inner demons is one that has caused several sleepless nights as of late. I fear these sleepless nights shall continue.

June 8, 1896

Today was not the first time I had ever been struck by a bullet, but it was the first time—and very likely the only time—I witnessed Holmes showing any sign of the sense of humanity or love that I have long since suspected he may lack. I am fortunate it was a superficial wound, one that will surely be healed in a short matter of time, but that seemed to provide Holmes with little reassurance in the end. Holmes confessed to it himself: the man responsible for wounding me would not have left that cellar alive should he have succeeded in taking my life.

We have not spoken of it since our return to Baker Street. Holmes retired to his room, and I suspect he will not emerge for several days, as is his regular routine. I have spent the last few hours reflecting upon the earlier events of today, and I do not believe I am any closer to understanding what exactly occurred.

As I have stated before, this was hardly the first time I had ever been shot. I am reminded of this fact anytime a dreadful chill descends upon London and my shoulder seizes up from the old bullet still lodged deep into the muscle there, leaving me in a great deal of agony. And make no mistake, while the mere graze of the bullet today had hurt tremendously, the pain had somehow not registered with me as Holmes whipped the man over the head with the butt of his pistol and proceeded to toss him aside as if he were as light as a feather.

I wonder if I have misjudged my old friend since his return, now that I have seen that he is indeed capable of feeling, however profusely he may deny it. At the very least, I now can attest to the fact that my old friend does care. That very well may have to be enough.

I didn't have a name for the feeling that had begun to creep over me as I closed the journal. It wasn't a good one. The remaining pages in the journal had either been crossed out with black ink, or ripped out entirely, leaving me without much else to go on.

But these entries alone were enough to confirm what was still (mostly) apparent: Watson cared deeply for Holmes. Seeing for myself the words written in Watson's own handwriting, I had a hard time believing that Watson would have had any ill intentions in his goal of keeping Holmes safe. He probably could have gone about things differently, like not locking Holmes in his office, for example, but Watson did care.

I looked up from the journal in my lap at Suruthi's approach. She had a journal in hand herself and was looking like she didn't know what to make of it either. I watched intently as she very slowly said words that I thought were, "What year do you have?"

"Eighteen ninety-six," I said. "Right after Holmes made his grand reappearance. Hang on, let me grab my hearing aids."

Once I grabbed the things and got them back in, I joined Percy, Suruthi, and Holmes on the floor in one very mismatched semicircle. Holmes had pulled out every journal from beneath the floorboards and they were now stacked neatly between us. There were about a dozen or so, all wrapped neatly with leather bands, but they were unlabeled, so it was anyone's guess what years the journals covered.

"Do you think these will do the trick, Holmes?" Percy asked cautiously.

Holmes was flipping so rapidly through the pages of one journal that I was sure he couldn't possibly be absorbing anything. "Yes, yes. I do think this will . . ."

And that was it for conversation.

I passed the first journal to Suruthi and took another from the stack. The journals were definitely out of chronological order, as the one I now started picked up about two years after Holmes's return.

January 24, 1898

It has been roughly thirty days since my beloved Mary has left me, and still the earth has not yet stopped spinning. My former rooms in Baker Street had already been prepared when I showed up on the doorstep. Mrs. Hudson had spent a considerable amount of time tutting about me, fixing tea, and had Holmes not intervened, she surely would not have stopped any time soon.

The only acknowledgement Holmes gave on the matter came later before we retired for the evening—a hand upon my shoulder, a hard squeeze, and a quiet, "I am sorry, John."

Strangely enough, I believe that was exactly what I needed to hear in that moment.

I will adapt to life as a widower; it is inevitable. And perhaps my having returned to Baker Street will lessen the ache some. But it is not the same. The light of my life was extinguished the day Mary died. Nothing will ever reignite it.

May 17, 1898

I have decided to take up my medical practice again, much to Holmes's displeasure—the reason, of course, being that he is in need of his "Boswell." I have attempted to reassure Holmes more than once that my practicing medicine will not interfere with his work, to which he replies that I am more than a fool than I let on. The urge to bludgeon him with one of his own massive chemistry volumes becomes overwhelming in these moments.

I have not said as much to Holmes, but there are times where I have found myself in a black mood of my own. It is weary upon the soul to witness the utmost depravity of human nature repeatedly, and with no apparent end in sight. The conclusion of our most recent case made this more apparent than ever. I truly believe that I could have saved that young woman, so brutally wounded at the hands of her own husband, had we arrived with enough time. I have seen death before, and death more gruesome than the young woman's to be sure, but I must acknowledge that hers has affected me most profoundly. She was so young.

Mrs. Hannah Collins had been her name, and her parents had poured their life savings into hiring Holmes with the hope that he would uncover the truth of the abuse their daughter was enduring. Holmes refused to be compensated, and whilst his skills were as finely tuned as ever, he still was not quick enough to save the young woman. We were not quick enough.

My military service made it very apparent that no one in life is ever able to save every individual, but by God, do I wish I could.

I do not know if this particular case weighs as heavily upon Holmes as it does myself and I dare not ask him. I only know that I must do what I can to heal the ache I feel deep in my bones. I want my two hands, however rough and calloused they are now, to treat the ill and tend to the wounded—to heal again. I am convinced the effort to achieve this will be worth it.

I only managed three entries in this journal before I encountered the same problem as before: the rest of the pages were blacked out.

"What year is that one?" Percy asked, motioning to the journal I held limply in my hands. "Eighteen ninety-eight," I answered. "Here, look for yourself."

We ended up swapping journals, and I ended up backtracking

with this one, reading a few entries from the end of eighteen ninety-six and into eighteen ninety-seven, about the case that led to what I knew would be Watson's short-lived marriage to a woman by the name of Mary Morstan. It was a little gut-wrenching to read about Watson's great love of Mary, knowing they would only have about eighteen months together. What sealed the deal was the very last entry in the journal before the remaining pages had been ripped out entirely. It was a short entry and written with a shaky hand, underlined three times:

November 2, 1897

On this day Mary informed me that I am to be a father.

This journal I passed on to Suruthi without a word. I could figure out for myself what must have occurred between Watson's last entry in eighteen ninety-seven and the beginning of eighteen ninety-eight.

I was about to reach for another from the stack when Holmes suddenly leapt to his feet with an exuberant shout of, "I HAVE FOUND IT!"

"*Cripes*, Holmes, would you pipe down?" Suruthi yelped as I clapped my hands over my ears.

"Never!" Holmes said happily, plopping himself down on the floor again. "Come, look at this! Read for yourselves!"

How I ended up on the bed beside Suruthi with Percy on the floor next to Holmes was *weird*, but reading over Holmes's shoulder was far from the strangest thing any of us had done lately.

"Do you see here?" Holmes said, pointing to the date of the first entry.

I had to lean in closer to make out Watson's neat, compact scrawl, but wasn't having much luck.

"August fourth, eighteen ninety-nine," Percy read aloud.

Holmes's excitement must've been contagious; I almost let out a shout too.

"That's right before *it* happened!" I said, tapping Holmes shoulder. "Well, whatever *it* is. You kept rambling on and on about the case with Violet Ramsey's weird death and when I asked, you told me the date was August seventh, eighteen ninety-nine."

"Indeed," Holmes said coolly without looking at me. "Let us continue, shall we?"

August 4, 1899

It would not be an exaggeration to say Holmes literally jumped for joy when Lestrade of all people visited Baker Street today, just as Holmes had finished reading the news article with the sensational headline of: WOMAN DROPS DEAD AT SÉANCE. As it so happened, this was the very same case Lestrade then presented to us.

Miss Violet Ramsey was her name, the eldest daughter of some minor nobleman, and engaged to be married this coming September. Needless to say, the nuptials will no longer be occurring.

Miss Ramsey had attended the séance in question with her betrothed, a Mister Everard Taylor, and another close acquaintance as yet unnamed. The current theory is that Miss Ramsey suffered from some sort of unknown health condition; why else would a perfectly healthy young woman barely into her twenty-first year of life expire so suddenly?

However, Lestrade tells us that could not be further from the truth. What was so conveniently excluded from the papers was that it was discovered during the postmortem not three hours later that Miss Ramsey's body contained not one drop of blood in her veins.

As a medical man, I am intrigued at how such a thing could be possible without some sort of grievous wound or some other injury that left the young lady bleeding out for a considerable time. From what we have read in the case notes Lestrade brought with him, the entire incident lasted less than a half hour.

Secretly I was relieved when Lestrade offered to let me examine the body myself without having to ask. Holmes had given me a knowing and rather smug look as we prepared to leave for Scotland Yard. It has been some time since our last case, and I will admit that my medical practice has more recently become occupied with several patients ridden with gout.

I will not admit this aloud to Holmes, but I am glad for the disruption of my tedious day-to-day routine, although I wish it had not come at the cost of Miss Ramsey's life.

August 6, 1899

Lestrade's retelling and the handwritten account by the constable who had responded to the incident had been accurate, much to Holmes's chagrin.

Only ten or so minutes into the séance hosted by self-professed medium Miss Adelaide Shaw and Violet Ramsey collapsed. Her betrothed at first thought it to be a fit of some sort, but the young man reported that she lay completely still moments after falling from her seat.

Upon examining Miss Ramsey's remains, I was shocked to find that not one wound or mark or even the smallest of scratches had been documented in the postmortem report.

This is a most curious and unfortunate case to be sure. Never in the entire time I have practiced medicine have I heard of such a thing occurring.

Thanks to Lestrade and his "damnable incompetence," Holmes and I were not able to see for ourselves the scene of Miss Ramsey's death before the sitting room in question had been thoroughly cleaned. This did not stop us from paying a visit, however, and I admit I was rather surprised when Miss Adelaide Shaw greeted us in the sitting room in question.

Miss Shaw is a rather plain young woman, not much older than Miss Ramsey had been, simply dressed and very humble indeed. And yet the young lady has already grown in popularity amongst the vast majority of London Society so enraptured by the many facets of spiritualism.

Miss Shaw was perfectly pleasant and appeared genuinely affected by the incident as she regaled us with her telling of the night of Miss Ramsey's death. She had been adamant indeed that she would never willingly do any harm to another human being and had been quick to send her immediate condolences to the Ramsey family.

Really, the only strange behavior the young lady exhibited was that she frequently kept fiddling with the bracelet she wore—an unusual thing with a leather band wrapped around a piece of silver and not something I have ever seen a well-to-do young woman wear.

Before departing, Miss Shaw invited us to attend a séance of hers so that we may witness for ourselves that no harm ever comes to anyone who participates. Holmes happily accepted her offer and the date has been set for the following week.

Miss Shaw's parting words had been, "The spirits are kind to those who treat them equally."

While it is obvious that Miss Shaw is a kind woman, I cannot say the same about any spirits. I do not think I even believe in any spirits. And what would they have to offer me as it were? Mary and our child are long gone now.

August 19, 1899

It feels as if for the first time in several days there is not some lead-weighted cloud suffocating me. Though I have not closed my eyes to sleep since, I feel well rested. Slowly I have begun to remember in bits and pieces the events of the night of August the twelfth, but I do not know if I . . . I am afraid I cannot trust what flashes across my closed lids when I blink. My hand protests even now as I attempt to write an account of what I do remember— what little that is.

Perhaps I am not ready.

August 30, 1899

I have just realized Holmes has not moved from his chair before the fire in over a fortnight. He sits exactly as he had the night of our return, but perfectly lucid when I remarked upon this.

"So it would seem, my dear fellow," was his response.

So it would seem.

September 22, 1899

Today when Mrs. Hudson had returned from her yearly holiday with her sister, she screamed upon the sight of us. I could not figure out why we would have elicited such a response. I followed her from the sitting room to the kitchen, where she fell into even more despair at the sight of rotten food in the cold box and the accompanying maggots. It is then that I recalled that Holmes and I have not stepped foot in the kitchen at all.

When Mrs. Hudson thrust a small looking glass into my hands so that I may reflect upon my own appearance, I saw the wound on my neck—a gash almost bone deep that I do not remember receiving. Mrs. Hudson's horror became clearer when I noticed for myself that there was no blood in this wound.

I can only think I must have sustained this injury some time ago, but I do not know when.

I spent time tending to the unnatural wound and sutured it closed with some difficulty, and still, no blood. Most unusual.

"You look positively horrific, Watson," Holmes told me as I had worked. This seemed to amuse him.

I commented that Mary would have thought the injury added character to my face.

"Perhaps," was Holmes's response.

He then proceeded to ask me to tend to the wound in his side even larger than my own had been, insisting that he did not remember how the injury occurred either.

"Most curious," was his singular response as I attempted to clean the wound that rather resembled teeth marks.

But there surprisingly wasn't much to clean, as Holmes appeared to have no blood either. Most curious indeed.

January 2, 1900

Our beloved Mrs. Hudson left this earth today and I cannot help but feel we are partially responsible—or rather, Holmes is responsible.

Prone to wandering as he has always been, Holmes went for one of his frequent walks about London, but at the most inopportune time. A fierce storm befell the city, bringing with it a most violent blizzard. It did not occur to me to go looking for Holmes until it became dark, and Mrs. Hudson pointed out that Holmes had been gone for some time.

"Ah, well, you know our Holmes, Mrs. Hudson," I had said to her. "He knows how to look after himself."

When Holmes did return the next morning, ice-cold and frostbitten but otherwise perfectly pleasant, Mrs. Hudson again screamed at the sight of him, only this time she appeared to have fainted. It brings me some pain to recount that she did not get up.

I put Holmes in front of the fire to thaw and a mere hour later, it was as if he had never set foot outside at all.

April 1, 1900

It is a curious thing that our first case in several months ended in Holmes meeting the finer end of a knife.

The lad responsible was barely older than a boy and green about the gills as he tried to convince us that he had been ordered to pickpocket the old man; his death had been entirely accidental.

The young boy had seemed surprised that he had done it, lunged forward to thrust the jagged knife into Holmes's chest. He had seemed horrified when

Holmes did not react, merely withdrew the noticeably clean knife with only a quiet grunt of effort.

The boy seemed rather content to be taken into custody.

"I say, Watson," Holmes had remarked upon our return to Baker Street. "I am rather miffed at the tear in this shirt."

Here I told my companion he should be more concerned with the fact that he had just been stabbed, to which Holmes replied that he had already put the whole ordeal from his mind and that the injury was one that had only "tickled" just the slightest bit. Nevertheless, I insisted he let me tend to him, which he grudgingly permitted.

I must confess it is a strange thing, trying to suture flesh so pale and corpse-like, but also strangely cleaner, as there was no blood to mop up.

"Wait just a second," Suruthi said, catching Holmes's hand before he could turn the page. "So not only did you sustain some side wound, but you also apparently beat hypothermia and were stabbed and survived that too?

"So it would seem," Holmes said, surprisingly calm.

"Oh, okay," Suruthi said. "If that's all then."

"Do we really need to keep reading?" I asked, feeling even more nauseated than before. "I think it's pretty obvious whatever happened to Holmes and Watson was because of that séance, and it left them in some kind of . . . shell-like state."

I was struggling with the urge to try and comfort Holmes after reading all that he had been through—Watson too—but *how*?

Even more confusing was wrapping my mind around the

fact that Ashley had somehow been responsible. What could she have possibly done that would leave Holmes and Watson in such a state?

This also meant that she had to be in some way responsible for the death of Violet Ramsey.

"Doesn't matter anyway," Percy said, taking the book from Holmes. "Look here, there's only one entry left, and it's from nineteen-eleven."

"What, a whole eleven years later?" Suruthi said. "What were you getting up to in that time, eh, Holmes?"

"Experimenting," a voice said behind us.

CHAPTER

AND I SUPPOSE YOU CONVENIENTLY FORGOT TO SHARE?

I wasn't the only one who screamed at Watson's sudden arrival.

Percy was stumbling his way to his feet while Suruthi outright fell off the bed, she'd started so badly at hearing Watson's voice. I only narrowly avoided landing on top of Holmes as I tried to get off the bed without my face meeting the floor.

Watson was leaning against the doorjamb, arms crossed, and seemed to be paying no attention to the fact his bedroom had just been ransacked.

"Please, continue," he said politely. "Far be it from me to stop you."

No one said a word for one tense moment, and Watson scoffed. "You might as well finish the last entry, for heaven's sake. You've already read everything else, haven't you?"

"*Yes*," Holmes agreed, somewhat suspicious of Watson's calm demeanor.

"Off you go then."

November 8, 1911

It comes and goes, my desire to write and chronicle my "adventures" with my companion, the great consulting detective Sherlock Holmes. Today it is still "gone." Though I have not picked up a pen to do so for some time now, I just had the strangest encounter and wish to document it.

It was an unusually bright day in London despite the season, and I desired a walk after Holmes informed me that I had been gazing longingly out the sitting room windows for several hours.

So off I went without a particular destination in mind. Paying tribute to my friend, I wandered for some time, up and down the surrounding streets, and somehow ending up near Grosvenor Square.

No sooner had I entered the park than I was being stopped by a woman who appeared as if she were looking at a ghost. The woman was unaccompanied and dressed plainly in black. She looked familiar in some way that I could not place, otherwise she would not have stood out as different from any other woman out for an afternoon stroll.

The first thing this woman asked of me was, "How are you alive?"

"I do not know what you mean, madam," I confessed.

My response seemed to upset the woman. She gripped my forearm when I attempted to offer her my arm to escort her home, and I saw that there was a ghastly burn scar on her wrist. Her skin was significantly marred and difficult to look away from, but her shout was loud enough to rattle my skull.

Most of what she shouted at me I could not make any sense of, but what I did understand sent a fierce chill down my spine, unfeeling as I have been these last dozen years or so.

Before the woman was led away by an incredibly mortified man who must have been her brother or husband, she had screamed, "I saw you die!"

Years of foolhardy attempts at ending my life through various means had me convinced that perhaps Holmes and I had somehow been cursed to walk this earth forever. It is somewhat reassuring to learn that we were meant to be dead after all.

There was a chilling silence in the room as we read Watson's last journal entry. Watson himself had gone to the desk and was investigating the content of the box we'd lugged all the way from Adele's shop.

"So…" Suruthi cleared her throat, sounding uncomfortable as she said, "I suppose we're going to talk about this now."

"What more must we discuss?" Holmes said, shutting the journal with a loud *snap*. "I believe Watson has said it all through these meticulous journal entries of his."

Watson made some noise of agreement as he started rifling through the packing peanuts in the box.

"Well, if you're not going to ask, I will then," Percy said, surprisingly bold. "In your last entry, the woman you wrote about was that medium, wasn't she? Adelaide Shaw."

"So it was," Watson said.

"So that means she *was* responsible for…whatever it is that happened to you," I said.

I couldn't tell if I was growing more excited as the pieces

began to fall into place, but something still wasn't sitting quite right with me. Watson was far too calm about having found his room turned upside down, and I could practically feel the fury radiating from Holmes where he stood less than a foot away from me.

"Correct me if I am wrong, Watson," Holmes began with a tremor in his voice, "but I believe you conveniently forgot to share any details of your impromptu meeting with Miss Shaw— then *and* now."

"Or just didn't mention it at all," Suruthi added in an undertone.

"Holmes, would you care to remind me of the outcome of the nineteen-ten case concerning Lord Harrington?"

Watson posed this question so casually that we were all taken aback. Watson spoke as if he meant to have a conversation about the changing weather, not something so clearly life-altering.

Holmes stared open-mouthed at Watson as he waited patiently for a response.

"You *do* remember the case I speak of, yes?" Watson said politely. "Lord Harrington and his attempted assassination in parliament? The poor man was certainly a right mess, showing up at our lodgings in Baker Street day and night, begging us to figure out who wanted him dead."

It was obvious that Holmes had absolutely no idea what Watson was talking about, and he was struggling to come up with a way around admitting this.

"Sherlock, you took a bullet for the man," Watson said, his expression turning grim. "Surely you remember."

"Of course I do," Holmes snapped. Out of the corner of my

eye, I could see Holmes's hand had begun to tremble. Though his pallor was usually an unhealthy one, he looked even more ill now. *"Of course I..."*

Watson stood and approached Holmes with an outstretched hand, lowering his voice when he spoke next. "I did not share this information with you, Holmes, because I did not wish to—"

"Do not say it was because you did not want to cause me undue stress or worry," Holmes said with a sneer. "As if I have never endured either before."

"I will not deny that you have," Watson said quietly. "But surely you must admit that there are times where you have been most—"

"Insane?" Holmes supplied angrily.

"Of course not!" Watson fired back, raising his voice to match Holmes's. "Occasionally erratic, perhaps manic even, but incredibly *reckless*! I cannot count the number of times I have seen you actively seek out danger with little concern for your personal safety, Holmes, and you know as well as I do that will wear on a person after a century."

"Dear Watson, *you* know as well as *I* that we do not—"

"We may exist as an empty shell of a human being, but that does not mean I can bare to witness the closest friend I have *ever* had the pleasure of knowing displaying such blatant disregard for their own life!"

"What does it matter?!" Holmes voice echoed like thunder. "What I choose to do with *my own life* should be of little consequence to you! Dare I ask if there is anything else you have hidden from me?"

"A rather foolish statement, to think that I should not care what you choose to do with your own life," Watson said calmly. "After everything we have endured together. I would have thought you would know me better than that."

Holmes converged on Watson like a predator closing in on their prey, and real panic had begun to take hold. I moved closer to Percy and Suruthi, and Percy reached for my hand at the same time as I reached for his. I squeezed his hand tight, willing myself to stay put and not flee in terror.

Whatever happened next, we were going to have to see this through to the end.

Holmes chucked the journal onto the desk with considerable force, almost undoing the binding on the thing, and it was as if the proverbial gauntlet had been thrown down.

"I demand you explain," Holmes said, struggling to keep his voice level. "*Now.*"

Watson's face had become a blank mask as Holmes loomed before him, and for one very tension-filled moment, he did not speak. When he did, it was a flat, "Very well."

"And what are we going to do when Holmes and Watson start to duke it out?" I whispered to the other two. "Make a break for it?"

"I don't know!" Suruthi whispered back, sounding panicked. "I don't want to witness them murdering each other, but I also *really* want to know what is going on here!"

"When you think about it," Percy said quietly, "this is more than a century in the making. It's going to take some time to . . . unpack everything."

No kidding, I thought.

As if sharing the same wavelength of thought, Watson

directed Holmes to the chair beside the desk. "This will not be an easy thing to explain. You might as well sit down."

Holmes did not sit down, instead fixing Watson with such an intimidating glare I felt a shiver go up my spine.

Watson brushed this off, picking up the journal Holmes had thrown, flipping through the pages. Holmes managed about one minute before he was loudly clearing his throat, a nonverbal demand to get on with it.

Watson tossed the journal aside on the desk and crossed his arms. "Am I correct in assuming you read each journal?"

"We read enough," Holmes answered at once.

Watson nodded. "Very well then. As you have already learned, our troubles began with the last case we took as . . . well, I do not know any other word to use but *mortal*."

I exchanged looks with Percy. This was a start.

"Holmes and I never paid much attention to any of the gossip rags publishing endless articles about a séance being hosted every other night or table tipping or connecting with the spirits or any other aspect of dealing with the occult. When the news of the death of a young socialite in attendance at a séance hit the papers, however, we began to pay attention."

Given what we'd read about the bizarre circumstances surrounding the death of Violet Ramsey, this was making perfect sense.

Watson went on. "Of course we seized the opportunity to meet with the self-proclaimed medium herself and investigate the sitting room where the séance had taken place." Watson paused to pass a hand over his mouth, debating his next words. "Adelaide Shaw was insistent that she had nothing to do with the death of the young woman, and I suppose I did believe her—at least, partially. She appeared earnest in her work and told us more than once that the spirits would never harm anyone."

"An absolute falsehood," Holmes interjected. "The young lady was lying throughout the entire conversation."

"And you remember all that?" Percy asked hesitantly.

"Of course I do," Holmes snapped without turning around. "She never once maintained direct eye contact, her respiration was increased, and she would not stop fidgeting with that trinket that adorned her wrist."

We all looked to Watson for confirmation, who merely nodded again.

"All true," he said. "I believe that *she* believed what she was saying, but something was obviously troubling her. When she invited us to attend her next séance, of course we accepted."

"Yes, yes, I remember," Holmes said, and he had begun to pace. "The night of August the twelfth, eighteen ninety-nine. It was raining and you were complaining about your shoulder, as always."

Watson sat back and let Holmes begin to fill in the pieces for himself as he paced, head down and hands clasped behind his back.

"I must confess I do not remember who else may have been in attendance that night, but the scene was perfectly set. Velvet tablecloth, one singular candle, the parlor room dimly lit, Miss Shaw already seated."

"Go on," Watson encouraged when Holmes faltered.

A few moments passed before Holmes resumed his story.

"We took our seats, as invited, and the butler closed the

door, but he . . ." Holmes's head snapped up as he turned back to Watson. "He locked the door."

Again Watson nodded.

"Miss Shaw explained how we were to proceed with the séance," Holmes continued, a frown taking over his face. "We were to stay seated and do not . . . we could not . . . *break the circle*."

CHAPTER

Rules Were Meant
to Be Broken

"Y ou broke the circle, didn't you?" Suruthi said, advancing on
Holmes. "You broke the circle and—"

Watson held up a hand to cut her off, watching Holmes
intently as he sagged against the wall, head falling into his hands.
Holmes was mumbling something unintelligible, and it was only
at another gentle nudge from Watson that he began to speak again.

"We *must* have broken the circle," Holmes said, then groaned
as if in pain as he dropped his head back against the wall. "But I
cannot remember how, or why we . . ."

"Because of that piece of silver Miss Shaw wore around her
wrist," Watson said quietly when the silence became too much
to handle.

"Because of the piece of silver," Holmes repeated, eyes fixed
on the ceiling. "It was the silver that . . ."

"Hold up a second," Percy said suddenly, catching us all by
surprise. "When you ran into Adelaide Shaw however many
years later, you wrote that she had a badly burned wrist, right?"

"Indeed," Watson answered. "A third-degree burn, at minimum, I would say."

I was expecting Percy to start pacing like Holmes. He was visibly excited, and I couldn't understand why when I personally felt myself rapidly losing any semblance of hope I had left from earlier this evening.

Because apparently Suruthi and Percy hadn't realized yet that Ashley's *wrists hadn't been burned.* I wasn't ready to think of the implications of what that meant.

"What are you on about, Percy?" Suruthi asked cautiously. "I don't like that look on your face."

Percy ignored her, carrying on with whatever piece of evidence he may have discovered. "She was using the coin as a conduit, wasn't she? That's why she wore it during the séance. She was using the coin as a conduit to better her chances of contacting *the spirits* or whatever."

Watson looked rather proudly at Percy for having come up with the big reveal on his own, and Holmes had gone slack-jawed as he stared at a spot on the wall. It was the same faraway look I'd seen before, which meant he was probably beginning to slip from the present.

"So, if you broke the circle then, I bet that must've seriously pissed off whatever spirits she'd managed to contact," Suruthi offered, now lost in thought too. "And then the spirits, what? Attacked you?"

The tension in the room as we waited for Watson to answer had become near palpable and I felt like squirming.

"*Well*?" Percy pressed when Watson remained silent. "*Is* that what happened?"

I felt myself begin to deflate when Watson grimaced.

"I cannot say with certainty that is what happened, but all of the research I have done would suggest so."

"Research?" Holmes said suddenly, his voice sharp. "What *research?*"

"Oh, don't give me that look, Sherlock," Watson said exasperatedly. "You have done your own fair share of research over the years."

"Which I have *always* made a point to share with—"

"Please, gentleman, can we not?" Suruthi interrupted. "*Please*. Just finish the story."

Holmes shot Watson a sullen glare but kept quiet, gesturing grandly for Watson to continue.

"Naturally I have conducted several decades of research at this point," Watson said. "And it was in a grimoire I found deep in the recesses of the Bodleian Library where I believe I encountered the truth." He paused to rub a hand across the back of his neck, sighing. "Mister Byers was correct, according to what I read in the text. The young lady was using that piece of silver as a conduit to better connect with . . . *the other side*, so to say. To what extent and for what purpose, I do not know. I doubt we will ever have a direct answer, but I speculate the young woman was doing it for both fame and fortune. From what I have been able to deduce, Miss Shaw was not born into wealth and nor were many advantages given to her early on in life. I suspect she used what skills she did have to make a name for herself, and that just so happened to be by capitalizing upon the spiritualist movement."

Watson's words hung heavy in the air.

For all I was in the know, Watson was making a great deal of sense in a way I didn't want him to. The type of information

Watson must've gained from conducting research in the Bodleian Library was unimaginable, and that also explained having a contact there: Joel the tour guide.

"*And*?" Holmes pressed impatiently. "On with it, Watson!"

Watson ignored this, speaking more to the three of us than Holmes.

"There is a certain delicate balance to this world that most are not aware exists. Some might call it the line between *good* and *evil*, but I don't think it's as simple as that. Regardless of what one refers to it as, surely there are those who are . . . less than thrilled when that balance is upset."

"Meaning what, precisely?" Holmes demanded with a scoff. It was clear he thought little of the turn the conversation had taken. "This speaks of lunacy, Watson."

"Perhaps so, but think about what the young woman was doing," Watson said, raising his voice to match Holmes's. "Regardless of what her intentions were, she was still charging a fee to . . . to . . . *perform* for the public, to channel the spirits or whatever you want to refer to it as. Granted, she was not the only one doing so, but perhaps if she had *angered* the wrong spirit . . ."

An unsettling feeling began to form in the pit of my stomach as Watson's words filled the silence.

"So, maybe if . . ." Suruthi took in a deep breath as if trying to steady herself. "If either of you broke the circle, then you were . . . punished."

Watson's grim expression deepened as he rolled his shoulder as if he were suddenly *very* uncomfortable. "That would be my assumption as well, Miss Kaur."

"Forgive me, Watson, but I don't believe I understand what our *punishment* was," Holmes said, overly polite. "Would you care to elaborate upon the finer details? Presumably you must have read a great deal in that *grimoire* of yours."

"A kind of ancient magical text," Percy muttered to Suruthi before she could ask.

"*Magic*," Holmes repeated, his derisive snort impressive. "My dear boy, surely you know that such a thing does not exist."

"Doesn't it?" Watson said quietly. "Look at us, Sherlock. We both know we should have died that night, and now think about all we have done and experienced over the last century. Would any of it have been possible without *some* type of magic playing a part?"

"Um, excuse me?" I interjected hesitantly. "I mean, *sirs*. There's something I'm still confused about."

Watson motioned for me to continue.

"If the medium was using that bracelet as a conduit, you broke the circle to, what? Take her bracelet? To see if she was *actually* channeling spirits or whatever?"

Holmes blinked a few times, his lips pressing together in a hard line. "Yes, I suppose so. Why else?"

"So, what then? The coin sucked out your life force?" Suruthi threw out, laughing nervously.

It was safe to say none of us were expecting Watson's answer to be a simple, "Yes."

After that, the only thing I could manage was an articulate, "*Huh?*"

"That is to say, I believe so," Watson clarified. "I consider myself to be intelligent enough, but even then I had difficulty interpreting what I read in the grimoire. Holmes and I may have broken the circle by touching the silver Miss Shaw possessed, but I am sure we very much remained seated at that table."

"So, let me get this straight," Percy said, a frown overtaking his features. "Whatever . . . ritual the medium had been doing ended up killing Violet Ramsey, but instead of doing the same to you both, you had your souls ripped out of you instead?"

"That is what I believe occurred, yes," Watson answered.

"But then why take your souls instead of killing you too?" I asked.

"Because there was no opportunity," Holmes said. His gaze was directed at Watson, but the glassy look in his eyes made it obvious he again was seeing something much different than the rest of us. "We were interrupted, weren't we, John?"

"Yes," Watson answered plainly. "It was the butler who had returned, presumably because of all the racket. I can't recall every detail, but I do remember there was so much *screaming* and a terrible chill that I felt deep in my bones, unlike anything I have ever experienced." Watson's voice trailed off into nothing as he fought to conceal a shudder. He cleared his throat a time or two before he tried to speak again. "When I finally came to, we were no longer in that drawing room in Miss Shaw's residence, but instead in some back alleyway a good distance from where we had been. Eventually I surmised that Miss Shaw must have believed us to be dead and tried to dispose of our bodies. Clearly that did not work, so I rousted Holmes, and we made our way back to Baker Street. A considerable amount of time had passed before we began to realize that something had happened to us that night."

And from what we'd read in Watson's journals, that time hadn't been enjoyable.

"*Jules*," Percy whispered. "You're hurting my hand."

I quickly dropped his hand with an apologetic look.

"Now I believe because Holmes had succeeded in ripping the piece of silver from the leather band Miss Shaw wore, she—"

"—got burned," Percy finished for Watson.

Watson nodded in response.

The thought occurred to me as Holmes walked heavily to the desk and dropped into the chair beside it, immediately reaching for the box with the typewriter. He had the thing unboxed in a matter of moments and had started messing around with the keys again, much like he'd done in Adele's shop the other day. The noise from the keys jamming had me wanting to cover my ears with my hands.

"If you were interrupted mid soul stealing, what happened to the parts that *were* taken?" I voiced aloud.

"Beg pardon?" Watson said, taken aback.

"What happened to the parts of your soul that were taken?" I said, somewhat impatiently. "Obviously you must have some bits left because you're still technically alive, aren't you? That must've meant all of Violet's was taken."

"Yes," Watson said slowly. "You are probably correct, Miss Montgomery."

"So, that being said," I continued. "Where's the rest of yours and Holmes's souls?"

"Have you not listened to anything I have said this evening?" Holmes suddenly said, looking right at me.

The speed with which he hefted the typewriter up was enough to have all of us leaping back in shock.

"Holmes," Watson started, reaching out to him. "What are you—?"

Holmes hurled the typewriter at the floor with such an astonishing amount of force that it seemed to shatter upon impact. He was on his knees the next second, slamming the pieces of typewriter again and again on the floor. By the time Watson had managed to wrestle Holmes back to his feet, all but dragging him away, all that was left were mangled bits of machinery.

"*Holmes*! What do you think you're doing?!" Watson yelled, struggling to keep him at bay. "Why would you—"

Holmes threw Watson off with another burst of that immense strength that had Watson stumbling back into the wall. On his knees again, Holmes started sorting through the broken pieces of the typewriter, frantically searching for something.

I caught a bright glint of light hitting some object just as Holmes snatched it up, shouting gleefully. His excitement lasted all of one second before he was cursing loudly, the object hitting the floor with a sharp *ping!*

Holmes was clutching his arm to his chest, his fingertips covered in angry red burns.

Suruthi's sudden gasp was impossibly loud in the room as she pointed a shaking finger toward Holmes. "*Oh my God.* Oh my God. It's the—that coin!"

"*What?*" Percy and I exclaimed.

Percy moved first, bending down beside Holmes to pick up the object he'd dropped almost like a literal hot potato. His quick yelp of surprise was enough confirmation that Suruthi had been correct.

"You're right, Suruthi," Percy said, sounding awed. "It's the coin."

"How can you be certain?" Watson cut in sharply.

"Because."

A shout of warning was on the tip of my tongue as Percy reached for the coin, but nothing happened—no cursing or burned fingertips this time.

"Look at the little design there," Percy said, the coin resting in the center of his palm as he held his hand out to Watson. "The symbol made up of the three rings? You can see the same one there in the photograph of Adelaide Shaw that I found."

I couldn't be sure how long the room was silent as we all stood staring at the coin still resting in Percy's palm. There didn't seem to be anything extraordinary about the thing. It was a little larger than a coin you might find in a bank, the edges a bit jagged, but it was overall plain. There had to be something *magical* about it though if Adelaide Shaw had used it as a conduit during a séance.

"They're in this, aren't they?" Percy said suddenly.

"What is?" Watson said distractedly. He hadn't once looked away from the coin.

"The pieces of your soul," Percy explained. "And Holmes's. Somehow they got trapped in this during whatever happened, and somehow the coin got lodged in that typewriter, maybe during all of the chaos Holmes was talking about. The chances are astronomical that the typewriter ended up in Jules's aunt's antique shop over a century later, but there you are." Percy glanced over at Holmes, smiling uncertainly. "I think you were right, Holmes. You must've been subconsciously drawn to the shop because that's where bits of your soul were."

"No, *don't*!" Watson lunged forward, grabbing Holmes's forearm, before he could take the coin from Percy. "You can't, it'll burn—"

"Let go, John." Holmes's voice was dangerously calm. His

face was blank as he stared at Watson, and that was somehow even scarier. "*Now.*"

Watson released his grip, but he definitely wasn't happy about it. Holmes slipped a silk handkerchief from his pocket and carefully took the coin from Percy. The barrier must've only partially worked; Holmes still winced as he wrapped the coin in the handkerchief, then returned it to his pocket.

It had become so quiet I could hear my pulse pounding in my ears and I was feeling as if I was about to take a tumble off the edge of a high building, my stomach was churning that much.

Suruthi broke the silence, voicing exactly what we all must have been thinking. "What now then?"

Holmes's answer was immediate. "We destroy the cursed thing."

Watson went slack-jawed, his eyebrows shooting up. His voice came out a croak as he repeated Holmes's words. "*Destroy it?*"

"Obviously," Holmes snapped, turning a glare on Watson. "What else?"

"But won't you—you know, *die* if you do that?" Percy said apprehensively.

"One can only hope," Holmes said, and the longing in his voice was unmistakable.

Holmes hadn't made it a secret that he was tired of the way he had been *existing* with Watson, and I couldn't really blame him. It had been a period of wakefulness for over a century for the man. I didn't want to imagine how exhausting that must've been, to see everything Holmes had and without a way to escape from the horrors of the world. Even if it solved nothing, an hour or two of good sleep always offered a clean slate for you to start over.

"Sherlock. We must consider every course of action as to how we proceed." Watson was speaking like he were addressing a small child, one hand extended toward him. "We cannot simply destroy—"

Holmes's thunderous expression was enough to silence Watson. "We can and we will."

Watson swallowed hard. Why did it look like he was getting nervous?

"*Sherlock*," he repeated, now imploring. "Please see reason, my friend. Everything I have read in that grimoire suggests that we might . . . we may meet a most . . . unfavorable end should that silver piece be destroyed, and not in the way you are hoping. We *must*—"

The only one who must have seen it coming was Watson, but even then, he wasn't fast enough to dodge Holmes's fist suddenly hurtling toward his face. There was a sickening crunch as Holmes's fist met Watson's nose, and then Holmes was slamming Watson up against the wall, forearm pressed into his neck.

I moved without thinking, grabbing the back of Percy's shirt to keep him from interfering.

"Your hesitation concerns me, John," Holmes said, that dangerous calm reappearing. "As I see it, there is *no* other course of action but to destroy that piece of silver. A simple solution of concentrated sulfuric acid should dissolve it in due time, and we should have whatever remnants of our souls returned to our being, at least that is what I suspect will occur. Then all that remains is to wait for the last century to catch up with us."

As if having anticipated Watson's reaction, Holmes caught Watson's fist rushing toward him open-handed. A full-out brawl unfolded from there.

Holmes clearly had the advantage, but Watson was holding his own, managing to get a few good punches in before Holmes knocked his feet out from underneath him, sending Watson crashing to the floor.

"*For crying out loud!*" Suruthi exclaimed, throwing up her hands.

She dodged my attempt to hold her back too and snatched the closest thing she could reach, what looked like an old cigar box, off the dresser. She threw it in the direction of Holmes and Watson.

The box collided with the side of Holmes's head, stunning him long enough for Percy to rush forward and drag him quite literally off Watson.

"That's *enough*, Holmes! Watson!" Suruthi was hands on hips as she glared at the two men. "Quit fighting like a couple of schoolboys and let's have a reasonable discussion about this, like the adults you're *supposed* to be!"

Holmes sounded only marginally breathless as he straightened up, fixing his shirtsleeves. "There is no discussion to be had. We will destroy that coin, and we—"

"No, I think we actually do need to have a conversation," I said, taking a step toward Watson. "Professor, is that Ashley's bumblebee pin that just fell out of your pocket?"

There was nothing but a tense silence in the wake of my question. No one spoke, and no one budged an inch; everyone's attention fixed on the bronze bumblebee pin that lay on the floor a short distance from Watson.

"I'm sorry," Suruthi finally said, her tone overly polite. "But I could've sworn you just asked the professor if Ashley's pin just fell out of his pocket."

"That's because I did." I pointed to the pin in question on the floor beside Watson where he sat, breathing harshly. It looked like Holmes may have gotten enough good hits in to break Watson's nose, but there wasn't a single drop of blood anywhere. Watson had yet to answer, and I was suddenly dreading it.

"Sir?" Percy spoke carefully. "There has to be a good explanation for this. Right?"

Watson remained silent.

"*John*," Holmes said sharply. "What the devil did you do?"

29

CHAPTER

VERITAS NUNQUAM PERIT

Watson used the desk to hoist himself up to his feet after scooping up the bumblebee pin, then offered it to me with an outstretched hand.

I didn't need to take a closer look. It was without a doubt Ashley's pin. How many other bumblebee pins had I seen recently?

"Can I see it, Jules?" Suruthi asked quietly.

I passed the pin over without a word.

"Ashley must've dropped this in your classroom, and you just picked it up, right? You were going to give it back to her," Suruthi said earnestly to Watson. "*Right?*"

We waited with bated breath for Watson to answer. When he finally did, what I heard made my heart skip a painful beat.

"I wish I could say that you were again correct, Miss Kaur."

I closed my eyes as I pressed a fist against my chest, trying to massage away the pain I felt blossoming there.

"Dare I ask why?" Holmes said, working to keep his voice level.

"You could," Watson said slowly. "But you would not like the answer."

"Well, as long as we're on a roll here, you might as well *tell the truth*, Watson!"

I hadn't meant to shout, but I thought it got my point across well enough.

There was a tic in Watson's cheek as his jaw locked, hands curling into fists at his side. He didn't seem able to meet the eyes of anyone in the room.

Holmes, apparently tired of waiting for a response, gripped Watson by the shoulder and forced him down into the chair at the desk. "I should be happy to assist in case you are having difficulty remembering, Watson. Your students and I discovered tonight that the missing girl and Miss Adelaide Shaw may very well be one and the same. What do you have to say on the matter?"

Watson seemed to deflate as he sagged against the desk, head falling into one hand. His shuddering inhale sounded like the last breath of a dying man.

"My students, though remarkably intelligent, would be incorrect."

Any last shred of hope I'd been holding on to shattered in that moment.

I rubbed at my eyes with the heels of my hands, inhaling sharply. There was no way this was happening. There was *no way* this could be happening. So what if it was some massive coincidence that Ashley looked exactly the same as Adelaide Shaw, and maybe I'd been mistaken, and Ashley's bumblebee pin hadn't been on the strap of her bag. Maybe it *had* fallen off in Room 217 at some point and Watson had found it and meant to give it back.

"I . . . I must confess I . . ." Watson's voice was a low rasp and I had to move closer just to hear what he said next. "I am not sure what I first thought upon seeing Ashley James enter my classroom, but the similarities between the two young ladies were . . . almost frightening indeed. So much so that I found myself . . ."

"Obsessing over the matter?" Holmes supplied. His response was practically dripping with sarcasm, but Watson seemed oblivious to it.

"That would not be inaccurate," he said after a moment of debate. "At first I tried to convince myself that I was overthinking things. Ashley James, at least in her mannerisms, was the exact opposite of Miss Shaw, and no burns seemed apparent on either of her arms. Ashley also presented herself as extremely confident and rather loud, whereas Miss Shaw had been mild-mannered and soft-spoken."

Out of the corner of my eye I saw Suruthi wince and Percy look as if he'd just had a bucket of ice water dumped on him, and I figured we now all had to be on the same page about this: Ashley and the medium were not the same person.

So where was she *now*? I had a sinking suspicion that by the end of this conversation we were going to know, and none of us were going to like the answer.

"That must've been it then," I said. "You realized Ashley and Adelaide Shaw weren't the same person and you just let it go."

The answer was evident on Watson's face before he'd even spoken. "No. No, I did not just *let it go*, Miss Montgomery. I couldn't. I agonized over my decision for several days, but ultimately knew it would be the safest choice."

"To do what, exactly?" Percy asked hesitantly.

"To observe," Watson said simply.

"Observe *what*?" Holmes demanded.

"Everything." Watson passed a hand through his hair, exhaling slowly. "I began to take notes on Ashley James to refer to and compare to what I had written of Miss Shaw in the past. Perhaps she had simply had some sort of cosmetic surgery to rid herself of the burn or yet again dabbled in some kind of magic to find a cure. But it . . . later, when I would revisit my journals, nothing made *sense*. I couldn't—I could not understand what I'd written, whether I was describing Ashley James or Miss Shaw, and it very quickly became *infuriating*. Yes, I would see Ashley regularly in my classroom, but I had no photograph of Miss Shaw. What then could I refer to after my classroom had emptied for the day and I was left alone to wonder by myself?"

"Is it just me," Suruthi murmured, leaning closer, "or does the professor seem a bit off his rocker at the moment?"

Or something, I thought.

"And this was something you believed I ought not be privy to, John?" Holmes asked Watson angrily.

"What would you have had me say, Sherlock?" Watson said, his voice pitching. "When, for the longest time, you went catatonic at the mere mention of the case Miss Shaw was involved in? Of course I could not have told you. No, I did the right thing. I was right to have kept my silence."

"Is he trying to convince us or himself?" I whispered to Suruthi, and she grimaced.

"Valid question," she muttered back.

Could the answer have been both?

Watson stood suddenly, converging on Holmes. I was worried for one second they were about to start fighting again, but Watson was only gripping Holmes by the arm, and *tightly*, his next words coming out in a rush.

"So, without any other reasonable explanation for the walking phenomena in my classroom, I knew ultimately that I must speak to the young lady myself. I also needed to continue gathering evidence of my own. Whatever evidence I managed to obtain would be invaluable later."

"I see." Holmes's voice was carefully controlled. "And once you came to this conclusion, what did you do?"

"Did you confront Ashley during that first conference we had over our manuscripts?" Percy suggested, sounding much more frantic than a moment ago. "That would have been the perfect opportunity, one-on-one like that."

"No, no, no, I had to talk to the young lady *away* from the classroom, you understand," Watson said. "Somewhere she would feel more . . . at ease, more willing to talk freely. When I overheard her desire to visit . . . what was it called?"

"The Narnia door," I answered uneasily.

"Yes, the very same," Watson said, nodding. "The Narnia door. Ashley had been complaining of nausea during the ride to Oxford, so I knew she would not think too much of my offering to accompany her to this Narnia door—as a concerned teacher, obviously."

Judging by the expressions on Percy and Suruthi's faces, I wasn't the only one becoming nauseated. Witnessing whatever *this* was, Watson's version of what I suspected was a confession I very much did not want to hear, had me feeling ill.

"However, I did not anticipate that *you* would be accompanying Ashley as well, Juliet." I felt a spasm of fear when Watson turned to face me this time. Hearing him use my full name when it had been nothing but *Miss Montgomery* from day one was a little disconcerting.

"Well, she said I could join her," I said, crossing my arms defensively. "I grew up reading those stories too."

"No doubt you did," Watson agreed. "But surely you can see where this posed a problem for me."

"And why is that, Watson?" Holmes asked. He had taken a step toward Watson, hand outstretched as if to stop him from taking another step closer to me. "I imagine the young lady here would have been perfectly fine should you have excused yourself to speak to this Ashley privately."

"Absolutely," I quickly agreed.

"By this point, I was doubtful Ashley would have a side conversation with me," Watson said, the corners of his mouth turning down into a frown. "Anyone could observe that the two of you were friends. Why would Ashley leave *your* side in order to speak with *me*?"

"Sounding a little jealous there, Professor," Suruthi said with a nervous chuckle.

Watson did not find this amusing. "I should think not. I am simply stating the facts of the case."

Percy looked as if he wanted to interject here, but Holmes beat him to it, encouraging Watson with a kind, "Please, do continue, John."

"Yes, I shall," Watson said. "Thank you. Yes, to continue . . . well, it was far too easy to follow you on your little trek across Oxford to find this fictional door. Fortunately for me, there was a small crowd assembled there, which I easily concealed myself in. And as the crowd began to disperse, I saw the perfect opening."

Watson began to pace, mimicking Holmes as he clasped his hands behind his back. In a matter of seconds, it seemed like he'd forgotten there were four other people present, waiting on pins and needles for him to keep speaking.

Percy had just mentioned that it had been about a century coming for Watson and Holmes to bring their various issues to the table for a discussion. Now I was thinking a nervous breakdown from Watson had to be a century in the making too.

"Juliet stepped to the side, making a considerable fuss about there being no reception, and as she was occupied with her mobile phone, I went quietly to Ashley to request a moment of her time."

Immediately I wanted to kick myself in the pants, because *of course* Watson had picked that moment to move in. It would have been the perfect opening, seeing as I frequently forgot I couldn't always tell how loud I was being.

"Did she, er, *go quietly* with you?" Percy asked, sounding anxious.

"At first," Watson answered, not once stopping with the pacing. "She was confused but happy to speak with me. It was a rather lovely day, before the rain, and the perfect opportunity for an afternoon stroll, and no one would have thought that strange. We spoke some about her manuscript, but I'm afraid her pleasant disposition did not last very long."

The nausea that had been building in the pit of my stomach was quickly replaced with dread.

The only one who hadn't visibly reacted to Watson's last statement was Holmes. "Is that perhaps because you said something to upset the young lady?"

"Of course not," Watson bit out. "I merely asked why she had chosen not to reveal her true identity yet. A fortnight was surely enough time to do so, and we certainly spent enough time together. When I said as much to her, she became very confused. Combative, even, when I repeatedly asked her to simply tell the truth. That is all I wanted from her, really. *The truth.* And yet she refused."

Watson stopped, hands now clasped behind his head, eyes fixed on the ceiling.

"In retrospect, I should have left it there. I could have made up some silly excuse about how I must have been mistaken, and would she please accept my apology?"

I was able to fill in the blanks when Watson hesitated.

I did not leave it there.

"I took us on a detour into an alleyway that was conveniently nearby and unoccupied—narrow enough for us to conceal ourselves in. Ashley made an attempt to return to Juliet, but I couldn't let the conversation end there. She hadn't given me enough time."

Watson didn't seem to need any further prodding to continue.

"I admit now that I perhaps used *too* much force in detaining her, but it was . . . too easy, almost. She wasn't a very strong young woman, and I . . . did not realize how forceful I was being, and she . . ." He cleared his throat, wiping his now sweaty palms down his pant legs. "Regrettably, she lost her footing and . . . hit her head against the brickwork in the alleyway when I attempted to grab her."

It was like a nightmare had begun to unravel right before my eyes the more the professor kept talking, and I was powerless to stop it.

"Naturally, I attempted to help the young lady to her feet. Being a former doctor, of course I knew that head injuries often appear worse than they are, given that they bleed far more easily than other wounds. So I was not necessarily concerned by all the blood."

"Regardless, you must have sought medical attention," Holmes insisted. "You cannot be too cautious in these situations, Watson."

"No, perhaps not," Watson agreed, his voice much softer. "She was frightened and disorientated. Of course she was. But even still, she refused to let me help her. I *wanted* to help her, but she wouldn't *let me*, and then Ashley . . ."

It was a miracle I didn't collapse then and there. My pulse was thrumming in my ears and my stomach was free-falling, but none of that mattered when I was frozen in place, unable to move so much as an inch.

"For God's sake, Watson, *speak!*" Holmes exclaimed, grabbing Watson by the arm before he could start pacing again. *"What happened?"*

It could have been a few moments or several hours by the time Watson brought himself to answer. I was torn between pulling out my hearing aids again and stuffing my fingers in my ears so I wouldn't have to hear what Watson would say, but I was still rooted to the floor, and I couldn't do anything. These words were going to come whether I wanted them to or not.

"I did not know . . . it had never been disclosed to me that . . . I did not know Ashley had asthma," Watson said in a rush, and the sound he made next made it seem like he was choking on a sob. "I didn't—I tried to find her inhaler, b-but it wasn't—she could not take a breath and—and I—"

Holmes kept remarkably calm when Watson was suddenly clutching at him for support, his voice raising as he said, "Holmes, you *must* understand, I never meant to hurt the girl. *Never.*"

When Holmes didn't immediately respond, Watson started to panic, curling his fingers into the front of Holmes's shirt, yanking him forward a step. "You believe me, don't you? *Don't you?*"

Holmes covered Watson's hands with his own, maybe to loosen his grip or pull him closer. "Where is the young lady now, John?"

I knew what had to be coming before Watson even spoke. I knew it, and yet it still cut bone deep when I heard it.

"Gone," was Watson's simple response. "I made sure of that."

"Gone where?" Holmes asked carefully. "Surely you know that you must tell me where she is."

"Gone," Watson repeated. Rather than on the verge of tears, he had suddenly become stoic, almost methodical as he finished his retelling of what had happened. "It was not without difficulty, I assure you. I had to enlist help, of course. Call in a favor. But Joel was easy enough to bring around after I reminded him that there were far worse things I could let slip about his dealings."

"Joel the tour guide?" Suruthi asked, her voice uneven. "That bloke in the red vest who looked like he wouldn't hurt a fly?"

Apparently we had been wrong. I had a difficult time imagining what could be worse than *murder*, however accidental—however *not in his right mind* Watson obviously was.

Because that was what had happened here. If Watson hadn't confronted Ashley alone, she would still be alive. How could I have missed this about the professor? After spending weeks in and out of his lectures, always so well put together and with the right thing to say.

One *would* have to become a very good actor after more than a century of existence.

Watson appeared to have not heard Suruthi, releasing his iron grip on Holmes's shirt and retreating to the desk, leaning against it for support. "It was inconvenient to be sure, staying hidden, but Joel arrived quickly enough, and we hid the body until I could return later to help dispose of it."

I couldn't help but shudder at that. *Dispose* of the body. To use Holmes's verbiage—this was abhorrent.

"*Where*, Watson? How in God's name did you manage to achieve this without being discovered?" Holmes asked, his voice barely level.

Surprisingly, it was Percy who answered before Watson could even open his mouth.

"The tunnels under the Bodleian Library."

"*What?*"

I couldn't tell if I had been the one to shout or if it had actually been Suruthi.

"There are tunnels under—"

"But how would you—"

"Apparently there are more than a few tunnels running under Oxford, and most of the ones under the Bodleian Library have been under construction," Percy explained, his gaze focused on Watson as he spoke. "That's what I've read, at least. I don't imagine they see much use, and since Joel gives tours at the Bodleian . . ."

"Correct assumption, Mister Byers," Watson said. "You cannot imagine the number of secrets one might uncover after spending decades exploring a place like the Bodleian Library."

The way that Watson sounded almost pleased with himself, that he had found such a clever way to cover his tracks, made me feel all the more sickened.

"So was it you or . . . or Joel who called me?" I said thickly, remembering that unsettling last call that came from Ashley's number. "I got a call from her phone, but no one was on the other line."

"Neither," Watson said. "Ashley had made the attempt to call you after she had fallen. I simply prevented her from succeeding."

I bit down on the inside of my cheek to keep from crying out, wishing I'd never asked.

"And when did you return to see to the young lady's remains?" Holmes continued, shifting uncomfortably where he stood.

"It took far longer than I would've liked," Watson admitted, rubbing a hand across his jaw. "Four days later, I believe. I spent a great deal of time running interference with the authorities the weekend following the . . . incident. And then Mister Maes's parents made an appearance, which I then had to—"

"It was that night then, wasn't it? When you did it," Suruthi blurted out. "No wonder you looked a mess that Monday. Because you hadn't . . ."

She stopped before her voice could pitch any higher.

I went over to the trunk at the foot of the bed and sat down when it felt like my legs were about to give out. Suruthi sat down beside me, resting her chin on my shoulder as she leaned into me. I was grateful for her presence. I had to stay anchored here somehow and see the rest of this out. I had to hear Watson finish.

"So you disposed of the body with the assistance of this Joel," Holmes summarized. "What happened next?"

"Well, in a way, nothing," Watson answered thoughtfully. "It did bring me some relief that the authorities were responding rather slowly. I suppose it was in my favor that the ordeal did present itself somewhat as a teenage runaway in a foreign country, and it certainly caused me no trouble to remind the authorities of this more than once. I was concerned when they went to search the dormitory where Ashley was staying, though I had already been through the place myself—wearing gloves, of course."

"Still missed the iPad," Suruthi muttered.

Watson heard her that time. "Yes, somehow I did. And yet once Holmes brought me the device, I realized I had precisely what I needed to conclude my business with the authorities."

"*How*?" I demanded incredulously.

"It was done simply enough," Watson said. "Joel used to dabble in the performing arts, as luck would have it, and this proved very useful indeed. As we already had the tablet, all that was left was to assemble a disguise for Joel to put on in order to conduct a video call with the authorities. Fortunately I have also learned a great deal about disguises over the years," Watson added with a wry smile for Holmes. "I had a masterful tutor, you see."

Holmes did not return the smile.

"It did not appear that they were overly suspicious," Watson continued, "but truthfully, I think they were relieved to have resolved the situation. A simple teenage runaway to an old family friend indeed. The whole thing was masterfully done, I assure you, Holmes. You would be proud."

Holmes looked far from *proud*. If I had to put a word to the expression on his face, I would say Holmes looked furious and betrayed—heartbroken, even.

"I am not proud, John," he said calmly. "However accidental the incident may have been, you deliberately went about covering up a young girl's death and proceeded to deceive the authorities. I fail to understand how such a situation would make me *proud*."

I wasn't sure what I was expecting Watson's response to be, but it definitely wasn't laughter.

"Perhaps you have a point, Holmes," Watson agreed. "But the alternative would have been far worse."

"Do enlighten me," Holmes requested, a hard edge to his voice.

Watson spread his arms wide. "Look at us, Sherlock. We haven't aged a day since August of eighteen ninety-nine. Could you imagine what the reaction would be to a man imprisoned who did not eat or sleep or age? So, you see, I *had* to do it."

Those words bounced around my skull for a painful moment, and I had to squeeze my eyes shut and try to steady my breathing. *Had to do it.*

If Watson truly believed he *had* to do it, then didn't it stand to reason that, if given the chance, he'd do it again? And all because he thought he was doing what was best to protect himself and Holmes, even if it had been at the cost of Ashley's life.

"I imagine your imprisonment *would* create quite the stir," Holmes allowed. "But rest assured, Watson, I intend to remedy this situation."

Holmes moved so quickly that one moment Watson was leaning against the desk and the next he was flat on the floor, clearly unconscious, Holmes standing over him. He did not look away from Watson until the dam that had been keeping my rapidly building grief at bay finally broke.

"Before the tears begin," Holmes said, "I might recommend you find a box of tissues first."

None of us made it that far. Once the tears began, they didn't stop.

30
CHAPTER

So It Goes

J ust so we're clear," I said to Percy and Suruthi. "I would've much rather spent my last day in London doing anything else *but* cleaning."

"Can't imagine why," Percy said teasingly. "What's more enjoyable than cleaning out an old flat that hasn't seen a good dusting since World War II?"

Seriously. I had difficulty keeping my own room at home organized, but going through Holmes and Watson's possessions, deciding which items were to be tossed, donated, or—surprisingly—given to the three of us, had me convinced my brain was going to start dribbling out of my ears.

This had been a daily occurrence since what I was referring to as *the night*—when we inadvertently stumbled across the truth of what had happened to our missing classmate as well as the old case Holmes had been attempting to solve for a century.

Watson's abrupt resignation from Ashford College and the remaining weeks of the writing seminar being cancelled had come as quite the disturbing shock to Thierry, who had promptly returned home to France without saying goodbye.

I'd thought my own fate would be something similar, but thanks to another private phone call between Adele and my mother, I was given permission to see out the rest of my time in London and catch my return flight home as scheduled—which now, sadly, was tomorrow.

So when I wasn't lending a hand in Dreams of Antiquity or playing the role of maid in Holmes and Watson's flat, I was with Suruthi and Percy, doing just about every touristy thing under the sun I could think of.

"We could always go ride the Underground for the evening," Suruthi said, pausing where she was clearing out an old trunk Holmes had dragged out of his room. Fortunately, this one wasn't full of spiders. "That way you can have another laugh every time the automated voice says, 'Now arriving at Cockfosters Station.'"

"That could get expensive," Percy said at the same time I pointed a threatening finger at Suruthi and said, "*Hey*, I've gotten pretty good about not doing that anymore."

"Well, I'd be happy to stay in tonight if you two would rather go on a date," Suruthi continued, her tone morphing into something a little suggestive. "You could enjoy a nice dinner, perhaps, or maybe find a new place to snog."

"If you're referring to this morning when Percy and I were *alone*, that's your own fault," I told Suruthi while Percy rolled his eyes.

"Yes, but I was *concerned*!" Suruthi said with false sincerity. "You'd been gone for a while, you see, and I just wanted to make sure you were being safe, so I—"

"Okay, okay, I think that's enough," Percy said loudly. "But it's not a bad idea," he added quietly, just for me.

It was very hard to keep from giggling at that, which had Percy grinning and Suruthi scoffing.

"I take full credit for whatever adorably nerdy relationship this is, by the way," she said, motioning at the two of us. "You two dancing awkwardly around each other this whole time, I swear. You'd better invite me to your wedding."

"Yeah, we'll get right on that," I said teasingly.

Obviously something like *marriage* wasn't even on the table, but seeing where this went with Percy—whatever long-distance thing we managed to come up with—was something I was very much looking forward to.

"I'm only agreeing with you, Jules," Suruthi said, trying and failing to smother a laugh.

"Well," Percy said forcefully, changing the subject. "We're just about done, believe it or not. This was the last of the rubbish from Holmes's room we had to go through, and he and Watson should be back from their solicitor's any minute now."

Unlike the first night I'd seen it, shrouded in darkness and coated in dust, the sitting room seemed more inviting with the sunlight washing through the open curtains. And now that some of the older pieces of furniture had been tossed out, there wasn't quite the same claustrophobic air either.

"Remind me again what they were supposed to be doing," I said, taking a seat on the sofa beside Percy.

Suruthi joined us last, throwing herself down on the sofa, her head landing in my lap. "Something about settling their affairs, I think. Can't imagine how many *affairs* they must have for as long as they've been . . . living."

"You know, I asked Holmes the same question," Percy said.

"The best I could make of his very confusing answer was that they've been pretending to *inherit* their own fortunes. And he did say Watson had a penchant for living frugally."

"Come again?" Suruthi and I said together.

"Well, it's not *that* difficult to forge documents," Percy explained. "Give it a few decades, tack on a *junior* to your name, and there you have it: you've essentially just inherited wealth from a close relative as far as anyone else is concerned."

"That's actually pretty smart," Suruthi said after a moment of thought.

"What are they going to do with all that money?" I asked, and I almost regretted it the next second.

We had been dancing around this subject for the last few weeks, after that initial discussion.

Holmes had not once wavered from his decision to destroy the silver coin that had been responsible for drawing out his existence for so long. When Watson eventually regained consciousness, he'd had no say in the matter.

Watson had no say either when Suruthi, Percy, and I had informed him that he was going to write a letter to Ashley's grandmother explaining *exactly* what had happened to her and what his hand had been in her death. The bumblebee pin, although far from a replacement for her granddaughter, would be returned to Edith as well.

None of this had been easy to digest, but *that* part had been the most difficult—the realization that Ashley really was gone.

Percy grimaced, rubbing his hands on his pant legs as if he were nervous about answering. "I—I told Holmes that the money should go to Edith. I don't know if he'll actually do it, but . . ."

"That's an excellent idea, Perce," Suruthi said quietly.

Percy shrugged, leaving it at that.

"She's right," I agreed. "It won't make up for any of what happened, but maybe it'll help ease some of her financial burdens."

We lapsed into silence after that.

Strangely, all of this didn't feel like closure, even though that was pretty much what we were helping Holmes and Watson with now. Once they'd taken care of their finances and we finished sorting and cleaning their flat, all that would remain would be for them to . . .

"Okay, I'm just going to say it," Suruthi said abruptly, sitting upright, spinning around to face us on the sofa. "I don't know how I feel about the fact that we're . . . helping Holmes and Watson prepare for death. Or at least that's Holmes's theory, but still. It's . . . sad."

Sad probably didn't even begin to cover everything that this was.

"That's because it is sad," Percy said. "On the one hand, we have a completely innocent girl who died, even if it was by accident, and on the other hand, we have two men who've spent more than one hundred years wandering around without their souls, not fully knowing what happened to them. I know you can't compare the two issues and some of this had to have been preventable, but they're both just . . . *awful*."

I rested my head on Percy's shoulder, taking in a deep breath. He kept quiet but still laced his fingers through mine, squeezing gently. I'd done enough crying the last few weeks. I didn't think I was capable of producing any more tears, but that didn't stop the fresh wave of grief from breaking over me.

"Well," Suruthi mumbled, swiping at her cheeks. "I guess there is one good thing that came about after all this."

Percy and I both sat upright, immediately on edge. What could've possibly occurred that was good about all this?

"What do you mean?" I asked suspiciously.

Suruthi managed a grin. "Holmes also made Watson turn Joel over to the police."

"*What*? When?" Percy demanded.

Suruthi shrugged a shoulder. "Not sure. Actually, I probably wasn't supposed to hear any of this, but I overheard their conversation just yesterday. Watson apparently phoned in an anonymous tip to the police about Joel that had something to do with embezzlement and illegally selling artifacts from the Bodleian. Needless to say, he's been placed on administrative leave pending a formal investigation."

"Oh."

I wasn't going to call that facing justice for his part in the aftermath of Ashley's death, but Joel would most likely be going to prison for a very long time after this.

And instead of prison for Watson . . . well, he was going to end up facing what I was willing to bet may have been his two biggest fears: losing Holmes and death.

"In the interest of full disclosure then," Percy said, shifting uncomfortably on the sofa. "I suppose now is a good time to tell you both that Watson gave me his journals."

"What, *all* of them?" Suruthi asked, her eyebrows shooting up in surprise.

The dozen or so diaries we'd first found hidden beneath the floorboards of Watson's bedroom like some tell-tale heart business was plenty, but there'd been at least a hundred journals we had managed to locate tucked away in various nooks and crannies around the flat since then. We'd already spent a good chunk of time on our hands and knees pulling up more floorboards, rummaging through cupboards or in closets, under various pieces of furniture, on the hunt for any small leather-bound journals.

"All of them," Percy confirmed with a nod.

"Wow," I said, blowing out a huff of air. "What are you going to do with them?"

Percy frowned. "To be honest, I haven't gotten that far."

"Do you even *want* to read them?"

"I'm . . . not so sure that I do," Percy admitted after a beat of silence. "Maybe. A part of me feels like I *have* to keep them even if I don't read them. And then there's another part of me that wants to chuck all those journals in a bin and set that bin on fire."

"Sounds perfectly reasonable to me," Suruthi said.

"Why do you feel like you have to keep them?" I asked Percy as gently as I could. "Because Watson said he wants you to have them?"

"No, it's not that," Percy said quickly. "At least, not completely. It's just . . ." He took in a sharp breath, then exhaled slowly. "Look at what we're helping them do, getting rid of all their things. If I don't take the journals, what's going to be left of them? If Holmes's theory is right and he destroys the coin like he wants to, that's it. They'll be gone and it'll be like they never existed in the first place. Well, not entirely. I know they've got all the Sherlock Holmes stories and novels, but everything that came *afterward*— everything that we experienced. Just . . . gone."

I had to swallow hard against the sudden lump stuck in my throat, making breathing difficult. I hadn't even considered looking at it from that angle. Suruthi looked just as lost as I felt.

Holmes and Watson *were* going to die—or at least Holmes was very determined to make it happen, ready for it as he claimed he was. Even if destroying the coin didn't work the way Holmes thought it might, I wouldn't put it past him to keep trying now that we had unpacked the events of that night where this first started.

It certainly felt like an end, but maybe not *the end*.

"I don't think that's necessarily true," I finally said. "They may not be around physically anymore, or all of their things might get thrown away, but *we* know the truth." I tapped a finger to my forehead. "I think we all know we won't be forgetting any of this any time soon."

"What are you saying, Jules?" Suruthi asked slyly, giving me a nudge. "Might this be the subject of your first novel?"

"Might be," I said, laughing. "What was that you said, Percy? *Write about my experiences*?"

"Something like that," Percy said, grinning crookedly.

My hand went up instinctively to start fiddling with my left hearing aid—a habit I hadn't entirely rid myself of yet. "Well, one could say we've had *a lot* of experiences this summer."

Most of them had been gut-wrenching and sad and full of heartbreak, but not all.

I let Suruthi's statement float around my brain as we got back to cleaning the rest of the sitting room. When I heard Holmes's heavy footfalls on the stairs outside the flat, followed by Watson's much quieter ones, I was halfway convinced that maybe I *would* write about everything that had happened this summer.

After that night when the truth had come out, I'd pulled out my journal and started writing the old-fashioned way because

I didn't know what else to do with the burning ache I felt radiating through my fingertips. Unbelievably, it worked, and my pen hadn't stopped moving. The one time I went back to read through the pages I'd written, I noticed the paragraphs were reading more like one of Watson's own journal entries.

Journaling had never been my strong suit, but this was a place to start. And maybe this would be something I'd actually finish. I wasn't going to count on *this* story—Holmes and Watson and every other strange or unnatural tale we'd managed to dig up—to be something, say, publishable, but then I wasn't sure that something like this should be published.

Even if Suruthi, Percy, and I were the only ones who ever read it, it would still be words on paper. It would still be a story that would not be forgotten.

ℰPILOGUE

"Well, it's about time you showed up!"

One of the Met's newest hires did his best to hold back a sigh of exasperation at the greeting. Of course it would be his luck that he'd pull *this* type of call right before clocking out for the night. He wanted to go home and relax in front of the telly with a drink before going to bed—not get yelled at by some angry pub owner.

But the young man knew complaining would get him nowhere; he was still a new recruit after all. Paying his dues was required.

"Apologies, sir," he said to the older man filling the doorway of The Bronze Archer pub. There was an angry flush to the older man's face as he wiped sweat from his forehead with a handkerchief. "What seems to be the problem?"

"The *problem* is that stench! It's driving away my business!"

"Stench, sir?"

Almost as soon as the words left the young man's mouth, he understood exactly what the pub owner was referring to. The smell of rotten eggs was quickly filling his nostrils, making the officer feel nauseated.

"Ah, never mind," he said as politely as he could manage. "I . . . see what you mean." *This* was what he'd been called here

332

for? He couldn't believe it. "Did you, er . . . forget to empty the bins, perhaps?"

The pub owner's face scrunched up in annoyance. "Are you daft? *Of course* I emptied the bloody bins."

"Of course, sir," the officer replied. He pulled out the small notebook he kept in the pocket of his trousers and began to jot down what the pub owner was saying—or rather pretended to. Now was as good a time as any to start his shopping list. "So, how can I—"

"You can help by looking in that flat upstairs," the pub owner interrupted, jabbing a finger up at the ceiling. "That's where the stench is coming from, I'm sure of it."

The younger man paused in his writing. "The flat upstairs is occupied?"

The pub owner gave a short nod, his jaw set. "For a long time now, I suppose, by two blokes." He frowned as he debated his next sentence. "Odd ones, they are. Keep to themselves mostly."

The new recruit couldn't deny that his curiosity was now piqued. "Odd how?"

"Dunno, do I? Seeing as they *keep to themselves,*" the pub owner said with an impatient growl. "But I haven't seen them in a while. Then that *smell* started up day before yesterday and it's only gotten stronger."

"I see," the young man said, slipping the notebook back into his pocket. "I'll look into this, if you'd be so kind as to direct me to the stairs."

The pub owner motioned for the officer to follow him, and together they exited the pub and walked around the corner from the main entrance. The owner pulled a set of keys from his apron pocket and fiddled around with a few before he selected the right one to unlock the door directly beside the alleyway.

There could be several reasons for bad smells, the young man thought as the pub owner stepped aside to let him pass through. *Needn't jump straight to the dead body assumption.*

It could just as easily be that the two men upstairs forget to empty *their* rubbish bins.

"There," the owner said, pointing to the door at the top of the narrow staircase. "That'll be them."

"Thank you, sir."

The stench of rotten eggs grew stronger as he approached the door, struggling not to gag. Perhaps these two men had several rubbish bins they needed to attend to.

The young man raised his hand to knock politely on the door, forcing himself not to pinch his nostrils shut. "Hello there! Is anyone home? I'm from the police and I'd like to speak with you about your bins."

He heard the pub owner give a scoff behind him and ignored it. When no response came from behind the door, he knocked again, more insistently this time.

Perhaps it was from the force of the knock or that it hadn't been fully closed, but the door gave way with a quiet groan, revealing a dimly lit entryway beyond.

This time the young man did slap a hand over his mouth and nose as he was hit full force with the unnaturally foul odor.

The pub owner cursed, his voice muffled as he called out from below, "Told you it was coming from this flat! I'm not going in there!"

The young officer didn't want to either. A feeling of unease settled deep in the pit of his stomach. He knew now that there was something else going on inside the flat that was far beyond a few nasty rubbish bins. A gas leak was another possibility, but still . . . nothing about this seemed *right*.

He tried to scrounge up whatever nerve he had left and all but shouted, "*Hello*?"

When the young man was met with nothing but eerie silence, he took a moment to gather his wits. *This is all a part of the job*, he reminded himself.

He crept forward into the flat, wincing when he heard the wooden floor creak ominously beneath his feet.

"Hello?" he called again. "Anyone here?"

His heart skipped through a few uneven beats as the silence stretched on, his pulse jumping as he took another step. He made it as far as the sitting room just around the corner and was met with the unexpected sight of what looked like a science experiment gone wrong.

A chintz armchair had been upended nearby, a coffee table overturned, and the drapes covering the windows were hanging on by threads.

The officer stayed put, feet planted firmly on the ground. The floor was covered in broken glass—shattered beakers, he presumed. Perhaps strangest of all was the gaping hole in the coffee table, as if some sort of acid had eaten away at the wood.

As the officer continued to catalogue his surroundings, he realized that the mysterious hole in the coffee table wasn't the strangest thing about all this.

It was the hand that lay on the floor, its skeletal fingers curled tightly around a blackened disc of metal the officer couldn't identify.

It was only because the owner of the hand was thankfully

hidden from view behind the sofa that the officer didn't lose his breakfast then and there.

It was a sight that would become permanently engrained in the young man's memory and the source of more than a few nightmares.

He used the toe of his boot to swing the door to the flat shut on his way out and addressed the pub owner now lurking at the top of the stairs

"I'm just going to nip outside for a phone call. Won't be a moment."

"What for?" the owner demanded as the now lightheaded officer passed him on the stairs.

He didn't answer, gasping in relief when the crisp, night air outside offered a reprieve from the stench.

Truthfully, the young man was now questioning his choice in careers, but there was nothing else for it now. He was going to have to ring the station for backup.

And here he thought this was going to be like every other normal, bland night he'd had for the last twenty-six years of his life. Clearly it was about to be anything but.

Acknowledgments

This project ended up being one of the hardest things I've ever written, so there are plenty of people to thank who helped get me to the finish line.

Firstly, my amazing agent, Shannon Hassan, and my fabulous editors at Blink YA, Katherine Jacobs and Mary Hassinger: Thank you for taking a chance on me and this story! I am so grateful for your support, guidance, and patience along the way. I sincerely think I'd be lost without you! It's been such a pleasure working with you and I hope we get to do it again in the future. Sara Merritt, Abby Van Wormer, and Jessica Westra, I want to thank you too for your help in all things marketing and for putting up with my reluctance to dabble in BookTok!

To my friends Samantha Duke, Brianna Schenkel, and Staci Nichols—thank you for your endless amounts of encouragement! I desperately needed it and your friendship. Megan Walker and Amy Bell, you deserve a special thanks for putting up with my panic-induced text messages about this story and for our amazing writing retreat. I don't know about you two, but I am really looking forward to going back to the lake house.

To my author friends Caroline Leech and Christina June, thank you for always being willing to answer my countless questions and/or making sure I didn't mess up the British slang...

ACKNOWLEDGMENTS

Mom, thanks for instilling a love of mysteries and Sherlock Holmes in me from such a young age. I wouldn't be where I am now if it weren't for you and Dad. I love you both.

Tyler, thanks for holding the fort down while I finished writing this thing—I know it wasn't easy. Our girls are a handful and you're a real champ for putting up with my random bouts of crying.

And to my other friends and family members too countless to name, I'm thinking of you too. You've helped and supported me in one way or another along my writing journey, and I'm so thankful to you all.

BLINK®